ADDICTION IS A GOOD THING

Ambassador Palvukin ... the game otherwise."

"Get up," said the Pre... a real game to play."

"There's still time," said Palv... watch. "I just want to finish—"

The Premier colored, and glanced angrily at the ambassador. "Who is this you are playing against on the computer, Palvukin?"

"An American named Schmidt, comrade Premier. He is a . . . er . . . tycoon. He is what they call here a 'pirate.' "

The Premier let his breath out with an audible hiss.

Spectators were drawing up chairs and seating themselves comfortably. People of varied races and nationalities were pouring out of the elevator and coming over to take a look at the game play. The premier's eyes were narrowed, and he glanced back and forth from the spectators to the board. "Hm-m-m," he said.

Along the lake, the little images of the ambassador's troops were steadily falling back, and the ambassador himself was groaning, "But I'll lose the whole district."

"You donkey," said the Premier angrily, "stop croaking and look confident. As far as all these people around us are concerned, the Soviet system is on trial on that board there. Now, start building railroads. And stop hanging onto that piece of worthless desert over there, and bring those troops back over here, where they can do some good. How did you get a supply line that long, anyway?"

"Well, he gave way there, so I pushed ahead, and—"

The Premier shook his head in disgust. "Bartov!"

"Yes, sir?"

"Go get some chairs. We're going to be here some time yet."

—from "War Games"

BAEN BOOKS
by Christopher Anvil

War Games
Pandora's Legion
Interstellar Patrol
Interstellar Patrol II
The Trouble with Aliens
The Trouble with Humans
Rx for Chaos

WAR GAMES

CHRISTOPHER ANVIL

edited by
ERIC FLINT

WAR GAMES

Copyright © 2008 by Christopher Anvil.

A Baen Books Original

Baen Publishing Enterprises
P.O. Box 1403
Riverdale; NY 10471
www.baen.com

ISBN: 0-978-1-4391-3350-7

Cover art by Alan Pollack

First Baen paperback printing, April 2010

Distributed by Simon & Schuster
1230 Avenue of the Americas
New York, NY 10020

Library of Congress Cataloging-in-Publication Data:
2008032555

Printed in the United States of America

10 9 8 7 6 5 4 3 2 1

★TABLE OF CONTENTS★

Acknowledgments

"Truce By Boomerang" was first published in *Astounding*, December 1957.

"A Rose By Any Other Name . . ." was first published in *Astounding*, January 1960.

"The New Member" was first published in *Galaxy*, April 1967.

"Babel II" was first published in *Analog*, August 1967.

"The Trojan Bombardment" was first published in *Galaxy*, February 1967.

"Problem of Command" was first published in *Analog*, November 1963.

"Uncalculated Risk" was first published in *Analog*, March 1962.

"Torch" was first published in *Astounding*, April 1957.

"Devise and Conquer" was first published in *Galaxy*, April 1966.

"War Games" was first published in *Analog*, October 1963.

"Sorcerer's Apprentice" was first published in *Analog*, September 1962.

"The Spy in the Maze" was first published under the title "The Problem Solver and the Spy," in *Ellery Queen's Mystery Magazine*, December 1965.

"The Murder Trap" was first published in *The Man From U.N.C.L.E. Magazine*, January 1967.

"Gadget vs. Trend" was first published in *Analog*, October 1962.

"Top Line" was first published in *Analog*, February 1982.

"Ideological Defeat" was first published in *Analog*, September 1972.

The Steel, the Mist, and the Blazing Sun was first published in 1980 by Ace Books.

"Philosopher's Stone" was first published in *Analog*, January 1963.

★THE★ PEACEKEEPERS' PROBLEMS

TRUCE BY BOOMERANG
★ ★ ★

Truce Supervisor B. H. Perkins lay hugging the dust as the barrage thundered overhead. The ground trembled beneath him. There was a taste of grit in his mouth and a bone-weariness in his limbs. From somewhere in the distance, a thin cheer reached him. Perkins raised his head and looked out from behind the shattered stub of a tree.

The glare on the sandy earth was blinding, but he saw it. A long column of sand-colored trucks was rumbling forward half-a-mile away. Further off he could see low clouds of dust churned up by advancing tanks.

Perkins turned his head and saw young Assistant Truce Supervisor Macklin studying the moving column with an expression of bitterness.

Perkins glanced around. Their jeep was fifteen feet away, where they'd left it when the bombardment

3

opened up. Then the shells had dropped practically down their necks. Now the barrage had lifted and moved forward. Perkins still had his life, if not his truce.

Macklin came to his feet and brushed himself off. "Now what do we do, sir?" he said angrily. "Should we go back and plead with them to take back their bombardment? Or do we go sit in the outer office and beg to be let in for an explanation?"

"That," said Perkins, "is all up to the Secretary General." He got in the jeep. Macklin sat down behind the wheel. They started back toward their headquarters.

On the way, they passed three columns of trucks loaded with troops. They were jeered twice, cheered ironically once. Passing the last column, a spray of bullets went over their heads.

Macklin stared straight ahead. "To do this job right," he said, "a man needs armored skin and the disposition of an angel."

Perkins grunted noncommittally. The trouble, he kept telling himself, was that he had nothing to offer but the *status quo*, and no one here wanted the *status quo*. Call the combatants A and B. Even assuming the two sides could be content with their present borders, how did A know that B would be peaceful five years from now? And how did B know that A would be peaceful twenty years from now? The *status quo* involved mutual distrust, and that prolonged mutual distrust was what neither side could stand. Neither wanted to live with a bomb at his ear, ticking now loud, now soft, now with a threatening boom and rattle, so neither could ever settle down and look ahead with any assurance.

Perkins' cheeks puffed out as he exhaled sharply. He just didn't see how it could ever be done. To guarantee peace, he needed to intimidate both sides, so that each knew the other would hesitate long before making trouble. And to do that properly, he needed the armed might of one or the other of the two great world powers. Yet, if either of those two powers moved in here, the other would be uneasy to the point where Perkins would need a seventy-two hour day just to keep *them* at peace.

Macklin leaned forward and squinted as the headquarters caravan came into view. Angrily, he said, "As if we didn't have trouble enough already, there's that So-and-So again."

Perkins shifted his position in the bouncing jeep. "Who?"

"I don't know. A correspondent, probably. Some unprepossessing-looking individual who thinks he has the answer to everything and wants to see you."

Perkins scowled. "He's been here before?"

"Several times. I've given orders that he's to be kept out, but he gets in, somehow."

Perkins leaned forward. As they came closer, he could make out a slight man sitting sidewise in a jeep, with a tarpaulin-covered trailer hooked on behind. Perkins cleared his throat. "I'm going to be busy for the next few hours, as you know. But I want you to send that man in to me at three-thirty."

"Sir, at best he's a correspondent with a bad case of swollen head. At worst, he's a crank."

"You said he thinks he has the answer to everything?"

"Oh, *he* thinks so."

"Then he's a straw," said Perkins, "and in the position we're in, we can't be above grasping at straws."

The day advanced discouragingly. It got hotter and dustier. The rumbling thunder in the distance grew loud and fell away, but never ceased. Heavy bombers roared low overhead. The reports coming in added to the proof that the attack wasn't cumulative, built up out of exasperations that burst loose here and there and spread from place-to-place. It was a fully co-ordinated offensive; the only discordant note, that set Perkins back in his chair, was a series of unexpected reports from a supposedly quiet sector of the boundary. Here, the *other* side had attacked at nearly the same moment, and with such force and effect that this, too, was clearly planned in advance.

Now the question was, who was the aggressor?

If A and B stand glaring at each other, growling mutual threats and insults, then A hits B on the jaw at the same instant B punches A in the stomach, who started it?

Perkins groaned and looked up to see Macklin, his face pale and gloomy, at the door.

"It's three-thirty, sir," said Macklin.

Perkins frowned, then remembered. "Send him in," he said.

Macklin stepped outside.

A thin, gray-haired man came in and looked at Perkins. After a moment, he said, "I got some stuff for you."

Perkins scowled.

The stranger said, "You want to end the war, don't you?"

"Of course," said Perkins, "but—"

"You'd better give a hand. Some of it's pretty heavy."

Perkins hesitated, then got up and followed his guest outside. It took twenty minutes to bring in the crates and boxes from the trailer. When they were all stacked up in Perkins' office, the stranger said, "O.K., now leave me alone. I got to put this stuff together."

Perkins, perspiring freely, stood outside the door.

"Sir," said Macklin, looking on. "I'm not sure I understand this at all. Why don't we just have this fellow escorted back to his starting place?"

Perkins looked at Macklin with a faint smile. "There's a great deal of wisdom in old sayings, my boy."

"Sir?"

"Beggars can't be choosers. Position is everything in life. A bird in the hand is worth two in the bush. A drowning man grasps at straws."

Macklin looked a little dazed.

" . . . All containing a great deal of truth," Perkins went on. "Our purpose here was to prevent fighting. We had a certain moral capital to expend in that direction. Ideally, we would have added to that capital, so that we would have been living, as it were, on the interest. The situation was such that we couldn't do it. We had to live on the principal. Now the principal is very nearly all consumed. I won't say that we're beggars, Macklin, but in this respect we're very close to it. Our position is precarious. Now this gentleman comes to us and asserts that he has the solution. He approaches the problem as a repairman might approach a television receiver that has gone out of order."

"The man's a lunatic," said Macklin.

"Quite possible," said Perkins sadly. "But he's a bird in the hand. And at least he's a sign that we have some moral capital left. He came to *us*, you see."

Macklin frowned and stated to speak.

Overhead, a jet roared, its heavy rumble making them both glance up apprehensively, then look at each other.

The door of Perkins' office opened.

"O.K.," said the slight, gray-haired visitor. "It's ready. You can come in now. No," he waved Macklin back. "Just *you*." Perkins came in.

Macklin stepped back angrily. Perkins closed the door, then turned around.

At first glance, Perkins was inclined to agree with Macklin that the man was a lunatic.

There seemed to be two large television sets face-to-face across the room. There were a number of smaller sets with blank faces ranked on Perkins' desk and chair and set on the floor nearby.

The gray-haired man looked at the apparatus gloomily. "Eight hundred and forty-two tests it took us to find out the thing isn't commercially feasible," he said.

"What *is* this?" Perkins demanded.

The man looked at him. "You've heard of the telephone?" he said sourly.

"Of course," said Perkins scowling.

"Well," said his guest, "some bright guy got the idea if we could send a voice over the wires, we could do it through empty space, using a carrier wave instead of a wire."

"Radio," frowned Perkins.

"Yeah. Radio. It worked. It turned into big business. And some guy sent *printing* over wires—teletype. And pictures—telephoto. And then, the idea was, send pictures without wires. Television. What a big business *that* turned into." He looked sourly at the assemblage in the room. "It was only natural somebody would think of this."

"I don't doubt it," said Perkins. "That's all very true. But what *is* this?"

"Matter transceiver," said his guest sourly.

"*Matter* transceiver?"

"That's right. Now, let me show you. London and New York are practically the same height above the center of the earth. No work has to be done against gravity to *raise* a package from New York to London. If a frictionless surface stretched from one to the other we could give a hard push at one end, the package would slide across the Atlantic and deliver up the hard push when it hit London on the other side."

Perkins goggled. "See here—"

His guest waved him silent. "Nearly all the trouble getting across the Atlantic comes from what amounts to so much friction. Shoving a ship through water is work. Millions of tons of water move to the right and the left and then back again as the ship goes by. You've got a track of turbulence and waste thousands of miles long. With an airplane, you've got the added work of holding the plane up against gravity all that time. You see what I mean? It's wasteful."

"Yes," said Perkins. "I'll concede that. But what does that have to do with us, here?"

Perkins' thin, gray-haired visitor looked sourly at the apparatus. "The idea was to transmit electromagnetically. 'There's no friction in radio waves,' as the boys used to say." He looked sharply at Perkins. "Do you think you could yell loud enough to be heard across the Atlantic?"

"Certainly not," said Perkins, startled.

"But you could yell into a microphone, have the pattern of your voice carried across the Atlantic as a radio wave, and your yell will come out a receiver on the other side before it could travel across the room under its own power. All right, the idea was to do the same thing with objects." He grew a little excited. "Think of the possibilities! The market would be world-wide. Shipping delays and spoilage cut to almost nothing." The gloom returned to his face.

Perkins, studying him with a frown, glanced at the apparatus curiously. "Hm-m-m," he said. He looked back at his guest. "Didn't it work?"

"Oh, after a fashion. We sent a block of lead two hundred miles and back and thought we had it licked. All we had to do was iron out the bugs. While we were doing that, someone even figured out a way to send and receive from the same instrument, to anywhere else in range. Meanwhile, we had refined the apparatus, and re-refined it, and refined it again, and it finally dawned on us that the bugs were built-in." He walked over to the nearest set and snapped it on.

Perkins blinked.

The desert stared out of the screen, bright and hot. Miniature tanks were grinding forward in a haze of dust and smoke. Their guns flared, and the roar of the explosions came as from a distance into the room. The picture was clear and detailed, and did not flicker at all. It was like looking through a hole into the desert itself.

"Incredible," said Perkins.

"Oh, it's great," said his guest sourly. "Now just try and *smell* that dust and smoke." He adjusted the set till the roar was deafening, and the muzzle of a hammering gun seemed less than ten feet away. Then he quickly readjusted it to a distant view, wiped his forehead, and looked up. "Smell anything?"

"I—No. I couldn't be sure, but I don't think so. The illusion was very convincing, other than that."

"Sure. It looks good. It sounds good. But there's a skin effect. Here. Put your hand in."

"I'll break the screen."

"No, you won't."

Perkins scowled, and reached cautiously toward the face of the receiver. Where he expected to touch the screen, he felt nothing but warmth. Frowning, he reached farther. There was a faint elastic resistance, and he pressed carefully against it. His arm went farther and farther into the set, feeling the warmth and the sunlight, and a sensation like that of a hand pressed into the side of a large, partially inflated balloon. Now, he expected to feel the back of the set. He moved forward, and suddenly he saw the other side of the set, and his arm wasn't there. He jumped back.

Now his arm was all right.

"Look here," he said. "What happened?"

"You reached through, into that space shown on the 'screen.' Or *almost* through. There's that skin effect I told you about."

"Do you mean, I could reach in there and *drop* something, and it would land in the desert?"

"No. It would be held right next to your hand when you tried to drop it. And when you pulled your hand back, it would fall out in the room here. The skin effect."

"I could feel the heat of the sun plainly."

"Sure, radiations go through all right. But not even anything as small as molecules can get through that skin unless they have high enough velocities and a long enough mean free path. That's why no odors get through."

"I don't follow."

"You can't *drop* a bullet through. But if you aimed a gun in there, you could *shoot* it through. You have to break through that skin or what you're trying to put through comes right back out again."

"Oh, I see. That was why you couldn't use it for . . . ah . . . matter transference?"

"That's half of it. We'd have had to pack the goods in artillery shells and shoot them through. But there's something worse yet."

"What's that?"

"There's a random distortion brought about by the circuit itself. We thought it was defective equipment, but we finally traced it back to the uncertainty principle. There isn't much we can do about that. If you send a watch through, it may or may not run when you take it out the other side. If you send cheese, it may have a slight off-flavor. A solid piece of lead, say, will change its shape slightly." He looked closely at Perkins. "Of course, if it's a bullet, that won't matter much."

Perkins looked back uneasily. "All this is of interest, no doubt, but what does it have to do with what's going on outside? And why are you here? Your interests, I judge, are purely mercantile."

His guest smiled and shook his head. "This is how you can *end* what's going on outside. As for what I'm doing here—I was sent. Somebody had to get it to you, and we wanted to try it out on the spot."

"But—why?"

"To make sure it worked. We want to end this war. Wars can spread, you know. And you can't do business in a crater."

"Fine, but—Look here. We have no need for this splendid equipment." Perkins gestured toward the machine. "Observation. This would be wonderful for observation. But, we're beyond that, don't you see?"

"You don't get it?" said his guest sadly. "I explained to you this is a *transceiver*." He walked resignedly to the set, adjusted it slightly, and said, "Go over there where you can't see it. Back there. Get in back of it." When

Perkins had followed instructions, his guest got down on the floor, reached up cautiously, and moved one of the controls. The thunder of big guns grew loud in the room, was joined by the mutter and cough of engines, and the whine of bullets. There was a burst from a machine gun, then another.

Abruptly, a line of holes appeared in the door and one wall of the room.

The thunder and crash receded.

Perkins stared at the holes.

"I told you," said his guest. "Skin effect. This is a transceiver. It makes a two-way connection and those bullets were coming in the right direction fast enough to get through."

Perkins wiped his forehead. He felt the glimmering of an idea starting to form. He glanced at the two big sets face-to-face.

His guest nodded approvingly.

Perkins thought, what each side needed was positive assurance the other side wouldn't start anything now or several years from now. Assurance that it would be deadly to start anything. In that way, each could relax; in time, good feeling might even have a chance to develop. In time—But *how*—

His guest walked over and spun around one of the big sets. He flicked it on and practically the same picture appeared as on the small set. He swung it back and locked it in place.

"The way it usually works out," he said, "soldiers don't start wars. Dictators start them. Cabinets start them. There's pressure of some kind and the war comes for emotional or political reasons. War is horrible today. That generally comes home as soon as anyone realizes *he* might have to fight the war. Then we get an inrush of cold common sense. The idea is, how to bring this common sense to the dictator, or the cabinet, so they don't see the war as an abstract symbol, but as solid bullets that may hit *them* any time."

He snapped on a second set, and there stood a famous figure studying a map. The famous man moved his hand here, and here. Assistants were rearranging pins on the map as he talked rapidly and earnestly with subordinates. The subordinates nodded. Orders were urgently repeated over phones. On the map, symbols moved, showing the general direction of massive forces approaching the battle area. A complex problem with many parts to be co-ordinated.

On the other set, tanks were burning. A man lying on the ground nearby was turning over in pain, his hand clenched over his face.

Perkins glanced from one scene to the other. The calm planner. The soldier in agony. "Horrible," he said.

"Isn't it? And for the time being, all that violence and suffering is just a symbol to the first man."

"Will this screen project an image directly into that one? Could we make him *see* the suffering?"

"Yes. We could."

"Still," said Perkins hesitantly, "people can become immune to the sufferings of others."

"If they're around it all the time, sure. If it flashes on them suddenly in normal surroundings, then disappears and comes back unexpectedly, that's different. But there's a more direct way—"

"What's that?" said Perkins.

His guest motioned him to the back of the room. He carefully readjusted the screens and stepped aside. He dove for the floor. The roar of guns and the whine of bullets filled the room. Bright flashes lit the far wall. Abruptly the roar was cut back, and Perkins hurried to look in the screens.

In one was the flash of a far-off battle.

In the other stood the famous figure, surrounded by frozen aides; the upper section of the wall nearby was pitted with holes sifting dust and plaster onto the floor.

Perkins whispered to his guest, "Is this two-way reception now?"

"Not on that screen. That's just receiving. But I can fix it."

"What will he see if you do?"

"Just as much as you see of him now, but not framed in a receiving set. It will be as if these two rooms were connected by a hole. Light and sound can pass through. You could even shake hands as if through an invisible rubber sheet."

On the screen, the famous figure was beginning to turn slowly. His aides moved their heads as if on rigid vertical pivots.

"Fix it," whispered Perkins.

The famous man's Adam's apple moved up and down. He stiffened his jaw and slowly turned farther around.

Perkins looked at him sternly.

Their eyes met.

"You broke the truce," said Perkins accusingly.

The face opposite him blinked, moved cautiously this way and that, as if trying to get things into focus.

"You must," said Perkins, his eyes narrowed, "withdraw your troops back of the boundary. Precise details will be settled in a radiogram I shall send you shortly. But the fighting must be completely ended by midnight tonight. Do you understand that?"

The well-known figure turned slowly and looked up at the wall behind him. As he watched, a piece of plaster near the ceiling gradually sagged and fell to the floor. Something embedded in the wall glinted dully, and he turned back toward Perkins.

Perkins looked at him coldly and unblinkingly and said nothing.

At length, the famous man cleared his throat. His voice a hoarse level whisper, he said, "All right. But see that *they* do the same."

Perkins inclined his head slightly. The scene vanished. Perkins looked at his guest and suddenly felt himself grinning. "And now," he said, "for the other side."

"Right." His guest was bent over the controls and looked up. "The angle of contact adjustments have to be made carefully. A martyr at this stage could cause trouble."

Perkins nodded and watched him make the adjustments.

This time there was speedy agreement, a halting flood of questions, and a faint baffled look of craft and determination. When it was over, Perkins said, "Now what?"

"Now after I get more equipment, I teach you how to operate this stuff. You can use it as transmitter, receiver, transceiver, and you have to know where to use which. And it's important to know how to make the settings quickly."

"I wonder if this will all work according to schedule," said Perkins thoughtfully. "There was a faint look of craft on the face of one of our principals."

"Oh, there's no predicting," said his guest. "In this age, people are likely to react fast to miracles. Maybe by tomorrow they'll have the nominal authority divided up into sixteen buck-passing committees. But in war, the authority has to center somewhere, and that is where to use this.

"At worst, things will get so complicated for them that they'll have to call off the war or go crazy. There are better ways for a man to spend his energy than planning on fighting a war. We just have to make that clearer."

Perkins looked at the apparatus. "What if there's a raid to capture this?"

"With practice, you can use them to put up an effective defense." He scowled. "But don't worry, we're covering you from a distance. We have a great many more of these defective apparatuses."

Perkins held out his hand. "I don't know how to thank you; I'll do the best I can."

"I'll bring you more of these. You've got to get men you can trust to operate them."

"I'll get them"

"Good. Eventually, we'll solve our original problem, and that should finally bring men close enough together so we'll have an end to these troubles." He turned to leave.

"I wish you luck," said Perkins.

His visitor turned and smiled for the first time. "Oh, we're making some progress. We've got a light-duty model of a new design going. It takes too much energy, but it has possibilities." He opened the door and strode out.

Macklin and two others were standing blank-faced outside the door.

"I'm sorry," said Macklin. "We heard the noise and came running. It was quiet when we got here. Rather than burst in, we looked through these bullet holes. And . . . well . . . we just stayed here."

"That's all right," said Perkins. "It'll make it easier for me to brief you." He stood for a moment watching his guest drive off in the jeep.

"I still don't see," said Macklin, "how that fellow got in here. I gave strict orders he was to be kept out."

"Well," said Perkins, turning away, "don't worry about it. We have work to do. And he has work to do. Perhaps some day he'll discover how to make his matter transmitter and then possibly everyone will be too busy to make trouble, and we'll be out of a job."

"No need to worry about *that*—" began Macklin, and cut off abruptly.

Perkins spun around, frowning.

In the distance, the jeep was stopped. The hood came down as Perkins watched, and a faint clang reached him. He and Macklin glanced at each other. There was the faint silvery flash of what looked like a brightly polished wire cable tossed into the trailer. The far-off roar of the engine reached them. The jeep started forward.

Perkins and Macklin blinked their eyes.

The jeep was gone.

Perkins grabbed Macklin by the arm.

"Let's get to work," he said.

A ROSE BY ANY OTHER NAME . . .
★ ★ ★

A tall man in a tightly-belted trenchcoat carried a heavy brief case toward the Pentagon building.

A man in a black overcoat strode with a bulky suitcase toward the Kremlin.

A well-dressed man wearing a dark-blue suit stepped out of a taxi near the United Nations building, and paid the driver. As he walked away, he leaned slightly to the right, as if the attaché case under his left arm held lead instead of paper.

On the sidewalk nearby, a discarded newspaper lifted in the wind, to lie face up before the entrance to the United Nations building. Its big black headline read:

U. S. WILL FIGHT!

A set of diagrams in this newspaper showed United States and Soviet missiles, with comparisons of ranges, payloads, and explosive powers, and with the Washington Monument sketched into the background to give an idea of their size.

The well-dressed man with the attaché case strode across the newspaper to the entrance, his heels ripping the tables of missile comparisons as he passed.

Inside the building, the Soviet delegate was at this moment saying:

"The Soviet Union is the most scientifically advanced nation on Earth. The Soviet Union is the most powerful nation on Earth. It is not up to you to say to the Soviet Union, 'Yes' or 'No.' The Soviet Union has told you what it is going to do. All I can suggest for you is, you had better agree with us."

The United States delegate said, "That is the view of the Soviet government?"

"That is the view of the Soviet government."

"In that case, I will have to tell you the view of the United States government. If the Soviet Union carries out this latest piece of brutal aggression, the United States will consider it a direct attack upon its own security. I hope you know what this means."

There was an uneasy stir in the room.

The Soviet delegate said slowly, "I am sorry to hear you say that. I am authorized to state that the Soviet Union will not retreat on this issue."

The United States delegate said, "The position of the United States is already plain. If the Soviet Union carries this out, the United States will consider it as a direct attack. There is nothing more I can say."

In the momentary silence that followed, a guard with a rather stuporous look opened the door to let in a well-dressed man, who was just sliding something back into his attaché case. This man glanced thoughtfully around the room, where someone was just saying:

"*Now* what do we do?"

Someone else said hesitantly, "A conference, perhaps?"

The Soviet delegate said coolly, "A conference will not settle this. The United States must correct its provocative attitude."

The United States delegate looked off at a distant wall. "The provocation is this latest Soviet aggression. All that is needed is for the Soviet Union not to do it."

"The Soviet Union will not retreat on this issue."

The United States delegate said, "The United States will not retreat on this issue."

There was a dull silence that lasted for some time.

As the United States and Soviet delegates sat unmoving, there came an urgent plea, "Gentlemen, doesn't anyone have an idea? However implausible?"

The silence continued long enough to make it plain that now no one could see any way out.

A well-dressed man in dark-blue, carrying an attaché case, stepped forward and set the case down on a table with a solid *clunk* that riveted attention.

"Now," he said, "we are in a real mess. Very few people on Earth want to get burned alive, poisoned, or smashed to bits. We don't want a ruinous war. But from the looks of things, we're likely to get one anyway, whether we want it or not.

"The position we are in is like that of a crowd of people locked in a room. Some of us have brought along for our protection large savage dogs. Our two chief members have trained tigers. This menagerie is now straining at the leash. Once the first blow lands, no one can say where it will end.

"What we seem to need right now is someone with the skills of a lion tamer. The lion tamer controls the animals by understanding, timing, and *distraction*."

The United States and Soviet delegates glanced curiously at each other. The other delegates shifted around with puzzled expressions. Several opened their mouths as if to interrupt, glanced at the United States and Soviet delegates, shut their mouths and looked at the attaché case.

"Now," the man went on, "a lion tamer's tools are a pistol, a whip, and a chair. They are used to distract. The pistol contains blank cartridges, the whip is snapped above the animal's head, and the chair is held with the points of the legs out, so that the animal's gaze is drawn first to one point, then another, as the chair is shifted. The sharp noise of gun and whip distract the animal's attention. So does the chair.

" . . . And so long as the animal's attention is distracted, its terrific power isn't put into play. This is how the lion tamer keeps peace.

"The thought processes of a war machine are a little different from the thought processes of a lion or a tiger. But the principle is the same. What we need is something corresponding to the lion tamer's whip, chair, and gun."

He unsnapped the cover of the attaché case, and lifted out a dull gray slab with a handle on each end, several dials on its face, and beside the dials a red button and a blue button.

"It's generally known," he said, looking around at the scowling delegates, "that certain mental activities are associated with certain areas of the brain. Damage a given brain area, and you disrupt the corresponding mental action. Speech may be disrupted, while writing remains. A man who speaks French and German may lose his ability to speak French, but still be able to speak German. These things are well-known, but not generally used. Now, who knows if, perhaps, there is a special section of the brain which handles the vocabulary *related to military subjects*?"

He pushed in the blue button.

The Soviet delegate sat up straight. "What is that button you just pushed?"

"A demonstration button. It actuates when I release it."

The United States delegate said, "Actuates *what*?"

"I will show you, if you will be patient just a few minutes."

"What's this about brain areas? We can't open the brain of every general in the world."

"You won't have to. Of course, you have heard of resonant frequencies and related topics. Take two tuning forks that vibrate at the same rate. Set one in vibration, and the other across the room will vibrate. Soldiers marching across a bridge break step, lest they start the bridge in vibration and bring it down. The right note on a violin will shatter a glass. Who knows whether minute electrical currents in a particular area of the brain, associated with a certain characteristic mental activity, may not tend to induce a similar activity in the corresponding section of another brain? And, in that case, if it were possible to induce a sufficiently *strong* current, it might actually overload that particular—"

The United States delegate tensely measured with his eyes the distance to the gray slab on the table.

The Soviet delegate slid his hand toward his waistband.

The man who was speaking took his finger from the blue button.

The Soviet delegate jerked out a small black automatic. The United States delegate shot from his chair in a flying leap. Around the room, men sprang to their feet. There was an instant of violent activity.

Then the automatic fell to the floor. The United States delegate sprawled motionless across the table. Around the room, men crumpled to the floor in the nerveless fashion of the dead drunk.

Just one man remained on his feet, leaning forward with a faintly dazed expression as he reached for the red button. He said, "You have temporarily overloaded certain mental circuits, gentlemen. I have been protected by a . . . you might say, a jamming device. You will recover from the effects of *this* overload. The next one you experience will be a different matter. I am sorry, but there are certain conditions of mental resonance that the human race can't afford at the moment."

He pressed the red button.

The United States delegate, lying on the table, experienced a momentary surge of rage. In a flash, it was followed by an intensely clear vision of the map of Russia, the polar regions adjoining it, and the nations along its long southern border. Then the map was more than a map, as he saw the economic complexes of the Soviet Union, and the racial and national groups forcibly submerged by the central government. The strong and weak points of the Soviet Union emerged, as in a transparent anatomical model of the human body laid out for an operation.

Not far away, the Soviet delegate could see the submarines off the coasts of the United States, the missiles arcing down on the vital industrial areas, the bombers on their long one-way missions, and the unexpected land attack to settle the problem for once and for all. As he thought, he revised the plan continuously, noting an unexpected American strength here, and the possibility of a dangerous counterblow there.

In the mind of another delegate, Great Britain balanced off the United States against the Soviet Union, then by a series of carefully planned moves acquired the moral leadership of a bloc of uncommitted nations. Next, with this as a basis for maneuver—

Another delegate saw France leading a Europe small in area but immense in productive power. After first isolating Britain—

At nearly the same split fraction of an instant, all these plans became complete. Each delegate saw his nation's way to the top with a dazzling, more than human clarity.

And then there was an impression like the brief glow of an overloaded wire. There was a sensation similar to pain.

This experience repeated itself in a great number of places around the globe.

In the Kremlin, a powerfully-built marshal blinked at the members of his staff.

"Strange. For just a minute there, I seemed to see—" He shrugged, and pointed at the map. "Now, along the North German Plain here, where we intend to ... to—" He scowled, groping for a word. "Hm-m-m. Where we want to ... ah ... destabilize the ... the ridiculous NATO protective counterproposals—" He stopped, frowning.

The members of his staff straightened up and looked puzzled. A general said, "Marshal, I just had an idea. Now, one of the questions is: Will the Americans . . . ah—Will they . . . hm-m-m—" He scowled, glanced off across the room, bit his lip, and said, "Ah . . . what I'm trying to say is: Will they forcibly demolecularize Paris, Rome, and other Allied centers when we . . . ah . . . inundate them with the integrated hyperarticulated elements of our—"

He cut himself off suddenly, a look of horror on his face.

The marshal said sharply, "What are you talking about—'demolecularize'? You mean, will they . . . hm-m-m . . . deconstitute the existent structural pattern by application of intense energy of nuclear fusion?" He stopped and blinked several times as this last sentence played itself back in his mind.

Another member of the staff spoke up hesitantly, "Sir, I'm not exactly sure what you have in mind, but I had a thought back there that struck me as a good workable plan to deconstitutionalize the whole American government in five years by unstructing their political organization through intrasocietal political action simultaneously on all levels. Now—"

"Ah," said another general, his eyes shining with an inward vision, "I have a better plan. Banana embargo. Listen—"

A fine beading of perspiration appeared on the marshal's brow. It had occurred to him to wonder if the Americans had somehow just landed the ultimate in foul blows. He groped around mentally to try to get his mind back on the track.

At this moment, two men in various shades of blue were sitting by a big globe in the Pentagon building staring at a third man in an olive-colored uniform. There was an air of embarrassment in the room.

At length, one of the men in blue cleared his throat. "General, I hope your plans are based on something a little clearer than that. I don't see how you can expect us to co-operate with you in recommending *that* kind of a thing to the President. But now, I just had a remarkable idea. It's a little unusual; but if I do say so, it's the kind of thing that can clarify the situation instead of sinking it in hopeless confusion. Now, what I propose is that we immediately proceed to layerize the existent trade routes in *depth*. This will counteract the Soviet potential nullification of our sea-borne surface-level communications through their underwater superiority. Now, this involves a fairly unusual concept. But what I'm driving at—"

"Wait a minute," said the general, in a faintly hurt tone. "You didn't get my point. It may be that I didn't express it quite as I intended. But what I mean is, we've got to really bat those bricks all over the lot. Otherwise, there's bound to be trouble. Look—"

The man in Air Force blue cleared his throat. "Frankly, I've always suspected there was a certain amount of confusion in both your plans. But I never expected anything like this. Fortunately, *I* have an idea—"

At the United Nations, the American and Russian delegates were staring at the British delegate, who was saying methodically, "Agriculture, art, literature, science, engineering, medicine, sociology, botany, zoology, beekeeping, tinsmithing, speleology, wa . . . w . . . milita . . . mili . . . mil . . . hm-m-m . . . sewing, needle work, navigation, law, business, barrister, batt . . . bat . . . ba—Can't say it."

"In other words," said the United States delegate, "we're mentally hamstrung. Our vocabulary is gone as regards . . . ah—That is, we can talk about practically anything, except subjects having to do with . . . er . . . strong disagreements."

The Soviet delegate scowled. "This is bad. I just had a good idea, too. Maybe—" He reached for pencil and paper.

A guard came in scowling. "Sorry, sir. There's no sign of any such person in the building now. He must have gotten away."

The Soviet delegate was looking glumly at his piece of paper.

"Well," he said, "I do not think I would care to trust the safety of my country to this method of communication."

Staring up at him from the paper were the words:

"Instructions to head man of Forty-fourth Ground-Walking Club. Seek to interpose your club along the high ground between the not-friendly-to-us fellows and the railway station. Use repeated strong practical urging procedures to obtain results desired."

The United States delegate had gotten hold of a typewriter, slid in a piece of paper, typed rapidly, and was now scowling in frustration at the result.

The Soviet delegate shook his head. "What's the word for it? We've been bugged. The section of our vocabulary dealing with . . . with . . . you know what I mean . . . that section has been burned out."

The United States delegate scowled. "Well, we can still stick pins in maps and draw pictures. Eventually we can get across what we mean."

"Yes, but that is no way to run a wa . . . wa . . . a strong disagreement. We will have to build up a whole new vocabulary to deal with the subject."

The United States delegate thought it over, and nodded. "All right," he said. "Now, look. If we're each going to have to make new vocabularies, do we want to end up with . . . say . . . sixteen different words in sixteen different languages all for the same thing? Take a . . . er . . . 'strong disagreement.' Are you going to call it 'gosnik' and we call it 'gack' and the French call it 'gouk' and the Germans call it 'Gunck'? And then we have to have twenty dozen different sets of dictionaries and hundreds of interpreters so we can merely get some idea what each other is talking about?"

"No," said the Soviet delegate grimly. "Not that. We should have an international commission to settle that. Maybe there, at least, is something we can agree on. Obviously, it is to everyone's advantage not to have innumerable new words for the same thing. Meanwhile, perhaps . . . ah . . . perhaps for now we had better postpone a final settlement of the present difficulty."

Six months later, a man wearing a tightly-belted trenchcoat approached the Pentagon building.

A man carrying a heavy suitcase strode along some distance from the Kremlin.

A taxi carrying a well-dressed man with an attaché case cruised past the United Nations building.

Inside the United Nations building, the debate was getting hot. The Soviet delegate said angrily:

"The Soviet Union is the most scientifically advanced and unquestionably the most gacknik nation on Earth. The Soviet Union will not take dictation from anybody.

We have given you an extra half-year to make up your minds, and now we are going to put it to you bluntly:

"If you want to cush a gack with us over this issue, we will mongel you. We will grock you into the middle of next week. No running dog of a capitalist imperialist will get out in one piece. You may hurt us in the process, but *we* will absolutely bocket *you*. The day of decadent capitalism is *over*."

A rush of marvelous dialectic burst into life in the Soviet delegate's mind. For a split instant he could see with unnatural clarity not only why, but how, his nation's philosophy was bound to emerge triumphant—if handled properly—and even without a ruinous gack, too.

Unknown to the Soviet delegate, the United States delegate was simultaneously experiencing a clear insight into the stunning possibilities of basic American beliefs, which up to now had hardly been tapped at all.

At the same time, other delegates were sitting straight, their eyes fixed on distant visions.

The instant of dazzling certainty burnt itself out.

"Yes," said the Soviet delegate, as if in a trance. "No need to even cush a gack. Inevitably, victory must go to communi . . . commu . . . comm . . . com—" He stared in horror.

The American delegate shut his eyes and groaned. "Capitalis . . . capita . . . cap . . . cap . . . rugged individu . . . rugged indi . . . rugge . . . rug . . . rug—" He looked up. "Now we've got to have *another* conference. And then, on top of that, we've got to somehow cram our new definitions down the throats of the thirty per cent of the people they *don't* reach with their device."

The Soviet delegate felt for his chair and sat down heavily. "Dialectic materia . . . dialecti . . . dia . . . dia—"

He put his head in both hands and drew in a deep shuddering breath.

The British delegate was saying, "Thin red li . . . thin re . . . thin . . . thin—This *hurts*."

"Yes," said the United States delegate. "But if this goes on, we may end up with a complete, new, unified language. Maybe that's the idea."

The Soviet delegate drew in a deep breath and looked up gloomily. "Also, this answers one long-standing question."

"What's that?"

"One of your writers asked it long ago: 'What's in a name?' "

The delegates all nodded with sickly expressions.

"*Now* we know."

THE NEW MEMBER
★ ★ ★

Badibax, Bongolia, March 15. Dr. Hodiroy Dabigam, newly elected president of the Republic of the United Bongolias, today presided in ceremonies during which the flag of the Bongolian Republic was raised over the Sanctuary, the principal building of the capital city of Badibax. The Sanctuary, built in the fourteenth century by European traders, was today rechristened Palace of the Presidents by Dr. Hodiroy, who was cheered by an enthusiastic crowd estimated by newsmen at around four thousand. Dr. Hodiroy announced that Bongolia will seek admission to the United Nations, in order to "take our rightful place in the councils of the mighty." Vice Admiral K. C. Baines, commander of the U.S. 34th Fleet, was among the American representatives at the ceremony, which was also attended by delegations from a number of other nations, including communist China.

New York, April 1ˢᵗ. The Republic of the United Bongolias today was officially admitted to the United Nations.

New York, April 2ⁿᵈ. Sodibox Gozinaz Hodiroy, head of the Bongolian delegation to the United Nations, today demanded that Bongolia be admitted to a seat on the Security Council. Mr. Sodibox charged that it is unfair to have only a comparatively few nations represented on the Security Council. "Who are they?" he demanded. "Is this right? They are few. We are many. Why should they have it and not we?" Mr. Sodibox, who spoke in native costume, also charged that many crimes had been committed against his country by the European traders who established themselves in the fourteenth century at the Bongolian capital, Badibax. Mr. Sodibox stated that it was not known just what nation these traders belonged to, but he charged that their presence had held back the development of Bongolian culture, reduced his nation to peonage and wreaked tremendous physical and psychological damage upon his people, damage which still manifested itself today. Mr. Sodibox demanded that reparations be paid by all the European nations, plus the U.S., Canada, Mexico, Australia, New Zealand and the "other colonialist powers responsible for the outrage."

Washington, April 4ᵗʰ. When asked today what the U.S. proposed to do about the Bongolian demand for reparations, the Secretary of State replied that he was a little puzzled by Mr. Sodibox's charge, insofar as the United States did not exist in the fourteenth century, when the alleged crimes took place. The fourteenth century, he pointed out, includes dates from the beginning of the year 1300 through to the end of the year 1399, and the American continent was not even discovered by

Columbus till 1492, one hundred years later. The United States, he said, sympathized with the Bongolian Republic, but naturally could not be expected to pay for crimes it had never committed.

New York, April 4th. Sodibox Gozinaz Hodiroy, chief of the Bongolian delegation to the United Nations, today charged the American Secretary of State with bad faith. In an impassioned speech, Mr. Sodibox declared, *"Look at my people!* Have they not suffered? It is the American imperialists who have committed this crime! They are responsible! And when they are called to account before the councils of the mighty they try to squirm out by some jugglery with numbers! Are numbers more important than the sufferings of my people!"

Washington, April 6th. In his news conference this morning, the President was asked his views on the Bongolian crisis. After a considerable pause, he replied that while the United States felt great sympathy for all who suffered from poverty and want, nevertheless the United States could not accept the blame for a crime committed by persons unknown, some four hundred years before the United States was founded.

Badibax, Bongolia, April 10th. Speaking before a roaring crowd officially estimated at some seventeen thousand, President Dr. Hodiroy Dabigam accused the United States of "treason to the principle of self-determination of the nations, treason to the principal of responsibility for past crimes, treason against race, religion, color, national origin, and the payments of past debts."

He likened the U S. President to a dog licking up the vomit of another dog, whom he identified as the U. S. Secretary of State. President Dr. Hodiroy warned that "the sovereign peoples of the world will not long ignore such insults as these." The Americans, he stated, are running dogs for the nations of Europe, which seek to escape their responsibility for the crimes against Bongolia, and the Americans moreover are descendants of these Europeans, and therefore in it with them. America, President Dr. Hodiroy warned, had best beware, lest the dispossessed nations of South America, Africa, Asia and all the world rise in one body, led by the Republic of the United Bongolias, and "claim the vengeance which has been unpaid now for six hundred years." At the climax of President Hodiroy's speech, the U.S. flag was burned, the Secretary of State was hanged in effigy, and an effigy of the American president was thrown into the streets to be spat upon, defiled and picked to pieces by the frenzied mob. In addition, three U.S. sailors were reported missing.

New York, April 11th. Sodibox Gozinaz Hodiroy, speaking to reporters, today charged that the riots in Bongolia "were fomented by the inflammatory speeches of the American President and Secretary of State, who are therefore personally responsible for them. They have caused them by their refusal to pay for their crimes." Mr. Sodibox was asked by one reporter for the date of his birth. Mr. Sodibox replied that he was forty-one years old. The reporter then asked Mr. Sodibox what he would do if he were charged with a rape that occurred fifty years ago. Mr. Sodibox refused to answer the question.

Washington, April 14th. Senator Clyde Deebling today called for "immediate full-scale economic aid to the Bongolian Republic," which he said "would otherwise be in danger of falling into the hands of the communists." In an unprecedented scene, Senator Deebling was booed for fifteen minutes and finally forced to sit down.

The view here is that the government of Bongolia is lucky not to have done all this a hundred years ago. But since war between the present-day U. S. and Bongolia, which in actuality is a moderately large island in the Sadinak Straits, would be ridiculous, we are in a predicament to know just what to do about it. A great many congressmen, meanwhile, report receiving angry telegrams from their constituents demanding to know what has happened to the American sailors.

New York, April 14th. A number of delegates from Afro-Asian countries are reportedly urging Sodibox Gozinaz, head of the delegation from Bongolia, to take it slower in his attacks on the U.S. These delegates, it is reported, feel that Mr. Sodibox is rousing antagonisms that will not help their efforts to obtain more economic aid from the U. S.

New York, April 14th. Sodibox Gozinaz Hodiroy, the Bongolian delegate to the U.N., today charged Great Britain, France, Spain, Italy, the Netherlands, the Soviet Union and Greece, with complicity in the attempt to avoid payment for the depredations of European traders who invaded Bongolia in the fourteenth century. Since it is not known exactly what nationality these traders were, Mr. Sodibox affirmed his government's position that "all alike must share in the responsibility." Mr. Sodibox estimates the damage done to Bongolia by the traders at two billion kittagotigs. The kittagotig is the new official unit of Bongolian currency. Its value is fixed by the Bongolian government at twice the value of the U.S. dollar.

Badibax, Bongolia, April 15th. No satisfactory answer having been received from the governments of Great Britain, France, Spain, Italy, the Netherlands, the

Soviet Union and Greece, President Dr. Hodiroy Dabigam, speaking to a frenzied rally estimated officially at 40,000 persons, stated that these nations, along with the United States and other guilty parties, owed the Bongolian Republic two billion kittagotigs, plus interest compounded annually at twelve per cent since the year 1300, for their "infamous crimes against the Bongolian peoples, crimes including rape, incest, murder, pillage, brutality, usury, extortion and seizure of lands public and private." At the climax of his speech, President Dr. Hodiroy personally hurled down to the mob effigies of the chiefs of state of Great Britain, France, Spain, Italy, the Netherlands, the Soviet Union and Greece, which were spat on, defiled and kicked around the public square. Later, the national flags of these nations were lashed with whips, pounded with clubs and then burned to the frenzied cheers of the mob.

New York, April 16th. Sodibox Gozinaz Hodiroy, chief of the delegation from the Republic of the United Bongolias, appeared in the U.N. General Assembly this morning, wearing his national costume, with the addition of four dried hands dangling from the front and rear of a strap worn across his left shoulder. These hands, Mr. Sodibox said, are "symbols of the suffering of my people at the hands of the foreign exploiters." When asked where these dried hands came from, Mr. Sodibox replied that they were obtained from "enemies of the state."

Washington, April 16th. "Unimpeachable government sources" state today that repeated queries to the Bongolian government about the fate of the three missing U. S. sailors have gone unanswered.

Badibax, Bongolia, April 17th. Persistent rumors are reported here that two white Americans and a Negro

American are being exhibited in wooden cages in a kind of carnival held on the outskirts of Badibax. Sharp-edged shells, it is reported, are thrown through the bars at the prisoners, and those who hit them win prizes. The description of these men matches that of the missing U.S. sailors.

With the 34th Fleet in the Straits of Sadinak, April 18th. A predawn raid by U. S. Marines this morning recovered the three U.S. sailors missing for more than a week. All three men are reported in serious condition, suffering from hunger, thirst, loss of blood and many deep and badly infected cuts.

New York, April 18th. In an impassioned speech before the U.N. General Assembly, Mr. Sodibox Gozinaz Hodiroy, his face smeared with blood and dirt, and wearing the Bongolian "suit of eighteen pleading heads," made an impassioned attack upon the United States for its "arrogant interference in Bongolian domestic affairs." He charged the U.S. with "aggression, provocation, trespass, and the theft of Bongolian Government prisoners." Mr. Sodibox likened the U.S. to a rich landowner who steals chickens from his impoverished neighbor. As Mr. Sodibox reached the climax of his speech, one of the dried heads slipped loose from its rawhide thong, fell on the table, and rolled off onto the floor. The General Assembly adjourned early, without voting on Mr. Sodibox's demand for a vote of censure against the U.S.

Badibax, Bongolia, April 19th. In an impassioned speech to a frenzied mob officially estimated at eighty thousand persons, President Dr. Hodiroy Dabigam accused the U.S. of "wanton naked aggression against the sovereign state of the Republic of the United Bongolias" and warned that "all oppressed peoples of the world will rise up behind the Bongolian martyrs and hurl themselves upon the American aggressors in a holy bonganap." (The Bongolian word "bonganap" is not directly translatable. It does not mean "war" or "crusade," but refers more to the slaughter of the enemy, followed by the breaking of the bones of the enemy dead. This is considered to cause further pain to those who have already been killed.) President Dr. Hodiroy further accused the American Marines of cowardice, charging that they came armed with modern weapons "only because they are afraid to fight like men, with spears, knives, and stranglewhips." (The "stranglewhip" is a long, slender cord with heavy knots at the end. It is said that skillful wielders of this weapon can coil it around an enemy's neck from behind, without coming close enough for him to hear their approach, then, by clever manipulation of the whip, the wielder can strangle the enemy to death without ever getting close enough for the enemy to strike back.) President Dr. Hodiroy further announced that he holds the U.S. president "personally and immediately responsible for this outrage and hereby demands a full and immediate explanation and apology for this unwarranted intrusion upon sovereign Bongolian territory. Otherwise the U.S. will be subject to retaliation by the full weight of Bongolian military might." It is reported that nearly four hundred Chinese communist technicians, military advisors and specialists in guerilla warfare have arrived in Bongolia since the beginning of the year.

With the 34th Fleet near the Straits of Sadinak, April 19th. Vice Admiral K. C. Baines, commander of naval forces here, has reportedly been petitioned by his contingent of Marines, many of whom wish to go ashore to Badibax in answer to the Bongolian president's accusation of "cowardice." The story is that the Marines would be happy to go after the Bongolians armed only with belts, bayonets, or barehanded and are confident they could "clean the place out in an hour." One enlisted man described the capital city of Badibax as "about a medium-sized town, with ocean in front, the jungle behind, the Kratigatik River to the west and the Chicago dump to the east."

New York, April 19th. Afro-Asian members of the U.N. are visibly shunning the Bongolian delegation. This appears to be in response to the widely quoted Bongolian claim that "Bongolia is the natural leader of the Afro-Asian bloc." Mr. Sodibox Gozinaz, speaking to reporters, today reasserted this position, charging that the other Afro-Asian nations "are backward and have no culture."

Washington, April 19th. Usually reliable sources here state that there is no truth to the rumor currently circulating that the U.S. plans a punitive expedition against the Bongolians. "We've got our men back, and that's what we were after." Asked about the personal feelings of high government officials toward the Bongolians, the spokesman refused comment.

Badibax, Bongolia, April 20th. Addressing a huge rally and speaking from the Palace of the Presidents, President Dr. Hodiroy Dabigam announced tonight completion of a new treaty with communist China. This treaty, President Dr. Hodiroy told the cheering crowd, provides for economic assistance and mutual aid and defense. Accordingly, said Dr. Hodiroy, he hereby calls upon communist China "to come at once to the aid of oppressed Bongolia." Amid the wild cheers of the crowd, officially estimated at one hundred thousand, President

Dr. Hodiroy declared, "we now call upon our pledged allies to hurl themselves at once into universal mortal conflict at all points with the mutual enemy who has sullied the soil of the Republic of United Bongolias. We will do the same, in turn, if our ally is ever attacked."

Peking, April 21ˢᵗ. No word has yet been announced here about the "American aggression" in rescuing three captured U.S. sailors from the Bongolians. There is also no word about the treaty.

Moscow, April 23ʳᵈ. A high Soviet official contacted here today was asked about the apparent predominance of Chinese communist influence in Bongolia. He replied smilingly that he understood that the Chinese were not perfectly happy with their new ally, but the Soviet Union "does not wish to interfere."

Badibax, Bongolia, April 24ᵗʰ. President Dr. Hodiroy Dabigam, addressing a wildly enthusiastic crowd officially estimated at a quarter of a million persons, called again tonight for the "immediate destruction by our Chinese allies of the American imperialists who committed rapine, murder, trespass and larceny against our people by their brutal armed aggression." President Dr. Hodiroy injected a new note into the demand by observing, "We have over four hundred Chinese here—they are in our power, remember."

New York, April 25ᵗʰ. The head of the Bongolian delegation, Sodibox Gozinaz Hodiroy, attempted to speak today, but the hall emptied so rapidly that he was left with no audience. Mr. Sodibox was wearing his "suit of eighteen pleading heads." A number of delegates, interviewed outside, stated that in their opinion the admission of Bongolia to the world body had been "premature."

Washington, April 26th. A number of U.S. senators and congressmen are reportedly agreed that the whole body of assumptions underlying the U.N. and many foreign nations needs to be re-examined. The "Bongolian mess" was the reason named by most of them for crystallizing this belief.

Peking, April 27th. In a formal warning to President Dr. Hodiroy Dabigam, the Chinese communist government today called for the immediate release of any Chinese nationals now held by the Bongolians as hostages. "Serious consequences may result," the Chinese warn, if these hostages are not immediately released unharmed.

Badibax, Bongolia, April 28th. President Dr. Hodiroy Dabigam, in an impassioned speech to an officially estimated half-million persons, today declared "bonganap" (war to the death, and then smash the enemy's bones) against the Chinese communists that he charged are trying to take over the island.

New York, April 28th. Sodibox Gozinaz Hodiroy, head of the Bongolian delegation to the U.N., today called upon the world body to unite in defense of a member nation and destroy communist China. The Chinese, Mr. Sodibox declared, are "heavily invading Bongolia despite heroic resistance by the Bongolian armed forces." No action was taken by the U. N., pending further information.

With the 34th Fleet in the Straits of Sadinak, April 28th. Firing from Bongolia could be heard tonight on board ships of the 34th Fleet cruising outside Bongolian territorial waters. If the Chinese are putting fresh "invasion troops" ashore here, they must be landing them from invisible ships. Aerial observation all day has revealed nothing remotely like a seaborne invasion force.

Badibax, Bongolia, April 30th. President Dr. Hodiroy Dabigam announced today that he has assumed "immediate full control over all Bongolian land, sea, air and space forces, with the rank of Field-Marshal General." President Dr. Field-Marshal General Hodiroy then announced completion of the successful bonganap against the Chinese communists by a "flank-attack combined with reverse enfilade fire by a seaborne invasion force of shock troops under my direct command." President Dr. Field-Marshal General Hodiroy then warned all states, singly and collectively, to consider this result of Bongolian Armed Forces in action and heed the warning. "China," he said, "is a large country. But we have defeated her crushingly."

Moscow, April 30th. Word of the Bongolian statement on their "victory" over "Chinese invaders" reached a group of leading Soviet officials at an informal reception here tonight. The Russians made no official statement, but were reported by the Americans present to have "gone into hysterics" after reading the Bongolian victory announcement.

Peking, April 30th. On the eve of the big May Day celebration, the mood of high officials in this capital can only be described by the image of a volcano pent up under a layer of ice five miles thick.

Washington, May 1st. Ships of the U.S. 34th Fleet, operating in the Sadinak Straits, are reported to have fished a large number of Chinese survivors out of the waters off Bongolia. Owing to the mutual anti-Bongolian sentiment, the Chinese appear to have talked freely to U.S. intelligence officers. What evidently happened was that the Bongolians, armed with weapons supplied by the Chinese, carried out a night sneak attack against the

Chinese, who were outnumbered and mostly split up into small groups to begin with. The Chinese were slaughtered piecemeal, no more than perhaps one out of five having gotten away, many of these seriously wounded.

New York, May 2nd. At a meeting of the Security Council today, it was unanimously decided to take no action on the Bongolian charge of Chinese aggression.

New York, May 3rd. Sodibox Gozinaz Hodiroy, head of the Bongolian delegation to the United Nations, today announced that "the free and sovereign nation of the Republic of the United Bongolias hereby breaks and severs all relations with the United Nations, unilaterally and irrevocably permanently withdraws from the United Nations and declares 'doziwak' (this word, "doziwak," does not mean "war" but a peculiarly devastating insult; it is not directly translatable from the Bongolian) upon the United Nations and all the members thereof." Mr. Sodibox, who donned his "suit of the fourteen angry heads" before speaking, immediately left the U.N. Building, followed by the rest of his delegation. Upon leaving the U.N. grounds, Mr. Sodibox was at once arrested by the New York City police, on suspicion of murder.

New York, May 3rd. The Police Commissioner denied today that the New York police had any intention of releasing Sodibox Gozinaz Hodiroy or his accomplices, "till we find out where all those dried heads came from. They got those heads off of somebody. The question is—Who?"

WASHINGTON'S
★HEADACHES★

BABEL II
★ ★ ★

The new Assistant Secretary of State doubtfully eased along the row of seats in the big dim room, and settled scowlingly into a chair beside the well-known Kremlinologist.

"Damn it, Bill," growled the Assistant Secretary, "if I'd known this was where you got your inside information—"

"Sh-h," said the Kremlinologist, raising a finger. "We're about to start."

At the front of the room, under a single clear light, Madame Sairo signaled to her assistants.

The room's overhead lights dimmed further. A blond boy dressed all in white rolled out on heavy casters a thing that at first glance looked like a big globe of the world set in a large holder, but on closer examination turned out to be a crystal ball about two feet thick.

47

Madame Sairo adjusted the big crystal, and took her seat.

The room fell silent. The Kremlinologists, the Far East experts, and the Government economists leaned forward attentively.

Madame Sairo gazed intently at the crystal, her mind focused on the question of the evening. For some time, however, she got nowhere, and when the mists finally did began to shred away, the scene that formed did not seem to be right. Frowning, she watched the unfamiliar man at the desk.

Elias Polk, trying to extract the sense of this latest report on the Esmer Drive, was stuck again on the section reading:

" . . . difficulty remains in the suffluxion of the tantron stream, and resultant violent node-regression. Yet any other approach obviously requires consideration of Hasebrouck's theory of complex particle-interaction . . ."

Polk's train of thought each time went off the track at that word "obviously." *Why* did any other approach obviously require consideration of Hasebrouck's theory?

Polk flipped on through the report.

There followed five pages of Hasebrouck's del, rodel, and pi-del equations, and then it all ended up with the words:

" . . . therefore, we unequivocally recommend construction of the 175–TEV tangential accelerator."

That followed from consideration of Hasebrouck's equations, and Hasebrouck's equations came in because "any other approach obviously requires consideration of Hasebrouck's theory . . . "

Why was it obvious?

Polk looked up exasperatedly at the reversed letters on the glass of the door, from long familiarity reading them as easily as someone in the hall outside:

PROJECT LONG-REACH
J. Elias Polk
Director

Polk squinted at the report, tossed it down, picked up some papers, and thumbed through them. He settled back, scowling.

The estimated cost of that accelerator was seventy-two billion, over nine years. But with that for the original estimate, the true cost would probably run well above a hundred billion, and it would take twelve years.

Even then, no one could be sure that would give them enough information to eventually straighten out the difficulty.

Polk glanced back at the report.

" . . . *obviously* any other approach requires consideration of Hasebrouck's . . . "

Frowning, Polk reached for the phone.

As the scene faded, Madame Sairo sat back blankly. Just what did *that* have to do with anything? What her clients wanted to know—

But there, a new scene was forming. She leaned forward hopefully.

The door opened, and Marcus Flint stepped out into the hall, the sheets of calculations and charts with their pretty colored lines clutched in his hand. He strode down the hall, and threw open a second door without knocking.

"Are you out of your head, Peters? What do you think I'm running here, a market report or an obituary column?"

Peters adjusted his thick lenses and set his jaw. "Our computer analysis showed the projected OJDA taking a nose dive through the TL, with our PF matrix-model running out of steam before the year is out. We're in for a depression that could jar your teeth, MF."

"Nuts. With this big spending for space projects—"

"That spending for space projects is increasing on our Chart III, there, to the point where it overshoots the stimulus role, and turns into a drain, pure and simple. Especially when you consider that Chart IV shows external and internal unidirectional cycle flow—"

"Will you, for God's sake—" Flint caught himself. "Look, I'll grant your expertise. Spare me this jargon, will you? What is external and internal unidirectional cycle flow?"

"Value tokens in unidirection circulation, external or internal to the national economy, unaccompanied by a reverse flow of actual-value services or goods, either essential, marginal, or redundant."

"*Unearned money?* Giveaway programs?"

Peters blinked. "Well—Yes, I suppose you *could* put it that way."

"All right, what about unearned money?"

Peters started to speak, hesitated, and shook his head. "I can't use that term 'unearned money.' It has extraneous moral connotations. The moral connotations block consideration of the purely economic factors per se."

"All right," snarled Flint. "Then what about this cycle flow?"

"We have a serious maladjustment of the reverse flow of actual-value units. Deferred payment of value tokens for actual-value units is not presently serious in itself. However, this continuing increase in the flow of value tokens with neither past, present, nor future correlated return flow of actual-value units creates an imbalance in the circuit flow, and that is serious."

Flint grappled with the statement, and finally quoted, " 'This grasping after unearned money will in time wreck the country.' I think Abraham Lincoln said that."

"He *did*?" Peters blinked, then squirmed uneasily. "But that term 'unearned money' implies a—"

"All right," snarled Flint, " 'unidirectional cycle flow.' Have it your own way. The point is, this projection of yours is so drastic no one will *believe* it. Its value, therefore, is nil. Moreover, jargon is great for mystifying people and impressing them with your expertise. But you've already accomplished *that*. It's a good idea to occasionally say something someone can understand, so he'll keep listening in hopes it will happen again. You've got this special lingo—"

Peters said stiffly, "Precise terminology is necessary, in order to express the special economic forces and relationships operative in the economy."

"You're carrying it too far. Nobody can understand it but you and a few other analysts who happen to use the same approach. Translate the final results into plain English."

Peters looked horrified. "That's as absurd as a surgeon trying to explain a complicated operation to a layman, using no special terms. What could he say? 'I got a knife out and slit his stomach open. Then I clamped the skin and muscle back out of the way, and went in after his append . . . this bag of—' "

Flint nodded. "That's the idea."

"But all the fine points would be lost! The expert would have to skip *every detail that the layman lacked the knowledge to understand*." Peters shook his head positively. "No. The only way to get the actual facts across is for the *layman* to study the matter until he acquires enough facts to *understand the expert's explanation*."

Marcus Flint leaned forward, the knuckles of his hand resting on the desktop.

"Doesn't it dawn on you that experts are proliferating like rabbits in this country? Just exactly where is any layman going to *get the time to study fifteen hundred different specialties so he can figure out what all these experts are talking about*?"

Peters spread his hands. "That isn't *my* problem. Don't blame me. *I* didn't make the world."

Madame Sairo sat back blankly. As the scene faded, she found herself like a pearl diver who surfaces with a few odd-shaped pebbles and no pearls. What was wrong?

But even as she groped for the cause of the trouble, a new scene was forming.

Ah, now, this looked more hopeful.

"Yes," she said quietly, "I have it. This is a distant land, and they are building. It is a tall structure—"

The Kremlinologists and Pekingologists leaned forward intently. The government economists looked shrewd.

The new Assistant Secretary growled, "Took her long enough."

"*Sh-h*," said his neighbors.

" . . . Yes," Madame Sairo was saying, "this is a tower of some kind. It is a very ambitious project, but this nation is great. It is—"

Someone murmured, "China?"

Another whispered, "A new atom-test project?"

The Assistant Secretary stared around in disbelief, trying to pick out faces in the gloom so he would know in the future whose advice had come out of this crystal ball.

Madame Sairo jerked back suddenly from the globe. She gestured imperiously.

The overhead lights came on.

She looked around the tensely quiet room, her expression serious.

"Gentlemen, I am afraid I must ask you to be very patient. You wish me to examine the next great world crisis. But there seems to be some difficulty here. I have been in contact with some events that appear irrelevant, and then with what apparently was a great *past* world crisis. Conceivably there is interference of some kind here. Or possibly some symbolism I do not yet understand. If you will be patient, I will try again."

Her audience quietly settled back.

The room lights dimmed.

In the crystal, a new scene seemed to swim into view.

But *this* seemed to be just a man and a boy, glaring at each other.

Patiently, Madame Sairo leaned forward.

Sumner Maddox said exasperatedly, "You look at the lives of outstanding men who've really succeeded in a big way, and you'll find that *most* of them got an early start. Now, I'm not trying to force you to decide what you want to do with your life. But you've got to decide for yourself, one way or the other, and pick *something*."

"But I *can't* decide," said Roger Maddox, looking baffled. "There just doesn't seem to be anything—It's all hazy. There's just nothing I want to—"

The elder Maddox grimaced. "Listen. Without half your opportunities or advantages your great-grandfather had already learned a trade and was making a living at your age. Now, no one expects you to do the same. *Your* generation can go to school till they're twenty-six, and—"

Roger Maddox abruptly flared up. "I *won't* go to school till I'm twenty-six!"

Sumner Maddox said placatingly, "I didn't say you *would*. I say you *could*. Anyway, that's a long way off. But you still have to decide—"

There was a brief tense silence.

The younger Maddox stared at a distant corner of the room. "Wait a minute. I see what's wrong. It used to be, that when someone was growing up, day after day he *saw* grown people at work. In Great-Granddad's day, you could *watch* what different people did, see with your own eyes how they lived, and what their work was good for. Then you could decide what you wanted to do, because you knew what the choices were. It was like stopping at a crossroads to decide which of three or four different towns to go to, when you'd already seen the towns, and knew what they were like. But now—Now it's like stopping at a crossroads to decide which of a hundred and seventeen different cities to go live in, *when you never really had a good first-hand look at any of them before*."

The elder Maddox frowned. "Well . . . you've got a point there. That's because things are more complex now. Each special type of work is harder to understand, there are more specialties to consider, and the grown-ups work in one place while the children are in school somewhere else. It's *got* to be that way, but—" He paused exasperatedly. "Now, how the deuce do we get around this? Let's see—"

The scene faded out. Before there was time to even try to evaluate it, another scene formed, and there were two men in uniform, in an office with a photograph of a long gray ship on one wall, and a photograph of what was apparently some kind of submarine on another wall.

Admiral Bendix ran his gaze down the list of officers and shook his head.

"I know every one of these men, and not one of them is fitted. For captain of the *Constitution*, we need someone exceptional. He has to have outstanding capabilities as a leader of men, plus unusual ability in all the skills of ship-handling. On top of that we need someone with the technical know-how to *comprehend the ship's drive*, so that he can get the most out of it and the technicians who handle it."

Admiral Hart leaned back, his hands clasped behind his head.

"We may need three men for captain, in other words."

"It has to be *one* man. The knowledge has got to be in one head when the clinch comes, because every bit of it is crucial. How can you decide, when you lack the knowledge to evaluate the factors involved? The captain has to make the decisions, and while he certainly doesn't have to know *everything*, he has got to understand the ship, the men, and the ship's drive. Unless he has the knowledge himself, he *can't* make the decisions."

Hart shook his head.

"We aren't going to find one man with all those skills."

"We've got to *have* one man with all those skills. He has to *understand* the technical limitations of the ship, and he can only do that *if he understands the drive*."

Admiral Hart sat up and looked Admiral Bendix in the eye.

"Do *you* understand the drive?"

Admiral Bendix looked flatly back.

"No. Do *you*?"

"No."

"But *we* aren't going to command this ship. Who-ever does—"

Admiral Hart waved his head irritatedly. "Look, to honestly understand that drive, you'd have had to start at about age twelve, and follow just the right course of study ever since. But you'd have had to follow it by luck or by predestination, because at that time, back when you'd have had to start, *nobody knew this drive could be built*. Did you ever look in any of those books? Did you ever try to talk to any of the people working on the project? And in about fifteen years, the thing may be obsolete." He lowered his voice. "I hear the Esmer Drive is going great guns. Who understands *that*?"

Admiral Bendix put the list down in disgust. "I sup-pose it wouldn't be too soon to start looking for one right now."

Hart nodded soberly. "But this still doesn't find us a man for the *Constitution*."

Exasperatedly, the two men went through the list again.

Elias Polk was staring at the man across the desk. "Damn it, can't you explain your reasoning any better than that? You want the country to put a hundred billion dollars into something you can't even explain?"

"How do I explain it to you when you don't understand the concepts involved? Once you understand those con-cepts, the solution is intuitive. I know the answer the same way I know where water will come out when I tip a pitcher. It's *obvious*."

Reginald Paxter slit the envelope, pulled out the glossy book advertisements, and glanced at the titles:

"Inverted Limits in Transient Field Problems."

"Operational Functions for Projected Relay Circuitry."

"Recent Developments in Kick-Back Ready-State Devices."

Paxter sneered. "Gibberish. Pure gibberish. Who would—" He paused. One more title caught his attention. His eyes lighted.

"Saro Integrals in Complex Space Matrices of Non-Orthogonal Form."

Eagerly he pulled over the order sheet and got out his checkbook.

"No, Mrs. Bennett," said the service manager with a hounded look, "it was the brake *lining*, inside the brake drum, that was bad. It was cracked, glazed—Before, all we had to do was *adjust* the brakes, that's why this time it cost—" The phone rang jarringly. "Excuse me just a minute. *Hello?*"

A familiar sarcastic male voice said, "Look, the starter you said you fixed. It doesn't work. When I tried to start the car this morning, it just groaned."

"Ah—Well, the trouble is, like I said when you were in here, your voltage regulator—"

"What's that got to do with the starter?"

"Well, you see, the generator puts electricity *in* the battery. The starter takes it *out*. The—"

"How did the *generator* get in this? Are you trying to tell me you've got to work on the *generator* now?"

"No, but the voltage regulator is—"

"A minute ago, you said the generator. Which is it?"

"The *regulator* decides what the *generator* output will be. If the regulator is bad, the generator can't put electricity in the battery. When you were in here, I was trying to tell you—"

"What's that got to do with the starter?"

"If your battery's dead, the starter can't turn the engine over."

There was a brief silence. "Well, there's *something* shot on this car. I had my brother push me all the way from Great Bend into town with the car in low-range, and the engine never caught once. I want that starter job done over, and this time find what's wrong."

The service manager seemed to see the bursting of innumerable bubbles before his eyes. "Look," he said, speaking carefully, "on your car, there's no rear pump in the transmission. You *can't* start it by pushing. You can ruin the transmission that way. You say you pushed it *all the way from Great Bend to town in low*?"

As the silence on the other end stretched out, he asked himself, didn't people know *anything* about the cars they drove?

Mrs. Bennett cleared her throat. "What did you mean when you said the brake linings were 'glazed'?"

Over the phone came a baffled voice.

"What's a 'rear pump'? Now . . . just wait a minute. What are you trying to pull, anyway? *What's the transmission got to do with the starter*?"

Madame Sairo sat back with a pained expression. She looked up from the globe, and glanced around the dimly-lit room.

"I am *trying* to learn of the next world crisis. I am concentrating on the next world crisis. I am trying to look into the future, and I am still making irrelevant contacts with past and present. Is there anyone here whose motives are not right?"

The Kremlinologists and Pekingologists squinted dubiously at each other.

The Government economists looked pious.

The Assistant Secretary sat back and sneered at the whole fraud.

Madame Sairo adjusted the globe, and without much hope.

Dr. Greenhaven peered at the knowledge-growth projection, and then at the distribution-of-intelligence curve.

"We seem to be running into some difficulty here."

"Obviously," said the Project Coordinator. "We now have teams of men attempting to do the jobs one man properly should do. This can only be carried so far. There is a delay each time knowledge must be transferred from one mind to another. If we have fifteen men, each with a different specialty, gathered around a table to help make a decision, we are in serious trouble. But we are worse off yet if we have a hundred and fifty men, each with his own specialty, gathered around that table. Knowledge is proliferating, Doctor. It is multiplying by leaps and bounds. If we aren't to have ten fragmented specialists where one stands now, what are we going to do about it?"

Dr. Greenhaven puffed out his cheeks, took another look at the charts, and said tentatively, "We must locate individuals capable of mastering this knowledge."

The Projects Coordinator looked bored.

"And," said Greenhaven, "educate them at an earlier age. If possible, we must specialize sooner, educate earlier and more intensively. If possible, we must select the most capable, rather than leaving them to blunder around on their own. We will have to separate types according to aptitude and potential skill. A deliberate *fractionation of the race* into useful types."

The Projects Coordinator at once looked interested. "Go on."

Madame Sairo watched the scene fade, and then hopefully looked into the crystal. *Now* she was seeing. But what did it mean?

There before her, as clear as if she were looking directly at it, was a tall something aimed at the sky, towering over the men in their coats of different styles and colors, working around the huge device.

Now it seemed to come closer to her, so that she was almost at the base of the device, and could see the people clearly.

Odd—They seemed to be separated almost according to physical types—or was that somehow the result of the similar clothes, similar facial expressions, and similar manner and air of those doing a particular job? Those at the—wiring?—seemed nearly all to be fairly tall and slender, with rather long faces, and penetrating blue eyes of an unusual cast, while those moving the machinery into place were mostly shorter, burlier types, and the others at the controls—

Puzzled, she leaned closer, trying to unravel the mystery, when a tall individual in a dark purple coat brushed past the—electronics men?—and then bumped a burly individual in a dark-blue jacket.

The purple-coated individual turned, holding the end of a long cable, and spoke irritatedly.

"Surry, fren?"

The blue-jacketed individual jerked his thumb back briefly at what looked like a large glistening maze of intertangled silver wires, set down into some kind of metal-lined pit, with large instrument panels nearby.

"Damn double-phased S-2 pit jerks more on hydrine than ever. Countercycles, shudders, creeps, unamit uknavit."

The blue-jacketed individual glanced around uncertainly, then his eyes widened. He seized the purple-coated individual by the arm.

"Damn doublefaced stupid jerk, eh? *Moron*, huh? Upurps gotcha nerv, *Tagibak!*"

The purple-coated individual looked at him coldly. He wrenched his arm free. "Right, Bluejack. Jerks, creeps, counter—"

"Bluejack" whipped the end of the cable around and landed a stunning blow.

The man in the purple coat staggered back, his hand to his face. Suddenly he screamed in rage.

Two tall, gray-coated individuals with a professorial air paused, frowning as if to try to get the scene into focus.

Another blue-jacketed individual, pulling a thick cable through a metal frame, whirled around as the man in the purple coat charged. Dropping the cable, the second blue-jacketed man rushed to the scene.

An otherworldly individual in orange and white looked down in pained surprise from an overhead ramp.

"Peace. Let us have peace. Brethren, what is the meaning of brotherhood if we cannot have peace? It is wicked to—"

Half-a-dozen purple-clothed individuals boiled out of the metal-lined pit and came on the run.

The two professorial individuals in gray glanced at one another in bafflement.

A short, plump man in a jacket, striped like black typewriter ribbon alternated with red tape, burst out of a little cubicle in the midst of a maze of pneumatic tubes, and still clutching a rubber stamp, a crumpled form filled out in quintuplicate, and a thick book with his finger holding the place, raced onto the scene.

"*Stop!* This voids the contract! Forbidden on worktime! *ARBITRATOR!*"

More blue-jackets were appearing from everywhere. One banged into a black-coated worker in his haste, and got rewarded by a smash over the back of the head with a socket wrench three feet long.

"There," said the blackcoat, beaming. "Stuckup bluejacket! Lectricity! Watsowunifulbout lectricty? I'll lectricity the sonsa—"

His voice choked off as a length of cable whipped around his neck from behind.

A plump individual with a pill bottle in one hand tore down the overhead ramp, his pastel pink coat flapping behind him.

"Here!" he shouted, "Let's ARBITRATE the differences! Friends, FRIENDS, let's SPLIT THE DIFFERENCE! The other side DIDN'T MEAN IT. They're *reasonable!*" He looked down at the boiling melee of bluejacks, purps, and blackcoats, then twisted the cap of the pill bottle, and shot three pills into his mouth. He chewed desperately, stuck the bottle in his side pocket, and waited till an air of calm assurance passed over his face like a mask. He pulled a tiny microphone on a cord from his pocket, plugged it into a socket on the rail of the ramp, and his voice seemed to come out from everywhere, calm, persuasive, assured.

"FRIENDS, THIS IS A MISUNDERSTANDING. *THEY DIDN'T MEAN IT*! THEY WANT TO BE *FRIENDS*. WE CAN SETTLE THIS BETTER—"

A blue-jacketed figure popped out of the mob, snarled, "Shutupjerk," and held a length of dangling cable near a small metal box on a pole. There was a large jagged dancing spark, a roaring noise, and then silence from the public-address system.

The bluejacket grinned, then thrust the cable against the leg of a purple-coated individual who had another bluejacket by the throat.

On the overhead ramp, the pastel-coated arbitrator looked puzzled, but spoke on with invincible assurance as a horde of burly individuals, their coats striped vertically like zebras, intermingled with the rest of the strugglers and began laying them out in all directions indifferently, only to be set upon by others, their zebra-stripes running horizontally.

In all directions, on high and low levels, struggling sets of individuals could now be seen pushing each other over the edge, choking, kicking, biting—

On the ramp, the arbitrator looked around, and paused. Worry crossed his face. He pulled out the bottle and tossed another pill in his mouth. He glanced at his watch. Ninety seconds passed and he was still worried. He took a last look around, jammed the bottle in his pocket and yelled, "POLICE!"

Below, the mob slammed into a wheeled machine, which mounted an insulated man-carrying stand on a long jointed metal arm.

The arm swung around sidewise, striking a tall heavy wire grid holding glistening beadlike objects of varying colors, shapes, and sizes. A large section of the grid wrapped around the stand and the metal arm. There was a loud sizzle, then a sheet of flame roared up, followed by a cloud of boiling smoke.

A dazzling spark, or blazing point of light, rapidly ate its way up the shiny cable into which a number of the grid wires fed, and traveled along the cable up the side of the towering device.

The arbitrator's gaze followed the climbing spark in bafflement. How did you split the difference with a thing like that? The facts of the matter began to penetrate his pill-given assurance. He glanced around.

A little group of scowling men in checked black-and-blue jackets, followed by a host of blue-clothed men armed with gas guns and billies, advanced at a fast walk down the ramp, trying to make out what was going on, and then one of the men in a checked jacket suddenly spread both arms, stopping those behind him. He stared up at the dazzling spark, just disappearing into the towering device, and suddenly grabbed a portable loudspeaker from a man behind him.

"She's going to blow! RUN! RUN FOR IT! *SHE'S GOING TO BLOW!*"

From the tall device, a feather of greenish smoke spurted out.

The men looked up in horror.

The greenish feather gradually grew darker and thicker. It came out with more force and began to reach farther out.

The mob boiled away in all directions, dwindled into little groups of men jumping off low towers and climbing up out of sunken pits, to sort themselves in like groups with almost a family resemblance, and sprint away in a desperate rush.

From the tall device, a green jet now reached out, with a whitish flame that lit the totally abandoned machinery below.

The whole scene began to dwindle, to fade entirely

Madame Sairo leaned back wearily. She sat in silence for some time, then shook her head.

As the bulk of her audience waited hopefully, and the Assistant Secretary looked on cynically, Madame Sairo spoke with considerable doubt.

"I am not sure our thoughts are all in harmony. It seems to me there has been some sort of interference.

"I have seen what was apparently remote antiquity. And I have looked upon a number of seemingly unrelated more or less current scenes which, however, now *do* seem to have some sort of connection, after all. And finally I have seen what I cannot believe was really the *next* world crisis, which is what you wish to know about; but then, if you are not in harmony, as I have warned you, it may confuse the issue under certain conditions. However, if I understand this, the sooner you know of the danger, the better."

Madame Sairo signaled to her assistants.

The overhead lights came on, and the blond boy in white wheeled away the big crystal.

"Now," said Madame Sairo, "I am going to tell you some ancient history. And let me remind you, 'History repeats.' "

At that moment, Elias Polk was studying the latest report on the Esmer Drive. This report was even worse than the one before. This one seemed so devoid of any human connection that Polk's mind could get no lasting grip on it.

Exasperatedly, he shoved the dictionary aside, flattened the report on his desk, and reminded himself that a human being on the other end of a pencil had originated the first version of this thing, and yet here it was, presumably in his own tongue, and he couldn't understand it.

Polk shook his head as a related thought occurred to him.

Science and technology were repeatedly branching, so that there were more separated specialties in each individual branch all the time.

All the curves showed that progress in each individual branch of science and technology was skyrocketing.

It was natural to suppose that this meant unlimited progress.

But what about the *connections* between the individual scientists, technicians, and people generally?

By shoveling coal fast into the firebox of a steam engine, and plotting the resulting speed, it would be possible to make a curve that rose and rose, heading up toward infinity, until the safety valve blew, or, barring that, until the metal of the boiler lost cohesion and let go in a hundred different directions at once, and the process came to a stop.

Polk picked up the report, and took a long hard look at it.

"It would be possible," he growled, "to carry this so far that nobody understands anyone in any other line of work, and *then* what will we have?"

He paused, frowning. Hadn't he read, or heard, somewhere, about some such thing?

Then he shook his head sourly, and tossed the report back on the desk.

Man was *headed* for the stars.

But he would have to be careful he didn't wind up in the Tower of Babel instead.

THE TROJAN BOMBARDMENT
★ ★ ★

General Pier S. Hardesty placed his finger on the map.

"Here, at Karnak City. A twenty-hour bombardment, and bombing round the clock until I say 'Stop.' Also at the road junction north of Hellcat Pass. I want the defenses there plastered."

Burns, the artillery officer, shook his head. "We can do anything you want to Karnak City. But we can't hit that road junction till we either capture both ends of the pass or get some kind of position on the south slope of the Hellcat Mountains. There's a little matter of lofting those shells over that mountain range."

"What's the matter?" Hardesty demanded. "You've got 915 mm. howitzers running out your ears."

"Yes, sir. But the shells have a somewhat different trajectory from what you might expect. I'd like to take the lot of these 915's and—" Burns told in short language what he would like to do with them. Hardesty listened critically, then shook his head.

"You couldn't do it," he said. "They wouldn't fit. Personally, I'd like to—"

The air officer put in, in a purring voice, "If Colonel Burns feels that his artillery can't make it over the foothills, I'm sure *we* can plaster this road junction, General. With any kind of explosive, incendiary or distractant you care to use."

"What we're up against is a collection of half-starved, communized fanatics here, and semi-lunatic do-gooders at home," said the general. "Personally, I'd like to take these Kazang rebels and slaughter the lot of them. But they pop down holes like rats, bob up somewhere else, to put a bullet through the back of your head, and if we give them what they deserve, everybody's afraid their coreligionists will rise up and the thing will spread instead of ending." He shook his head. "So—we're using distractants only."

"Yes, sir," said the air officer. "Well, *we* can reach that road junction, sir."

Burns, the artillery officer, said, "*Live* distractants. They have to hit the junction with a reasonable facsimile of pinpoint accuracy."

"We can—"

"*Without jarring.*"

"Ah."

"Parachutes won't work. Vaned containers induce nausea and make a bad psychological effect. Our 915's have a rotating base and tip, stabilized canister and proximity-controlled shortlife superrotating pop-out blades. They land the load *gently.*"

The air officer snorted. "But at the beginning, this same load starts off how? It's *shot out of a gun.*"

Burns nodded. "Using microtimed charges and safety vents to insure smooth acceleration, with internal cushioning in the canister, rocket-assist units, and a barrel proportioned to fit a coast-defense gun instead of an honest howitzer. These 915's may burn the ears off an artilleryman now and then, but they don't hurt the charge."

The air officer shook his head in disgust. "What a war."

General Hardesty eyed him speculatively. "Can you air-drop these distractants on that road junction?"

"Well, sir—"

"Our canisters," said Burns helpfully, "are armored, to prevent unfortunate incidents."

The air officer said in disgust, "No, sir. I'm afraid we can't compete under these conditions. Not yet, at least."

"All right," said Hardesty. "Let's get this mess straightened out and get squared away. First we hit Karnak City. Twenty-hour bombardment and bombing around the clock, until I'm satisfied they've had it. There's three battalions of the Kazang Death's Head Elite Guard holed up in there, and they aim to make a house-to-house defense and then afterward claim we desecrated the temple when they left. We want to be sure they're well softened up before we move in."

"Yes, sir. As—the charges?"

"A, B and C, but no D. I have to reserve D for that road junction." He eyed Burns coldly.

"Sir," said Burns, "the 915's just won't reach that junction. That's all there is to it. But if you decide to soften it up with A and B distractants, out of 155–S howitzers, we can do that for you."

Hardesty nodded. "All right. Hit the pass with A and B for a couple of hours, then walk on back and plaster the junction."

"When we move up later," said Burns, "we can hit the junction with all the D you want. Ah, that is, with as many D canisters as you can load."

"All right. That will have to do it."

Burns saluted and left at a trot. The air officer saluted and ran off in a different direction.

A perspiring individual in fatigues, with "Correspondent" sewed at his shoulder, scribbled frantically in a notebook and eased closer to the scowling general.

"Ah—General Hardesty. May I ask, sir, how do you feel about the effectiveness of this new and advanced means of—er—settling international conflicts?"

"I've been directed to use it," said the general, "and I'm using it."

"Yes, sir, but how do you *feel*? What is your *assessment* of the *effectiveness* of this method?"

Hardesty squinted at the correspondent like a large dog eyeing a small porcupine. The fellow was a nuisance, all right. And there was no question but that Hardesty could obliterate him. But in the process, he might collect some painful mementos that would fester for a long time afterward.

"It works," said Hardesty abruptly, "in the short run. In the long run, I foresee some difficulties."

"H'm. Might I ask, sir—"

"I can't tell you what's going to go wrong without tending to precipitate the very thing I want to avoid. Just stick around. You'll see."

"M'm." the correspondent was scribbling fast in his notebook. The general suddenly wondered how much of that was going to be legible later and how many illegible sections would be bridged over by the correspondent's imagination. He glanced at his watch and saw that there

were still a few moments till the 105's opened up and
the air arm went into action. He frowned back at the
notebook. "What system of shorthand is that you're
using?"

"Shorthand? Oh, my own, general. I leave out all the
vowels and capitals, and don't bother with the punctu-
ation."

The general nodded. "Just as I thought."

Underfoot, the ground jumped.

A few moments later someone shouted, "Drones
out, sir!"

The general nodded.

A thunderous concussion rolled out across the flat
green land and echoed back from the hills ahead. There
was a continuous trembling underfoot. Dark forms
blurred into the sky, to vanish in the direction of Karnak
City, the Kazangs' ancient capital and religious center.
With a roar, the aircraft began to take off.

Someone shouted, "Drones transmitting, sir!"

The general nodded and walked fast for the TV shack.
The correspondent stayed close at his heels.

"Sir!" shouted the correspondent. "Would you say this
new and more sophisticated means of—ah—settling dis-
putes is an outgrowth of the spectacular increase in our
productive capacity, consequent upon progressive scientific and technological advances, and the rationalization
of productive methods?"

"I suppose so."

"Would you say that it represents a hopeful development in relations between states and differing ideological
systems and viewpoints?"

"That I don't know." The general ducked past a guard
and through a doorway. Behind him, there was an angry

outburst as the guard stopped the correspondent. The general ran down a flight of steps, turned a corner, went by another guard, and through another doorway. Before him were about a dozen big TV screens, arranged in a semicircle, with operators adjusting the screens for clarity and speaking through headphones to the drone-controllers overhead. Roughly half of the screens were already lit.

The nearest lighted screen showed a street of small shops, with a trench across the street, the heaped-up dirt forming a parapet, and the crowded figures of Kazang rebels armed with tommy-guns and bazookas peering out over the dirt. Down the street, others looked out from barricaded shops. One of the men pointed up and shouted, as a small parachute drifted down, supporting some kind of dangling burden.

Instantly a fanatical-looking soldier raised his gun and shot at it, creating a dazzle of flying fragments and a splash of something dark on the front of the parapet. A second soldier bent over the parapet, straightened, and shouted something. The first soldier took aim toward another parachute drifting down. A third soldier changed grips on his gun and smashed the first soldier over the head.

The small parachute drifted closer, and was immediately snatched from the air. For an instant, its burden was clear on the screen—a bottle suspended on a cord and labeled:

Govt. Issue
WHISKEY
For offensive use only.

More and more parachutes were drifting down, and more and more enemy troops were rising from holes to snatch them out of the air.

Officers appeared, shouting furiously, to be hit on the head by drifting bottles labeled, "Govt. Issue—RUM— For offensive use only."

The populace was now reappearing in the streets, to snatch at drifting bottles.

Discipline and order were clearly giving way, save where one grim and burly officer dealt out a savage harangue and then cautiously tried a sip from a bottle, and spat it on the ground. Obviously he was warning that it must be poison. Now, however, a surprised look crossed his face, and he tried again. He raised his eyebrows, took off his helmet, eyed the bottle with a frown, and tried a third sip.

More small parachutes were now drifting down, marked with concentric stripes, where the first had been in solid colors. These latter bore small cartons lettered:

Govt. Issue
CIGARETS°
For offensive use only.

°Caution: May be harmful to your health.

The general watched alertly. Surely in this religious capital *something* would happen to prevent the distractants from working unhindered. But if it was going to happen, it would have to happen fast. The troops had not left their posts yet, but they were making good use of every drifting opportunity as it wafted by.

Now came a third set of parachutes, marked with varicolored rays and bearing boxes of assorted sizes, that troops and populace alike tore open, at first warily, and then with wild abandon.

Inside was a variety of different things, some boxes holding big flashlights that lit up brightly, others containing box cameras, and others clocks, already showing the correct time. All of these things were somewhat large and breakable, but useful and good by local standards.

The general glanced from screen to screen. To his experienced eye, it now seemed clear that resistance in Karnak City would fold up without any serious struggle. So much for that. But there was still the pass on his left front. Once he had that, and the road junction beyond, any counterattack would have to proceed by awkward detours. But the road junction was held by an enemy general who knew exactly what the situation was, and he was there in person.

From behind General Hardesty came the sound of loud arguing, and then the correspondent, shoving passes and authorizations back into his pocket, thrust into the room and stopped to stare at the screens. From his face, it was evident that he had heard the theory of this procedure but had never seen it in action before.

"Ah—ah—*General*," said the correspondent. "Ah—this is a bombardment with A, B, and C charges?"

"Correct."

"But no D charges?"

"That's right. No D."

"A is—ah—"

"Liquor."

"And B?"

"Cigarets. C is bulky breakable objects of local value."

"Why bulky and breakable?"

"When the enemy soldier has something bulky and breakable that he values and wants to hang onto, it cramps his style considerably. Picture yourself trying to fight a war with a portable TV in one hand."

"I see. What is a D charge?"

"Stick around. You'll see."

"And the object of this 'distraction attack' is—?"

"According to the book: 'Vast quantities of wealth and productive effort are expended in the production of munitions, only a tiny fraction of which ever strike a living target. Much is wasted, even in attacks upon inanimate objects. Where these objects are hit, valuable structures are destroyed and must be replaced at considerable expense by the victors, when they occupy the conquered territory. A railroad, for instance, destroyed in the attack, must be replaced in the occupation. This all creates much waste and duplication of effort. *Desirable* objects, however, like the Trojan horse, will be actively sought by the populace, and *each one* will, in effect, strike its target. A more desirable way to block a road or railroad is to place thereon an object of great value to the defender, who will feel impelled to remove it carefully. Much can be accomplished by using objects of *local* value to block facilities of *national* value. In this way, one interest in the country can be led to oppose another. By judicious use of this method, a chaotic situation may be created wherein the united enemy fragments into local groups. Since comparatively little killing of the enemy is involved, the actual aggressor using this method incurs comparatively little ill-feeling. It is a method which, of course, can by effectively used only by a highly productive and well organized power, with highly developed technology and reliable and flexible transportation system.' "

The correspondent wrote urgently in his notebook, then looked up. "And this method is what we're using?"

"Exactly."

"What if someone shoots at our men?"

"If it's serious, shoot back."

"Doesn't that create ill will?"

The general shrugged. "Consider this present setup. An inefficient but at least anti-communist government is overthrown by fanatical communist rebels, who seize the capital and drive the legitimate but inefficient government to the coastal city from which they now rule what's left of the country. The efficient but communist rebels take over, have a blood purge, exterminate anyone unfortunate enough to have possessions, and make so much bad feeling that they're afraid of being overthrown themselves, so they efficiently create a murderous dictatorship. Meanwhile, the legitimate government invokes our mutual-defense treaty and urges us to come in and slaughter every rebel Kazang with a head on his shoulders. Are you under the impression that anybody can do anything in a such a setup without creating bad feeling of *some* kind?"

The correspondent blinked. "Yes, I see."

He scribbled desperately in his notebook, and the general said, "Why not a tape recorder?"

"I had one, but I got too close to one of those 915 mm. howitzers. Now, General, when you explained the theory of distraction warfare, you said 'according to the book.' Is there another explanation?"

"Sure. Have you ever heard of Sheridan's ride?"

"I've heard of it, but I don't know what it was."

"Sheridan's troops were defeated by a Confederate force under the command of Early. Sheridan was away at the time, but rode to the battlefield, turning his retreating troops back as he went. When he reached the battlefield, he found Early's troops, who were suffering from want and hunger, plundering his camp. While they were still in a state of disorder, Sheridan attacked and routed them. Throughout history, armies capable of standing great deprivation have been *torn apart by sudden plenty* and then quickly defeated. This has almost always happened by accident. The present idea is to use it *on purpose*. So far, it seems to be working. But believe me, it goes against the grain."

"But doesn't this method strengthen the enemy?"

"What—liquor, cigarets and cameras, delivered to him when he needs maximum alertness? Strengthen him? How?"

"Don't you ever use food?"

"Certainly, after we've got control of the place, or for some definite purpose. The idea is to cause the maximum distraction at just the time he can least afford it, if you follow me."

The correspondent frowned, and nodded. The general glanced briefly at the screens, then looked back at the correspondent. Somewhere, the general had heard the saying, "He is a fool who cannot hide his wisdom." Now was this correspondent really such a dolt as he seemed to be, or was he merely *seeming* to be a dolt in order to get his victim to lower his guard. And *then* what would happen? Would he send back such a report that the do-gooders would all complain because the poor Kazang rebels were being fed liquor instead of a balanced diet?

"Ah—" said the correspondent—"these reports of—immoral practices—"

"What reports of immoral practices?"

"There have been rumors."

"Get to the point."

"Well, it's said that on some battlefields, beautiful women have been driven along ahead of the troops."

"That was the Kazang's stunt, not ours."

"H'm. Well—"

The general glanced at his watch. A few moments before, he'd noticed another screen flicker on. That view was of the pass. Out of the corner of his eye, he took occasional glances at the screen as the correspondent asked more and yet more questions. Was this method moral? Was it humane? Wasn't it really, in a way, more cruel than to shoot a man? Was it *fair*? Meanwhile, disorganization at the pass progressed rapidly. Now the attacking troops approached, ignoring the liquor with a disinterest that spoke volumes for the regulation chemical in their bloodstreams that would make them sick if they drank that particular brand. And then the troops were in the pass.

Somewhere the TV observers watched the effect of the bombardment further ahead, taking pains to see that the bombardment was accurate, as usual, and that it was having a real and not only an imagined effect. But that collection of staggering drunks, guns lost or slung at their shoulders, packs bulging and bottles in both hands gave testimony that Intelligence had correctly estimated the tastes and psychology of the Kazang ordinary soldier. The best general officer of the Kazang, back at that crossroad, was another matter. Again General Hardesty glanced at his watch.

" . . . so don't you feel," the correspondent was saying, "that really this is a heartless and callous exploitation of human weakness, human frailty, to subvert the mind and morals of your opponent from his true loyalty, to degrade . . . ."

"Phew," said the general. "Not enemy, but *opponent*. How did you degrade an opponent who delights in torture, who in peacetime considers himself clever if he strains ditch-water for a particular type of intestinal parasite, then bribes a servant to put it in his competitor's food? We are supposed to use only the most knightly of methods, while our own men are carried off by the thousands, bloated from barbed darts, smeared with the dung of specially infected monkeys? Is that your argument?"

"Well, of course, they are primitive. It's up to us—"

The conviction was gaining ground with the general that this particular correspondent, actually was a real, genuine, Grade-A boob. In that case, the fellow's boobishness could be put to use.

". . . if not more honorable," he was saying now, "to first send them a note stating clearly your own intentions and frankly asking them for theirs. Then you could *offer* them, freely and openly, an equivalent amount of goods to what you are using now. That is, *if* they would agree to step back a distance, as it were. Then, they would get something and we would get something, and it would be honest and aboveboard and both would profit."

"How?"

"Why, in that they would give a little, and we would give a little, and—"

"And when they wanted more, they'd grab territory, and we'd bribe them to give part of it back again?"

"Well, what's the difference between that and his present method?"

"This present method does *not* give them what they need to make trouble. It gives them what the individual soldier momentarily *wants*. What they need and what they want can be two entirely different things. We use that fact to split them wide open. While they're split wide open, we move in. Before they know what hit them,

we do our best to set up an honest government, which
is something this country hasn't seen for the last one
thousand years."

The correspondent appeared momentarily dazed.

The general glanced at his watch, and frowned. "Outside, the artillery should be getting set pretty soon to let
fly with those D-charges. Better stay down here when
they load them."

The correspondent looked crafty and shot out the door
and up the stairs.

The general shook his head. A genuine boob. Already,
on one of the screens, the first of the gigantic howitzers
was rolling toward the pass. By the time the fellow got
to the spot where the big howitzers *had* been, they'd be
set up elsewhere, and the view would then be coming
in on the screen.

The general watched the screen with interest. Already
the road junction was coming into view as the drones
moved forward. For such a valuable piece of real estate,
it didn't look like much. To left, and right, the north-
south road, a long strip of dust, stretched out over the
mountain slopes, high above the low, wet ground.
Straight ahead, the east-west road gradually descended
from the pass onto the one reasonably solid causeway
through swamp and jungle to the neighboring state of
Cuchang. The Cuchang and Kazang mutually despised
each other, and if one threatened to make progress, the
other kicked his feet out from under him out of sheer
jealousy. But, having the same religion, they obviously
might unite to flatten any outsider with the gall to bring
a new idea into the region. It followed, the general concluded, that he had better get a firm grip on that nearby
narrow gateway from Cuchang into Kazang. Unfortunately, the Kazang had a general of their own who had

already got a grip on this road center and intended to keep it himself. How to pry him loose?

Already, the screens showed the pass, from end to end, and the nearby slopes dominating it were in friendly hands. Already, the bombardment of the road center—using these shells originally intended to shoot supplies into besieged outposts—was producing a whirl of gaily colored parachutes.

But not a single individual reached out to sample the temptations offered him.

Obviously the enemy general had his troops well under control.

There was a faint distinct jolt underfoot.

Someone murmured, "There go the nine-fifteens."

On the screen, a new type of shell spun down, the sunlight flashing on its whirling rotors. Then another and another dropped down, till they seemed to be landing everywhere.

General Hardesty watched closely. This was the acid test.

From behind him, a familiar voice said, "Those are the D charges?"

"Yes."

The correspondent said, "What's going on?" He sounded intent and serious.

The general said, "Whoever has that crossroad controls whether troops move north and south on that road and whether they go east and went on the Cuchang road."

"Can't they go cross-country?"

"Yes, of course, but the country is bad. The Kazang general who had that road junction wants to hold it till help can come across from Cuchang. We want to take it away from him. But he's dug in. If he can hold it till the Cuchang get their armor across, he can make trouble for us. We have to split his position wide open *now*. Once we break up his position, we can get through to blow up the causeway. This will present the Cuchang with something of a problem."

"But how are you going to capture that position, if their general can keep his troops in order? But, then, how can he control—"

General Hardesty watched the screens. "Either he's convinced them that anything we send is poisoned, or he's got some special troops who'll shoot anyone they see so much as reach for the stuff."

"So these D charges are to crack their resistance?"

"That's the idea."

"What are they? Explosives?"

"No."

"Gas shells? Tear gas?"

"No."

"You say they're live, right?"

"That's right."

"Hordes of plague rats?"

Hardesty snorted. "That would be bright, wouldn't it? We're here, too. Wouldn't it be shrewd of us to start a thing like that with us in the middle of it?"

"Then what is inside?"

"Bear in mind, we supply what they want. Not necessarily what they *need*, but what they *want*. What does any soldier of any nationality, with weeks of hard labor and deprivation behind him, and stuck in some desolate hole—what does he want?"

"I don't—"

On a nearby screen, a tall figure appeared out of the ground, walked slowly out toward one of the brightly-colored "shells," and turned to shake his fist. He appeared to be looking out of the screen almost straight at Hardesty. Silver insignia glinted at his collar as he glared angrily back toward the pass. Then he bent at one of the shells, worked a release of some kind, and the top swung up.

A slender woman in a long black dress slit up both sides rose up out of the shell and threw her arms around him.

General Hardesty glanced at the correspondent. "That's his wife. We captured her two weeks ago." He studied the correspondent's face. "We only get the best value out of the D shells toward the end of a campaign, and a lot depends on Intelligence."

The correspondent stared at the screen. Men were appearing from the earth like ants and snapping open the big shells. Out of each climbed someone the men seemed very glad to see.

"How do they know—"

"Each of those shells has a loudspeaker; each one is labeled, and this bombardment was preceded by dropping leaflets and an armored broadcast speaker."

The general smiled. "So now you see, we reunite families, and promote romance, at considerable expense to ourselves. Isn't *that* considerate of us?"

The screen had taken on the look of a huge picnic. Into the midst of this reunion dropped a barrage of freshly heated food, swinging on parachutes.

And in the midst of the confusion, there raced down the road in a cloud of dust half-a-dozen loaded jeeps with no drivers visible. The first four blew up. The last two bounced, crashed, swerved, made it to the crossroad and started back.

"Remote-control," said the general. "To check for mines."

The two remaining jeeps again roared up the road, and this time successive little groups of jeeps boiled up the road after them, bristling with guns. Behind the jeeps came a gigantic howitzer.

From the direction of the jungle swamp and Cuchang, a big tank crawled up the road. Then, as the driver got a look at the howitzer, the tank turned around and headed back to Cuchang again.

"Just barely in time," said the general.

The correspondent was still staring at the reunited families, feasting on the specially provided meal fired at them in place of bullets.

"Phew," he said. "Now I see it. It's all calculated. They always get what they want when it so happens that what they want will wreck their position. Holy—"

Then his eyes widened even further.

The general nodded. Not a boob after all, he thought. Now, had he earlier just made believe he was a boob?

Or had he actually been one, and now the shock had jolted him out of it?

"And," said the correspondent, *"that's the flaw!"*

"The what?"

"What's wrong with this. The long-range drawback of the short-range advantages you spoke of."

The general nodded slowly. "And what is that?"

"What happens," said the correspondent slowly, "is we make this *too* satisfactory, *too* painless. Just suppose—"

The general listened critically. Here it came. The very thing that he had to throw out of his mind every night in order to get a little sleep.

"Here we are," said the correspondent, "trying not to be brutal. We've hit on a system that actually makes it *pleasant* for the opposition to get beat. It's an expensive method, but wars are always expensive. The difference with our method is it's comparatively bloodless and even pleasant. It's designed to *make no unnecessary enemies.* Half the trouble in the world comes from the enemies you made in the last fight."

"Yes," said the general. "That's it. And—"

"And," said the correspondent, "now that we've got this comparatively bloodless, pleasant way of waging war, this is still ruinously expensive, however, what do we do if—"

The general nodded. "Go on."

"What do we do," the correspondent concluded, "if we *make it so pleasant that everyone wants to fight us?*"

On the screen, the liquor bottles whirled past like snowflakes in a blizzard. The correspondent listened alertly, and the general listened with him.

But no one stepped forward to provide an answer to that question.

PROBLEM OF COMMAND
★ ★ ★

Colonel Martin Grainger read the top-secret document through slowly in the privacy of his office, shook his head gloomily, slapped the papers down on his desk, and walked over to look out the window. All he saw of the outside was a blurred image of sky, ground, and building. The blurring, he was vaguely conscious, came from an unworthy weakness; the tear ducts in his eyes were preparing for that release from unbearable stress granted to women and small children. The tightness in his throat came from the same source. As this knowledge touched the edge of his mind, he stiffened, dismissed the idea before it had a chance to become fully conscious, and grimly faced the fact that now not even a lifetime's work would ever be crowned with the only reward that meant anything to him.

There was a friendly rap at the door. It was the rap of an ally, in a competition where allies were necessities, whether Grainger liked it or not.

"Come in," he called, and he was relieved that his voice was clear and unemotional, as always.

The door opened, and a trim man of about sixty, the two stars of a major general on his jacket, stepped into the room, nodded and smiled.

Two hours ago, Grainger could have smiled back naturally. Now he forced a smile.

"Good afternoon, sir."

The older man smiled at him.

"Think you can handle it, Mart?"

Grainger kept his face blank.

"I'll do my best, sir."

"I know you will." He sat on the edge of Grainger's desk. "Don't be ill at ease, Mart. I wouldn't have picked just anyone to do this job." He rapped out a cigarette, automatically started to offer the pack to Grainger, laughed and said, "I forgot; you don't use them." He snapped the lighter, paused and looked at Grainger quizzically, "You don't object?"

"Of course not, sir."

"Don't be so formal, Mart. I'm Al, remember?"

"Yes . . . Al."

"That's better." He blew out a cloud of smoke. "What do you think of the plan?"

Grainger reminded himself that he desperately needed this man's friendship.

"It's a very logical plan . . . Al."

"I'm glad you say so." He stood up, still friendly and apparently unconscious of the gap of rank between them. "You'll be charged with the actual execution of Phase I.

I've already talked the plan over with Lyell Berenger, and he's agreed that the best moment for the attack is the 30th, at 0300—Moscow time. Our preparations should be complete by then. If we wait, there is no assurance we'll retain the advantage. It could be the atomic monopoly, all over again."

"Yes, sir."

The general stubbed his cigarette out in the clean, unused ashtray on Grainger's desk. He crossed the room and, scowling, studied Grainger, who came to attention. When the general spoke, his voice was sharp, with an undertone of sympathetic concern.

"What is this, Mart? You're capable of this job. *I* picked you, remember? Out of the herd. There were brighter ones, and there sure were smoother ones. But I'm not a fool, Mart, and I never would have picked you if I didn't know you could do the job. You've got the stuff. That's elementary. You also have a quality that is none too common these days, if it ever was common. You aren't easily swept along, and you don't bribe. I know that. Therefore, I can trust you. Don't panic on me." He paused a moment, then laughed. "I know what you're going through, Mart. I know how I felt with my first independent command. But I would never have given you this responsibility if I hadn't had complete faith in both you *and* the plan. You're going up there in a few minutes to see Lyell Berenger. What of it? He has three stars, sure." He studied Grainger's face. "Mart, what I'm trying to tell you is, you're at a ceiling, and you've got to get through it. *You* are three-star material. But you'll never get the first one, you'll fall farther and farther behind your class, you'll be passed over for promotion, you'll retire with the same rank you have now—*if* you go into that office *scared*. This is too important to entrust to a man who lacks confidence. Mart, what is it?"

Grainger drew a deep breath.

"Sir, the plan is wrong."

The general stepped back. He started to speak, changed his mind. He looked Grainger flatly in the eyes. "If you tell that to Berenger, I'll see you retired on corporal's pay."

"If you can do it, that's your privilege." Grainger's voice carried an unintended rasp of hard defiance.

The general stared at Grainger, and for a moment his eyes seemed to mist over. He turned away. "I'll never trust another human being."

"Al." Grainger, who never relied on emotion, acted before he could stop himself. He caught the general's arm. "I'm not attacking you. But that plan won't work."

"That plan is my baby. You attack that plan and you attack me."

"I never saw it before yesterday. I'd have told you—"

"Who do you think you are? I didn't submit that plan for your approval. You were to familiarize yourself with it, and prepare to carry it out."

On Grainger's desk, the phone rang imperatively.

The general scooped it up. His entire bearing and *personality* changed instantly. His voice conveyed friendliness and respect, with a warmth that it seemed impossible to counterfeit.

"Sure, Lyell," he said, with a laugh at some question Grainger couldn't hear. "A little buck fever, maybe. He'll be right up."

He hung up, and looked at Grainger. "No one gets to my position without the capacity to forget. You can still have that first star, Mart."

Grainger nodded, but couldn't bring himself to speak. He picked up the plan from the desktop, slid it into a flat tan case, turned, and feeling the general's gaze in the center of his back, left the room.

Lieutenant General Lyell Berenger was a strongly-built man, engaged, when Grainger came in, in an argument with his daughter. The relationship was obvious at first glance in the girl's jaw, nose, regularity of features, and bearing. She was handsome rather than pretty, and though she was attractive, she was also formidable.

"Yes," she was saying exasperatedly, "but as far as I'm concerned, he's got as much backbone as a bowl of mush. I'll grant you, he's got brains, tact, education, tact, upbringing, tact, culture, tact, a good build, tact, and everything else a man needs except a backbone. He's never said anything but just the right thing since I've met him. I can't bear him."

"But, Babs," said Berenger, "somebody's got to give."

"How did he get *you* to start in on me? I'll bet he was very *tactful*."

"Not at all; I just wondered."

"I'll bet."

"You can't stay single forever, Babs. If your mother were alive, she'd tell you—"

"Now just how do you know what Mother would tell me? Are you going to try to convince me you can think like a woman?"

Berenger changed color. "No, but the trouble with *you* is, you think like a man!"

"What's that got to do with it? That's neither here nor there. You said if Mother were alive she'd tell me—"

"She *would*."

"And *I* want to know," said the girl remorselessly, "how do *you* know what she'd tell me? *Can* you think like a woman? You just admitted you can't. Therefore you can't possibly know what Mother would tell me!"

Father and daughter glared at each other.

"Get out of here," said Berenger. "A man can stand only so much in one day."

"I stepped in because you asked me to," said the girl, unintimidated.

"Well," said Berenger, "that was my mistake." He spotted Grainger, who had been listening in fascination to the argument. "Just what are you doing in here, Colonel?"

"Sir, I thought you wanted me to come straight up. The outer office was empty and this door open. I was preoccupied, and I'm afraid I stepped in without thinking."

"You could have had the decency to step out again."

Grainger briefly shut his eyes. Downstairs, "Al" was at this moment calculating where to sink the knife in, and now, before the plan itself was even brought into the conversation, he had succeeded in offending the one man whose opinion of it was vital. For just a moment, he felt the anguish of a lost dream.

For the better part of his life, Grainger had wanted that one star more than he had wanted anything else. Women, liquor, and dice didn't tempt him. He had never married, and he wasn't interested in anything but soldiering. That had gotten him through O.C.S. and lifted him from one rank to another not too far behind competitors who had gone to the Point. But the closer he came to the center of power, the slower it lifted him, and now he could see that he would never make that first star. The silver eagle would be the zenith of his career, and he didn't think he would remain at the zenith long. And if he couldn't have the star, the hell with it. He might just as well get it over with.

"Colonel," Berenger was saying evenly, "I'd appreciate an apology."

"Sir," said Grainger, "I've come straight from a fight with one general, and I might as well have a fight with another."

The girl, just opening the door to go out, turned around again.

Berenger blinked, "Al didn't say anything."

"I don't disagree with him, sir. I do disagree with the plan."

"It's his plan."

"I don't think it's going to work."

"Have you discussed this matter—"

"Sir, I just finished discussing it with him. That's what the argument was about."

Berenger glanced at his daughter, his face expressionless.

"Get out of here, young lady. And I mean right now."

This time, she went out.

Berenger picked up the phone, changed his mind, and put it down again. He looked at Grainger.

"Do you realize what you're doing?"

"I realize that this plan calls for a surprise attack on the Soviet Union, using a completely new scientific device. The aim is to hamstring Russian nuclear-delivery capability, immobilize Russian armor in Eastern Europe, and by progressive stages sabotage all Russian heavy industry, transport, light, power, and means of communication. That is Phase I."

"And you don't think it will work?"

"No, sir."

"Why not?"

"For two reasons, sir. First, it's an attack without a real reconnaissance. Second, it's an attack without a defense."

"You don't claim to know more about this device than the scientists, I hope."

"I don't claim to understand the *modus operandi* of the device at all. *How* it works is beyond me. But a man doesn't have to understand how an internal-combustion engine works to be able to use it. I know what this device is supposed to do, and on that basis I know that this plan is *dangerous*."

"Are you sure you really *do* understand it?" said Berenger. "How long have you had to study it?"

"Yesterday and today. It takes a certain length of time to cut through the technical phraseology. It's only in the last two hours or so that I've been able to see it clearly enough to realize what's wrong."

Berenger frowned. "This has a peculiar sound, Colonel. Men with far greater experience and technical knowledge have concluded that the plan was sound."

"It wasn't up to them to actually carry it out. The parts look right but the whole is no good."

"All right," said Berenger. "If there's something wrong with this plan, now is the time to find it out." He frowned a moment at Grainger, who was still standing, and glanced around. "Pull up a chair, Colonel. The one by the door is comfortable."

"Thank you, sir." Grainger turned to get it, and the door, which was open a crack, moved slightly, as if in a slight breeze. Grainger picked up the chair, set it down, and saw Berenger studying the door. As Grainger sat down, Berenger stood up, looking past Grainger, and said, "Perhaps if you'll move the chair a little to your right, there'll be less glare."

Grainger did as he was told, but there was no glare worth mentioning in either place. The only sunlight was slanting in to one side of both of them, and Grainger's back was turned slightly toward it.

Berenger opened up a drawer of his desk, leaned back as if to rest his feet on it, changed his mind, and swung his chair in the other direction.

"Suppose," said Berenger, "that you start with a brief description of the device itself."

"It's known as a 'displacement device.' It consists of three parts: circuit 1, circuit 2, and the sending coil. When an object is placed in the focus of the sending coil, and a current is passed through the two circuits simultaneously, the object in the sending coil will be 'displaced.' That is, it will be transported through something called 'Zeta space,' and will reappear in normal space in a different location. At the same moment, if the light in the new location is intense enough, the light will overcome what is called 'barrier potential,' be displaced in the reverse direction, and appear as a flicker in the sending coil. This flicker can be resolved to give a visible image of the new location. The device causes a slight structural rearrangement in the objects sent, but this is only harmful in the case of the higher animals, which suffer nervous damage, and die quickly."

Berenger nodded approval. "Now, tell me, what if there is a physical object already in the space to which another object is sent by the displacement device?"

"Liquids or gases are moved aside, just as a stone thrown through the air or into a pool will move liquids or gases out of its way. But if a solid already occupies part of the space, only so much of the object in the coil will be sent as will emerge in space not already occupied by a solid object. It seems to me there must be borderline cases, but I don't know enough to say anything about that."

Berenger nodded, frowning. "Now just give a brief résumé of the plan itself."

"The plan is very simple. It involves sabotage on a massive scale. For the purpose, there are batteries of SFD units; that means, 'Spotter-Flasher-Displacement' units. Now, again, I haven't been given the technical details. All I know is that a 'spotter' unit is one that uses the flicker in the coil to detect an object and 'lock onto' it. The 'flasher' provides the extra light needed to overcome the so-called barrier potential, so that the spotter unit can work. Meanwhile, the 'displacer' unit is programmed to displace a metal slug that will block a fuel line, or a quantity of special glue that will bond moving parts together, or whatever else seems suitable to cause the greatest disablement in the shortest possible time. Each one of the SFD combinations can be programmed to handle a particular type of target.

"Now," Grainger went on, "the first step is sabotage of Russian missiles. Closely following that is sabotage of the Russian bomber force. Next, the immobilization of their Eastern European armored forces—such of the Russian armor, that is, as might try a strike against Western Europe. Next follows sabotage against Russian industry, transport, light, power, and communication. That is Phase I."

"Don't you think it will work?"

"Sir, I was laid up in a hospital one time, and all I had for entertainment was a book that made a comparison between war and chess. It told how you should go about a winning a game of chess *strategically*. I think I remember enough to give you an idea. First, you isolate one wing of your opponent's forces. Second, you bring the bulk of your power to bear against the isolated wing, maintaining only enough power on the other flank to hold off the enemy. Third, you crush the opponent's isolated forces with your superior concentration of power. Fourth, you wheel your mobile forces into the conquered battleground, and strike your diminished enemy with overwhelming force from the flank. Fifth, you grind up any remaining pockets of resistance piecemeal."

Berenger grinned. "What's wrong with that?"

"Not a thing. But what's the *other* side doing all this time?"

"And your objection to this present plan?"

"The same thing. This plan assumes they're as helpless as a cow in a slaughterhouse. All it tells us is how to slice up the corpse. It's all very logical, so far as it goes. The fine details are excellent. But what if the corpse fights back? The basic assumption throughout is that we now have a monopoly of the displacement device. But how do we *know*? We could find out by using the SFD units in a reconnaissance sweep just before the attack."

"Haven't you read the reasons for not doing that, in the plan itself?"

"Yes, sir. To maintain secrecy until the last moment. 'Premature use of the device would reveal our intent.' It certainly would create a sensation. But all that would be visible would be the dazzling burst from the flasher units—so many beams of brilliant light displaced through Zeta space to provide illumination for the spotter units. Certainly, if it were done long before the preparations were complete, it would serve as a warning. But the point is that it *wouldn't* be done before preparations were completed. It would, therefore, serve only as a shock and surprise, *unless they have the device themselves*. In which case, sir, we'd be a lot better off if we found it out."

Berenger said, "You mentioned another objection?"

Grainger frowned for a moment. Why, he asked himself, was the general so apparently unconcerned? If what had been said so far was true, the plan was badly at fault. Grainger knew it. Certainly Berenger, with his far greater experience, must also see it.

"Go on, Colonel," Berenger prompted.

"Yes, sir. The first objection is that we are striking without a proper reconnaissance, when there is no real reason why we shouldn't make such a reconnaissance. The second objection is worse yet. We're striking without having a real defense. Sir, under Paragraph 17, of the second section of these plans, there is mention of the 'necessity for exerting maximum force in the early stages of the attack.' The argument is that by doing so, we will knock out the enemy missile and bomber forces, and thus be safe from counterattack. But *again*, this assumes that the enemy has no developed defenses using the new device. How do we know this? We can't know it unless we carry out a reconnaissance."

"You've been all over this," said Berenger.

"Yes, sir, but not from this particular viewpoint: What happens if the enemy has a few dozen nuclear bombs or warheads ready to throw at us, *from each of the several displacement installations we haven't located because we didn't look?* Then what? This device removes an object from ordinary space, displaces it through Zeta space, and returns it to ordinary space at a location depending on the setting of variable circuit elements in circuits 1 and 2, the amount of energy available, and so on. And when this object reappears, it is already in the target area. It doesn't follow a trajectory so that you can try to hit it on the way down. It's already there. There's nothing to prevent it from going off instantaneously on arrival. The trajectory has been through Zeta space, and it's clear from the plan that there is no way to follow it through that."

"I think," said Berenger, "that you made some mention of Paragraph 17, in the second section?"

"Yes, sir. This paragraph is in explanation of the need for absorbing our own nuclear strike force displacers into the SFD units at the height of that attack. Sir, this is precisely when we'd need them."

"You're speaking of the displacement devices we now have assigned to our nuclear-delivery units."

"Yes, sir. If we convert these displacers for use with SFD units, merely for sabotage purposes, what do we do in the event of an enemy threat to counterattack using his own hidden displacement devices? What do we do in the event of an actual enemy attack?"

"As you said yourself, Colonel, there's no defense against that. What can we do in case of an attack anyway?"

Grainger stared at the general dizzily. He hadn't heard of this device till yesterday, and he hadn't unwound the complexities of it till a couple of hours ago, and now he had to *explain* it.

"Sir," he said patiently, "I admit, if they attack with everything at once, I don't see *what* we can do. But there are two objections to converting the nuclear displacers to SFD units. In the first place, they might . . . the Russians, I mean . . . might deliver a limited nuclear blow in reprisal for our sabotage. If we then responded with a limited nuclear attack in an unimportant region, they would see we were prepared to strike back, and we both might be able to work our way out of the mess. But if we can't strike back except by more sabotage—if our only choice is to either go on as we had been going, or else quit—they could work us into a corner in no time. They might even decide to end the trouble permanently. That's one of the things that's wrong with breaking up our own nuclear displacement units in order to strengthen the attack."

"What's the other?"

"They might know we'd done it without *having* to test us by a nuclear blow. They'd know by spying on our displacement units, using their devices."

"I can assure you," said Berenger, "we've had no word of any such use of their devices—if they have them. You remember, they can only use the device for spying purposes with an auxiliary light source. We keep the light in our displacement installations well below the intensity needed to enable them to spy. And we would immediately detect any auxiliary light source."

"Sir, this is an age of automation and miniaturization. I don't claim to have the technical knowledge to know whether small electronic devices would suffer from the same rearrangement of structure that damages the nervous system of a living creature when it's displaced. It seems to me that a proportion of such devices would be undamaged and usable. In that case, spy devices could be placed in our displacement installations *without* any flash of light. They could be put in more or less blindly, disguised as other things—lab tools, cigarette butts, whatever seemed most suitable, and in whatever place seemed best from study of the architecture of the outside of the building. The spy devices would then provide the information needed, perhaps by relaying it through other units outside."

Berenger nodded slowly. "Do you have any further objections to your superior's plans, Colonel Grainger?"

Grainger winced. "I have others, sir, but I think these are sufficient."

Berenger reached for the phone, then paused. "What would *you* do, if you were making the plan?"

"Multiply our SFD units further, do everything possible to find out if the Russians do or do not have the device, plant disguised spy devices wherever there appears to be such an installation, and do everything possible to find a defense against the displacement device. The present plan looks good when you read it off, Paragraph 1, Paragraph 2, Paragraph 3. But, sir, the nature of the device described is such that the plan won't stand up to analysis."

"And yet, you claim no great specialized knowledge of displacement devices?"

"Sir, I don't need specialized knowledge of cars to know that if I push on the accelerator the thing will go faster. I don't know the first thing about the chemical reactions that take place in a muscle, but that doesn't keep me from using it."

Berenger nodded. "All right, Colonel. I've listened to you. Now, if you wish to retract your statement, and if you will agree to go along with the plan as stated, I won't call your superior officer and describe the gist of this conversation to him. If you refuse, I will have to do it." He reached for the phone.

Grainger stared, "I'll resign my commission before I'll go along with this plan."

Berenger picked up the phone.

The outer door opened up, and the general's daughter stepped in. Her eyes were slightly widened as she looked at her father.

Berenger pressed down the bar in the phone's cradle, and said, "Just where were you?"

"In a chair right outside the door of this office. I heard the whole thing." Her eyes flashed. "You can't order *me*. If you go through with this, I'll see that it reaches every newspaper in the country."

Berenger glanced from his daughter to Grainger.

Grainger was looking at the girl in admiration. As she glared at her father, her fine, regular features, and the slight flush of emotion, gave her beauty. And there was no questioning the fact that she had a good figure. True, that look of iron will-power—or self-will, whichever it was—was enough to scare off almost any man. On the other hand, she was a challenge, far different from any of the girls Grainger had known. And there was no questioning the fact that she had a mind—albeit a highly independent one.

"Hm-m-m," thought Grainger, studying her.

A flicker of hope passed across Berenger's face, then vanished as he spoke into the phone.

"Hello, Al? Your protégé is up here, and he's just torn your plan to shreds. Moreover, he refuses to go along with any part of it." Berenger smiled. "Quite a stab in the back, isn't it? . . . Yes . . . Yes . . . No, nothing personal, he just doesn't like the plan, that's all . . . I'd come up if I were you. Sure, we can arrange it . . . Yes, come up and help me plan the court-martial. Maybe we can nail him for direct disobedience to orders, insubordination and"—he glanced at his daughter—"divulging confidential information to unauthorized persons . . . All right, Al." Berenger put the phone in its cradle.

His daughter was watching him in puzzlement. She started to speak, then changed her mind.

Grainger was watching the interesting play of emotions across her face.

Berenger said, "Out, Babs."

She didn't move, but stood watching him in puzzlement, her mind obviously sorting things over.

Berenger glanced at Grainger, "Colonel Grainger, would you remove this intruder before she wrecks the routine completely. Watch out for her. She knows judo."

Grainger got up. "That's all right. I know judo, savate, karate, aikido, yawara, ate-waza, and Shanghai Municipal Police close-combat."

She blinked at him, and suddenly smiled. She had a nice smile, "I'll go peacefully."

"Get her out of here," said Berenger. "Make sure she doesn't stay in the outer office. Put her on the elevator."

"Yes, sir."

Grainger walked her out into the hall.

She said, "Do you know what he's up to?"

"I don't have any idea. I'm completely lost. But I never heard of two generals getting together and arranging a court-martial *that* way, so I'm not going to give up yet."

"He's not angry with you at all. He's pleased with you. And there's something else, but I can't put my finger on just what he's trying to do." She glanced back. "I wish I had some way to know what happens. He'll delight in teasing me and not telling me a thing."

Grainger made a quick decision. A few minutes later, he was back in Berenger's office, with the two generals studying him quizzically. Assuming he got through this, he reminded himself, he had a date with Berenger's daughter.

"Sir," he said to his superior, "I'm sorry. But that displacement device just doesn't fit in with those plans."

He expected a rebuke, but got a smile instead. "It doesn't actually fit in with *any* war plans—yet."

"I don't understand, sir."

"We have such a device—with a few points of difference. And the Russians have it, too. Use of it creates a detectable disturbance, like the tremor and shock wave created by nuclear devices. The result is, *we* know they have it. And *they* know we have it."

Grainger frowned. "Sir, what are the points of difference?"

"Range is one. The curvature of normal space is too gradual to allow use of the device on the planet, or even in the way we'd like to use it, within the solar system. Whatever we send ends up *too far out*. In addition, there's a theoretically explainable, very slight random effect, negligible when considered over the enormous range of the device, but nevertheless measured in a great many Earth diameters. Incidentally, we estimate this error by the highly expensive process of boosting out an entire pre-packaged displacement installation, complete with self-contained power supply, and preset to send back a series of objects whose radiations we then struggle to detect. The scatter is impressive. If we tried to hit Moscow with this thing, we could kick up a fuss in the asteroid belt. and consider ourselves lucky, at that. About all the device is really good for right now is getting rid of radioactive waste. It's fine, for that purpose. And we're trying to develop it into a tool for space travel. But for warfare on Earth, it's as worthless as a 21–inch gun in close combat."

Grainger thought it over. "And the plan?"

"What we've just been speaking of is a device that operates outside of normal space. This present device doesn't happen to use the theoretical Zeta space mentioned in the plan. But how do we know the Zeta space mentioned in the plan doesn't actually exist? Or if not that, something equally capable of serving the purpose? A great many devices predicted long ago, and ridiculed for a generation or more, have now come into existence. We have atomic devices, rocketships, and heat rays. We begin to become wary. What's coming next? To be capable of higher command, a man seems to need the capacity of a sea captain. While the technological deck heaves and lunges under his feet, he has to stay upright."

Grainger nodded.

Berenger said, "Do you realize what it involves to try to keep up with this new technology? Despite the best technical training available, it's impossible for even the specialists in a given field to keep up with *their own field*. And *all these* fields can affect war. Do you see what that means? Until we have some means of multiplying the present rate of learning so that it can begin to keep up with the advances of technology, we have to expect new advances to be flung at us from time to time that we can't possibly understand as a scientist understands them. In the First World War, there were commanders who never did figure out the meaning of a machine gun. In the Second, we had teams of technicians and scientists going out to explain the devices. That's important. But now we have reached the point where it becomes glaringly obvious that one of the most important requirements of higher command is *the ability to cut through technicalities, and quickly sense the possibilities of even the most fantastic new technological devices*. And this will very likely have to be done *under stress*."

Grainger blinked. "So the plan was a *test*?"

Berenger nodded. "We put you under the highest stress we could manage, let you think you'd be ruining your career if you gave an honest answer, let you have a scene with your commanding officer, and after you'd won, we offered you a hole to crawl back into; but you came through anyway. We've had others fail."

Grainger felt himself pale as he realized how close a squeak this had been. All he would have had to do to disqualify himself was to think only of getting a promotion.

Berenger noted his expression, and grinned. He reached in a drawer and took out a pair of silver stars.

"Here, put these in your pocket. Al will want to pin them on, but I can give them to you. It may take a little while, but don't get impatient.

"The papers can come through fast when we find the right man *these* days."

UNCALCULATED RISK
★ ★ ★

Lieutenant General Lyell Berenger held to the opinion that life would have been much simpler if the human race had never invented Science. General Berenger occasionally tried, as he was trying tonight, to prove this proposition to a friend or acquaintance. Berenger was vaguely aware, as he talked, of the high-pitched laughter in the room, the occasional clink of glasses, and the surflike murmuring of voices around him. In his hand he absently held a glass, two-thirds of the contents of which he had tossed into the fireplace at the first opportunity, and which he had now forgotten. His attention was concentrated on his friend, Senator Vail, who was trying inconspicuously to unload his own glass into a pot holding a kind of lacy fernlike plant.

"In the old days," Berenger said, noting with suspicion the tolerant smile on the senator's face, "back, say, in the time of the early Romans, a soldier's job was difficult and demanding. The army had to be well-equipped, strong, and well-trained. The general commanding needed to be alert, and to know his job thoroughly. The same holds true today. The difference is this: In those days, virtue was rewarded. If a soldier did what he was supposed to, the odds were very great that he would win. In modern times, it's all a hodge-podge. The cause, as the cause of a lot of our troubles, is this pet of yours, Science."

Vail smiled. "Come on, now, Lyell, don't tell me you aren't happy whenever one of our technical teams beats the Russians to the punch."

Berenger nodded. "Yes, and I'm grateful that we were the first to get nuclear fission. But think back a while. How did it seem when the Germans came out with rocket-planes, flying bombs, and V-2s? The trouble is that you can't predict who is going to get what, or when. Military calculations can be completely unhinged by some mild individual who hardly knows one end of a gun from the other, and cares less."

"True," said Vail, who had now succeeded in transferring half his drink to the hapless plant, "but what is going on is doing more than merely upset your plans. Each scientific advance increases the power and well-being of the race as a whole."

"I don't object to Science, within bounds," said Berenger. "But I have reservations as to its violent, uncontrolled, headlong nature. Look, Vail, you speak of 'beating the Russians to the punch.' Doubtless they think of it the same way. It's a race. But where *to*?"

"To greater power and well-being. Obviously, the greater our capabilities, the more we can do. If we race someone, that means we both get there faster. You want to work it all out before we take a step. At that rate, we'd still be figuring out the implications of gunpowder, and wild-eyed theorists would be making radical predictions to the effect that some day in the next two thousand years steam engines would begin to replace the horse— in certain applications."

Berenger nodded. "It would probably be just that bad. But now consider one aspect of this 'race' you like so much. It is *uncontrollable*. Because it is a competition, neither side can stop. The side that stops, loses. Therefore each side *must* go on. Isn't that so?"

"Right. And a good thing."

"O.K. But when you speak of winning an ordinary race, you have in mind a definite physical goal. Suppose, instead, you took a group of men out into the wilderness and told them simply to run, and if any one got ten yards ahead of his nearest opponent, that one would instantly win, and could impose his will, if he so desired, on the other runners. That is more what this race is like, isn't it?"

Vail scowled. "Yes. Go on."

"Ten yards," said Berenger, "is no great distance. In the race we're in, a small definite lead can be conclusive. Now, if either side takes the lead, the other must run faster. Running faster, it is likely to cut down the lead the other side has, which will in turn force the other side to run faster. So it goes."

Vail nodded. "There's something to what you say. It could, in theory, get out of control. But actually, of course, both sides are pretty hard-headed, and this, combined with the natural inertia of human beings, keeps the process from running out of control."

Berenger said, "It may be that the *process* isn't running out of control. But in any race where you are not running on a beaten track, there is the possibility of a sharp surprise to the individual runners. The runners may go very fast, but they take as their standard of performance their position relative to the other runners. None of the runners knows the territory ahead. Now, what happens if, during some desperate spurt, the leader suddenly arrives at the edge of a ravine? *Then* what?"

"A purely rhetorical question," said Vail, smiling. "The scientists are often afraid the military men will do something irresponsible, so I shouldn't be surprised to find a military man afraid the scientists will do something irresponsible. Meanwhile, both sides think politicians are irresponsible. Nobody thinks the other man knows his business. But he does."

"You've missed the point," said Berenger. "It isn't irresponsible for a scientist to make discoveries. That's his business. But making discoveries is like running through unknown territory. Do it too fast and sooner or later, you're likely to get a severe fall."

Vail nodded, grinning. "We politicians learn to use words, but to look to reality. The situation you describe *sounds* convincing, but it doesn't fit in with reality. Tell you what. If you're free next weekend, why don't you come on out to Iowa with me and see a scientist in action on a real project. It's part of the race between us and the Soviets. Nothing spectacular, but pretty effective, all the same. It'll get your head down out of the clouds and onto solid ground. What do you say?"

Berenger smiled. "I don't think I want my head 'on solid ground,' Vail, but yes, I can get away next weekend. I'll take you up on that."

That was how, the next weekend, Lyell Berenger came to find himself on the edge of a flat windy field with

Senator Vail and a short broad man who'd been introduced as Dr. Franklin Green. The college tower was visible in the distance, but Dr. Green had eyes only for the field, where a tractor was churning methodically back and forth.

"Soil texture," said Dr. Green, stopping to pick up a handful of the rich-looking soil and crumbling it in his fingers, "soil texture is an important matter to the farmer. If the texture is right, rainfall is absorbed, the working of the soil is easy, and plant development takes place naturally. With the wrong texture, everything goes wrong. Now, you've seen this. Let me show you the control plot."

They plodded across the yielding, somewhat spongy soil to a strip of arid ground with a surface like cracked cement. Dr. Green looked at them significantly. "*This* plot wasn't treated. The one you've just seen was. Suppose you gentlemen were farmers. Which plot would you rather farm?"

Berenger glanced from the soft, yielding, even-textured plot to the hard-surfaced plot. Something began vaguely to disturb him. He heard Vail say, "Well, I have no doubt which *I* would rather work, Doctor. Is your texturing agent so effective on *all* soils?"

"Not entirely, I'm sorry to say. But we are working at it steadily. We expect to have it ready for commercial use by early next year. First we have to make tests on a variety of soil types."

Vail said, "What do you expect will be the effect on farming in general?"

Dr. Green said, with a hard effort at modesty, "It should increase the yield, in some cases very considerably."

Berenger and Vail were on the plane the next day before Vail got around to saying triumphantly, "What did you think of *that*?"

Berenger said, "I thought we already had surpluses."

"Yes," said Vail, "and there you hit the sore point on the head." He lowered his voice, "But, you see, some of our allies and a considerable number of the neutrals don't share that problem. They desperately need food. It takes a long time to increase yield by conventional methods. You have irrigation projects, huge quantities of farm machinery to ship overseas, and all kinds of technical training programs to carry out. It's a slow process, it may go head-on against local prejudices, and while you're carrying it out, people are starving. But this new process holds out the possibility of increasing yields by, say fifteen percent the first year. It will fit right in with local customs, since nearly everyone is used to adding manure to soil. It isn't expensive, it won't use much shipping space, and it is *immediate*. Now what do you have to say?"

Berenger was silent for a while. Finally he said. "I'll be frank with you. There's something about it I don't like."

"Too big an advance?" Vail looked at him curiously.

Berenger shook his head. "I don't know what it is. I just have an uneasy feeling about it."

Vail smiled, and settled back on his seat. "Not I," he said. "It makes *me* very happy."

Berenger was back at work the next day, and the incident soon slipped into the back of his mind. As the months rolled by, with shifts and changes in foreign affairs, new surprises in technology, and the continuing need to fit these variables into the overall picture, he in time forgot the incident entirely. He was reminded of it by a newspaper article, which first discussed the development in general, then went on:

" . . . Thus Dr. Green's development of the Catalytic Texturing Agent will largely do away with problems caused by too-heavy soils. Best of all, from the point of expense, the effect is permanent. The texturing agent, operating on an entirely new principle of ionic interchange, actually generates more of itself over the course of time from the chemicals of the surrounding soil. The proper 'dosage' is scientifically determined by soil analysis, to assure that regeneration of the catalyst proceeds at a rate just sufficient to restore that used up in the course of the soil-conditioning operation. In explaining this, Dr. Green, winner of the McGinnis Medal for Agricultural Chemistry, remarked . . . "

Berenger read back carefully over the article, then, frowning, read on: "Winner of the McGinnis Medal for Agricultural Chemistry, remarked, 'Any catalyst is theoretically capable of handling an unlimited quantity of material. But in practice, the catalyst usually becomes "poisoned" and ceases to operate. In this instance, the poisoning is offset by the generation of new catalyst. This effect must not, of course, be allowed to proceed too rapidly, or it could have most disagreeable consequences. That is easily avoided by the use of proper initial testing procedures, as had been demonstrated repeatedly in field tests, in all types of soil . . . ' "

Berenger looked up from the paper, sat back, and thought it over. Scowling, he glanced at his watch, picked up a phone, and tried to call Vail. Vail, it developed, was away on a trip, but would be back by early next week. Berenger put the phone down again, thought some more, then picked the phone up and called long distance for

Dr. Franklin Green. In due time, Green came on the line. Berenger first reminded Green of his previous visit, then said guardedly. "I don't ask you to reveal anything that might be classified, Doctor. You understand that?"

"Of course," came Green's voice. "There isn't much that *is* classified about this project, General. It's all perfectly straight agricultural chemistry. We've evolved a new twist that should be useful, that's all."

"Yes," said Berenger, "but I notice that you say the generation of new catalyst mustn't be allowed to proceed too rapidly. Can you tell me, without revealing classified information, what happens when catalytic regeneration *does* proceed too rapidly?"

Green was silent a moment, then said, "Well, you understand, that is amply guarded against by proper preliminary tests."

"Yes," said Berenger, and waited.

Green said, "There's really no need of any such eventuality *ever* arising in practice."

"I see."

"Newspaper reports tend to be somewhat sensational. Actually, we've never had that happen in the field."

"I see," said Berenger. "But—if this information isn't classified—what takes place when it *does* happen?"

There was a considerable silence. Berenger could hear faint voices in the background. Then Green said, "General, I wonder if you could come down here for a few hours this weekend?"

Berenger was silent a moment.

Green said, "I can *show* you, much better than I can tell you. If this seems important to you, I hope you can come down here."

"Yes," said Berenger. "Thank you for the invitation, Doctor. I'll be there."

The college looked about the same as when Berenger had been there last, but Dr. Green seemed preoccupied. He opened the door to the darkened laboratory, snapped on the lights, stood aside for Berenger, then locked the door behind them. He led Berenger the length of the room, and up several steps to a small laboratory. Inside, on a soapstone-topped bench, sat a very large brown-enameled earthenware crock. Green locked the door behind them, and lifted the lid of the crock. "Here it is. See for yourself."

Berenger glanced in at a gray-brown glop that looked about the thickness of molasses.

"This is what happens if you add too much of the catalyst?"

"A great deal too much," said Green. "That was made by adding, originally, one liter of conditioner to one liter of untreated soil."

Berenger glanced into the mammoth crock again. Green, he noticed, seemed willing to give him information on request, but he certainly wasn't volunteering it. "So," said Berenger, "You had two liters to start with?"

"That's right."

"You've got a lot more than two liters here now. What did you do then?"

"We were disturbed at the results of the experiment. Naturally, we had to allow for a possible malfunction of the equipment used to spread the texturing agent. We also had to consider the possibility that a quantity of the agent might be spilled accidentally. If this caused a breakdown of the soil at the spot where the accident happened, it could result in a . . . a mudhole. We wanted to avoid that."

"Yes," said Berenger patiently, "but where did the rest of this stuff come from? You say you started out with a liter of dirt and a liter of catalytic agent. A liter is roughly a quart. This is a lot more than two quarts."

Green nodded sourly. "We added a large quantity of untreated soil."

"And the soil did what?"

"There you see it."

Berenger looked in at the glop. "You mean the original muck transformed the untreated soil into more of itself?"

"As far as we can tell, something like that happened."

"What would happen if we added some more dirt to this?"

"I'd have to try it to know."

"Does this look any different from the stuff you had when you added one liter of texturing agent to one liter of soil?"

"There's more of it, that's all."

Berenger thought this over, and fought off the urge to profanity. Carefully, he said, "Let's say, as a hypothetical case, that a farmer had a container of this texturing agent and dropped it. Would he get a mudhole?"

"Apparently."

"Then what would he do?"

"He would have a serious problem."

"Could he collect the muck in . . . say . . . an empty drum, and then put it in his spreader and spread it over the same number of acres he'd originally planned to treat?"

"No," said Dr. Green uncomfortably, "I'm afraid that wouldn't be the thing to do."

"Why not?"

Green hesitated, then said, "The reaction is so complex that, frankly, I don't know how to explain what happens. Normally, the agent is vastly diluted by the soil. When it is used in so large a concentration, the agent itself seems to undergo a change. The result is this— substance. If this were spread over a field, I hate to think what it might produce."

"Suppose it were worked into the soil finely?"

"If the ionic complex itself were broken up, that of course would stop it. If not, each small particle would still be of the same substance. Not the texturing agent, but the substance the concentrated texturing agent and the soil had reacted to form. As far as I can see, the process would not be stopped. It would be accelerated."

"There would be more of this stuff, then? A whole field of it?"

Green hesitated. "I'm afraid so."

"And this would then spread to adjacent fields?"

Green shrugged helplessly. "All I can say is, we added the dirt, and there you see the result. We didn't mix it. We just added it."

"How long did it take?"

"About forty minutes before the reaction was complete."

"So it *would* spread?"

"Apparently."

"Where would it stop?"

"I don't know."

Berenger drew a deep breath, and let it out slowly. In the back of his mind was the awareness that the texturing agent was even now being manufactured. No doubt, it was being loaded onto trucks, transported, unloaded, transferred to ships tied up at docks, perhaps even already being unloaded at foreign ports. His natural instinct was to do something fast. Get on the telephone, bulldoze his way to the highest available authority. Every second might count.

With an effort, he pulled out a laboratory stool, and sat down. He glanced at Green, who now looked very pale. Berenger said, "What have you done about it?"

Green shook his head. "The possibility of something like this never occurred to me. It was one of my graduate students who thought of this experiment. It seems an obvious thing to try, now, but to begin with we had only small amounts of the texturing agent to work with. Later, I supposed as you did, that if the agent were mixed with too little soil, it would merely be a diluting of the agent. I was very angry when I learned of this crude experiment, which was only carried out *after* the agent was in commercial production. Before, it was too expensive. When I finally did realize what this might mean, I tried to explain the situation to the president."

"The President?"

Green shook his head. "The president of the college. He decided I was suffering from overstrain, and refused to take the matter seriously. I wrote a letter to the head of the corporation producing the agent, and got a letter back assuring me that they were using proper safeguards in shipping the agent, and congratulating me again on its discovery. Several days later, I received a whole drum of the texturing agent, compliments of the company. Gradually I began to think perhaps I *was* suffering from overstrain. I locked up the laboratory here, and tried not to think of it."

Berenger noted that his own hammering pulse was beginning to quiet down again. He could now see clearly what he had only sensed before: Any effort on his part to get this picture across would have to be done carefully, or he, Berenger, would also get sent off for a rest cure.

But to do it carefully would take time. While he was doing it carefully, trucks, trains, and ships would be in motion, increasing the likelihood of spillage.

Green said shakily, "It looks bad to you, too, doesn't it?"

Berenger said, "Suppose spillage makes just one mud-hole? Small animals will track it around locally. Bits of muck stuck to men's shoes can easily end up forty miles away in an hour. And you said it only took forty minutes for a batch of fresh dirt to get converted to muck?"

Green nodded.

"How long would it take you to carry out complete laboratory tests, check your results, find out how this stuff reacts when finely divided in a comparatively large quantity of earth, how it reacts when treated with various chemicals, what effect heat and cold have on it, and anything else that seems useful?"

Green shook his head, "General, it would take several years to do a thorough job. But I can get my best graduate students and have a rough idea in the next eight or ten hours."

Berenger got up. "Good. I'll get to work right away and see what I can find out."

The next eight hours Berenger spent in long-distance phone calls, and some nerve-wracking calculations. He discovered that the soil texturing agent was already well-dispersed in stores and warehouses across the United States. Eight ships carrying sizable quantities of the agent in drums were at sea, destined for ports in Europe, Asia, Africa, and South America. The first of these cargo ships was due to dock in London in twelve hours, and others now in American ports were regularly taking on the texturing agent as part of their regular cargoes. There seemed to be no existing legal machinery that Berenger could put in motion to stop the shipment or sale of the substance.

Senator Vail, Berenger discovered, was on a hunting trip in the Canadian woods, and to get in touch with him would be no easy matter.

The president of the chemicals corporation manufacturing the agent was on a cabin cruiser fishing in Long Island Sound, no one knew exactly where, and the cabin cruiser was not equipped with a ship-to-shore radio.

Berenger paused to think things over. He was accumulating information rapidly, but he had yet to discover any way he could do anything about it. Fortunately, since it was the weekend, it was unlikely that any of the texturing agent would be sold. But for the same reason, it was hard to get hold of anyone who might know what to do about the situation.

Berenger paused to think what he could do himself. No doubt, he had enough rank so that he could create a stir in the effort to stop the shipments. He could probably even stop, or delay, *some* of the shipments. But, he thought, if a pile of dynamite has twenty lighted fuses eating their way toward it, it isn't enough to put out even nineteen of the twenty fuses. They *all* have to be put out, or the end result will be just the same as if none at all had been put out. And he did not by any means have the authority to stop all the shipments.

Next, Berenger tried to consider who he might reach who would have the authority to stop the shipments.

To begin with, many of the consignments of texturing agent must by now have changed ownership, so that the actual owners would be citizens of various foreign nations. These nations would have different regulations, and to stop all the shipments by any legal procedure would almost certainly be too complicated. After thinking this over it was clear to Berenger that there was probably no individual on the face of the earth with the legal authority to stop all the shipments.

Berenger then tried to think who might have the practical physical power to stop the shipments. This quickly narrowed down to one person. The eight ships at sea could almost certainly be stopped, and most of the sales in the United States in some way blocked, by only one man: the President. But he would never do it without being convinced.

Berenger thought the thing over and could see that it would take more than the assurances of Dr. Franklin Green to convince the President that drastic action was needed. Berenger's own word would mean nothing. A colleague need only say, "I didn't realize you were a soil chemist, Lyell."

Berenger looked at it objectively and saw how it would work out. He could hear a voice saying to the President, "There's a general out here, sir, who claims that the world's about to be eaten up by some kind of fertilizer. Shall I . . . ah . . . get the M.P.s, sir?"

If it turned out that Green was mistaken, Berenger would never live this down if he lived to be two hundred years old.

Frowning, Berenger sat back to consider Green. Maybe Green *was* in need of a rest cure.

At that thought, Berenger felt both a sense of exasperation over wasted effort, and sudden relief from tension that he hadn't realized was growing unbearably tight.

And the more he thought of it, the more likely it seemed that Green *was* unbalanced.

And in that case, there was no need to do anything.

Just then, the phone rang.

Berenger warily lifted the phone from its cradle. "Hello?"

"General Berenger?"

"Right here."

"This is Franklin Green. I think you ought to come down to the lab right away."

Berenger frowned. "I'll be right there." He hung up, thinking that now at least he should find out definitely whether the man was right or wrong.

Green met Berenger at the door to the laboratory, drew him inside, and locked the door. Inside, three pale young men in lab coats stood at one of the long benches. They looked up nervously as Berenger came in, and Green made hurried introductions.

Berenger interrupted to say sharply, "What did you find out?"

Green said, "Let me show you." He pointed to several bucketfuls of dirt at the far end of the bench. "We put samples of that in these glass dishes, and added small quantities of the transformed texturing agent to each dish. Some we put in in lumps, others we worked carefully into the soil. There you see the result."

Each of a line of the glass dishes contained the same kind of brown-gray glop that Berenger had seen earlier.

"Worse yet," said Green, "we put a little of this transformed agent into a flask, poured in ordinary tap water, decanted the water over the soil, and look here. The soil is changed just as in the other cases. It was a little slower, that's all."

Berenger felt as if an iron band were tightening around his chest. "What about the effects of chemicals?"

Green shrugged. He removed the top of a bottle of sulfuric acid, and carefully poured it over one of the dishes of glop. The substance swelled up, and gave a faint hissing sound as the acid poured into it. Next, he poured a sodium hydroxide solution over one of the dishes. The gray-brown glop shrank slightly, and cracked, leaving the solution in a pool on top of it.

"Now," said Green, "we have found one hopeful thing. We tried ordinary tap water, as I mentioned. We also tried to obtain a solution, or dispersion, in a saline solution." Green pointed to a dish of damp, but unchanged dirt. "Nothing happened." He glanced around. "Jerry. Show the general what you discovered."

One of the graduate students took a paper heaped with tiny white crystals, shook it over a dish of gray glop, and stirred methodically. The grayish color vanished, the texture changed, and then Berenger was looking at ordinary dirt.

"So," said Green. "The process can be reversed. But you have then sowed the soil with salt."

Berenger shook his head. "Can you show me the actual change, from dirt to glop."

Green glanced at one of his graduate students. "Arthur."

The student spoken to put some dirt from a bucket into a clean dish, took a small lump of glop from one of the other dishes, and began working it carefully and methodically into the dirt.

Berenger watched tensely. After a considerable time had passed, his attention began to waver. With an effort, he held his gaze on the dish, and shifted it from one part to another to try to avoid the hypnotic affect of Arthur's ceaselessly-working hand.

Just when it began to happen, Berenger could not say, but suddenly the dirt was no long dirt, but the gray-brown stuff that looked and acted like a kind of thick muck.

Berenger drew a deep breath, and straightened up. "Did you duplicate the experiment that started all this?"

Green nodded. "The same result."

"Did you use a different batch of the texturing agent?"

"Yes, we used some from the complimentary drum the manufacturer sent us. So it isn't just a freak side-effect from one batch of the agent."

Berenger said, "What about heat and cold? What effect do they have?"

"Cold seems to have no effect whatever, except that the substance becomes somewhat more stiff. Intense heat, however, reverses the reaction."

Berenger said tensely, "You're sure of that? Heat reverses it?"

In answer, Green lit a burner, and held it so that the flame played on the surface of one of the samples. Where the flame heated it, the gray color was gradually replaced by the look of ordinary dirt. Green took the burner away. The gray coloration gradually returned.

"The heat," said Green, "only penetrated a thin layer. But we heated one sample in an oven. That sample didn't change back, though it became extremely crumbly."

"Did you try adding water?"

"Yes. The soil absorbed it quite well. But it didn't change . . . or hasn't yet, at least."

Berenger looked around at all the samples. The graduate students were standing around looking at the floor, as if they thought they had committed some criminal act.

Green said tensely, "You've got to stop the shipments."

Berenger shook his head, "I don't have the authority."

"Take it to someone who has the authority. Why don't you take it right to the President?"

"For the same reason that you can't simply walk over there and convince the president of your own college. To function at all, the head of an organization has to recognize and weed out crackpots and alarmists. Anyone who walks in and tries to get action on this will get automatically hustled right out again. To convince the President, I'd have to build up a case first."

"Can you do that?"

"It would take too long." Berenger glanced at his watch.

"Four hours from now, the first cargo ship will reach Britain. While I'm building my case, shipments will be moving over the Canadian and Mexican borders. Stores will be selling the stuff, and farmers using it. Ships will dock in Africa and South America. While I convince the men who will have to convince the President, this stuff will spread out over the globe. By the time they have him convinced, it will be too late for him to do anything."

Green said, "But there's *got* to be something we can do."

"How is this stuff manufactured? Under a patent?"

"No. The company decided the process was sufficiently unusual to justify trying to keep it a trade secret."

"Did you publish any account of the process?"

"No, I wanted to be sure what I had first. Then I was persuaded not to publish." Green's voice climbed. "But the important thing is, *how can we stop the shipments*?"

Berenger said, "Let me take another look at that stuff that formed first."

"But what does that—" Green saw Berenger's expression, hesitated, then led him down to the little laboratory. He locked the door behind them. "This was just so we could talk alone, wasn't it? What are you thinking?"

"What will happen if we take that stuff out onto the campus and plant it?"

Green swallowed. "It will start the reaction. In time, the whole campus will be affected."

"How fast will it happen?"

"It will depend on how finely we divide it. But what good will that do?"

"Can we make a horrible example? Can we have the grounds one sea of spreading muck?"

"Yes," said Green. "But, General, we *can't* do that."

"All right," said Berenger. He sat on the edge of a stool and glanced at his watch. "The first ship docks in London in about three hours and fifty-four minutes. We can go at the problem in slow stages and gamble the whole world. Or we can run the risk here that we will have to run anyway as soon as the stores open on Monday."

Green looked down. In a low voice, he said, "How will we stop it?"

Berenger said grimly, "If heat will stop it, we can stop it all right."

Green nodded slowly. "Yes, I see." He hesitated, then said, "All right."

It was about 4:00 in the morning when Berenger sent for the paratroops. At 5:00 he got through to the Army Chief of Staff, who listened, and then exploded, then listened again.

By 5:30, the college buildings were evacuated, and the headlights of cars competed with the gray light of dawn as excited reporters were held back by police from the expanding edge of the slop. By 6:30 the paratroops had blocked the roads, and the sound of crashing bricks told of buildings toppling as the soil at their foundations softened. By 7:00 the word had gotten to the President, who rejected the whole idea angrily, and sent singed aides scurrying to unload their own wrath at the "hoax." By this time, the Pentagon was receiving direct reports from the paratroops.

At 8:00, a new set of envoys reached the President, bringing photographs, statements of witnesses, and a statement by Dr. Green. The paratroops reported that the perimeter now appeared to be moving out at the steady rate of about one-and-one-half feet per hour. A penciled notation added the calculation that this would amount to an increase in the diameter of the affected area of seventy-two feet every twenty-four hours, with no end in sight. A brief analysis of the situation by Lieutenant General Lyell Berenger, fortunately on the scene, pointed out the impossibility of transport through such muck as this, the danger of it being seeded in new localities, the dangers of hysteria as the muck spread, the political effects of shipments of similar materials being sent overseas, and the desirability from every viewpoint, of immediate drastic action to end the trouble before it had time to gather any more momentum.

The President looked over the photographs and the reports, glanced at an appended list of ship sailings, read Berenger's recommendations through again, and looked at the Army Chief of Staff.

"Is Berenger reliable?"

"He always has been, sir."

"I want to talk to some of these people on the scene. And I want to be very sure they are the people they represent themselves to be."

"Yes, sir."

At 8:35, the urgent message went out to the British Prime Minister.

At 8:55, British troops were racing the police for the docks.

By 9:00 all the ships still at sea were notified, and the United States Navy was in hot pursuit of one that refused to change its course.

By 9:25, the FBI was at work tracing down all the smaller shipments of the texturing agent.

By 9:40, there was a panic in Chicago, as an excited newscaster announced that a "wall of annihilation is approaching at supersonic speed from the state of Iowa."

By 9:55, the college and its surroundings had been forcibly evacuated by troops and police. By this time, also, the warning message had been received in the capitals of the NATO nations, the Soviet Union and Japan.

By 10:00, the President was speaking to the nation, and as he spoke the first jet bomber was already on its way. At the conclusion of his speech, he was handed a slip of paper, and announced that a hydrogen explosion had destroyed the college and surroundings, and was believed to have burned out, by its intense heat, the action of the catalyst.

By 10:55, the Premier of the Soviet Union was receiving Intelligence reports on the situation, and looking it over from a variety of unpleasant angles.

By 11:00, the Pentagon was beginning to subside toward normal, and the Army Chief of Staff was pouring questions at Berenger, at the end of which he gazed off into the distance and remarked, "So, now if we want to we could drop one drop of this stuff anywhere we want to, and eight hours later have a pool of glop twenty-four feet across. It would be tough on people who depend on stretched out rail and road communications, wouldn't it?"

"Yes, sir," said Berenger. "But I'd hate to start it. They could do it back."

"Oh, but I was just looking at it from their point of view, to see how it strikes them. Besides, they don't yet *know* they could do it back."

And several weeks later, Berenger was talking to his friend, Senator Vail.

"You know, Lyell," said Senator Vail, "that experience kind of knocks the spots off your argument. There's been no activity from the Crater, and the whole business seems to have faded away to nothing. We're still competing with the Russians, and I believe we are all running just as fast as ever. I thought that fall was supposed to finish us."

Berenger smiled and shook his head. "I don't expect to convince you that Science is, inherently, unavoidably, and of its own nature, deadly dangerous. But there's one thing you ought to recognize."

"What's that?"

"When you think it's necessary, you run a risk. But you have to use the right names when you label things."

"What of it?"

"You haven't used the right name for that experience."

Vail frowned. "What do you mean?"

"That wasn't a fall," said Berenger. "Far from it."

He thought a moment, then added, "*That* was only a stumble."

★MOSCOW'S★ DILEMMAS

TORCH
★ ★ ★

Moscow, April 28th—Official sources here have revealed that the firing of a huge intercontinental ballistic missile is scheduled for the annual Soviet May Day celebration.

New York, May 1st—Seismologists report violet tremors occurring shortly after 8:00 a.m. G.M.T. this morning.

Washington, May 1st—The Soviet May Day missile is suspected here to have been the first of the new "groundhog" type, capable of penetrating underground shelters. But no one here will comment on certain rumored "strange characteristics" of the blast.

New York, May 2nd—Seismologists report repeated tremors, apparently from the site of the blast of May 1st. One noted seismologist states that this is "most unusual if the result of a bomb explosion."

Moscow, May 2nd—There is still no word here on the May Day blast. All questions are answered, "No comment."

Mew York, May 3rd—Seismologists report tremors of extraordinary violence, occurring shortly after 1:00 a.m., 1:35 a.m., and 1:55 a.m., G.M.T. this morning.

Washington, May 3rd—The Atomic Energy Commission this morning assured reporters there is no danger of the world "taking fire" from recent Soviet blasts.

Chicago, May 3rd—The world may already be on fire. That is the opinion of an atomic scientist reached here late this evening—"if the initial blast took place in the presence of sufficient deposits of light or very heavy metals."

Los Angeles, May 3rd—The world will end by fire on May 7th, predicts the leader of a religious sect here. The end will come "by the spreading of fiery fingers, traveling at the speed of light from the wound in the flesh of the Earth."

Tokyo, May 4th—A radioactive drizzle came down on the west coast of Honshu, the main Japanese island, last night. Teams of scientists are being rushed to the area.

New York, May 4th—Stocks fell sharply here this morning.

Paris, May 4th—A correspondent recently arrived here from the Soviet Union reports that rumors are rife in Moscow of tremendous flames raging out of control in Soviet Siberia. According to these reports the hospitals are flooded with burned workers, and citizens east of the Urals are being recruited by the tens of thousands to form "flame legions" to fight the disaster.

London, May 5th—The British Government today offered "all possible assistance" to Moscow, in the event reports of a great atomic disaster are true.

New York, May 5ᵗʰ—Seismologists report repeated tremors, from the site of the shocks of May 1ˢᵗ and 3ʳᵈ.

Tokyo, May 6ᵗʰ—A heavy deposit of slightly radioactive soot fell on Honshu and Hokkaido last night.

Moscow, May 6ᵗʰ—There is no comment yet on the May Bomb or on British, French and Italian offers of aid.

New York, May 7ᵗʰ—Seismologists here report tremors of extraordinary violence, occurring shortly after 8:00 p.m. G.M.T. last night

Washington, May 7ᵗʰ—A special Senate committee, formed to consider the atomic danger in the U.S.S.R. announced this morning that it favors "all reasonable aid to the Russians." The committee chairman stated to reporters, "It's all one world. If it blows up on them, it blows up on us, too."

Washington, May 7ᵗʰ—The Atomic Energy Commission repeated its claim that the earth could not have caught fire from the recent Russian explosions.

Tokyo, May 8ᵗʰ—Japanese fishermen to the northeast of Hokkaido report the waters in large areas black with a layer of radioactive soot.

New York, May 8ᵗʰ—Seismologists report repeated tremors from the region of the severe shocks of May 1ˢᵗ, 3ʳᵈ, and 7ᵗʰ.

Washington, May 9ᵗʰ—The United States has offered special assistance to Soviet Russia, but the latest word here is that no reply has been received.

Washington, May 9ᵗʰ—Responsible officials here indicate that if no word is received from Moscow within eighteen hours, and if these shocks continue, a special mission will be sent to Russia by the fastest military transportation available. "We are not," said one official, "going to stand around with our hands in our mouths while the world disintegrates under our feet."

Seoul, May 9th—It is reported here that the radioactive soot that plastered Japan and adjacent areas has fallen even more heavily in North Korea. The Communist Government is reportedly trying to pass the soot off as the work of "Capitalist spies and saboteurs."

Washington, May 9th—The United States government has reiterated its offer to the Soviet Union of "prompt and sympathetic consideration" of any requests for aid.

New York, May 10th—Seismologists here report repeated tremors from the region of the earlier shocks.

Moscow, May 10th—It has been impossible to reach any responsible official here for comment on Western offers of assistance.

London, May 10th—The British Government today urgently recommended that the Soviet Union seriously consider Western offers of assistance.

Washington, May 10th—No word having been received here from Moscow, an experimental Hellblast bomber sprang from her launching rack bearing a nine-man mission to Moscow. Word of the mission's departure is being sent the Russians by all channels of communication. But it is said here that if no permission to land is given, the Hellblast will attempt to smash through to Moscow anyway.

Tokyo, May 10th—Another load of soot has been dumped on Japan today. This batch is only slightly radioactive, but scientists are not happy because they do not know what to make of it.

Seoul, May 10th—Riots are reported in Communist North Korea as the "black death" continues to rain down from the skies. It is not known whether the soot has caused actual death or merely panic.

St. Paul, Minn., May 10ᵗʰ—A light powdering of black flecks has been reported in snow that has fallen near here in the last twenty-four hours.

Moscow, May 11ᵗʰ—A United States Hellblast bomber roared out of the dawn here today bearing a nine-man mission. The mission was greeted at the airfield by a small group of worn and tired Russian officials.

Minneapolis, May 11ᵗʰ—Scientists report only a trace of radioactivity in the "tainted snow" that fell near here yesterday. The scientists reiterate that the radioactivity is not present in dangerous amounts.

Tokyo, May 11ᵗʰ—Considerable deposits of radioactive soot and ash landed on Japan yesterday and last night. Japanese scientists have issued warnings to all persons in the affected areas. The Japanese Government has delivered a severe protest to the Soviet Embassy.

Hong Kong, May 11ᵗʰ—Reports here indicate the Chinese Communist Government is making representation to Moscow about the soot-fall following the Russian May Day blast. According to these reports, the North Korean Government is being overwhelmed with the people's angry demands that the Russians cease "dumping their waste on their allies."

New York, May 12ᵗʰ—The American mission that arrived here yesterday has disappeared into the Kremlin and has not been seen or heard from since.

Washington, May 12ᵗʰ—The United States Government reports that it is now in close contact with the Soviet Government on the situation in Siberia.

Seoul, May 13ᵗʰ—It is reported here that the government of Communist North Korea has issued a twelve-hour ultimatum to the Soviet Union. If the dumping of fission products continues beyond that time, North

Korea threatens to break off relations and take "whatever other measures prove to be necessary."

Paris, May 13th—Repeated efforts by the French Government have failed to produce any response from Moscow. French atom scientists have offered to travel to the Soviet Union in a body if their services can be of any use.

Washington, May 14th—A Soviet request for American aid was received here early this morning. Reportedly, the Russians asked for ten thousand of the largest available bulldozers or other earth-moving vehicles, equipped with special high-efficiency filters for the air-intake mechanisms.

London, May 14th—The British Government reports receiving a request for large numbers of specially-equipped earth-moving vehicles. Red tape is being cut as fast as possible, and the first consignment is expected to leave tomorrow. However, there is still no explanation of what is going on in the Soviet Union.

Washington, May 14th—A special meeting of the Senate committee investigating the May Bomb is scheduled for tomorrow, when the American mission is expected to return.

New York, May 15th—Repeated tremors are reported here from the region of the severe shocks of May 1st, 3rd, and 7th.

Washington, May 15th—The Senate Committee on the May Bomb met today, and questioned members of the American mission that had just returned.

Senator Keeler: Gentlemen, what's going on over there?

Mr. Brainerd: They're in a mess, Senator. And so are we.

Senator Keeler: Could you be more specific? Is the . . . is the earth on fire?

Mr. Brainerd: No. It's not that, at least.

Senator Keeler: Then, there's no danger—

Mr. Brainerd: The earth won't burn up under us, no. This thing was set off atomically, but it goes on by itself.

Senator Keeler: What happened?

Mr. Brainerd: They tried out their groundhog missile on May Day. They had a giant underground shelter built, and they wanted to show what the groundhog would do to it. The idea was to show there was no use anyone building shelters, because the Russian groundhog could dig right down to them.

Senator Keeler: Did it?

Mr. Brainerd: It did. It blew up the shelter and heated it white hot.

Senator Keeler: I see. But why should that cause trouble?

Mr. Brainerd: Because, unknown to them or anyone else, Senator, there were deep deposits of oil underground, beneath the shelter. The explosion cracked the surrounding rock. The oil burst up through the cracks, shot out into the white-hot remains of the underground chambers, and vaporized. At least that's the explanation the Russians and Dr. Dentner here have for what happened. All anybody can see is a tremendous black column rising up.

Senator Keeler: Do you have anything to add to that, Dr. Dentner?

Dr. Dentner: No, that about covers it.

Senator Keeler: Well, then, do any of my colleagues have any questions? Senator Daley?

Senator Daley: Yes, I've got some questions. Dr. Dentner, what's that black stuff made of?

Dr. Dentner: Quite a number of compounds: carbon monoxide; carbon dioxide; water vapor; saturated and unsaturated gaseous hydrocarbons; the vapors of saturated and unsaturated non-gaseous hydrocarbons. But the chief constituent seems to be finely-divided carbon—in other words, soot.

Senator Daley The world isn't on fire?

Dr. Dentner: No.

Senator Daley: The oil fire can't spread to here?

Dr. Dentner: No. Not by any process I can imagine.

Senator Daley: All right, then, I've got a crude idea. Why not let them stew in their own juice? They started this. They were going to scare the world with it. O.K., let them worry about it. It'll give them something to do. Keep them out of everybody's hair for a while.

Senator Keeler: The idea has its attractions, at that. What about it, Doctor?

Dr. Dentner: The fire won't spread to here, but—Well, General Maxwell has already considered the idea and given it up.

Senator Daley: Why's that?

General Maxwell: Set up an oil furnace in the cloakroom and run the flue in here through that wall over there. Then light the furnace. That's why.

Senator Daley: The stuff's going to come down on us?

Dr. Dentner: It seems probable. There have already been several light falls in the midwest.

Senator Daley: I thought it was too good to work. O.K. then, we've got to put it out. How?

Dr. Dentner: They've already made attempts to blow it out with H-bombs. But the temperature in the underground chamber is apparently so high that the fire reignites. The present plan is to push a mass of earth in on top of it and choke out the flame.

Senator Daley: Don't they have enough bulldozers? I mean, if it's that simple, why don't they have it out?

Dr. Dentner: It's on a large scale, and that produces complications.

General Maxwell: For instance, the air is full of soot. The soot gets in the engines. Men choke on it.

Mr. Brainerd: The general effect is like trying to do a day's work inside a chimney.

General Maxwell: And the damned thing sits across their lines of communications, dumping heaps of soot on the roads and railroad tracks, and strangling anyone that tries to get past. The trains spin their wheels, and that's the end of that. It's a question of going way around to the north or way around to the south. There's a severe cold wave in the north, so that's out. They're laying track to the south at a terrific pace, but there's a long way to go. What it amounts to is, they're cut in half.

Senator Daley: It seems to me we ought to be able to make a buck out of this.

Mr. Brainerd: It's a temptation; but I hate to kick a man when he's down.

Senator Daley: ARE they down?

Mr. Brainerd: Yes, they're down. The thing is banging their head on the floor. They're still fighting it, but it's like fighting a boa constrictor. Where do you take hold to hurt it?

Senator Daley: Just back of the head.

Mr. Brainerd: That's the part they can't get at. Meanwhile, it crushes the life out of them.

General Maxwell: The idea is to fight the main enemy. If they don't beat it, we'll have to. And it will be a lot harder for us to get at it than it is for them. The idea is, to pour the supplies to them while they're still alive to use them. Otherwise, that volcano keeps pumping soot into the air and we get it in the neck, too.

Dr. Dentner: There's one more point here.

Senator Daley: What's that?

Dr. Dentner: Neither their scientists nor I could understand why a stray spark hasn't ignited the soot. It must be an explosive mixture.

General Maxwell: If that happens, it will Make World War II look like a garden party.

Mr. Brainerd: Like a grain-elevator explosion a thousand miles across.

Senator Daley: Well—All right, that does it. What do they need?

Mr. Brainerd: We've got a list here as long as your arm for a starter.

Senator Daley: Then let's get started.

Senator Keeler: Let's see the list. And I'm not sure the rest of this shouldn't be secret for the time being.

Senator Daley: Right. Let's see what they want first.

New York, June 8th—The first ten shiploads of gang-tracks, bores, sappers, and hogger mauls raced out of New York harbor today on converted liners, bound for Murmansk. A similar tonnage is reported leaving San Francisco for Vladivostok tonight.

Tokyo, June 14th—The evacuation of another one hundred square miles of Honshu Island was completed early today.

Hong Kong, June 27th—Reports reaching here from Red China indicate that the Chinese Communist Government is moving its capital south from Peiking to Nanking. Relations between Red China and the Soviet Union are reported extremely bad.

New York, June 28th—According to the U.N. Disaster Committee meeting here this morning, over three billion dollars worth of supplies has thus far been poured into the U.S.S.R. in Operation Torch.

Tokyo, July 2ⁿᵈ—The Smog Belt is reported extending itself southward. Officials here fear that this, combined with the unseasonable cold, will swell the mounting casualty list still further.

Seoul, July 9ᵗʰ—Severe fighting is reported between the North Korean People's Army and Russian troops defending the border region south of Vladivostok.

New York, July 18ᵗʰ—Three specially-built high-speed dual-hull transports left here this morning bearing three Super-Hoggers of the Mountain-Mover class.

London, July 23ᵗʰ—The furnaces of Britain's yards and factories are blazing as they have not in three generations, to finish the last four sections of the huge Manchester Snake, which will be shipped in sections to France and assembled for its overland trip to the Soviet Union. Work has been aided somewhat here by the unusually cool summer weather.

Skagway, Alaska, August 2ⁿᵈ—The Pittsburgh Mammoth rolled north past here at 2:00 a.m. this morning.

Nome, August 5ᵗʰ—The Bering Bridge is almost complete.

Moscow, August 6ᵗʰ—The 20ᵗʰ, 21ˢᵗ, and 40ᵗʰ Divisions of the Soviet 2ⁿᵈ Red Banner Flame Army marched in review through Red Square today before entraining for the East.

Nome, August 8ᵗʰ—The Pittsburgh Mammoth crushed past here at dawn this morning. Crowds from up and down the coast, their faces hidden behind gas masks and soot shields, were on hand to see the mammoth roll north toward the Bering Bridge. Tank trucks in relays refueled the giant.

Headquarters, Supreme High Command of the Soviet Red Banner Flame Legions, September 21ˢᵗ—Final Communiqué: The campaign against the enemy has ended in victory. Nothing remains to mark the site save a towering monument to the bravery of the Soviet citizen, to the supreme organization of the war effort by the high officials of the Soviet Government, and to the magnificent output of Soviet industry. Help also was received from countries desiring to participate in the great Soviet effort, which has resulted in this great victory. Work now must be begun with unhesitating energy to return the many brave workers to their peacetime stations.

London, September 22ⁿᵈ—The consensus here seems to be that naturally we cannot expect credit, but it is at least a relief to know the thing is over.

Washington, September 22ⁿᵈ—After talking with a number of high officials here, the general feeling seems to be: After this, we are to go back to the Cold War?

Moscow, December 3ʳᵈ—Winter here seems to be taking hold with a vengeance. Temperatures of a hundred degrees below zero are being reported from many regions that normally do not record even remotely comparable readings till the middle of January. It looks by far the severest winter on record. Coming after all the trouble this spring and summer, this is a heavy blow.

Ottawa, Canada, December 8ᵗʰ—The cold here in Canada is unusually severe for this time of year.

Washington, December 10ᵗʰ—The Senate Committee on the Russian May Bomb explosion reconvened briefly to hear expert testimony today. Bundled in heavy overcoats, the senators listened to testimony that may be summed up briefly in this comment by a meteorologist:

"No, Senator, we don't know when these fine particles will settle. The heavier particles of relatively large diameter settle out unless the air currents sweep them back up again, and then we have these 'soot showers.' But the smaller particles remain aloft and screen out part of the sun's radiation. Presumably they'll settle eventually; but in the meantime it's a good deal as if we'd moved the Arctic Circle down to about the fifty-fifth degree of latitude."

When asked what might be done about this immediately, the experts suggested government aid to supply fuel to people in the coldest locations, and it was urged that fuel stockpiles be built up now, as unexpected transportation difficulties may arise in the depths of winter.

Underground Moscow, December 17th—The Soviet Government is reported making tremendous efforts to house millions of its people underground. Much of the equipment used in fighting the Torch is fitted for this work, but deep snow and the severe cold have hamstrung the transportation system.

New York, January 15th—National Headquarters of the Adopt-A-Russian Drive has announced that their drive "went over the top at 7:00 tonight, just five hours before deadline."

Prince Rupert, Canada, January 22nd—Three polar bears were reported seen near here last Friday.

Washington, February 3rd—Scientists concluded today that things will get worse before they get better. Settling of the particles is slow, they say, and meanwhile the ocean—"the great regulator"—will become colder.

New York, March 10th—Heavily dressed delegates of the former "Communist" and "Capitalist" blocs met here today to solemnly commemorate the ending of the so-called "cold war"—the former ideological phrase—in the strength of unity. The delegates agreed unanimously on many measures, one of them the solemn pledge to "Remain united as one people under God, and to persevere in our efforts together till and even beyond the time when the Cold War shall end."

DEVISE AND CONQUER
★ ★ ★

Sergei Vladimirov sat at the steering wheel near the bustling street corner, conscious of the hurrying crowd, the new-style cars, a huge sign reading "Close-Out Sale," and P. Grulov.

P. Grulov was in the passenger's seat beside him. P. Grulov was a small man with thick glasses and an air of absolute rightness. When P. Grulov spoke, subordinates nodded eager agreement. When he commanded, they sprang to obey. When he was irritated, they cringed.

Sergei Vladimirov was a subordinate of P. Grulov and P. Grulov was irritated.

"Look there," snapped Grulov. "Do you see that across the street? What sort of incompetence is this? We leave you in charge for a year and a half, because we trust you. We raise your pay and rank, heap medals on

147

you, give your family a nice house to live in—and this is how you repay us! You bungler, explain *that* to me!" Grulov angrily pointed across the street.

Vladimirov looked where he pointed. "There is a crowd of shoppers, but nothing unusual."

"Nothing *unusual*! Look there! Do you see those two men? There they go, arm-in-arm!"

Vladimirov groaned. "I see them."

"This is an American city, is it not?"

"Yes, comrade." Vladimirov could feel the iron jaws of logic begin to close on him.

"And these," said P. Grulov, making a gesture to indicate the crowd, "are Americans, are they not?"

"Yes. Yes, this is true."

"And there are two kinds of Americans, are there not?"

"Well, comrade—about that."

"No evasion. Remember your teachings at the Special School. There are two kinds of Americans. Name them."

Vladimirov groped mentally for some way out. "Capitalists and workers, exploiters and—"

P. Grulov's voice carried a bite. "None of that! You evade. I am speaking of your teachings at the Special School."

"Oh."

"There are two kinds of Americans. Name them."

"Exploiters, and—and exploited."

"Very good. Now be more *specific*."

Vladimirov drew a deep breath. "Those of European, and those of African descent."

"You are squeamish, Vladimirov. Why go around the problem? Speak out! Why do you hesitate? Look here, my friend, this is the *Americans'* problem. *You* don't have to worry about it. Let them twist and turn. *You* don't need to find soft words and easy expressions. Not European and African, Vladimirov. *White and black*. There, *now* we have it. Think bluntly. Be more than blunt. Call a spade a dung-fork. You are a saboteur, Vladimirov. It is your job to throw matches into other peoples' racial gasoline." He eyed Vladimirov sharply. "That is right, is it not?"

Vladimirov nodded miserably. "Yes, Comrade Grulov."

P. Grulov scowled. "Or am I being too subtle for you? Let me be more plain about it. America, Vladimirov, is made up of many races. Ideally they will all separate like a pack of mixed dogs and cats and tear each other to pieces. Divide and conquer, you see?"

Vladimirov gripped the steering wheel, and nodded.

P. Grulov went on. "At home, there are some who disagree. I am happy for you that you are not one of them, Vladimirov."

Vladimirov swallowed nervously.

Grulov said, "Ideally, from the Americans' viewpoint, these different races will all say, 'I'm American. Nobody better try to turn me against my country, or I'll smash his head.' "

Vladimirov nodded dutifully. "Yes, that is what the Americans want."

"You realize," said P. Grulov, "that they have been very fortunate. They have had a very large measure of that. We are alone here, and I can say it. They have been truly 'the melting pot of races.' You know that?"

"I know it."

"Let us be very realistic, Vladimirov. How have they been able to do this? First, they have had *a great deal of work that needed to be done*. Second, they had a frontier. Third, they had a philosophy. The philosophy struggles on under great ideological handicaps; the frontier is gone, except for a little piece here and there, mostly in Alaska; and the abundance of work, Vladimirov, is running out, thanks to the new machinery and the automation. The melting pot was a blast furnace, in the memory of living men. What is it now? All that is left is the remaining heat from the past, and the American philosophy which tries to keep it going. It is not enough I am talking to you very frankly. *Ideas are essential, but they alone are not enough.* They must be implemented, made real, provided with actual material means. This American melting-pot has been a real thing, a very real frustration to us. It is a cliché, it is hackneyed, it is a set of words used so often the meaning is all but rubbed off, but nevertheless, it has been a real thing. But now the heat is almost out. *Now is our chance!* Now is the time to drive in the wedges! Now is the time to find the planes of cleavage and split all these races wide open. American against American, Vladimirov. And what do *you* do but slump here with your hands on the wheel and mutter excuses! Speak up for yourself! What are your plans? How will you make up for this disgraceful defeat, *if* we permit you to try? Do you think we have grown so broadminded we will not punish incompetents and worse? Do you know how quickly you can lose your rewards? Speak up!"

"Comrade—"

"Why have you failed? *Look!*" He pointed: "And look there!" He pointed again. "Don't sit there staring at the instruments! Look out! See where I point!"

Miserably, Vladimirov raised his head, and looked out vaguely at the shoppers going by.

Furiously, P. Grulov commanded. "Focus your eyes! *Look* at those people. Now, you see what I mean?"

Vladimirov forced himself to obey, and gradually he saw.

"There," said Grulov, "go two young men, talking intently. They have some plan, perhaps for a sale of merchandise. They are making a 'deal.' To use your weak-kneed phrase, Vladimirov, one is 'of European descent,' and the other is 'of African descent.' Right?"

Vladimirov groaned. "No. You don't understand—"

"I understand well enough. It is your job to keep them *at each other's throats*. You have the money, you have the training, you have the false identity, so your acts can never be traced back to us—"

"Comrade—"

"And I come over here, to check discreetly, and what do I find? Here they are, walking around in each other's arms! There go three women, chattering like hens! There is no self-consciousness, no stiffness! Look over there! This time, two men, well-dressed, talking casually. And, great ghost of—"

"Comrade," pleaded Vladimirov, "I meant well. But a terrible misfortune befell us."

"Horrible! Horrible!" roared Grulov. "This time it is a whole group, all going off on a picnic together! And no one is *doing* anything!"

"I couldn't help it," Vladimirov was pleading.

"Shut up!" snapped Grulov, abruptly getting control of himself. "This is incredible. I can see what you are up against. But it is a very simple matter to fix, just the same."

"No," said Vladimirov earnestly, "that's just it. It *isn't* simple. It's tricky. It's so subtle you don't know who's behind it. It is a very tricky, underhanded, peculiarly American—"

"Sh-h!" Grulov looked around. "No need to get hysterical, comrade. We have our duty, and it is very simple, and we *will* do it. Now, at the moment, I don't see any suitable opportunity, but there will be one, and I will show you. I have experience at this. Start the car."

Vladimirov shook his head resignedly, and did as he was told.

P. Grulov said, "There is a simple little key word, Vladimirov, and if you only use it at the right time, you can set off an explosion. There are, in fact, several key words that can be fired off in various directions, like rockets. But for this present problem, one specific key word in particular is suitable. I will show you how to use it. Be ready to drive off at once. This is a very crude technique, Vladimirov, but it is, at least, sure to work."

Vladimirov braced himself to make one more attempt to explain the trouble, but Grulov said, "Ah, here we are. Splendid."

A tall, extremely dark young man was coming down the sidewalk.

Grulov threw his coat in the back seat, yanked his tie to one side, unbuttoned the top button of his shirt, sprang out, took his hat off and put it on aslant. He swaggered across the sidewalk. In a loud voice, he said, "Out of my way you—" and then P. Grulov used the key word.

The young man glanced at him in puzzlement, then smiled uncertainly, "I am dark, aren't I?"

Grulov looked momentarily stunned. Recovering fast, he shouted, "Tell *me* to get off the sidewalk, will you, you—" In quick succession, he spat out half-a-dozen powerful adjectives, and tacked a key word on the end.

The young man looked at him blankly, then shook his head in wonderment and shoved past.

Grulov shouted insults after him, freely mixed with keywords.

Nothing happened.

Now genuinely furious, Grulov accosted an extremely dark young matron, screaming insults at her. An elderly red-faced man, chewing tobacco and carrying a large cane, reversed the cane, shot it out, caught Grulov around the neck by the crook and yanked him away from the woman, who walked past with her nose in the air.

Grulov, rubbing his neck and staggering, stared after the woman, unable to speak.

The crowd moved on again.

A burly man paused to snap at Grulov. "Just where in the hell have you spent the last year and a half?"

Another passerby said menacingly, "Better go home and sleep it off, buddy. The market in used nightmares is damned low around here right now."

A third, an imposing man with broad shoulders and pale complexion, gripped Grulov by the shirt front and growled, "Use that word on *me* and see what happens."

A fourth bystander, who had been lounging against a telephone pole, now straightened up, and growled, "Seems to me there was something funny about his accent. Let's hear him say all that over again."

Vladimirov set the parking brake and shot out of the car. Explaining earnestly that his friend didn't mean it, that he had these spells now and then, that he was sick, that he was under the influence of strong drink, and that he wouldn't do it again, Vladimirov got Grulov safely back into the car.

The people on the sidewalk followed his departure with hard glares, as Vladimirov shot away from the curb and got lost in the traffic. When they were well away from the place, on the way back to his apartment, Vladimirov stopped at a drugstore for iodine, liniment, sore-throat remedies and other supplies. Then he parked his car in the lot near the apartment, helped Grulov, who had yet to say a word, into the elevator, then down the corridor and into the apartment. There he painted Grulov's various scratches, and gave him a large spoonful of the sore-throat remedy.

Grulov gagged and choked. "Phew." He sat up, looked around, and whispered, "Incredible. Who would have believed it?" Then he sank back dizzily.

Vladimirov loosened Grulov's shirt, picked up the bottle of liniment, and eyed the label, which read:

" . . . its soothing warmth penetrates deep into sore and aching muscles . . . "

Vladimirov poured some into his hands, winced, and went to work on the dazed Grulov with it. Grulov suddenly got his voice back:

"What are you doing to me? Where am I? *Nothing you can do will make me talk!*"

"Steady, comrade," said Vladimirov, his hands burning. "You are among friends."

It was some moments before the situation became clear to Grulov, who suffered further temporary confusion as Vladimirov explained that the liniment was really all right, and showed Grulov the label, with the words "for external use only," and the warning that it was illegal to drink it. Grulov wonderingly stared at the label, massaged his throat and sat up. He straightened his glasses regretfully.

"I apologize to you, Comrade Vladimirov. You truly had difficulties. I see that now."

"It has been very discouraging," Vladimirov agreed.

"It is incredible. I do not look forward to reporting this. You, at least, were spared *that* problem, since there was to be no contact—nothing that could possibly be traced."

"For which, frankly, I was grateful. And yet, very uneasy. Word of this should have been sent back at once."

"Yes." Grulov got up gingerly. "Fantastic. Our plans plainly count on them to fly at each other's throats. Instead, here they are, going around arm-in-arm. Yet it looked so promising a little while ago! The melting-pot must have had more heat in it than we thought. Look here, Vladimirov, what did it? Was it the civil-rights movement?"

Vladimirov shook his head sadly, thinking of the shock still ahead for Grulov.

Grulov said hopefully, "Something purely *local*, perhaps? Something others of your group may not have run into?"

"No, comrade. It came out very quietly. With no fanfare. It was very subtle. Very underhanded: Maybe it hit me first, I don't know. But it's widespread now."

Grulov said, with a sort of nervous dread, "It wasn't—ah—ah—'brotherly love,' was it?"

"Not that I know of."

"Government action! The courts, perhaps?"

"No. All these things had their effect, but it wasn't this that hurt."

"An 'executive order,' perhaps?"

"No, comrade."

"Some new 'grass-roots' movement?"

"No."

"Was it the churches, then?"

"Not that I know of. As I say, all these things had their influence. They were troubles to us. But we were making progress anyway."

P. Grulov frowned. "This is a very serious problem, Vladimirov. Here we have an ideal situation from our viewpoint. Splits and divisions in our opponent's camps are to be encouraged—quietly and unobtrusively, of course. This was made to order for us." Exasperatedly, Grulov said, "With automation, with nine jobs for ten people, we could *count* on it to get worse." Plaintively, he added, "Is that not true, Vladimirov?"

Vladimirov said patiently, "It is true, Comrade Grulov."

"And what has happened? How has this great store of trouble and embarrassment in our opponent's camp vanished into thin air? How has it just disappeared?"

Gently, Vladimirov said, "I understand your feelings, Comrade Grulov. It is very sad."

Grulov blew his nose and sat down. "You are sparing me some blow, Vladimirov. All right. Let's have it. Obviously they have out-generaled us. How did they do it?"

Vladimirov reached into the paper bag from the drugstore.

Grulov eyed the iodine, liniment, and sore-throat medicine, and winced.

Vladimirov handed him a wasp-waisted bottle with a shiny gold-edged green label bearing in large letters the trade-name "SUNBLOX," and beneath it the slogan "Suddenly you don't burn!"

Squinting at this, Grulov discovered that the bottle held so-and-so many ounces, contained such-and-such chemical constituents and was a long-lasting quick-acting lotion for the "positive protection of sunburn, by nature's own tested remedy."

Grulov put the bottle down and looked up questioningly at Vladimirov, who handed him a second bottle like the first, except that the label read "UNBLOX," and had the slogan, "When sunburn is no problem."

Grulov felt a pulse beat at his forehead, swallowed hard, and set the second bottle by the first. "Surely, Vladimirov—"

Vladimirov shook his head. "Steady, Comrade. This is the way the Americans do things. They must have figured the whole thing was basically caused by differences in the amount of heat and sunlight over a long period—so they worked out a way to control the process at will."

"You don't mean to tell me—"

"I'm not trying to tell you anything, comrade, except that this whole problem, that promised to blow their whole country up into one huge anarchy, has all been kicked out from under our feet by a couple bottles of sun-cream."

"Are you sure it works?"

"Try it."

P. Grulov sat and glared at the bottles as if they were enemies. Finally he reached out, and uncapped the SUNBLOX. Muttering to himself, he rolled up his sleeves, poured some into his hand, and smeared it on his forearm. Vladimirov handed him a paper towel, and Grulov wiped off the excess. Gradually, his forearm came to look as if he had spent a solid summer on the beach. Grulov smeared on some more cream. Then another dose. Grimly determined to test the potential of the stuff, he repeated the treatment till his arm was blacker than anything Vladimirov had seen before. A long session at the sink then convinced Grulov that soap didn't budge it.

Vladimirov held out the UNBLOX, Grulov smeared it on. After half-a-dozen applications of this, he was back where he had started from.

Vladimirov said apologetically, "You can understand what it was like, Comrade. The capitalists have, of course, been selling sun-tan cream for a long time. There has even been stuff that would give you a tan *without* the sun. This cream was advertised as operating on 'Nature's own principle of solar protection.' It sold in huge quantities. There's another version, called SUNBLOX with REPELZZ, that also repels bugs. Naturally sportsmen smeared it on good and thick. Then, comrade, if some other sportsman who didn't know about it came along and used a key-word, he got flattened. Meanwhile, young people took to using it as a prank. The demand was unprecedented. For a time, UNBLOX was selling at around seventeen-fifty a bottle."

"I can see you certainly had a problem," admitted Grulov, staring at the bottle.

"What was there to do? It went from bad to worse, until the situation became so confused that if I used a key-word in a mixed crowd, I never knew who would hit me."

Grulov shook his head gloomily.

Vladimirov added wearily, "Undoubtedly, comrade, it was the cursed 'profit motive' at work. Our loss is some capitalist's gain."

"It seems incredible that such disastrous things could happen without reaching our ears."

"Would members of our provocations units break discipline to report? And then, who wished to be the one to bear the bad news? Worse yet, seeing it from the outside, who would really know what was happening until it was too late?"

For a considerable time Vladimirov and Grulov sat in gloom, then at last, Vladimirov said hesitantly, "They *still* have unemployment."

"It isn't enough. In a struggle like this, any advantage to either side tilts the balance, and tends to accumulate new advantages. Most of the energy the Americans wasted in this problem is now freed. They can apply it to other things. We *must* have some compensating advantage, or—"

Vladimirov snapped his fingers. He rummaged through a bureau drawer, and handed Grulov a large brown pill-bottle.

Grulov scowled. "And what is this?"

"We have, at times, had—ah—difficulties with certain of our Asian comrades."

Grulov winced. "But what has this bottle to do with that?"

"Read the label."

Grulov squinted at it: "SWEETRES'N. Take two tablets each, before conferences."

"What's this?" said Grulov.

"They came out with it a few months ago. The Americans use these pills at contract talks."

"What can we do with them? And how do you pronounce that trade name?"

"Well, as for what we can do, I was thinking if we invited the Chinese comrades to a banquet, ground up several dozen of these pills and put them in the food . . . The name on the bottle is pronounced 'Sweet Reason,' comrade."

" 'Sweet Reason,' " murmured Grulov. He looked from the bottle to Vladimirov. "You are not fooling me? These will *work*?"

"I understand that they have worked for coal miners and operators, longshoremen and ship owners, and even for the executives and workers at a factory out west, where they had been bombing and shooting each other for seventeen years." He hesitated. "Of course, as for whether they will work on the *Chinese comrades*—"

"Anything would be worth trying," said Grulov.

"They cost a dollar eighty-nine cents a bottle. I think there are fifty pills to a bottle."

Grulov dug into his pocket.

"Get a big supply. You may have to go from store to store. Several dozen bottles would not be too many."

Vladimirov started out.

"Wait," said Grulov, "there is one other thing."

"Yes, comrade?"

"The Americans seem very thorough in the drug line. And—there is no escaping it—I *still* have to report that we have failed here. Is there anything that you could— say—*squirt* at your superior, and then he is reasonable? Feeding him pills might be too slow."

Vladimirov looked intent. "I hadn't thought of that."

P. Grulov lay back, and winced with pain. "Think about it now," he said testily. "Keep your eyes open for a change."

Vladimirov blinked. "Yes, Comrade Grulov."

"Don't just stand there," snapped P. Grulov, getting back into form. "*Move.*"

Vladimirov gently shut the door.

If, he told himself fervently, he only *could* find such a drug, he knew exactly who to try it out on first.

WAR GAMES
★ ★ ★

Nikolai Bartov, the Premier's personal interpreter, was afraid the ambassador had gone over to the Americans. That was about all it would take to make this trip to the United Nations the worst week Bartov had ever lived through.

The trouble had started over West Rindelia, an insignificant strip of tropical jungle presided over largely by malarial mosquitoes, and coveted by the communist overlord of East Rindelia. Diplomats who had visited the two Rindelias called them "the key to nowhere—the pesthole of Southeast Asia." Veterans who had struggled and sweltered in the Rindelia jungles in 1944 remembered West Rindelia as "Purgatory" and East Rindelia as "Hell". No one wanted either place except for the Rindelians, who were loud in their demands for help and that was the trouble.

Experts who claimed to understand such matters called the Rindelian affair a "prestige crisis." The United States, they said, had let Russia put a wall through divided Berlin, and had thus lost prestige. The Russians had let the United States clamp a blockade on Cuba, and had thus lost prestige. Any sensible person might suppose that this evened matters, and the two were back where they started from, but the experts claimed this wasn't so. According to the experts, these two events climaxed a long series of backdowns by both sides, and malcontents and exasperated allies in each camp were accusing their leaders of having lost their nerve. For either side to back down in Rindelia might shatter the confidence of its allies, permanently damage its prestige, and thus prove a large scale disaster.

Bartov did not know how much truth there might be in this. But he did know that the Premier showed no sign of giving way. And the American newspapers that Bartov had studied gave every sign that this time the Americans would not yield an inch. The result was a severe strain on the nervous system, which got worse daily, and now rose to a new climax as the Premier, about ready to leave the Embassy for the U.N. building, demanded to know where Ambassador Palvukin was.

Bartov happened to know where the ambassador was, but he joined the rest of the Premier's party in a glum silence as everyone tried to look blank and inconspicuous like students when the teacher asks a tough question.

The Premier's voice rose angrily. "Where is he? *Where's Palvukin?*"

Someone hesitantly cleared his throat. "I believe he was over at the American electronics exhibition. They have a game . . . ah . . . a strategy computer on display over there."

"Send somebody over to get him."

"We have done it. He won't come."

"He *what*?"

"He says he's too busy playing the game. He can't be disturbed. He won't come."

The Premier's expression changed from exasperation to amazement to a look of suppressed rage. He glanced at his watch.

"We'll drag him out by the ears. Come on!"

They went out the door to the street, and piled into the waiting cars. There was uproar and confusion as the police discovered they weren't going to the U.N., but to the Electronics Exhibition. Then this was straightened out, and the procession got in motion. Bartov glanced out at the huge gray buildings gliding past, then the car pulled to the curb.

"Here we are," said someone. They all got out in front of a building with a monster plate glass window behind which was visible a large room with people grouped around exhibits, and stacks of advertising folders piled up on every table in sight.

"Let's go," growled the Premier, and in a compact group they shoved open the wide all-glass door.

The Premier looked around narrowly. "Where is he?"

Bartov spotted a directory on the wall across from the entrance, and read:

"War Games Computer—2nd floor."

He translated this, then spotted an arrow lettered "Elevator". The Premier was silent as they went up. The door slid open, and they stepped out into a large room where a sense of excitement tingled in the air.

The Premier immediately growled, "There he is."

They headed across the room toward a sort of big table with two men seated at opposite sides and groups of watchers looking on alertly. The man on the far side of the table was Palvukin, the ambassador. He had a worried look as he hunched over a set of controls.

As the Premier, his face determined, strode towards Palvukin, Palvukin leaned forward, and speaking English said tensely to the man across the table, "I'll attack with missiles if you don't break off your advance."

The other man smiled coolly, "You use missiles, and so will I."

The Premier glanced sharply from one to the other of them. They both looked perfectly serious.

Bartov squinted at the table. A second look showed him it was no ordinary table, but looked more like a photographic map, in three dimensions. Geographical features were shown in relief; lakes, rivers, and mountains stood out clearly, as did cities, roads, railroads, and forests. He bent over the table, to see that the actual view was apparently under the surface itself, which seemed to be made of some very clear plastic. The effect was that of looking at an actual scene from a considerable height, and the illusion was remarkable in its detail. A pall of smoke seemed to hang over a heavily industrialized region near where Bartov was standing.

A tiny train was crawling through a mountain pass, moving away from one industrialized region towards another.

So absorbed in examining details, Bartov almost missed it when the Premier asked a question, and for a moment he wasn't sure who had spoken, or whether the question was meant for him. Then he realized that

Palvukin had the cover off a gray-enameled box that housed a control board lettered "Nuclear Missiles."

The Premier, scowling, put the cover back on the box again.

"But," pleaded Palvukin, "I've got to. Look, here." He pointed at a big lake, along the borders of which it was possible to see tiny tanks, armored troop carriers, and motorized artillery, crawling steadily forward. Around them was a large faint blue arrow, like those used in newspaper diagrams of military maneuvers. Looking around, Bartov could see a number of these arrows, which must represent advancing troops, and also a number of straight lines which apparently marked stationary portions of the front. It was easy to see that Palvukin had gotten himself into an unenviable position.

Palvukin was complaining again. "I'll *lose* otherwise."

"Get up," said the Premier, as if to a child. "We have a real game to play."

"There's still time," said Palvukin, glancing at his watch. "I just want to finish—"

Someone coughed. "Comrade Premier. Excuse me. Look there."

Several men in Arab headdress and robes had wandered over to the table, and were looking interestedly at the people on both sides of the board. A number of other Africans and Asians were looking on intently.

A voice with a British accent carried across the room. "The Americans are quite clever with games, you know. Baseball, Monopoly, strip poker. Somehow, they manage to devise games that capture the attention."

The Premier eyed the Afro-Asians intently. They were now leaning across the board, and it was clear from their gestures and facial expressions that they knew which side was winning. They glanced covertly at the Premier and his party, then with respect to the lone individual seated on the other side of the table.

The Premier colored, and glanced angrily at the ambassador. "Who is this you are playing, Palvukin?"

"An American named Schmidt, Comrade Premier."

"Who is he? What does he?"

"He is a . . . er . . . tycoon. He is what they call here a 'pirate.' "

The Premier let his breath out with an audible hiss.

The spectators were drawing up chairs and seating themselves comfortably. People of varied races and nationalities were pouring out of the elevator and coming over to take a look. The Premier's eyes were narrowed, and he glanced back and forth from the spectators to the board. "Hm-m-m," he said.

Bartov moved over to study what was happening on the board.

Along the lake, the little images of the ambassador's troops were steadily falling back, and the ambassador himself was groaning, "But I'll lose the whole district."

"You donkey," said the Premier angrily, "stop croaking and look confident. As far as all these people around us are concerned, the Soviet system is on trial on that board there. Now, start building railroads. And stop hanging onto that piece of worthless desert over there, and bring those troops back over here, where they can do some good. How did you get a supply line that long, anyway?"

"Well he gave way there, so I pushed ahead, and—"

The Premier shook his head in disgust. "Bartov!"

"Yes, sir?"

"Go get some chairs. We're going to be here some time yet."

Bartov hurried off after chairs.

An hour had crept past, and the Premier had divided up various tasks amongst his party, who now sat near various controls, giving suggestions to Palvukin in low voices. The solitary financier across the board had delivered several additional hard jolts, captured the main rail and road junctions north of the lake, and driven in a wedge that in effect divided the front into two halves. Palvukin, perspiring freely, would now have been licked, save for the alternate rail line the Premier had had him construct further back, which enabled troops to be shuttled from one of the separated fronts to the other. This, however, involved a delay that Schmidt was taking full advantage of, to get control of more and more territory by a succession of rapid blows, first against one front, then against the other.

"We can't match him," said Palvukin. "He goes a short distance. We have to go a long distance."

"Have patience," said the Premier, "and keep building factories, like I told you to."

A large part of another hour crept by, and the financier was glancing from the board to the poker-faced group that sat across the table from him, nothing moving but their eyes and their lips, as Palvukin jumped from one control to another, like a marionette operated by several dozen pairs of strings. Schmidt frowned at the board, and Bartov, following his gaze, could guess what the man was thinking.

The financier's "troops" now held a large, roughly circular arc of "Red" territory. He could still concentrate large enough forces to push farther at any selected point. But as he pushed in one direction, the counterthrust started from another direction, to threaten the flank and rear of his attack, and force him to break it off before it accomplished anything. Meanwhile, the factories were steadily rising in sectors out of his reach, and the games computer was taking full account of the fact that his supplies came from a great distance, while his opponents' supply lines were short. Worse yet, the game went along steadily, with no pause while first one side moved and then the other, and as the opposition now had a number of shrewd minds calculating various angles at the same time, his relative overall position was deteriorating steadily. He had, for instance, apparently set up his industries on a basically better plan than the ambassador, but the computer repeatedly gave realistic notice of bottlenecks here and tie-ups there, and it was impossible to devote his attention to these things and to the steadily-progressing battle at the same time.

"Hm-m-m," he said, and settled back. After a little while, he glanced around and spoke briefly to someone standing nearby. That person moved off quietly, and the financier again devoted his attention to the board. His military action now began to take the form of short sharp thrusts apparently intended to do nothing more than keep his opponent off balance and on the defensive. Bartov noted, however, that an accelerated improvement of the road-net now began to take place on the financier's side of the board. Bartov did not see what good this was going to do. The initiative was plainly passing from one side to the other, and more roads were not going to solve the problem.

A half hour or so passed, and one of the diplomats glanced at his watch, and said to the Premier, "We are going to be late."

"Don't worry, we can finish this up soon, now." The board was studded with monster industrial complexes on the "Red" side, all joined up by interconnected railroads. The other side showed accelerated growth, and an impressive multiplication and improvement of the road net, together with the shady outlines of what might become a huge industrial expansion. But the actual productive capacity for war goods had now dropped below the "Red" productive capacity, and enormous quantities of war material were piling up behind the lines.

Leaning forward, Bartov could see the tiny symbols of tanks, guns, and troop carriers, stretched out in huge parks, ready to be moved forward when needed.

"We could attack," said Palvukin, in an awed voice.

"Not yet," said the Premier. "When we hit him, we want to hit him so hard we break his back. Keep him stretched out for now. Remember, many people are watching this. Once we smash him, then I can say in my speech that even on an American scientific computer we have proved the superiority of communism over capitalism. Just a little longer, and the time comes."

The "Red" buildup proceeded at a furious pace.

Possibly sensing what was to come, the opposing forces began to fall back.

"Now," said the Premier.

The "Red" troops, massively reinforced, started heavily forward, in a sweep designed to trap a large number of the opposing troops.

The board of the War Games Computer now showed the massive red arrows, and a number of wavering blue lines falling back fast.

Leaning over the board, Bartov could almost believe he was an observer in a plane, watching a great offensive. The setting was unfamiliar, the geography actually matching that of no country on earth, but the movement of the vehicles was complete down to the representation of churned mud in some sectors of the front, and clouds of blowing dust in others.

The "Blue" forces were in full flight, withdrawing so fast that they were pulling well ahead of the pursuit.

"We have won," said Palvukin.

Bartov grinned with pleasure, and looked across to see the expression on the face of the capitalist.

The capitalist had moved into another chair, and was now apparently devoting himself to industry and road-building. The troops were apparently being directed by a big elderly man in a conservative suit, smoking a corn-cob pipe.

The Red troops were falling steadily behind the fleeing Blue troops.

"Why is this?" said the Premier. "Surely we can go faster than that! Palvukin, put the question to the computer."

Palvukin asked the question. The computer unreeled a length of tape reading: "ROADS THICKLY MINED. SUCCESSIVE WAVES OF TANKS HAVE CHURNED GROUND INTO MUD. HEAVY WEAR ON TANK ENGINES IN SOME REGIONS DUE TO DUST AND INSUFFICIENT PROVISION FOR AIR CLEANERS ON ENGINES."

The Premier glared at an inoffensive scholarly-looking man. "Milkov, you are in charge of tank production. Why is this?"

"I had no idea it was necessary to attend to such fine details, Comrade Premier. Anyway, we have such a production that these little things cannot stop us."

Bartov, observing the huge onrush of the Red armies, nodded agreement. What could possibly stop that? He felt a wave of elation. Somewhere in his mind, an invisible band struck up the *"Internationale."*

He glanced across the table to observe the effect of this crushing defeat on the capitalist-imperialists.

The American financier was working in intense concentration. The elderly man apparently handling the troops for him had a calm contemplative look, and as he turned to say something to the financier, Bartov got a brief profile view of the bold nose and jutting corncob pipe.

Chills and fever swept over Bartov in successive waves. In his mind's eye, huge naval armadas closed in on tropical islands, and a long peninsula, almost completely conquered, fall apart at a sudden thrust from the sea.

The Premier gave a low exclamation.

Bartov glanced at the board. The "Red" troops were now well into enemy territory. The Blue troops, moving over the excellent road net, were reorganizing fast. As Bartov watched, one of the Blue armies swung rapidly around, and bit into the flank of the Red advance. A confused whirl developed, and then the red arrow outlining the advance disintegrated.

The Premier had put some questions to the computer, which now unrolled its length of tape; Bartov peered over the Premier's shoulder, to read: ENEMY STRATEGIC DISPOSITIONS SUPERIOR. ENEMY TACTICAL HANDLING OF TROOPS VASTLY SUPERIOR.

Bartov tried to tell the Premier who was across the table. The Premier silenced him. "Go get Marshal Malekin. And hurry up!"

Bartov forced his way through the crowd around the table and hurried out.

Finding Malekin, even with the help of the Embassy staff, was no easy job. He was eventually located at the

U.N. Building, stupefied with boredom, as nothing was going on there and nearly everybody had gone off to watch some game on TV. He supposed it was either baseball or football, he didn't know which, and couldn't care less. For Bartov, the business of getting the actual picture across to him was like trying to drive spikes into concrete using the bare fist as a hammer. Bartov's desperation finally roused him, but as he went along toward the electronics exhibit, he kept saying, "What's the sense of it? It's only a game, isn't it?"

"Yes, but it's a very realistic game."

"Bah! You have been humbugged by the Americans. There is a little man inside this machine, and you can't win. I remember when I was a boy, they had a machine that was supposed to play chess. There was a man inside of it."

"But this is scien—"

"It's all a joke. Listen, when the Hitlerites invaded, what do you think stopped them? Tactics? It got cold, that's what really stopped them. Tell me, is there any weather on this calculating machine of yours?"

"Yes, Comrade—"

"What about disease? I remember once when a whole troop of cavalry was laid out flat on its back from—"

Bartov had the sense of terrific pressure building inside him. "Can I say just one thing?"

"Go right ahead, my boy."

"On this fake machine . . ."

"Exactly what it is."

" . . . The Premier made a big tank attack, and it slowed down . . ."

"Naturally, the American midget inside didn't want the Premier to win."

" . . . And when the Premier wanted to know why the attack slowed down, a length of tape came out of the machine with a message on it."

The marshal looked interested. "What did it say?"

"It said the retreating enemy had heavily mined the roads, the tank tracks were grinding the earth into muck, and in other regions the churned-up dust was wearing the tank engines out fast because no good air cleaners had been provided for them."

The marshal frowned. "Did the enemy have difficulties like this?"

"He seemed to."

"Hm-m-m. I want to get a look at this computer."

The room as they came in was even more thickly packed than when Bartov had left. He and the marshal shouldered their way across the room, and one look at the board confirmed his worst fears. The captured ground had been lost, and the Blue forces were slicing deep into Red territory. The Red forces appeared to be still moderately numerous and well-supplied, but their disposition suggested a tin bucket with the sides kicked in.

The marshal stared at the board, bent over it closely, grunted, and looked up with an odd expression. The others were eagerly explaining to him how it worked. The Premier said, "We can supply the troops and give them the right general directions, but when the fight comes, everything seems to depend on particulars and timing. We don't have that. You have to supply that, or we are going to get beat."

"I talk into this microphone?" growled the marshal.

"Yes, or you can work this control board if you prefer."

"All right. Leave it to me."

The Red forces, still retreating, began to straighten themselves out, clinging to natural barriers, and striking at any exposed flank that presented itself.

The fight gradually stabilized until a heavy air attack knocked out a great many rail lines on the Red side of the board. It proved impossible to do as much damage to the huge road net on the opposite side of the board.

The marshal then tried dropping a nuclear missile on an enemy jet-engine factory. There was a stir all around him. One of his own jet-engine plants blew up in a hideous glare accompanied by a dull clap and thud that shook the table. The marshal grunted and looked across the board. There were several more Americans over there now. They all seemed to be closely concentrated on the job in hand. Bartov, watching the marshal, could guess his thoughts. From his aggrieved look, he was thinking, "Why are you attacking us?" Then his face cleared as he remembered that it was, after all, just a game. He devoted himself to it, and showed satisfaction as he gradually drove the over-extended Blue forces back. Then their positions were solidly stabilized, and he was unable to get any advantage. A big war-production struggle was getting under way, and the marshal was settling down to a lengthy war of attrition when a younger general, one P. Rudov, appeared at his shoulder, looked over the board, and said, "Bah! All that is old-fashioned. Here, let me show you something."

The marshal glanced at the Premier, who nodded.

P. Rudov took his seat. The board rapidly took on a fantastic appearance as vertical envelopment became the rule of the day. Paratroop drops appeared to outflank previous drops of enemy forces, which in turn were defending against previous drops to protect forces attacked by former drops of enemy troops. Both sides teetered on the brink of disaster or sudden victory, but nobody could figure out which it would be. Rudov resorted to tactical atomic weapons to clarify the situation, and his opponent responded with the same thing, pressed down and running over, and the situation resumed its previous uncertainty. New weapons began to appear as each side got renowned scientists busy feeding suggestions into the computer. Some obscure Red expert took a crack at spreading a special type of influenza among the enemy, but it unexpectedly reacted through some odd chain of events, and instead of hitting the enemy went through the Red side of the board like a mowing-machine through a wheat field. Malekin personally knocked the expert senseless and when the expert came to, the Premier spoke to him in such a way that he passed out again.

Meanwhile, the Blue forces offered a remedy which was partially effective in stopping the spread of the disease. The interlocked mazes of mutually-enveloped airheads were then disentangled and got loose from one another during a temporary truce, following which the two sets of players now grown large enough and official enough to run their own real countries without further help, stared at each other across the board.

At some point, on one side or the other, for some reason, somebody smiled.

Suddenly, both sides looked from the board to each other, the wise experts controlling the little figures, and began to laugh.

As by one impulse, without settling which side was to win the game, they got up, and left the board.

Both sides left the room together, arm in arm, and the good fellowship, despite the language differences, was tremendous.

But then, when they had got down to their cars and split up in groups to go to the U.N., the Premier growled, "It doesn't make any difference. We're in the same place we were in before we played it."

"I still can't see a war over Rindelia," said the marshal.

"No, but then what do we do?"

"It's too risky. Nobody knows who will win, and meanwhile we've got one foot in a beartrap."

The Premier scowled. "They can't back down. Neither can we. Where is the way out of it?"

Gloom descended, and was not dispersed by the proceedings at the U.N. Here the Premier tried alternately thrusting out an olive branch and a loaded cannon, had no particular success with either one, and then waved missiles, satellites, and spaceships in a warning that had a number of neutrals glancing at the exits. When it was over, Bartov had to admit it created a picture in the light of which Rindelia looked remarkably not worth fighting over.

He glanced at the Americans to see how they were taking it, and got an unpleasant shock. The Americans were all looking at the Premier with expressionless faces, and an ugly light in their eyes.

The U.N. session produced no compromise. That evening came word that the Americans were moving into— not Rindelia—but bases threatening the communist state that had organized the Rindelian guerrilla war.

The Soviet Union issued an ultimatum ordering the immediate withdrawal of these troops.

The United States responded by placing all its forces on a worldwide alert.

The Soviet Union pointed out with biting crudeness the vulnerability of U.S. cities to Soviet missiles.

Large numbers of U.S. nuclear bombers rose into the air.

It suddenly dawned that the unthinkable was happening.

"All this over Rindelia—this dunghill!" cried the Premier. "Have they gone insane?"

It was Marshall Malekin who broke the impasse. "We can't just sit still while this goes on! We have pushed them too far on this, and the only way out is to either attack head-on, which is no good now, or stop pushing and back-pedal fast."

"I won't give way to them on this."

"What if we could fight the war in Rindelia without losing a man?"

"It won't stay confined to Rindelia. The way things are, it will spread like lightning."

"You want that?"

"No! But I won't—" The Premier looked startled. "What are you thinking?"

"I will tell you. It all depends on just how mad they are, and whether they are still susceptible to reason. But there is one thing on our side, thank heaven!"

"What is that?"

"The Americans will trust their own computer."

The extreme crisis lasted for another six hours.

Then the terrified world had a chance to draw an even breath. Rindelia would be either partitioned or left whole. But the rest of the world could watch the struggle in peace.

Across the big board of the War Games Computer, newly set up to accurately represent Rindelia and surrounding territory, the two sets of uniformed and plain-clothed figures glared at each other. The huge fleet moved in, and the volunteers swarmed across the border.

The war was on.

SORCERER'S APPRENTICE
★ ★ ★

To say that Ambassador Smernov was in a bad frame of mind would have been an understatement. It was obvious to Vassily Kuznetzov, Smernov's assistant, that the ambassador was as hot inside as he was outside, and in this Caribbean climate that was no small achievement. Kuznetzov eyed the ambassador with the practical gaze of a farmer living on the slope of a volcano. From the preliminary rumblings, tremors, and the general impression of pressure building to the danger point, Kuznetzov could not escape the impression that the ambassador was about to erupt.

Two tanned and grinning boys ran past the construction project carrying a banner. Smernov gripped Kuznetzov by the arm.

"Look at that!"

Kuznetzov unhappily stared at the sign:

YANKEE SI! CUBA NO!

The breeze shifted momentarily so that instead of the rush of the surf and the *putt*-cough of a small fishing boat bobbing off-shore with engine trouble, there came to them the roar of the bulldozers clearing jungle back in the hills, and the pound of hammers and whine of saws in the housing project.

The ambassador glared at the buildings going up, stared at the backs of the two boys and their banner, looked down angrily at the new wharf running out into the harbor, looked back at the steadily-laboring workers and the rising buildings, and spat out a four-foot length of profanity.

Kuznetzov winced and took on the look of a man outdoors in a strong wind.

The Caribbean sun beat down on them, its glare almost a physical attack.

Smernov gripped Kuznetzov by the arm. "You see the wharf out there?"

Obviously Kuznetzov saw it. "Yes, Mr. Ambassador," he said.

"You see those buildings going up?"

"Yes. Yes, Mr. Ambassador."

"All right. Good. You have eyes in your head. Now, did you see that road we drove in on this morning?"

"Yes, Mr. Ambassador."

"Six months ago," said Smernov furiously, "that road wasn't there. And this wharf is new. And that housing project you're so complacent about—*that's* new. And you know who's putting them up?"

"Why, the Americans, Mr. Ambassador."

Smernov glared at him. "*Who?*"

Kuznetzov stammered, "Why, surely the Americans. I mean, the capitalist-imperialists. The monopolis—"

Smernov lit up like a volcanic glare. He let his breath out in a hiss, and stared off at the green hills in the restful interior. The changing patterns of fluffy clouds that cast dark moving shadows across the hills provided some distraction, until one of the shadows in moving on let the sun shine on the new dam rising in the interior.

Smernov grunted, and looked back at Kuznetzov. "You've missed the whole point," he said. "Take another look at those workers."

Kuznetzov polished his glasses, wiped the sweat off his forehead, and studied the scene. The rhythm of the workers was unmistakable. No one raised in this tropical heat and humidity would work like that. Then Kuznetzov scowled and looked again, studying the features of the workers, the faces and arms swarthier than he thought a few months of sun could make them. And yet—there was still, he told himself, something unmistakably Yankee about the way they moved. And they were dressed like Americans. They seemed to be working in six-hour shifts on the job, and as they changed shifts now, in midday, the men coming on were wearing palm-tree shirts, and carrying cameras to the big shacks where they changed to their working clothes.

Kuznetzov squinted.

Satisfied that he was right, Kuznetzov studied the expressions of the workers, the way they moved, their manner of greeting each other, their look of pride in themselves and their work.

Smernov said, "Well?"

Kuznetzov shrugged. "They are Americans."

"And you are a donkey," said the ambassador. "In the first place, if you open your ears, you can tell that they are talking Spanish. In the second place, they are too eager about their work. In the third place, they aren't using enough machinery. And in the fourth place, it is only American *tourists* that go around carrying cameras. There are more cameras going back and forth to work here than on any one hundred American building sites. What do they want to take cameras to their *work* for? It is only people who have newly acquired such possessions who carry them around for the pleasure of ownership and for prestige."

Kuznetzov stared at the men going off shift.

"I didn't think of that."

"Well," said the ambassador, "we are going to get to the bottom of it. These people were born here. They shouldn't be working like that. They should be growling about the *latifundia* and trying to think up some way to get a government pension. Every other way to earn an honest living should have been closed up to them. Meanwhile, the Americans should be pumping in money, which the local dictator will stuff in Swiss bank accounts, and use to pay his guards to keep the people from killing him for not correcting all the trouble nature and three hundred years of bad management have piled onto their heads. And the American Banana Company should be hand-in-hand with the local dictator, because if they aren't he will wreck their business in self-defense, and meanwhile they make a good scapegoat for him, since he can privately blame all the troubles in the country on them." The ambassador beamed. "What do you think of that?"

Kuznetzov wasn't sure what he thought of it, so he said politely, "Yes, Mr. Ambassador."

The ambassador squinted at all the activity going on despite the heat, and growled, "The problems in a country like this are so complicated, Kuznetzov, that the Americans *cannot* solve them. As I have just explained to you. In fact, it is so complicated that there is no way out except to smash the whole thing and start all over from the ground up. But the Americans won't do that. So, there is no one left to clean up the mess except us. Do you understand?"

"Yes, Mr. Ambassador."

"The trouble with the Americans is that they believe in peaceful evolution. But what this place needs is violent revolution. So—" The ambassador sucked in his breath sharply, and stood like a man paralyzed, watching something take place near the construction project.

Kuznetzov was vaguely aware that a big expensive car had been parked in front of a rough building with a small American flag on it. The car had pulled forward to a wider place in the road, near the construction work, and backed around with a multitude of flashes from the slanted windows and polished trim. It had then started to drive away. It had, however, backed up again, and Kuznetzov vaguely supposed the driver wanted to ask something of the workers in the project. Hw saw, now, however, that a young man had gotten out of the back of the car, wearing black trousers and coat, and was talking with a group of the workers, who crowded around looking friendly and excited.

Abruptly the man talking to the workers took off his black coat and tossed it in on the rear seat of the car. He took off his string tie, folded up the arms of his elegant shirt to the elbows, tossed the tie into the back of the car, and took a hammer one of the workmen handed him.

Immediately, both front doors of the car opened up. A man in chauffeur's uniform popped out one side, and a bodyguard with slab face, huge physique, and a drawn gun, surged out the other side. The shirt-sleeved young man with the hammer waved them away. They expostulated with him. Finally, they tried to take him by the arms and drag him back to the car. The workers immediately cracked the guard and chauffeur over the heads and knocked them senseless.

In the abrupt silence, two Spanish sentences carried to the ambassador and Kuznetzov:

"It is bad teeth that make such bad temper. Take them to the Yankee aid station."

Several workmen picked up the chauffeur and the bodyguard and carried them into the rough building where the car had been parked.

Smernov and Kuznetzov looked at each other blankly.

The renewed sound of hammering came from across the way.

Smernov took a hard look at the flag on the building, then back at the young landowner and the friendly workers.

Kuznetzov was now beginning to get the picture. "Something is certainly very much out of the ordinary here."

"Something underhanded is going on." The ambassador looked as if he had been punched in the stomach. "There is some trick here." He looked back at the rough building where the workers were just coming out after carrying in the chauffeur and guard. He looked hard at the small flag. "And right there," he said, "is where we will find out what it is. Come on."

Kuznetzov followed him across a stretch of cleared ground to the building, then up the steps and in the door, which sounded a gong as it opened.

Inside was a long counter to the right, with shelves laden with thick pamphlets behind it. Above the counter was a sign:

Information. Reliable. Inexpensive.

Directly ahead was a flight of steps, with a sign reading "Trading Post."

To the left were two barber chairs, three dentist chairs, and a closed door marked, "Doctor." The two barbers were playing checkers, and a pair of dentists were laboring at the opened mouths of the guard and the chauffeur.

A man appeared behind the counter to the right. "May I help you gentlemen? How about a copy of the Do-It-Yourself Master Guide? Or a Concrete Handbook? Our works are very complete."

Smernov said, "What we'd like is something on ideology."

The clerk looked blank. "Ideology? Let's see—Does that have to do with bathrooms?"

Smernov cleared his throat. "I mean, dialectics."

"Oh, dialectrics. Hm-m-m. I think we have something here." He looked vaguely at the shelves, pulled out two or three titles at random, then opened a door into a back room. "Oh, Jim—"

A second man appeared. The clerk turned back to the ambassador. "This is the manager. He'll take care of you."

The manager smiled. "You'd like something on dialectrics? Did I hear that correctly?"

"Dialectics. What we are looking for is something on ideology."

"Oh, I see. We don't have much call for that." The manager seated himself at a desk, pulled out a file of some kind, flipped through it rapidly, and said, "How about some of these: 'How to Decommunize Your Country,' 'Beating the Reds to the Punch,' 'How to Foul Up Street Demonstrations,' 'Six Dozen Stunts that Jolt the Pinkoes.'" The manager looked up. "Am I on the right track?"

Smernov stared at him, then abruptly came to life. "Yes. That's what I'm looking for. We'll take all of those."

Kuznetzov said in a low voice, "Do we want to have *those* things in our luggage?"

Smernov murmured, "Don't be silly. This isn't the bad old days. Besides, after we read them, we'll chop them up into little pieces, burn them, grind up the ashes, and flush them down the sewer a little at a time."

The manager got out a list about half as long as a man's arm, and came over with it. "Just check the books here you want, write your name and address on top, and we'll send in for them. We haven't had much demand for that selection lately, so we'll have to make a special order."

Kuznetzov and the ambassador looked at the list. There appeared to be about a hundred titles, culminating with a work on "How to De-Communize a Communist."

The manager said, "It will only take about four days to get them. Take the order sheet along if you'd like, and look it over."

The ambassador cleared his throat. "Yes. Thank you."

"Anything else we can do for you?"

"No. No, this is fine."

The manager smiled pleasantly, and moved off into the back room.

Smernov folded up the order sheet, looked at the sign, "Trading Post," glanced at Kuznetzov, and led the way up the steps.

The "Trading Post" proved to be a small store jammed to the rafters with hammers, axes, machetes, kegs of nails, cameras, portable radios, carpenter's saws, bow saws, power saws, sun glasses, California-type shirts, big straw hats, shovels, hoes, women's dresses, and a huge stack of mail-order catalogues.

Finding nothing that answered their question there, they went downstairs, looked around again, and walked outside. The ambassador got out the order list, and squinting against the glare, looked it over.

"I just don't believe," he said frowning, "that their propaganda could have been *that* effective. This has all been too subtle. There is still something—"

The door opened up, and the chauffeur and the guard staggered out and headed for the car. They were almost there when they stopped and looked at the construction project. They paused and looked at each other. They started for the car, and the chauffeur even got the door open. But then the guard drifted off, stopped one of the workers, and began pleading for the use of his wheelbarrow. The guard ended up proudly shoveling dirt into the wheelbarrow.

The chauffeur, like an iron bolt under the influence of an electromagnet, now began to drift from the car to the construction project. About halfway there, he paused, looked at the car, snapped his fingers, went back to the car, jacked up the front end, went into the building he'd just come out of, reappeared carrying a grease gun, and crawled under the car.

Kuznetzov mopped his forehead. Smernov scratched his head.

With a *bang*, the motor of the fishing boat out in the harbor started, and they watched it chug out into the ocean. Everywhere they turned, people were busy.

Smernov murmured, "First, the dentist operates on them, then they come out here and go to work. It seems insane, but—" He looked at Kuznetzov, cleared his throat, and spoke in the syrupy tones of one who is overly considerate of another's welfare. "Vassily Kuznetzov, my friend, didn't you say your wisdom tooth was hurting you the other night?"

Gloomily, Kuznetzov trudged across the road to enact his role as guinea pig.

He went up the steps, opened the door, went in, and encountered the gaze of the clerk behind the counter, the checker-playing barber who happened to be faced in his direction, the two dentists rinsing down little bowls affixed beside their chairs, and two other men, apparently the other dentist and the doctor, who were standing outside the door of the doctor's office, and stopped talking as Kuznetzov came in.

The tail end of their conversation registered on Kuznetzov as he shut the door:

" . . . Tone that thing down the next batch they send or there's going to be some heat exhaustion around here."

Kuznetzov looked at one of the dentists, and cleared his throat.

The dentist standing with the doctor immediately said, "Trouble with your teeth, sir?"

"A wisdom tooth that gives me an occasional pain."

"Swollen at all?"

"Oh, no."

"Well, if you'll just come over here and sit down, I'll take a look at it."

Kuznetzov settled into the dentist's chair, feeling all the customary sensations that go with this procedure. The dentist bent Kuznetzov's head back onto a head rest, shone a light in his mouth, and groped at his wisdom tooth with a long steel explorer which caught in a hole, and gave a gritting sound. The dentist straightened up and reached for something out of Kuznetzov's range of vision.

Vassily Kuznetzov wished earnestly to get out of this place.

Something swabbed his gum, and the next moment there was the pressure of a hypodermic needle. The dentist removed the needle. "Been here long?"

Kuznetzov was perspiring freely. "A few weeks."

The dentist laid out an assortment of drills, selected one, and held it up to examine it closely. "Nice country, don't you think?"

Kuznetzov eyed the drill. "Yes. But the people surprise me."

"How so?"

"They're so . . . busy."

"They're hard workers. You didn't expect them to be?"

"Well—"

"How's the gum? Numb yet?"

"Just a little."

"It'll be ready in a minute or so. We have efficient drugs these days. What science can do, given time and a good idea, is really wonderful."

He had the drill tightened in its chuck now, and checked to be sure his instruments were all at hand. He tapped one of these tools against Kuznetzov's gum, and Kuznetzov reported unhappily that he felt nothing. The dentist leaned forward and reached into Kuznetzov's mouth.

There promptly followed a whine, a grinding vibration, a squirt of water, and Kuznetzov was spitting out little bits of tooth and old filling. The dentist began a good-natured, one-sided conversation.

"Now, lean back, and just relax . . . This may buzz a little, but it won't hurt . . . Yes, our drugs are certainly efficient. Science and a good idea, given time, can do some wonderful things . . . A little wider, please. Tell me if this hurts . . . What we need most, in science or just about anything else, is a good, sound, workable idea. We've got a lot of people working on techniques now, but we need people to work on ideas, too. Why, it's ideas that make a people great. Not ideas alone, of course. It takes work. 'One per cent inspiration, and ninety-nine per cent perspiration,' as Edison said . . . Open a little wider . . . But without the one per cent inspiration, you can perspire from now till doomsday, and just get a backache out of it . . . Hurt? . . . You see, the right idea makes all the difference. But it has to be put into effect through practical measures. Why, it wasn't so long ago that the world was loaded down with knights, dukes, barons, and so on, not chosen by worth but because some ancestor twenty generations back was worth something. Gunpowder and the rise of manufacture helped unload that setup. Next came the same general kind of thing, only with huge inherited wealth instead of inherited rank as the gimmick. Universal suffrage was the little device that damped that one down. But next came . . . Better spit that out, and rinse out your mouth."

Vassily felt of the tooth with his tongue, and found a hole larger than he had realized the whole tooth to be. Extremely uneasy, he sat back again.

"Yes," said the dentist cheerfully, "we have one trouble following another, but the big trouble that caused

most of our other troubles, with noblemen, bored play-
boys, selfish-type pressure groups, and so on, is that these
people want *something for nothing*. They want to take
out of the general fund without putting in. That's wrong.
Wherever a nation has been great in some line of activity,
there have been a large number of people confident that
if they added enough to the general fund, they would be
rewarded, either in wealth, fame, the advancement of
their cause, or whatever else they were interested in.
When people think they can get something for nothing,
or when they think they will get nothing back for their
something—that they will be suckers, in other words—
the system breaks down. And when you've got a state set
up so the people on top want something for nothing, and
the people on the bottom expect nothing for something,
or vice versa, then, my friend, you have a mess, and no
aid program, no technical advice, no exhortation to new
efforts, is going to work until there is a big enough group
of people confident that if they do their best for the
cause, they will get fair treatment. The problem is—how
to get these people? . . . Spit that out please, and we'll
fill it, and you'll be all set."

Kuznetzov leaned back again, and the dentist began
to put some form of material into the filling. This part
was different from what Kuznetzov had experienced
before, and seemed to require extra care and concentration.

"Hm-m-m," said the dentist finally. "There, now keep
your mouth wide open . . . Yes, the problem is, how to
get this group of people—we might call them reciprocators
—who trust each other to work along a variety of lines
for the general good, and who are prepared to give an
honest day's work for an honest day's pay. Who, in fact,

are uncomfortable if they don't give an honest day's work for an honest day's pay. And who know they're uncomfortable if they don't work. The more of these people you have, the stronger your position is. You see, when you have enough of these people in the right positions, the country starts progressing of itself, and no radical movement can get anywhere, because it serves no useful function." The dentist put a mirror on a stick in Kuznetzov's mouth. "There, I guess we're ready to finish."

Vassily Kuznetzov was conscious of something strange, but unable to say exactly what it might be.

The dentist reached for a new tool, and began packing the cavity. "Yes," he said, "science and a good idea are a wonderful combination. Usually the idea is *within* science, for the development of science or technology. But then, too, science and technology can be used to convey ideas—the radio, and television, for instance. But how often do they spread the ideas of mutual trust and the willingness—eagerness—to do a good day's work and give a fair return? Not often. But, of course, new discoveries are continually being made. And we know, from practical experience, that somehow, thoughts often seem to be contagious. It might be possible some day, to duplicate the impulse thrown off by a brain thinking certain admirable thoughts. It would be a kind of radio set, designed to affect, not the external ear, but whatever it is in a man that picks up mood, atmosphere, and reacts to that communicable zest and eagerness when conditions are just right for progress. Such a device could probably be quite small. We've seen what transistors have done for radio sets. We can even guess that the device would probably need to be located, or have a part of itself located, very close to the man to be affected by it. Possibly it would even be located inside his own head . . . There, now. Bite on this piece of paper. Gently. How does that feel. All right? Fine. Let's see now. Yes . . . Yes . . . O.K., pay the cashier at the counter on the way out. Our fees are very reasonable. If you have any trouble with that, let me know. It should be all right."

Kuznetzov dazedly paid, and went out, passing on the way a man who looked like some kind of bandit and was being carried in tied up with rope.

Kuznetzov stopped on the road outside the building, and looked around. The world appeared somehow to be different to him. He took a breath of air. He was conscious of its freshness, despite the heat. He became aware of the possibilities of life. Look, he found himself thinking, at all the things he could do, and the only thing that was required of him, of *any* man, was to give a fair return.

A pretty girl walked by, and Vassily smiled at her. She smiled back, and Vassily beamed.

A pale, rather unhealthy-looking man crossed the road.

"Well, Kuznetzov?" he demanded.

"Oh," said Vassily, recognizing him. "Hello there, Smernov."

The ambassador looked jarred.

Kuznetzov looked around. His muscles felt the need of work, his brain cells the need of the stimulation of a problem. He was a man, wasn't he? He must earn his keep. Now then, what to do? He would have to find some regular line of business that would keep him supplied with reliable opportunities for work.

The ambassador was scowling at him. This expression had once seemed formidable. Vassily, however, was now well aware that an honest person who improves himself, and does his daily work regularly, needn't cringe to any man.

The ambassador cleared his throat threateningly. "Kuznetzov. Snap out of this! What happened in there?"

"Hold your horses," said Vassily in an equable, pleasant tone. "I'm trying to think."

Smernov's jaw fell open, then snapped shut again.

Abruptly, Vassily remembered that he had been a communist. And what was communism but the desperate effort to solve by radical means the problems that arise where there are too many people who want something for nothing, and too many people who expect to get nothing for something.

"Kuznetzov," said the ambassador, a note of alarm in his voice, "do you feel all right? What did they do to you in there?"

"It's hard to explain. Do you remember the question a reporter put to Premier Khrushchev on his visit to America: If communism is to succeed capitalism, what is it that is to succeed communism?"

"Yes. Yes. What of it?"

"Well," said Vassily. "*I* know what is to succeed communism. And you must not resist it, because it is the crowning success that allows for a large degree of the withering away of the state, which, after all, is what communism is aiming at. Correct?"

"What?" said Smernov.

"Yet," said Vassily, "it looks like individualism, and it *is* freedom, but it is also communism in the highest sense, because everybody is working for the common good, to each according to his need, from each according to his ability, but with no spongers or loafers, and no one man always getting the milk at the hind end of the cow while another man always has to fork the hay in at the front end, and it is capitalism, too, because that is what it is based on, capital, but—"

"Brain-washed," said the ambassador, awed.

"But," said Vassily, scowling, and feeling the discontent from unused muscles, and from brain cells sitting around doing nothing, "what to do?"

Vassily was intensely conscious that the best food is that eaten when a man is hungry, and the best rest that taken when a man is tired, and the best way to get hungry and tired is to *work*. But now, how the deuce—?

The ambassador was squinting at him perplexedly, and now abruptly drew a deep breath. "Kuznetzov. Enough of this! I warn you that there are severe penalties for this form of behavior! And I will not hesitate to bring them down on your head! For the sake of monolithic party unity—right or wrong, Kuznetzov—I will . . . "

Vassily scowled at the ambassador. "But that is not ideologically sound, Comrade."

"What's that?" Smernov's face turned purple. "You have been corrupted. Come along." He seized Kuznetzov by the arm.

Kuznetzov whipped loose and knocked the ambassador out. The pleasurable sensation resulting from this activity assured him that he was on the right track. He picked Smernov up and carried him up the steps. "My apologies, comrade ambassador, but you were ideologically all blocked up." He carried Smernov inside.

On the way in, the ex-bandit went out, muttering, "Got to find *work*."

Kuznetzov looked at the nearest dentist.

"My friend," he said, "has a troublesome tooth."

The dentist helped ease Smernov into his dental chair. "Leave it to me. We will cure him."

Vassily went outside, conscious of the beauty of the day, and of all the possibilities of life.

But there was still that irksome problem of finding work.

He *could* go down and work on the housing project, and that was all right, but this was, strictly speaking, not his own country. To a degree, he would be evading his duty. And that would never do.

He was still wrestling with the problem when the ambassador came out looking dazed, glanced around at the world as if seeing it with new eyes, smiled at a pretty girl going by, flexed his arms, and looked meditatively down at the construction work.

Vassily eyed him warily.

The ambassador grinned, and banged his fist into his hand. "We're through here. No point in trying to fight this. But Vassily, do you remember that collection of zoot-suited drones we saw in Moscow, who have contrived to avoid doing any work?"

Their eyes met. The idea sprang from one to the other.

"Just the thing!" said Vassily.

As with one mind, they went back, located the manager, and put the idea to him.

"Ah," said the manager, nodding approval. "Yes. what you're talking about is what we call an 'associate dealership.' There's no trouble arranging that, and let me tell you, it will clean up your problem as slick as a whistle. Here, come into the back room, and I'll make the arrangements for you."

"You don't mind," said Vassily, "helping out . . . ah . . . 'iron curtain' countries?"

"No, no," said the manager, "we understand each other, and it's all one world now. Besides—"

He glanced a trifle furtively around the room at a set of exerciser springs dangling from the wall, a neat desk and file case with all work obviously done right up to the minute, a complex kit-type radio set half-built, with a dozen completed sets stacked up in a corner.

"Besides," he said, "ah, though of course this solves all our production difficulties, and we've really whipped the distribution of wealth problem to a frazzle, there's still"—he lowered his voice—"a little question about the proper distribution of *work*." He laughed, then changed the subject by showing them a couple of simple confidential dealership forms. He then arranged all other details right on the spot, and escorted them to the door.

Here he paused, to speak in the low voice of a conspirator. "Now, I've helped you get started, so if you fellows run into any problems, especially any nice big tough ones with a lot of work in them, *bring them to me first.—O.K.?*"

Vassily was thinking that if he ran into any nice big problem with lots of work in it, he would keep it for himself. The manager, however, did not wait for any answer, but immediately said, "Swell. That's settled. Say, now, wait here just a minute. I've got something for you."

He disappeared into the back room, and came out carrying two nicely-finished short-wave portable radio sets. "Seven bands, swell reception. You pull up this antenna here, see? I make these from kits in my spare time. Have to keep busy. You know anybody could use one? Wait a minute."

Loaded down with portable radios, Vassily and the ambassador made their way to where they had parked their car, in one of the few shady spots around the development.

"I don't know," muttered the ambassador, "there's something about this that makes me uneasy. Here, let me carry that for you."

"No, no," said Vassily. "However, if you'd like me to carry yours—"

"Hands off," growled Smernov. "This is *my* work."

They arrived at the car, and loaded the radios into the back seat.

The ambassador said, "I'll drive going back . . . Move over."

Vassily's muscles were aching for exercise.

"No, *I* will drive."

"Who's in charge here?"

"Who cares? I am your assistant. Therefore, this is *my* job. You get in back and figure out what we will do next."

The ambassador grumbled to himself and climbed in.

Vassily was hoping the car wouldn't start. Then he could go back, buy some tools, and tear it all down and put it together again. Perversely, it caught with a bang on the first turn. He swung it around and started up the road. This, he acknowledged, was better than nothing, but modern cars are so easy to drive that he failed to get much satisfaction from it.

About halfway back to town, they passed a labor gang felling trees.

Vassily slowed the car somewhat.

The ambassador said, "It might be a nice gesture, you know, if we—"

Vassily slammed the car to a halt.

They sprang out and advanced upon the workers.

Intimidated, two of the workers gave up their axes.

Vassily and Smernov set to work with a will. As they settled to the job, the trees began to topple to a satisfying rhythm. They were just getting nicely lathered, however, when the workers demanded their axes back.

The edge, at least, being taken off their need for activity, they returned to the car, and out of a feeling of well-being attempted to give away a few portable radios.

The workers declined. "Thank you. But as we have not earned them, they would not be satisfying."

Vassily and the ambassador drove on, the ambassador this time insisting that Vassily ride in back.

"I don't know," said the ambassador, swinging them around a curve. "There is more to this than meets the eye at a first glance."

"But you must give them credit. They have solved the problem of increased production. One willing worker is worth far more than one who is driven. And this way, *all* workers are willing workers."

"Yes, true enough. But do you remember the fairy tale about the assistant to the magician? He got the broom carrying water—or was it a magic pot boiling porridge? In any case, at the beginning he did not have enough, but at the end he was driven out by a colossal surplus."

"Oh, well, I wouldn't worry about that. That's a long way off, and—"

The car straightened out at the end of the curve, which shifted the portable radios piled on the seat, and all but crowded Vassily off onto the floor. Suddenly thoughtful, he rearranged them so he would have some room.

The ambassador cleared his throat.

"I just hope," he said, "that when *this* pot boils over, they know the right spell to stop it."

★FREE★
ENTERPRISE
AT WORK

THE SPY IN THE MAZE
★ ★ ★

Richard Verner leaned back in his office chair with the alert look of a big cat as, across the desk, Nathan Bancroft, a quietly dressed man of average height, spoke earnestly.

"Last Saturday, Mr. Verner, a technician at one of our most highly classified research laboratories got away with the plans for a new and secret type of laser device. The scientist who invented the device evidently tried to stop him, and was stabbed to death."

Verner nodded intently.

Bancroft went on. "To understand the situation that's come about, you have to know that the region around this laboratory has a great many caverns. These are connected in a gigantic system of natural tunnels, rooms, crevices, and underground streams that have never been thoroughly mapped or explored.

"The technologist who stole the plans is an ardent speleologist—cave explorer. Possibly one reason for his hobby is that he suffers from hay fever, and cavern air is pure. In any case, over a period of years he's spent entire days in an underground complex of branching tunnels known as the Maze of Minos. A number of cave explorers have been lost in there, and the local people shun it. The only known expert on this underground maze is the murderer himself.

"Now, there's no question, Mr. Verner, but that this spy expected to be far away before the theft of the plans was discovered. But, by sheer good luck, the director of the laboratory discovered what had happened, and immediately notified the police. The police were lucky too—they spotted the technician's car just after the call came in. But then we all ran out of luck. The technician, taking the plans with him, escaped into this cavern—this Maze of Minos."

"And got away?" said Verner.

"Got clean away," said Bancroft. "The tunnels branch off in all directions, and of course it's as dark in there as the blackest possible night. He simply vanished."

Verner nodded again. "He's still in there?"

Bancroft said glumly, "Yes, he's still in there. We have a great many men on the spot, doing nothing but watch the known exits. But there's always the chance that he'll find some new way out, or knows of one, and get away. Meanwhile, we desperately need those plans. With the inventor dead, there are certain details we can clear up only from those papers. Yet, if we should get close, he just might take it into his head to destroy them. What we want to do is get to him before he realizes we're near. But how? How do we even *find* him in there?"

"Is he starving?"

"Not likely. He probably has caches of food for his longer explorations. And there's water in the caverns, if you know where to look."

"You want to get him alive, and by surprise?"

"Exactly."

"But he knows you're hunting for him in the cavern?"

"Oh, yes. We've brought in lights, and before we realized what we were up against, we set up loudspeakers and warned him to give up, or we'd come in after him. If he understood what we were saying over all the echoes, this must have amused him immensely. We could put our whole organization in there and get nothing out of a grand-scale search but sore feet, chills, and a dozen men lost in the winding passages. The thing is a standoff, and he knows it."

Verner asked thoughtfully, "And what brings you to me?"

Bancroft smiled. "We've consulted cave explorers, geologists, and all kinds of specialists without finding what we want. Then one of our men, who knows General Granger, remembered his saying he'd been helped in that mess at the hunting lodge by a 'heuristician.' We got in touch with Granger, who recommended you highly. We didn't know exactly what a 'heuristician' was—but we're prepared to try anything."

Verner laughed. "A heuristician is a professional problem solver. I work on the assumption that nearly all problems can be solved by the same basic technique, combined with expert knowledge. Some of my cases are scientific, some involve business situations, and others are purely personal problems. The details vary, but the basic technique remains the same. If the case interests me enough to take it in the first place, and if the necessary expert help is available, I can usually solve any problem—though sometimes there's an unavoidable element of luck and uncertainty."

"Well," said Bancroft, "we have plenty of experts on hand—all kinds. And I hope this problem offers enough of a challenge to interest you."

Verner nodded. "And we'd better lose no time getting there."

Many cars and several big trucks were parked outside the main cavern entrance. From outside, electric cables coiled into the brilliantly lighted mouth of the cavern, and there was a steady throb of engines as Verner and Bancroft walked in.

"Generators," said Bancroft. "We're trying to light this end as brightly as possible, and extend the lights inward. But it's a hopeless job. I'll show you why."

They pushed past a small crowd of men, who nodded to Bancroft and glanced at Verner curiously, and then they were in a brightly lighted chamber in the rock, about forty feet long by ten high, and twelve to fourteen feet wide. Here their voices and footsteps echoed as Bancroft led the way toward the far end, where a faint breeze of cool air blew in their faces.

"So far, so good," said Bancroft, stepping around a tangle of cables and walking through a narrow doorway cut in the rock. "But here we begin to run into trouble."

He stepped back to show a long brightly lit chamber where fantastic frieze-like shapes dipped from the ceiling to meet fairy castles and miniature ranges of mountains rising from the floor. Here the electric cables that lay along the floor fanned out in all directions, to wind around huge pointed cones into the well-lighted distance.

Wherever Verner looked, the stalactites and stalagmites rose and dipped endlessly, with new chambers opening out in different directions, and as Bancroft led the way, they clambered over the uneven slanting floor past waterfalls of rock, through little grottoes, and by shapes like thrones, statues, and weird creatures from fairyland.

For a long time they walked in silence except for the echoes of their own footsteps. Then suddenly it was dark ahead. The last giant electric bulb lit the shapes of stalagmites rising, one behind the other, till the farthest ones were lost in impenetrable shadows.

A gentle breeze was still in their faces—cool, refreshing, and pure. Somewhere ahead they could hear a faint trickling of water.

"Here," said Bancroft, "we come to the end of our string. These tunnels branch, then open out into rooms, and the rooms have galleries leading off from them, and out of these galleries there are still more tunnels. They twist, wind, and occasionally they even rejoin."

His voice echoed as he talked, and he pointed off to the right. "Over there, somewhere—I think that's the direction—there's an eighty-foot sheer drop with a little stream at the bottom, and from the wall of this drop other tunnels open out in various directions and on different levels. There are eyeless fish in the stream, and a kind of blind salamander—very interesting, but our problem is the complex of all those tunnels. A man who knew where he was going could pick the one tunnel he wanted out of a dozen or so at any given place. But we have to follow them all. And every so often they divide again or—look up there."

Bancroft pointed to a dark opening above a slope like a frozen waterfall.

"Probably that's another one. This whole place is honeycombed, filled with diverging and connecting tunnels. It's like trying to track down someone inside a man-size termite's nest. We thought he might have left some trace, some sign of where he'd gone. We thought we could follow him with dogs. We forgot that he's practically lived in here during his spare time ever since the laboratory was set up.

"There's a superabundance of clues. Dogs have followed one track through the dark right over the edge of a sudden drop, and been killed. We can find signs that he's been just about anywhere we look. We found a pair of sneakers at one place, and a cache of food at another." Bancroft shook his head. "Let's go out. There are some people you'll want to meet, now that you've seen what it's like in here, what our problem is."

Outside, in the warm fall night, a group of men quickly gathered around Verner and Bancroft.

One, an old man in dungarees and checked shirt, was well known locally as a cave explorer. A tall man in gray business suit was the director of the government laboratory, and he repeatedly sneezed and blew his nose. A boy in dungarees and old leather jacket told how he had seen the murderer-spy enter the cave, after crossing a nearby field; he was sure it was the man they were looking for.

"Heck, we all knew him. We'd often see him go in here. He knows more about these caves than anyone—well, except maybe Gramps Peters here."

The old man laughed. "Don't fool yourself. I know old Minotaur, at the other end of this, like I know the back of my hand. But this Maze—I admit I don't know it. I was in here maybe ten years ago, got lost, wandered around for five days, drinking the water in an underground stream, and finally made my way out of a collapsed sinkhole miles away from here. That was the end of the Maze for me. Now, this man you're looking for is a different animal. He's as good as lived in there."

The laboratory director sneezed and blew his nose again. "One reason he spent so much time there, especially in the fall, was the pure air of the caverns. He was, if anything, even more allergic than I am. He once told me that the only place an active man could find recreation out of doors in the fall, if he suffered from hay fever, was inside a cave."

Bancroft said, "We're watching all the known exits. We've sent teams of men through those tunnels, and we've only begun to grasp the difficulties. Somehow, we've *got* to locate him—but how?"

Verner glanced at the old man. "There seems to be a slight, steady current of air in there. That doesn't come from the outside, does it?"

"Gramps" Peters shook his head. "These passages are complicated, but in this part of the cavern most of the passages slope a little uphill. Up at the other end is what they call the Minotaur. There's an underground riverbed there; no river—that's eaten its way farther down—but there's this gentle flow of cold air. I suppose the air comes from the outside somewhere, maybe from hundreds of miles away, but you wouldn't know it by the time it gets here. It seems to flow into the Minotaur, and then branch out through the Maze. It's always fresh and cool. If you get turned around in a passage, that gentle breeze, when you come to a narrow place, will tell you which way you're headed."

When Verner was finished asking questions, Bancroft took him aside.

"You see now what we're up against, Mr. Verner?"

"I suppose you've got infrared equipment?"

"Yes, and if we knew where he was, it might help us find our way to him in the dark without warning him. But it won't help to send teams of men prospecting at random through all those tunnels. The last time we tried it we found nothing, and three men were seriously injured when they came to a sudden slope." He looked at Verner tensely. "Do you have *any* suggestion, any idea at all?"

Verner nodded. "If we're lucky. and if what we've been told is true, we *may* have him out of there in a few hours."

"If you can do that, you're a miracle worker."

"No miracle at all—just common sense. But this is a case where we'll need a little luck, But we'll have to work from the upper end—from the Minotaur."

The passages of the Minotaur were larger and looked less complicated than those in the Maze. Here the gentle current of cool air seemed stronger, steadier, and could sometimes be felt even in comparatively wide passages.

Verner and Bancroft waited tensely, and then down the passage ahead came a small group, carrying a struggling man who was swearing violently.

"*Find* him?" said one of his captors, grinning. "All we had to do was follow the sounds he was making. He was sitting by a cache of food that would have lasted a week, with the plans still in his pocket."

Bancroft was looking at Verner, but he didn't speak. An awful choking and strangling from the prisoner made

Bancroft turn in amazement. The choking and strangling noises were interspersed with violent sneezing.

Down the passage the men had stopped thrashing the stacks of ragweed, which had sent thick clouds of pollen drifting through the passage and into the Maze. The pollen had unerringly found its target—the murderer-thief who suffered from hay fever.

THE MURDER TRAP
★ ★ ★

Richard Verner sat back in his desk chair, and turned the knife thoughtfully in his hands. The hilt was checked to give a firm grip, and as he closed his fingers around it, it fit snugly into his palm, the curved guard resting lightly against his thumb. The tapering double-edged blade felt razor-sharp, and its tip was like a needle's point.

Verner slid the knife into its sheath, and handed it back to the colonel, who sat across the desk, in the client's chair.

"A formidable weapon," said Verner.

The colonel, a man of about average height, with a look of intense self-discipline, rolled the knife in a piece of khaki cloth, and snapped a heavy rubber band around the outside.

"The man who owned it was formidable."

"So I understand." Verner glanced at the hand-written note the colonel had brought with him:

Dear Mr. Verner:

This will introduce Colonel Andrew Sharpe of the U.S. Army. Colonel Sharpe is head of a training school for selected cadets chosen from among certain of our Asian allies.

The colonel's most effective instructor at the training school was an officer you may have heard of—Steve "Tiger" Banks. I had only a slight personal acquaintance with Major Banks, and knew him mostly by reputation. He had an implacable hatred for terrorists of any variety. He was a ruthless and formidable fighter, and on several occasions led guerrilla penetration teams deep into territory controlled by communist terrorists. There he struck such fear into the hearts of the terrorists themselves as to cause widespread desertion from their cause. Major Banks was one of the few westerners of modern times to strike the imagination of Asiatics, who gave him his nickname "Tiger" because of his ferocity in attacking terrorists.

Major Banks was working with Colonel Sharpe on a plan which could have a very great effect on our efforts to defeat communist subversion in Asia. Several weeks ago, however, the major was found dead in his room, and his death was ruled suicide. Colonel Sharpe does not believe it was suicide.

I would appreciate any help you could give Colonel Sharpe.

With many thanks for all your help in the past—

> Sincerely,
> Martin Grainger

Colonel Sharpe cleared his throat. "As you may know, Mr. Verner, one of the toughest problems in fighting guerrillas is their ability to blend in with the rest of the populace. In the daytime, you may distribute food to a certain individual, and that same night, he may heave a bomb through your window. If the guerrilla could be picked out from among the other people, it would be an enormous help. Major Banks put a great deal of work and ingenuity into the attempt to solve this problem."

Verner nodded thoughtfully. "And he was teaching his technique for doing this?"

The colonel smiled ruefully. "I'm afraid I can't answer that question, Mr. Verner. That's classified information."

"I see. But at any rate, Major Banks was working on this, and now Major Banks is dead."

The colonel nodded. "And the men who examined the circumstances say that Major Banks committed suicide. I don't believe it; but I have no way to disprove it. I want you to disprove it, Mr. Verner. Then I want you to nail the killer for me."

Verner nodded. "Did General Grainger explain to you that I'm not a detective?"

"The general said you're a heuristician—that is to say, a professional problem-solver. He said that you consult with other experts when necessary, but that your own specialty is the solving of problems. He said that you have a special technique you can use to solve any kind of problem, so long as the facts are available, that he had seen this technique in action, didn't claim to understand it, but it worked. That's good enough for me, Mr. Verner. I don't care how you do it. Just run this murderer into the ground for me."

Verner leaned back. "When did the death take place?"

"A little over three weeks ago. It was a Sunday evening, and Major Banks had gotten back from a weekend trip. Captain Ramsey, another instructor, became worried about Banks, and spoke to me. I phoned Banks, got no answer, and Ramsey and I went over and knocked on Banks' door. There was no reply. The guard on duty told us Major Banks was inside, alone. We called, got no reply, and smashed in the door. Major Banks was on his back on his bunk, stabbed through the heart with his own knife. There was no one else in the room. The windows were shut and locked from inside. The door had a bolt, and two locks, put there apparently by different people who have used the room in the past."

The colonel frowned. "The door works by a knob, has an ordinary latch that clicks shut when you close it, and can be opened by turning a knob on the inside or out. There is a keyhole under the knob, which should work the lock bolt that slides out next to the latch; but this keyhole has, for some reason, been plugged with putty and painted over.

"About ten inches above the knob, there is a tumbler lock which can be worked by a key from the outside, or by an oval brass knob on the inside. When the lock is on, the oval knob is straight up and down. To draw back the bolt and release the lock, you turn the knob to the right or left, and snap down a little stud, which holds the lock open. To lock it again, you press up the little stud, and the lock snaps shut. Above this lock there is an ordinary sliding bolt. Due apparently to settling of the building, this sliding bolt is hard to shove into place.

"I mention all this detail, Mr. Verner, so you'll understand what I mean when I say that when we went in, the door had been locked from inside. It had been locked by snapping up the stud of the second lock I've mentioned—the one with the oval brass knob."

Verner nodded. "That's clear, Colonel. The keyhole of the lower lock was plugged, so that it couldn't be used. The uppermost of the three, the bolt, was hard to shove home. It was the *middle* lock, which worked by a key outside, or an oval knob inside, which had been locked."

"Yes. Exactly."

"Did *this* lock work easily?"

"Yes. It was only the bolt that stuck."

"And the door itself shut easily?"

The colonel nodded. "It did. Now, you see the situation. Major Banks was dead. The windows were locked from within. No one was in the room. There was no other way in or out beside these windows and the door. There was a guard outside who had heard Major Banks snap shut the lock from inside. This guard had seen no one go in or out the door since that time. The natural assumption is that Major Banks killed himself."

"What about the windows? How were they locked?"

"The ordinary type of window-fastener."

"One large pane in the upper and lower sash, or several?"

"Six in each sash."

Verner thought a moment. "Suppose the killer had already loosened one pane, and, after stabbing the major, had climbed out the window, reached through and locked it, put the pane back, held it in place with a couple of glazing points or thin brads, and then stuck dried putty in position using a fast-setting glue? The window would then be locked, apparently from the inside."

The colonel blinked, then said with a smile, "And you're not a detective?"

"Of course not. The problem is, how could a killer have got out? This strikes me as a possible method."

"Yes. What surprised me was that you thought of it so quickly. Well, there are two difficulties. The first is that the ground outside the windows had been soaked by a heavy rain, and was very soft. There were no impressions in this soft earth."

Verner's eyes narrowed in thought. "How far is any road, sidewalk, or other solid surface from the building itself?"

"About five feet, I should say."

"The major's room was on the first floor?"

"Yes."

"What is the building made of?"

"It's faced with red bricks. Why?"

"The windows are set in? There are moderately wide sills?"

"Yes. What does this matter?"

"What was to prevent the murderer from resting one end of a heavy board on the walk and the other end on the sill, and using this board to support his weight as he worked on the window? That way, his footprints would never appear in the soil below the window."

The colonel blinked. "Good Lord! But no, Mr. Verner. Those windows were examined very carefully. They hadn't been tampered with."

"You're sure it wasn't just assumed that whoever went out that way would have been taking too great a risk, so he wouldn't have done it?"

The colonel smiled. "That assumption was made, yes. You see, there are other buildings about a hundred feet away in front, and perhaps fifty feet away to the side. It wasn't quite dark, but Major Banks' lights were on, and his shades down. Whoever went out the window would have been outlined against that light. But I was convinced that this was a murder, and it seemed reasonable that the killer must have gone out a window, however unlikely it seemed. So I had those windows examined very carefully. No one had tampered with them, Mr. Verner."

"That brings us back to the door. There was only one door?"

"Yes, and this opened into the first-floor corridor. There was a guard who could see the door all the time."

"How far away?"

"Just across the hall, facing the door."

"It was his job to guard the major's door?"

"No, it was his job to sign cadets in and out. As it happened, there were only three cadets who went out, for help from their instructors. Two cadets came in, to see Major Banks. Also, two cadets from upstairs came down to see Major Banks, though they, of course, didn't sign out, since they didn't leave the barracks."

Verner frowned. "The same guard was on duty all the time?"

"Yes, and here again we run into a blank wall. The guard is perfectly reliable. He insists that he did not leave his post, and that he had the major's door in plain view all the time."

"Except when he was signing cadets in or out?"

"Yes, but even then he would have heard the door open. Besides, that was too short a time to be significant."

Verner sat up. "Just a minute, Colonel. Grant that the guard could see the door plainly. Still, it wasn't his job to watch it. He had no special interest in watching that door. If he had been distracted—"

The colonel shook his head. "No, Mr. Verner. You see, he did have a special interest in watching that door. I may as well explain to you that Major Banks was moody at times. Action stimulated him. Without the stimulus of action, he became severely depressed at times. Now, when Major Banks was depressed, he was barely civil. If he found anyone neglecting his duty, in any way, he could be savage in his reprimands.

"Major Banks was a highly trained fighting man, and he regarded the extermination of terrorists as his personal aim and duty. He wasn't really happy as a teacher, although he could see the importance of what we were trying to do. Now, on this particular Sunday evening, Major Banks had just gotten back from attending the funeral of his divorced second wife. The cadets who had come over to see Major Banks found him in a black mood, and warned the guard. The two cadets who came downstairs to see him said that he was more depressed than they'd ever seen him.

"When they came out, Captain Ramsey happened to be coming in to see Banks. The cadets tried to warn Ramsey, but Ramsey called to Banks and rapped on the door. Without a word, Major Banks snapped the lock shut from inside. Now then, the guard, outside in the hall, was aware that Major Banks had a tendency to come out of these fits of depression by giving a terrific tongue-lashing to whoever he found being slack in his duty. No,

Mr. Verner, the guard was on his toes, wide-awake, and acutely conscious of Major Banks' door."

Verner frowned, and looked off at a far corner of the room. "Did the major often snap his lock shut when someone knocked at his door?"

"No, but this wasn't the first time. After he got over his depression, he would apologize for any such rudeness. If he felt that he'd been too severe in his treatment of a cadet, he'd be especially considerate to him. It was his version of an apology. He never lost his control to the point of striking anyone. He never spoke insultingly to a cadet or to another officer. He was, however, barely civil, and sometimes not that.

"To snap the lock shut in Ramsey's face was exactly the kind of thing he *would* do. When he was in this mood, he always wanted to be left alone. But the longer he was left alone, the worse he got. Ramsey knew it, and had come over to get him out of it. Banks knew why Ramsey had come over, and he resented it. I imagine that Banks was incapable of saying one friendly word to Ramsey, and rather than have a fight he would regret, he locked the door. That was the last contact any of us had with him."

Verner sat back, frowning.

"There was no sound from the room later on? Nothing the guard noticed?"

"No. There'd been a thunderstorm earlier, but it had died away by then, so that any exceptional sound would have been noticed. Of course, there were quiet sounds all around—sounds of chairs scraping, occasional low voices, the sound of a water tap being turned on—but nothing particularly noticeable from Major Banks' room. We questioned the guard closely about this."

Verner leaned back, resting his right elbow in his cupped left hand, his right hand gently massaging the faintly perceptible bristle at his chin.

"You mentioned that the cadets tried to warn Ramsey. Do your cadets speak English?"

"Fluently. And Ramsey understands *their* tongue. But what they said only made him the more anxious to get to Banks."

"The guard, Colonel. Could he have entered the major's room?"

"Not without a key. You remember, it was locked from inside."

"Yes, but if the major came out, delivered a worse tongue-lashing than ever before—"

The colonel thought a moment, then shook his head. "He would have been overheard by the cadets upstairs and down the hall. They heard nothing of the sort."

"Was this a cadet guard?"

"No. He was one of our own men. He is perfectly trustworthy. He understood Major Banks' moods, and sympathized with him."

Verner looked at the colonel.

"Sympathized with him?"

The colonel blinked. "Didn't I explain this? No, I didn't. You see, Mr. Verner, Major Banks' first wife and their little son were killed by a terrorists' fire-bomb, tossed through a window of their house. The major got there too late to save them. It would have been better if he'd never seen it at all. To the best of my knowledge, he never had these severe fits of depression before. Given a situation like that, a man will often blame himself that his family was exposed to danger."

Verner sat very still as the colonel talked, then looked off at a far corner of the room.

"You're satisfied the major didn't commit suicide?"

"I'm sure of it. More than that, Mr. Verner, I'm convinced that the people who investigated this murder let themselves fall out of the frame of mind of criminal investigators, and instead fall into the frame of mind of amateur psychologists. On this basis, they decided that Major Banks, for the reasons I've just mentioned, had suicidal tendencies. Therefore, they did not dig as deep into the evidence as they should have."

Verner nodded. "That's possible. I have to admit, this sounds very much like suicide to me."

"You didn't know Steve Banks."

"No. Did your investigators know him?"

"Of course not." The colonel added ironically, "They were impartial, Mr. Verner. They could observe the problem with a degree of detachment, not blinded by any personal knowledge of Major Banks' character."

"What do the other officers think?"

"They're divided on the question. But that's neither here nor there."

Verner sat back, his eyes closed to mere slits. The colonel waited tensely.

Finally Verner said, "Colonel—" and paused.

"Yes?"

Verner's eyes came open, and he looked across the room, frowning.

"When you went into the room, you saw the major, lying on his bunk, dead?"

"Yes."

"What else did you see?"

The colonel frowned. "Banks' suitcase was open on a chair beside the bunk. A partly-eaten liverwurst sandwich, wrapped in wax paper, was on his desk. His cooler was overturned on the floor by the door, with clumps of frozen ice-cubes strewn around on the rug. The shades were down at all the windows. A lamp on the desk was turned on. A floor lamp was on. The door of his locker was open. That about covers it, I'm afraid."

"Did the major overturn furniture when he was depressed?"

"Not very often. But I understand he once reduced a solid oak chair to splinters. There are dents on the floor, the steel bed frame, and the wall, where the chair hit."

Verner thought that over in silence. Finally, he said, "Why did he happen to have a cooler in his room?"

"It was a picnic cooler, Mr. Verner. He'd had to drive quite a long distance over the weekend. He said he could drive much further, and stay awake better, if he ate as he drove, instead of stopping at eating places. He'd load up the cooler before he started on a trip of any length."

Verner leaned back, studied the far wall. Finally he stirred, glanced back at the colonel.

"You're right, Colonel. This could have been murder. Provided what you've told me is strictly accurate, and provided chance happened to favor the killers."

The colonel's eyes widened. "Killers? You don't think it was one person?"

"I don't see how it could have been."

"Who did it?"

Verner, frowning, raised his hand. "Just a minute. The problem you gave me was to find out if a murder actually occurred, and, if so, to run down the person or persons responsible. Isn't that right?"

"Yes. That's right."

"Seeing how a murder could have happened is not the same thing as proving it did. In this case, I'm afraid it's going to be next to impossible to prove anything by the usual methods. We're going to have to trap the killers, and they will almost certainly have thought this through too thoroughly to be easily tricked. To prove this is going to be—" He leaned back, scowling, as the colonel twice began to speak, and each time changed his mind.

Finally, still frowning, Verner said, "It's first going to be necessary to go to your school."

The colonel said ruefully, "I'm sorry, Mr. Verner. The location of the school is classified. I can't reveal it."

Verner said irritably, "If you want this solved, I am going to have to be on the spot."

"Very well. I can take you there. But you can't see anything that will reveal the location."

"I couldn't care less about the location. But I have got to be in that room. And while I'm there I want the guard, two cadets, and Captain Ramsey on hand."

"What do you intend to do?"

Verner looked at the colonel thoughtfully. "It's a little early to say. But would you object if I brought along some scientific friends?"

The colonel looked blank. "What good will that do?"

"I think General Grainger may have mentioned that I use my own methods."

The colonel thought a moment. "Bring anyone you want, Mr. Verner. But they are not to know the location of the school. They will need to be prepared for certain indignities."

On the day agreed, Verner, along with a chunky, square-built friend named Bartlett, and two men wearing rimless glasses, with sober faces and an air of intense abstraction, waited in Verner's office. Verner stood looking out and down through the Venetian blinds as, below, a tan sedan pulled to the curb, and the colonel stepped out, and glanced up. Five minutes later, they were all on their way to the airport. A few minutes after that, they, with several small crates, were being loaded onto a light plane. Immediately after that, they were heavily blind-folded.

The colonel's voice said regretfully, "I hope you'll excuse the melodrama, gentlemen, but if any one of you should attempt to look out, he will do it only once. I have strict orders to protect the location of the school, and the location of the school will be protected."

Throughout the trip that followed—by plane, car, a second plane, a speed boat, and at last several army Jeeps—the blindfolds remained firmly in place. When they were removed, Verner, Bartlett, and their two com-panions found themselves in a room about twelve feet wide by twenty long, containing a bunk, a desk, a chair, and a steel clothes locker. The walls of the room were painted a light cream. There were two windows along one side of the room, and one window at the end. Heavy tarpaulins of dark-green canvas blocked any view from the windows. From outside could be heard the faint scrape of branches, as a light wind brushed tree limbs across the face of the building.

The door of the room was on the long inside wall, directly across from one of the two windows on the oppo-site wall. Seated on folding chairs across the end wall of the room was a U.S. Army sergeant, two young men with close-cropped black hair and olive complexions, and a U.S. Army captain. Against the adjoining wall stood two strongly-built military policemen with holstered .45 auto-matics at their belts.

The colonel said, "Well, gentlemen, here we are. The door of this room will not be opened until you've finished your work here."

Verner looked the room over intently, then relaxed, and nodded. "That shouldn't take long, Colonel. It's a matter of comparatively simple routine. Now, let me introduce Dr. Grant Dwight Richmond of the Massachusetts Institute of Technology, and Dr. Seaman R. Smith of the California Institute of Technology. Drs. Richmond and Smith are nuclear physicists, and both have done a great deal of work in the structural analysis of steel under severe stress. Most of this work is classified, but I think I can mention that our nuclear submarines can go a little deeper than they might be able to otherwise, thanks to the work of Drs. Richmond and Smith."

The onlookers looked impressed. Dr. Smith cleared his throat, and said, "I suggest we set this apparatus up at once. That really is the larger part of the work."

The colonel said, "If you need help, gentlemen—"

"No, no, Colonel. We're quite used to this."

The crates came apart easily, and as the two men took out several black-finished boxes and a large folding tripod, Verner said, "This also is classified information, but as a certain part of it has become public recently, I think I can give you a rough idea of the part that is not yet public. As you probably know, it is possible to identify quite a few substances by their radiations, their spectra. It has been found possible to detect very small quantities of substances by neutron bombardment, followed by analysis of the resulting radiation, using a gamma-ray spectrometer. In each case, radiation is involved, but of course the newer process is much more flexible and sensitive for everyday use. It has been used a number of times to convict criminals, using very small samples as evidence."

The colonel was nodding, as if he were familiar with this. The captain worriedly watched the two scientists take out a long shiny tube with a black flexible hose at one end, and a sort of ring-shaped lens around a hole at the other end. The two scientists then pressed a red button on the side of a black-finished box. In turn, they looked through an eye-piece on the back.

Dr. Richmond glanced around the room, then back at his companion. "I think we'd better start with a calibration. We don't know what the background radiation is here."

"All right, Dwight. Let's use the metal rails on that bunk."

Dr. Richmond glanced at the colonel and the little group seated along the wall.

"The flash you will see is not the zeta-radiation. There's no real danger, so please don't be alarmed."

Dr. Smith smiled. "It's just for preliminary activation. There's actually no danger at all. We've done it dozens of times."

The colonel glanced uneasily at Verner, the captain looked around the room nervously, the two MP's glanced yearningly at the door, and the cadets intently watched the two scientists, as if trying to memorize their every move.

Dr. Richmond carried his black box with a small lens on one side across the room and set it on the tripod. He spread the legs of the tripod further apart, aimed the lens at the metal side rail of the bed, peered into the black box, and said, "All set, Rod."

Dr. Smith raised his shiny tube, with its long flexible black hose trailing across the floor to one of the crates, and held it close to the rail of the bed.

"Got the background," said Dr. Richmond. "Go ahead, and we'll get the flux."

Dr. Smith glanced around. "This is in no sense evidence, is it, Colonel?"

The colonel said blankly, "What's that?"

"The bed is not evidence."

"No. Of course not."

There was a *snap* and a blinding flash.

Dr. Richmond said apologetically, "There'll be no need for that again. We're zeroed in, now, so to speak. Again, gentlemen, the light is not the radiation. But if I were you, Colonel, I would dispose of the side rail of this bed. There's no harm in brief exposure. But don't let anyone sleep in the bed. Remove that side rail and bury it in a dump, or somewhere out of reach. I'd advise that you bury it at least eight feet deep, just to be safe."

The colonel blinked, started to speak, and Verner interrupted gently. "Dr. Richmond and Dr. Smith are the two leading structural radiation analysts in the U.S., Colonel. What they are able to do amounts practically to a re-creation of the precise history of any sample of metal. Several saboteurs and a number of inefficient workmen have been trapped by their methods. When you consider the importance of our nuclear submarines, Drs. Smith and Richmond are two of the most valuable scientists in the U.S. In fact—"

Dr. Richmond was moving the tripod back across the room, to set it in front of the door. The two scientists bent briefly over the tripod. Then Dr. Smith said gently, "Mr. Verner, if you would just give more of the technical aspects, and less personal information, I think it would be of greater interest."

"Well," said Verner, "what this amounts to, is a re-creation, step by step, of every significant physical and chemical change that a given piece of metal has undergone within the limiting time-period of—"

Dr. Smith was aiming his shiny tube at the lock, and Dr. Richmond was carefully adjusting his black box. The MP's were glancing from the door to the bed with no very happy expression. The two cadets had their heads together, talking fast and low in their own tongue. The captain leaned forward and said urgently, "Sir, there's an MP on the other side of that door!"

"Hold it!" shouted the colonel He leaned out the door, barked a few crisp orders, shut the door, glanced at Verner with an unreadable expression, and then everything was interrupted by a second less bright flash.

"Perfectly harmless," said Dr. Smith. "I wouldn't care to leave my hand on that lock for more than a few hours at a time, but I doubt that anyone will. Anything of interest, Dwight?"

"We seem to have a very brief temperature minimum here that seems quite anomalous. It's so brief I'll have to expand the baseline. Let's have that gauge."

Verner said, "Dr. Richmond seems to have found an anomalous temperature minimum. This means an abnormally low temperature has been applied to that lock, or to some part of it, within the limiting time-period. By expanding the baseline, he can find how long this low temperature lasted, and the heat-transfer effected during that time. From this he can deduce in what way the low temperature was created. That is—"

The two scientists were bent at their instruments.

"Odd," said Dr. Richmond. "This is obviously not a case of air-cooling.

"Look, the latent heat of fusion must have been around 79 to 80."

"Ice," said Dr. Smith.

The colonel said anxiously, "What are they saying?"

"Evidently," said Verner, "a piece of ice was pressed against some part of that lock within the limiting time-period. Now Dr. Richmond will calibrate the baseline, and find out just when this took place. In time, by checking every piece of metal, we will be able to deduce—"

The rest of the sentence was lost in a paralyzing yell, a shrill sound accompanied by the suddenly bursting of the two cadets from their chairs, straight for the silent figures of the two scientists bent at their instruments. The two cadets had their hands raised, the flat edges ready to deliver the *karate* chop that could stun or kill a man.

The two MP's, startled, had scarcely time to step away from the wall. The colonel was coming out of his chair in a surprising display of speed. But nothing in the room compared with the two scientists.

Dr. Smith whipped around in a blurred movement too fast to be seen, and rammed the end of his shiny tube into the nearest cadet's midsection. Dr. Richmond bent slightly at the knees, caught the second cadet by a fistful of shirt front, and in a rapid sequence of movements spun him over his head and slammed him to the floor. The cadet succeeded in partially breaking the fall, but then smashed into the wall. The first cadet, bent from the blow in the midsection, paused before Dr. Smith for a brief fraction of a second, and in this brief instant, Dr. Smith cracked him over the head with his shiny tube.

The two MP's were now getting into action. The colonel was on his feet, wide-eyed, staring at Verner, who hadn't moved an inch, and then at Bartlett, who had a little tear-gas gun in his hand. The colonel's face suddenly split in a grin.

"By God! The whole thing was a fraud!"

Verner smiled. "There's nothing like science, Colonel. Never underestimate it."

The colonel stepped over to the black box on its tripod. "If there's anything in this box, I'm a Marine."

Dr. Richmond said, "Then you've got the wrong uniform on, Colonel. Press that red button at the side."

The colonel found the red button, pressed it, and looked through an eye-piece in the back of the box. Before him, a series of neatly-printed lines lit up in red:

Richmond: "I think we'd better start with a calibration. We don't know what the background radiation is in here."
Smith: "All right, Dwight. Let's use the metal rails on the bunk." (check bunk)
Richmond: (turn to watchers) "The flash you will see is not the zeta-radiation, there's no danger, so please don't be alarmed."
Smith (smile reassuringly) "It's just for preliminary activation. There's actually no danger at all . . ."

The colonel swore and straightened up. He glanced at the captain, "Take a look at this, Ramsey. Push this little button, and see what's in there."

As the captain bent to stare into the box, the colonel turned to Verner. "You're wasting your time as a heuristician. You could be the greatest confidence man ever seen in the western hemisphere."

Verner, smiling broadly, said, "Well, it fooled them, Colonel, and it solves your problem. You see what happened, of course?"

"Yes, of course I see what happened. They thought these two scientists were methodically tracking them down, and they decided to act before it was too late. You'd built these two all-time close-combat experts, or seventh-dan judo masters, or whatever they are, up into the two most valuable scientists in the United States. Naturally, this pair of communist saboteurs—the cadets—having finished off one of our greatest guerrilla-warfare experts, and seeing that they were about to be found out anyway, jumped at the chance to score some more points by killing our scientists before we could stop them. So they sprang headfirst into the trap."

The colonel, beaming, thought a moment. "You apparently already knew how they'd made Major Banks' death look like suicide. But there was no way to *prove* it. So you trapped them into thinking it was being proved right before their eyes. But how did you know what they'd done?"

Verner smiled. "It was a simple matter, Colonel. Obviously, if anyone *had* murdered the major, and if the facts you stated were true, the two cadets must have been lying. They claimed to have last seen the major alive. No one had entered or left his room since they had left it, until the major was found dead. It follows that he either committed suicide, or else he was *not* alive when they left him. Since no one else could have entered the room unseen, no one else could have committed a murder."

"Yes, it follows. But the ice against the lock—If that was false, it would have been a dead giveaway—"

"Why?" said Verner. "For all the cadets knew, someone might have put ice, for some reason, against the lock.

All that conversation would have been so much gibberish to them, they would merely have been confused, not alarmed, unless they knew it were true."

"I still don't quite follow it," said the colonel. "What the deuce has ice to do with the question?"

"The door lock was snapped from within, you remember?—Without a word from Banks. This suggests the possibility that he was already dead. Then, who snapped the lock? No-one went in or out after the door was locked, and no-one but Banks was found in the room. It follows, if Banks was already dead, that no one snapped the lock. How, then was it done? Some gadget or device might have been used to do it. I could think of several possibilities, but none that would not leave something inside the room, to be found when the door was opened. You said there was no special confusion. It follows that if any device had been used it would have been seen. It would have exposed the murder the moment it was noticed.—Unless it wasn't noticed because it was expected."

The colonel was frowning. "And—"

"Colonel, there was Major Banks' overturned cooler, and ice from it strewn around by the door. What if the cadets pushed the stud of the lock up, as if to lock the door, but held the oval knob back so the lock couldn't work, then fitted in a piece of ice, to hold back the knob while they left the room?"

The colonel swore, and crossed to look at the lock. He pushed the stud up, and turned the oval knob. The door unlocked. While he held the knob turned, the door stayed unlocked.

He let go of the knob, and the door locked with a snap. He looked around.

"They could have fitted that ice between the knob and the hand bolt above it."

Verner nodded. "When you mentioned that bolt above the lock, and the ice, it made murder a distinct possibility. To hold open the lock, there has to be a prop, and there has to be something to rest the prop against. In this case, there were both."

"So, when Ramsey here rapped on the door, he jarred the ice loose?"

Verner nodded. "Whereupon it fell to the rug inside the room, and the lock snapped shut. This must have been much better than the cadets had expected. They could only have expected the guard to hear the snap of the lock. After killing the major, they would have to leave, then quickly change their minds and come back, knock, and hope that the ice jarred loose.

"But the captain came along, and the way it worked out couldn't have been better for them. The ice, meanwhile, having fallen on the rug near the other ice, was apparently just one more piece from the cooler. Since the cooler was overturned, there seemed nothing unusual about the ice on the floor."

The colonel nodded. "Yes, I see it now." He glanced around at the cadets, now sullenly handcuffed, with the MP's watching them closely. The colonel's gaze hardened. Then he looked at the two scientists who already had their crates repacked and were ready to leave.

The colonel smiled. "What recruits they would make! Or are they already in some branch of the service? Where the deuce did you get them?"

Verner smiled.

"I'm sorry, Colonel. That's classified information."

GADGET vs. TREND
★ ★ ★

Boston, Sept. 2, 1976. Dr. R. Milton Schummer, Professor of Sociology at Wellsford College, spoke out against "creeping conformism" to an audience of twelve hundred in Swarton Hall last night.

Professor Schummer charged that America, once the land of the free, is now "the abode of the stereotyped mass-man, shaped from infancy by the moron-molding influences of television, mass-circulation newspapers and magazines, and the pervasive influence of advertising manifest in all these media. The result is the mass-production American with interchangeable parts and built-in taped program."

What this country needs, said Dr. Schummer, is "freedom to differ, freedom to be eccentric." But, he concluded, "The momentum is too great. The trend, like

235

the tide, cannot be reversed by human efforts. In two hundred years, this nation has gone from individualism to conformism, from independence to interdependence, from federalism to fusionism, and the end is not yet. One shrinks at the thought of what the next one hundred years may bring."

Rutland, Vt., March 16, 1977. Dr. J. Paul Hughes, grandson of the late inventor, Everett Hughes, revealed today a device which his grandfather kept under wraps because of its "supposedly dangerous side-effects." Dubbed by Dr. Hughes a "privacy shield," the device works by the "exclusion of quasi-electrons." In the words of Dr. Hughes:

"My grandfather was an eccentric experimenter. Surprisingly often, though, his wild stabs would strike some form of pay dirt, in a commercial sense. In this present instance, we have a device unexplainable by any sound scientific theory, but which may be commercially quite useful. When properly set up, and connected to a suitable electrical outlet, the device effectively soundproofs material surfaces, such as walls, doors, floors, and the like, and thus may be quite helpful in present-day crowded living conditions."

Dr. Hughes explained that the device was supposed to operate by "the exclusion of 'quasi-electrons,' which my grandfather thought governed the transmission of sound through solid bodies, and performed various other esoteric functions. But we needn't take this too seriously."

New York, May 12, 1977. Formation of Hughes QuietWall Corporation was announced here today.

President of the new firm is J. Paul Hughes, grandson of the late inventor, Everett Hughes.

New York, Sept. 18, 1977. One of the hottest stocks on the market today is Hughes QuietWall. With demand booming, and the original president of the firm kicked upstairs to make room for the crack management expert, Myron L. Sams, the corporation has tapped a gold mine.

Said a company spokesman: "The biggest need in this country today is privacy. We live practically in each other's pockets, and if we can't do anything else, at least QuietWall can soundproof the pockets."

The QuietWall units, which retail for $289.95 for the basic room unit, are said to offer dealer, distributor, and manufacturer a generous profit. And no one can say that $289.95 is not a reasonable price to pay to keep out the noise of other people's TV, record players, quarrels, and squalling babies.

Detroit, December 23, 1977. Santa left an early present for the auto industry here today.

A test driver trying out a car equipped with a Hughes QuietWall unit went into a skid on the icy test track, rolled over three times, and got out shaken but unhurt. The car itself, a light supercompact, was found to be almost totally undamaged.

Tests with sledgehammers revealed the astonishing fact that with the unit turned on, the car would not dent, and the glass could not be broken. The charge filler cap could not be unscrewed. The hood could not be raised. And neither windows nor doors could be opened till the unit was snapped off. With the unit off, the car was perfectly ordinary.

This is the first known trial of a QuietWall unit in a motor vehicle.

Standard house and apartment installations use a specially-designed basic unit to soundproof floor and walls, and small additional units to soundproof doors and windows. This installation tested today apparently lacked such refinements.

December 26, 1977. J. Paul Hughes, chairman of the board of directors of the QuietWall Corp., stated to reporters today that his firm has no intention to market the Hughes QuietWall unit for use in motor cars.

Hughes denied the Detroit report of a QuietWall-equipped test car that rolled without damage, calling it "impossible."

Hartford, January 8, 1978. Regardless of denials from the QuietWall Corporation, nationwide experiments are being conducted into the use of the corporation's sound-deadening units as a safety device in cars. Numerous letters, telegrams, and phone calls are being received at the head offices of some of the nation's leading insurance companies here.

Hartford, January 9, 1978. Tests carried out by executives of the New Standard Insurance Group indicate that the original Detroit reports were perfectly accurate.

Cars equipped with the QuietWall units cannot be dented, shattered, scratched, or injured in any way by ordinary tools.

Austin J. Ramm, Executive Secretary of New Standard Group, stated to reporters:

"It's the damndest thing I ever saw.

"We've had so many communications, from people all over the country who claim to have connected QuietWall units to their cars, that we decided to try it out ourselves.

"We tried rocks, hammers, and so forth, on the test vehicle. When these didn't have any effect, I tried a quarter-inch electric drill and Steve Willoughby—he's our president—took a crack at the center of the wind-shield with a railroad pickaxe. The pickaxe bounced. My drill just slid around over the surface and wouldn't bite in.

"We have quite a few other things we want to try.

"But we've seen enough to know there definitely is truth in these reports."

New York, January 10, 1978. Myron L. Sams, president of the Hughes QuietWall Corporation, announced today that a special automotive attachment is being put on sale throughout the country. Mr. Sams warns that improper installation may, among other things, seize up all or part of the operating machinery of the car. He urges that company representatives be allowed to carry out the installation.

Dallas, January 12, 1978. In a chase lasting an hour, a gang of bank robbers got away this afternoon with $869,000 in cash and negotiable securities.

Despite a hail of bullets, the escape car was not damaged. An attempt to halt it at a roadblock failed, as the car crashed through without injury.

There is speculation here that the car was equipped with one of the Hughes QuietWall units that went on sale a few days ago.

Las Vegas, January 19, 1978. A gang of eight to ten criminals held up the Silver Dollar Club tonight, escaping with over a quarter of a million dollars.

It was one of the most bizarre robberies in the city's history.

The criminals entered the club in golf carts fitted with light aluminum—and transparent-plastic covers, and opened a gun battle with club employees. A short fight disclosed that it was impossible to even dent the light

shielding on the golf carts. Using the club's patrons and
employees as hostages, the gunmen received the cash
they demanded, rolled across the sidewalk and up a ramp
into the rear of a waiting truck, which drove out of town,
smashing through a hastily-erected roadblock.

As police gave chase, the truck proved impossible to
damage. In a violent exchange of gunfire, no one was
injured, as the police cars were equipped with newly-
installed QuietWall units, and it was evident that the
truck was also so equipped.

Well outside of town, the truck reached a second roadblock. The robbers attempted to smash through the
seemingly flimsy barrier, but were brought to a sudden
stop when the roadblock, fitted with a QuietWall unit,
failed to give way.

The truck, and the golf carts within, were found to be
undamaged. The bandits are now undergoing treatment
for concussion and severe whiplash injuries.

The $250,000 has now been returned to the Silver
Dollar Club, and Las Vegas is comparatively quiet
once more.

New York, January 23, 1978. In a hastily-called
news conference, J. Paul Hughes, chairman of the board
of Hughes QuietWall Corporation, announced that he
is calling upon the Federal Government to step in and
suspend the activities of the corporation.

Pointing out that he has tried without success to suspend the company's operations on his own authority, Dr.
Hughes stated that as a scientist he must warn the public
against a dangerous technological development, "the
menacing potentialities of which I have only recently
come to appreciate."

No response has as yet been received from Washington.

New York, January 24, 1978. President Myron L. Sams today acknowledged the truth of reports that a bitter internal struggle is being waged for control of the Hughes QuietWall Corporation.

Spring Corners, Iowa, January 26, 1978. Oscar B. Nelde, a farmer on the outskirts of town, has erected a barricade that has backed up traffic on the new Cross-State Highway for twenty miles in both directions.

Mr. Nelde recently lost a suit for additional damages when the highway cut his farm into two unequal parts, the smaller part containing his house and farm buildings, the larger part containing his fields.

The barricade is made of oil drums, saw horses, and barbed wire. The oil drums and saw horses cannot be moved, and act as if welded to the frozen earth. The barbed wire is weirdly stiff and immovable. The barricade is set up in a double row of these immovable obstacles, spaced to form a twenty-foot-wide lane connecting the two separated parts of Mr. Nelde's farm.

Mr. Nelde's manure spreader was seen crossing the road early today.

Heavy road machinery has failed to budge the obstacles. The experts are stumped. However, the local QuietWall dealer recalls selling Mr. Nelde a quantity of small units recently and adds, "But no more than a lot of other farmers have been buying lately."

It may be worth mentioning that Mr. Nelde's claim is one of many that have been advanced locally.

New York, January 27, 1978. The Hughes QuietWall Corporation was today reorganized as QuietWall, Incorporated, with Myron L. Sams holding the positions of president and chairman of the board of directors. J. Paul Hughes, grandson of Everett Hughes, continues as a director.

Spring Corners, Iowa, January 28, 1978. Traffic is flowing once again on the Cross-State Highway.

This morning a U.S. Army truck-mounted earth auger moved up the highway and drilled a number of holes six feet in diameter, enabling large chunks of earth to be carefully loosened and both sections of the barricade to be lifted out as units. The wire, oil drums, saw horses, and big chunks of earth, which remained rigid when lifted out, are being removed to the U.S. Army Research and Development Laboratories for study. No QuietWall units have been found, and it is assumed that they are imbedded, along with their power source, inside the masses of earth.

The sheriff, the police chief of Spring Corners, and state and federal law enforcement agents are attempting to arrest Oscar B. Nelde, owner of the farm adjacent to the highway.

This has proved impossible, as Mr. Nelde's house and buildings are equipped with a number of QuietWall units controlled from within.

Boston, February 1, 1978. Dr. R. Milton Schummer, Professor of Sociology at Wellsford College, and a severe critic of "creeping conformism," said tonight, when questioned by reporters, that some of the effects of the QuietWall units constitute a hopeful sign in the long struggle of the individual against the State and against the forces of conformity. However, Dr. Schummer does not believe that "a mere technological gadget can affect these great movements of sociological trends."

Spring Corners, Iowa, February 2, 1978. A barbed-wire fence four feet high, fastened to crisscrossed railroad rails, now blocks the Cross-State Highway near the farm home of Leroy Weaver, a farmer whose property was cut in half by the highway, and who has often stated that he has received inadequate compensation.

It has proved impossible for highway equipment on the scene to budge either wire or rails.

Mr. Weaver cannot be reached for comment, as his house and buildings are equipped with QuietWall units, and neither the sheriff nor federal officials have been able to effect entry onto the premises.

Washington, D. C., February 3, 1978. The Bureau of Standards reports that tests on QuietWall units show them to be essentially "stasis devices." That is to say, they prevent change in whatever material surface they are applied to. Thus, sound does not pass, because the protected material is practically noncompressible, and is not affected by the alternate waves of compression and rarefaction in the adjacent medium.

Many potential applications are suggested by Bureau of Standards spokesmen who report, for instance, that thin slices of apples and pears placed directly inside the surface field of the QuietWall device were found totally unchanged when the field was switched off, after test periods of more than three weeks.

New York, February 3, 1978. Myron L. Sams, president of QuietWall, Incorporated, reports record sales, rising day-by-day to new peaks. QuietWall, Inc., is now operating factories in seven states, Great Britain, the Netherlands, and West Germany.

Spring Corners, Iowa, February 4, 1978. A U.S. Army truck-mounted earth auger has again removed a fence across the Cross-State Highway here. But the giant auger itself has now been immobilized, apparently by one or more concealed stasis (QuietWall) devices.

As the earth auger weighs upwards of thirty tons, and all the wheels of truck and trailer appear to be locked, moving it presents no small problem.

Los Angeles, February 5, 1978. Police here report the capture of a den of dope fiends and unsavory characters of all descriptions, after a forty-hour struggle.

The hideout, known as the "Smoky Needle Club," was equipped with sixteen stasis devices manufactured by QuietWall, Inc., and had an auxiliary electrical supply line run in through a drain pipe from the building next door. Only when the electrical current to the entire neighborhood was cut off were the police able to force their way in.

New York, February 5, 1978. Myron L. Sams, president of QuietWall, Inc. announced today a general price cut, due to improved design and volume production economies, on all QuietWall products.

In future, basic QuietWall room units will sell for $229.95 instead of $289.95. Special small stasis units, suitable for firming fence posts, reinforcing walls, and providing barred-door household security, will retail for as low as $19.95. It is rumored that this price, with improved production methods, still provides an ample profit for all concerned, so that prices may be cut in some areas during special sales events.

Spring Corners, Iowa, February 6, 1978. A flying crane today lifted the immobilized earth auger from the eastbound lanes of Cross-State Highway.

A total of fourteen small stasis units have thus far been removed from the auger, its truck and trailer, following its removal from the highway by air. Difficulties were compounded by the fact that each stasis unit apparently "freezes" the preceding units applied within its range.

The de-stasis experts must not only locate the units. They must remove them in the right order, and some are very cleverly hidden.

Seaton Bridge, Iowa, February 9, 1978. The Cross-State Highway has again been blocked, this time by a wall of cow manure eighty-three feet long, four feet wide at the base, and two-and-one-half feet high, apparently stabilized by embedded stasis units, and as hard as cement. National Guard units are now patrolling the Seaton Bridge section of road to either side of the block.

New York, February 10, 1978. Representatives of QuietWall, Inc., report that study of stasis devices removed from the auger at Springs Center, Iowa, reveals that they are "not devices of QW manufacture, but crude, cheap bootleg imitations. Nevertheless, they work."

Spring Center, Iowa, February 12, 1978. The Cross-State Highway, already cut at Seaton Bridge, is now blocked in three places by walls of snow piled up during last night's storm by farmers' bulldozers, and stabilized by stasis devices. Newsmen who visited the scene report that the huge mounds look like snow, but feel like concrete. Picks and shovels do not dent them, and flame throwers fail to melt them.

New York, February 15, 1978. Dr. J. Paul Hughes, a director of QuietWall, Inc., tonight reiterated his plea for a government ban on stasis devices. He recalled the warning of his inventor grandfather, Everett Hughes, and stated that he intends to spend the rest of his life "trying to undo the damage the device has caused."

New York, February 16, 1978. Myron L. Sams, president of QuietWall, Inc., announced today that a fruit fly had been kept in stasis for twenty-one days without suffering visible harm. QW's research scientists, he said, are now working with the problem of keeping small animals in stasis. If successful, Sams said, the experiments may open the door to "one-way time-travel," and enable persons suffering from serious diseases to wait, free from pain, until such time as a satisfactory cure has been found.

Bonn, February 17, 1978. Savage East German accusations against the West today buttressed the rumors that "stasis-unit enclaves" are springing up like toadstools throughout East Germany.

Similar reports are coming in from Hungary, while Poland reports a number of "stasis-frozen" Soviet tanks.

Havana, February 18, 1978. In a frenzied harangue tonight, "Che" Garcia, First Secretary of the Cuban Communist Party, announced that the government is erecting "stasis walls" all around the island, and that "stasis blockhouses" now being built will resist "even the Yankees' worst hydrogen weapons." In a torrent of vitriolic abuse, however, Mr. Garcia threatened that "any further road blocks and centers of degenerate individualism that spring up will be eradicated from the face of the soil of the motherland by blood, iron, sweat, and the forces of monolithic socialism."

There have been rumors for some time of dissatisfaction with the present regime.

Mr. Garcia charged that the C.I.A. had flagrantly invaded Cuban air space by dropping "millions of little vicious stasis units, complete with battery packs of fantastic power," all over the island, from planes which could not be shot down because they were protected by "still more of these filthy sabotage devices."

Des Moines, February 21, 1978. The Iowa state government following the unsuccessful siege of four farm homes near the Cross-State Highway today announced that it is opening new hearings on land-owners' compensation for land taken for highway-construction purposes.

The government appealed to owners of property adjoining the highway to be patient, bring their complaints to the capital, and meanwhile open the highway to traffic.

Staunton, Vt., February 23, 1978. Hiram Smith, a retired high school science teacher whose family has lived on the same farm since before the Revolution, was ordered last fall to leave his family home.

A dam is to be built nearby, and Mr. Smith's home will be among those inundated.

At the time of the order, Mr. Smith, who lives on the farm with his fourteen-year-old grandson, stated that he would not leave "until carried out dead or helpless."

This morning, the sheriff tried to carry out the eviction order, and was stopped by a warning shot fired from the Smith house. The warning shot was followed by the flight of a small, battery-powered model plane, apparently radio-controlled, which alighted about two thousand yards from the Smith home, near an old apple orchard.

Mr. Smith called to the sheriff to get out of his car and lie down, if the car was not stasis-equipped, and in any case to look away from the apple orchard.

There was a brilliant flash, a shock, and a roar which the sheriff likened to the explosion of "a hundred tons of TNT." When he looked at the orchard, it was obscured by a pink glow and boiling clouds, apparently of steam from vaporized snow.

Mr. Smith called out to the sheriff to get off the property, or the next "wink bomb" would be aimed at him.

No one has been out to the Smith property since the sheriff's departure.

New York, February 25, 1978. Mr. Myron L. Sams, president of QuietWall, Inc., announced today that "there is definitely no connection between the Staunton explosion and the QW Corp. stasis unit. The stasis unit is a strictly defensive device and cannot be used for offensive purposes."

New York, February 25, 1978. Dr. J. Paul Hughes tonight asserted that the "wink-bomb" exploded at Staunton yesterday, and now known to have left a radioactive crater, "probably incorporated a stasis unit." The unit was probably "connected to a light metallic container holding a small quantity of radioactive material. It need not necessarily be the radioactive material we are accustomed to think of as suitable for fission bombs. It need not be the usual amount of such material. When the stasis unit was activated by a radio signal or timing device, high-energy particles thrown off by the radioactive material would be unable to pass out through the container, now in stasis, and equivalent to a very hard, dense, impenetrable, nearly ideal boundary surface. The high-energy particles would bounce back into the interior, bombarding the radioactive material. As the population of high-energy particles within the enclosing stasis-field builds up, the radioactive material, regardless of its quantity, reaches the critical point. Precisely what will happen depends on the radioactive material used, the size of the sample, and the length of the 'wink'—that is, the length of time the stasis field is left on."

Dr. Hughes added that "this is a definite, new, destructive use of the stasis field, which Mr. Myron Sams assures us is perfectly harmless."

Montpelier, Vt., February 26, 1978. The governor today announced temporary suspension of the Staunton Dam Project, while an investigation is carried out into numerous landowners' complaints.

Moscow, February 28, 1978. A "certain number" of "isolated cells" of "stasis-protected character" are admitted to have sprung up within the Soviet Union. Those that are out of the way are said to be left alone, on the theory that the people have to come out sometime. Those in important localities are being reduced by the Red Army, using tear gas, sick gas, toothache gas, flashing searchlights, "war of nerves" tactics, and, in some cases, digging out the "cell" and carrying it off wholesale. It is widely accepted that there is nowhere near the amount of trouble here as in the satellite countries, where the problem is mounting to huge proportions.

Spring Corners, Iowa, May 16, 1978. The extensive Cross-State Highway claims having been settled all around, traffic is once again flowing along the highway. A new and surprising feature is the sight of farm machinery disappearing into tunnels constructed under the road to allow the farmers to pass from one side to the other.

Staunton, Vt., July 4, 1978. There was a big celebration here today as the governor and a committee of legislators announced that the big Staunton Dam Project has been abandoned, and a number of smaller dams will be built according to an alternate plan put forth earlier.

Bonn, August 16, 1978. Reports reaching officials here indicate that the East German government, the Hungarian government, and also to a considerable extent the Polish government, are having increasing difficulties as more and more of the "stasis-unit-enclaves" join up, leaving the governments on the outside looking in. Where this will end is hard to guess.

Washington, September 30, 1978. The Treasury Department sent out a special "task force" of about one hundred eighty men this morning. Their job is to crack open the mushrooming Anti-Tax League, whose membership is now said to number about one million enthusiastic businessmen. League members often give Treasury agents an exceedingly rough time, using record books and files frozen shut with stasis units, office buildings stasis-locked against summons-servers, stasis-equipped cars which come out of stasis-equipped garages connected with stasis-locked office buildings, to drive to stasis-equipped homes where it is physically impossible for summons-servers to enter the grounds.

Princeton, N.J., October 5, 1978. A conference of leading scientists, which gathered here today to exchange views on the nature of the stasis unit, is reported in violent disagreement. One cause of the disagreement is the reported "selective action" of the stasis unit, which permits ordinary light to pass through transparent bodies, but blocks the passage of certain other electromagnetic radiations.

Wild disorders broke out this afternoon during a lecture by Dr. J. Paul Hughes, on the "Quasi-Electron Theory of Wave Propagation." The lecture was accompanied by demonstration of the original Everett Hughes device, powered by an old-fashioned generator driven by the inventor's original steam engine. As the engine gathered speed, Dr. Hughes was able to demonstrate the presence of a nine-inch sphere of completely reflective material in the supposedly-empty focus of the apparatus. This sphere, Dr. Hughes asserted, was the surface of a space totally evacuated of quasi-electrons, which he identified as "units of time."

It was at this point that the disturbance broke out.

Despite the disorder, Dr. Hughes went on to explain the limiting value of the velocity of light in terms of the quasi-electron theory, but was interrupted when the vibration of the steam engine began to shake down the ceiling.

There is a rumor here that the conference may recess at once without issuing a report.

Washington, D.C., August 16, 1979. Usually reliable sources report that the United States has developed a "missile screen" capable of destroying enemy missiles in flight, and theoretically capable of creating a wall around the nation through which no enemy projectile of any type could pass. This device is said to be based on the original Everett Hughes stasis-unit, which creates a perfectly rigid barrier of variable size and shape, which can be projected very rapidly by turning on an electric current.

Other military uses for stasis devices include protection of missile sites, storage of food and munitions, impenetrizing of armor-plate, portable "turtle-shields" for infantry, and quick-conversion units designed to turn any ordinary house or shed into a bombardment-proof strongpoint.

Veteran observers of the military scene say that the stasis unit completely reverses the advantage until recently held by offensive, as opposed to defensive, weapons. This traditionally alternating advantage, supposed to have passed permanently with the development of nuclear explosives, has now made one more pendulum swing. Now, in place of the "absolute weapon," we have the "absolute defense." Properly set up, hydrogen explosions do not dent it.

But if the nation is not to disintegrate within as it becomes impregnable without, officials say we must find some effective way to deal with stasis-protected cults, gangsters, antitax enthusiasts, seceding rural districts, space-grabbers, and proprietors of dens. Latest problem is the traveling roadblock, set up by chiselers who select a busy highway, collect "toll" from motorists who must pay or end up in a traffic jam, then move on quickly before police have time to react, and stop again in some new location to do the same thing all over. There must be an answer to all these things, but the answer has yet to be found.

Boston, September 2, 1979. Dr. R. Milton Schummer, Professor of Sociology at Wellsford College, spoke out against "galloping individualism" to an audience of six hundred in Swarton Hall last night.

Professor Schummer charged that America, once the land of the co-operative endeavor, is now "a seething hotbed of rampant individualists, protestors, quick-rich artists, and minute-men of all kinds, each over-reacting violently from a former condition which may have seemed like excessive conformism at the time, but now in the perspective of events appears as a desirable cohesiveness and unity of direction. The result today is the fractionating American with synthetic rough edges and built-in bellicose sectionalism."

What this country needs, said Dr. Schummer, is "coordination of aims, unity of purpose, and restraint of difference." But, he concluded, "the reaction is too violent. The trend, like the tide, cannot be reversed by human efforts. In three years, this nation has gone from cohesion to fractionation, from interdependence to chaos, from federalism to splinterism, and the end is not yet. One shrinks at the thought of what the next hundred years may bring."

TOP LINE
★ ★ ★

Tokyo, January 3. Once again, Japanese auto production has outstripped all competition. In the words of Setsui Tamizake, outspoken head of giant NKF Auto Industries, "We are the best."

Detroit, January 4. In a packed news conference, Frank B. Service, president of the troubled U.S. automaker Colossal Motors, admitted to another loss of over two billion dollars, "due to a lack of customer appreciation of the merits of our new Z-car."

Washington, D.C., January 6. Legislation to further restrict foreign imports is reported still stuck in committee. The main objection is that foreign goods are often cheaper, so that stopping these imports would further accelerate inflation.

★ ★ ★

New York, January 7. Interest rates are rumored to be on the way down again. On the rumor, the Dow-Jones Industrial Average today soared more than seventeen points, to 467.79.

Kapungoola, January 8. The price of oil is going up again. Delegates to the Oil Producers Price Adjustment Congress today agreed to an immediate five-dollar-a-barrel increase, blaming "renewed inflation in the oil-consuming nations."

Detroit, January 8. G. Bates Merritt, former president of bankrupt Mammoth Motors, today warned that, "this country can't continue to support foreign manufacturers." Speaking to a meeting of the Auto Industry Emergency Council, Mr. Merritt stated, "What we need is a partnership of Capital, Labor, Government, and the American consumer. The Japanese succeed because their government backs business, and their consumer never gets a chance to squander his money on all kinds of foreign goods. Either we voluntarily stick together, or we're all going down the rat-hole together, involuntarily."

Silicona, Calif., January 11. Edwin A. Storch, inventor of the lattice-channel-junction technology that has revolutionized the booming microelectronics industry, was today questioned about the Detroit situation by veteran financial reporter Rupert Neal:

Q: "Mr. Storch, should we shut out foreign auto imports?"

A: "No, we ought to obsolete them."

Q: "How do we—"

A: "Quit this step-by-step fooling around, and redesign from the ground up. The last large-scale innovator the auto industry had was Henry Ford."

Q: "You're saying Detroit is out of date?"

A: "I'm saying the whole auto industry is out of date."

Q: "How about the Japanese?"

A: "Hard-working, efficient people."

Q: "What about their cars?"

A: "They're dinosaurs."

Q: "They're profitable, aren't they?"

A: "So was Detroit, when it was turning out two-ton gas-eating monsters with nothing new but the chrome trim. You're talking about profit, the so-called 'bottom line.' "

Q: "That's the name of the game, isn't it?"

A: "Which game? I'm talking about progress."

Q: "You can't separate the two, can you?"

A: "Are you kidding? They used to have two-wheel brakes on cars. Rickenbacker saw the opportunity for improvement, and built cars with four-wheel brakes; there was a whispering campaign that four-wheel brakes were unsafe, and his car was finished right there. Chrysler saw that streamlining would be an improvement, and then the customers didn't like the style. If innovation was the same as profit, all successful businessmen would be inventors. They aren't the same. But we can beat the imports if we obsolete them."

Q: "Would you say that you, yourself, combine innovative and business skills?"

A: "I'm not a businessman. When I got the idea for LCJ technology, I wasn't strictly even in the microelectronics industry. I just thought I saw a way to revolutionize microprocessors."

Q: "And it worked, didn't it?"

A: "True. But if I'd had to be a businessman, too, I don't know. I went to a banker, thinking to get some backing, and he said, 'Mr. Storch, I don't understand a word you're saying. And I have serious doubts. You suggest too large an improvement from your idea. You are basically a chemist, experienced mainly in coatings —durable surface coatings, I believe—*not* in micro-electronics. And you don't have an actual working model to show me. But never mind. I'm going to give you a name and address, and a note to take with you. The man I am sending you to is a·venture capitalist. He may decide to risk some money, and find you a partner to take care of the ten thousand business details you've never dreamed of. If he says "yes," come back.' "

Q: "Did he say 'yes'?"

A: "Luckily."

Q: "But, now, you're saying Detroit can't beat the imports, or what?"

A: "I'm saying the whole fight so far is a waste of effort. We need a new product."

Q: "Why don't *you* make it?"

A: "I'm an innovator, not a businessman. I see the technical part, but that's all."

Q: "Why not get the government to help?"

A: "The government wants to keep Detroit afloat. What I want is a car that's not another dinosaur."

Honolulu, January 14. Jacob L. Arnow, the American financier, today ceded control of the Interislands Restaurant and Hotel chain to Oceanasian Development, a foreign-dominated investment organization believed to be controlled by Setsui Tamizake, head of NKF Auto Industries. Mr. Tamizake, reached in Tokyo, refused comment on his role in Oceanasian Development, but said, "Arnow is just a drop in a receding American financial sea. He should have seen this, and his losses would have been smaller."

San Francisco, January 15. Jacob Arnow, the financier, was questioned here by reporters as he debarked from the *Islands Belle*:

> **Q:** "Mr. Arnow, did you hear what Tamizake said about you?"
> **A:** "I care more about what he did to me."
> **Q:** "Is it true that you lost ten million dollars?"
> **A:** "That's none of your d—d business."
> **Q:** "What's your answer to Tamizake?"
> **A:** "I won't answer him in words."
> **Q:** "Mr. Arnow—"
> **A:** "Out of my way."
> **Q:** "Mr. Arnow, why did you come back by boat instead of a plane?"
> **A:** "To think over something I saw in the paper."

Washington, January 17. Renewed concern is being expressed here over the size of the Federal budget. And inflation appears to be accelerating again.

Zurich, January 18. The dollar resumed its vertical fall today, on word of lower interest rates in the U.S.

Washington, January 19. Dr. H. Walter Schoen, new head of the Federal Reserve Board, denied that he intends to lower interest rates. "To assure a stable dollar," said Dr. Schoen, "it is essential to maintain realistic interest rates above the rate of inflation."

Zurich, January 21. The dollar rebounded today on news of higher U.S. interest rates ahead.

New York, January 21. Panic struck Wall Street on word of another jump in interest rates. The Dow-Jones Industrial Average plunged thirty-eight points to a new low of 396.

Detroit, January 23. Frank B. Service, head of troubled Colossal Motors, today blasted "chaotic conditions in the financial markets" for the continuing problems facing CM. "How," Mr. Service demanded, "are we supposed to plan ahead? You can't borrow money without going broke paying the interest. You can't sell stock to raise money, because the stock market has turned into some kind of city dump. If you've got foreign subsidiaries, you have to juggle dollars, pounds, francs, marks, and yen, and you don't know what any of them will be worth three months from now." Explaining a new wave of firings, layoffs, and plant closings, Mr. Service said, "It's the only way to stay in business. We just can't ignore the bottom line."

Tokyo, January 31. A delegation of Japanese businessmen is reported to have prevailed upon outspoken NKF head, Setsui Tamizake, to change his speech before the Asia-America Friendship Society. Mr. Tamizake's original speech is rumored to have contained the words, "to America belongs the past, and to us the future." In his revised welcoming speech today, Mr. Tamizake said, "We of Asia honor the great deeds of America's past, and aim to build our future upon heights you have known before." Mr. Tamizake then took the delegates on a tour of the gigantic NKF Auto Industries Main Plant.

Silicona, Calif., February 16. Edwin Storch, inventor of the lattice-channel-junction technology and chairman of LCJ Corporation, today confirmed rumors that he met recently with financier Jacob Arnow. Asked the reason, Mr. Storch replied, "Oh, Jake and I like to go fishing together."

New York, February 17. Financier Jacob Arnow, questioned about a possible venture with hard-coatings and microelectronics wizard Edwin Storch, admitted contacting Storch last month. Rumor has it that the two men discussed producing a new type of car. Arnow refused comment on these rumors.

Detroit, February 17. Auto industry officials here discount rumors of a new car. "If anyone could do it," said one auto executive, "CM would do it. Their new Z-Car is first-rate, but in this economic climate, it doesn't sell. A newcomer would be wiped out."

Washington, April 20. The Administration is reported putting pressure on the Federal Reserve to bring down sky-high interest rates.

Geneva, April 21. The dollar plunged again on fresh rumors of a drop in U.S. interest rates.

★ ★ ★

Washington, June 20. Word is circulating here that the latest economic figures are unusually bad.

Seraloa, July 1. The Quarterly Conference on Oil Price Readjustment today announced a price increase of fifteen dollars a barrel. Abu Sinkad Selou, chairman of the conference, warned, "The wasteful oil-consuming states must control their appetites." Chairman Selou also announced agreement on a new cut in oil production, "to save our irreplaceable resources."

Washington, July 2. Well-informed sources here warn of serious consequences if the renewed sharp oil-price increases continue.

Salambang, July 15. During a press conference, Seroo Seleen Tarabanda, oil-state firebrand and this month's price-adjustment chairman, jeered at rumors from Washington of possible "serious consequences" to new price increases: "If they had the power to dare to create 'serious consequences,' they would create serious consequences. If they had even the possibility, they would deliver a plain warning, publicly or in private to us. They do not possess even the possibility. So they make rumors. This is to soothe their simpleminded public. Confused, are they not?"

Washington, July 20. Recent comments by Seroo Seleen Tarabanda, chairman of this month's Oil Price Readjustment Conference, have hit this city like a pan of dishwater over the head. Senator Graham G. Young, chairman of the Foreign Affairs Committee, seems to express the general reaction: "You put enough heat on any explosive situation, and it's likely to blow up in your face. Tarabanda has now lit the fire."

Salambang, July 31. Seroo Seleen Tarabanda, Chairman of the new Monthly Conference on Oil Price Readjustment, defiantly announced "an initial monthly price adjustment of thirty-five dollars a barrel, 'to make up in advance for decreased purchases by the oil wasters.'" Many delegates are reported to have protested the increase, but to have been voted down.

Washington, August 1. Senator Graham Young of the Foreign Affairs Committee met this morning with the President, reportedly over the latest oil price increase. The senator is believed to have urged strong action, including military measures, if necessary.

Moscow, August 2. The Soviet Union today warned that "any interference" with the oil states "will be crushed."

London, August 4. There are persistent rumors here of a new U.S. weapon, due to be tried out on whoever raises oil prices the highest. Fantastic though the rumors seem, usually reliable sources believe there is substance of some sort behind it.

Norfolk, August 7. The newly formed U.S. Second Fleet is being fitted with what are spoken of as "normal weapons improvements." Spokesmen denied rumors of new weapons.

Washington, August 8. The President, in his news conference, refused to confirm or deny the truth of rumors of a new weapon.

★ ★ ★

Paris, August 10. Surprisingly detailed reports are said to have reached French naval circles of an American device which "essentially reproduces Archimedes's sunweapon." The American weapon, according to these reports, involves a tremendous concentration of the sun's rays, by means of metallized film. The U.S. Embassy here has dismissed the rumors as "pipe-dreams, pure humbug."

Oil City, Sultanate of Tazar, August 16. Intense nervousness is evident here, in the light of recent rumors. Seroo Seleen Tarabanda, fire-brand head of last month's price meeting, is extremely unpopular here. A typical reaction was that of Abu Said Ha'ak, a leading politician: "Tarabanda would stick pins in a tiger to prove he is dead, and thereby wake him up. Would it have cost him money to be polite?"

Zurich, August 16. Dr. Heinz Bittendorfer, world-renowned economist, refused today to predict the outcome of the present world economic situation. "It is a hive of enraged bees. Who can say what will happen?"

Washington, August 16. The Defense Department revealed today that the heavily reinforced Second Fleet has entered the Mediterranean. Asked why, a spokesman replied, "To maintain the peace."

Moscow, August 16. In a strongly worded statement, the Soviet Union warned that "any imperialist interference with peace-loving nations will be crushed with an iron fist." Moscow is rumored to have sixteen divisions of airborne troops ready to move "at a moment's notice."

Oil City, Sultanate of Tazar, August 18. Tazar today announced a fifteen-dollar-a-barrel discount in its oil price. The Tazar foreign office earnestly denied asking for Soviet or U.S. protection, saying, "So far as we know, the peace here is not in any danger. We just want to live quietly."

Sabadang, Golduhar, August 20. The Sheikh of Sabadang today cut the Sheikhdom's oil price by twenty dollars a barrel, "for competitive reasons."

Washington, August 21. Most Congressmen report that their constituents show no gratification at the recent drop in oil prices. "They're mad," said Congressman Nicholas Veale, "and they're waiting for some new stunt."

Paris, August 28. As yet, no sign has been found of Seroo Seleen Tarabanda, oil-state firebrand who arrived here during a visit earlier this month. Police spokesmen offer little hope for his safety. "We are not the only ones looking for him. We are just the only ones he can afford to be found by."

New York, September 15. The prime rate dipped today. It is now below thirty percent at most major New York City banks.

Washington, October 1. The steep drop in oil prices is reported to have had little impact in lowering inflation, as the drop merely cancels the preceding steep increases.

Detroit, November 2. Frank B. Service, president of Colossal Motors, today held a news conference at which he announced the first of the new "Q" cars. "With gas again below $5.50 a gallon," said Mr. Service, "we expect the consumer back in the marketplace." Mr. Service admitted that this has not happened yet.

Tokyo, December 15. Setsui Tamizake, outspoken head of giant NKF Auto Industries, has admitted to a falling off of sales, though NKF has further increased its market share. Mr. Tamizake suggested no reason for the sales decline.

Bernhardt, Minn., December 20. Professor Charles Arden of the Bernhardt World Analysis Clinic today reported "recent studies conducted by the Clinic indicate an 'oil psychosis' that is becoming worldwide. There has been so much trouble from oil that people are actually becoming sick of it." Dr. Arden also reported that studies carried out for auto manufacturers suggest that the automobile itself has acquired a negative image. "People now equate the auto with Expense, Breakdown, Recalls, Pollution, Inflation, Shortages, and Waste. This isn't encouraging for an early upturn in car sales."

Zurich, January 4. Dr. Heinz Bittendorfer, world-renowned economist, warned today that the world may be slipping into a deep depression. "In present circumstances, a depression is only too possible. We have very high interest rates, continuing inflation, tight credit, and extremely high fuel prices. There is, moreover, the *feel* of a depression. There is a sullenness, a grayness. I think that is it, a depression. And I do not know the cure."

New York, January 5. Financier Jacob Arnow, in a rare appearance on Wall Street, was questioned by reporters about the statements of Dr. Heinz Bittendorfer, the renowned Zurich economist:

Q: "Is Bittendorfer right?"

A: "I'm not an economist."

Q: "You're a financier, aren't you? Isn't that the same?"

A: "They have theories. We're stuck with the reality."

Q: "You've got an opinion?"

A: "Who hasn't?"

Q: "Stop stalling. Is Bittendorfer right?"

A: "Look at the papers. Where's the Dow-Jones Industrials? 316 yesterday, wasn't it? What do you need an economist for? Sure we're in a depression. What else could it be?"

Q: "Since you're a financier, isn't it your job to get us out of it?"

A: "You're a newsman. Is it your job to get me good news?"

Q: "You know what I mean. *Isn't* it?"

A: "Well, the government isn't paying me for it. My first job is to make money, or I wouldn't be a financier very long."

Q: "What about the new car?"

A: "No comment."

Q: "Bittendorfer doesn't know how to end a depression. Do you?"

A: "Yes, and so do you. So does Bittendorfer. You end a depression when people see something worth so much more than what it costs that it starts the money flowing again."

Q: "How can something be *worth more* than it costs? Isn't everything 'worth' what it costs?"

A: "No. That's just the price. The worth of the thing is different. If something will do a lot more for you than the money it costs, the odds are you'll find some way to buy it. When things generally are worth more than their prices, and people realize it, they'll buy, and enough of that will end any depression. You start with bargains."

Q: "What's stopping it from happening now?"

A: "Look where the oil price is. Look at the interest you have to pay if you borrow money. Look at the price they put on the Q car they were sure would sell. Look around, and you tell me where there's a bargain anywhere in this high-price place."

Q: "How about the stock market?"

A: "Sure, once we come out of this mess, this will have been a great time to buy. Meanwhile, it *could* go down another hundred points. Hop right in, why don't you?"

Q: "If you know so much, why don't *you* end it?"

A: "No comment."

Q: "*Can* a so-called financier end it?"

A: "*If* he finds the right innovator."

Sabadang, Golduhar, February 24. The Sheikh today refused to lower prices by the additional $2.50 per barrel reported of other producers. "I do not need more dollars," the Sheikh is reported to have said. "If they will not buy at this price, I will cap the wells. The oil, once burnt, is gone forever. They can print endless dollars. Therefore, the oil is worth more than the money."

Washington, June 11. The Administration today reported that the Armed Forces are at last up to full strength. The economy is so bad there are still plenty of volunteers looking for at least some job. In the words of the Treasury Secretary, "We are in a stagflated depression, and I don't see which way is out."

★ ★ ★

New York, August 25. The Dow-Jones Industrial Average slid fractionally below 300 today, then rebounded, to close at 302.46. (See our special article, page D4.—"Can It Go Lower Than Zero?")

Skogosh, Wisconsin, September 29. There has been a small business here for years that has produced a type of ultra-tough resin for specialty use in industry. As the economy has declined, orders for this resin have *increased*. The small shop has gradually expanded, at the urging of its customers, and now employs over two hundred and fifty persons. The owner cannot explain why orders have increased. Today he received a huge new order and must expand again to keep up.

Washington, October 15. The latest Economic Conference has ended in another blind alley. This time, not even a report is to be issued.

Zurich, October 21. Dr. Heinz Bittendorfer, world-renowned economist, announced today that, after a careful computerized study lasting more than six months, "No way out of the Stagpression exists. Everything is too well balanced on a low level. I cannot explain it to the layman. To the scientifically educated, I would suggest the comparison of entropy. We are falling economically to a state of maximum entropy."

New York, October 21. The stock market today collapsed 29.79 points, to a new low at 181.86.

New York, October 22. Financier Jacob Arnow today called a news conference to announce the production of a new vehicle, the "Star," named from a combination of the first letters of inventor Edwin Storch's name and that of Mr. Arnow. Arnow also stated—and he insisted that he was serious—that the bottom of the economic cycle has now been reached. Mr. Arnow claimed that the Star vehicle "will lead the way upward in an economic advance possibly equal to that following World War II." He then answered questions put to him by skeptical reporters:

Q: "Mr. Arnow, don't you have any model, or at least some pictures, of this new car?"

A: "We're keeping the details secret."

Q: "Why?"

A: "It's a new concept."

Q: "Does it run on wheels?"

A: "Yes."

Q: "Does it have an engine in it?"

A: "Ye-es."

Q: "Does the engine run on gas or oil?"

A: "No comment."

Q: "What's so new about it?"

A: "It will get over a hundred and forty miles to the gallon in favorable conditions."

Q: "What are favorable conditions?"

A: "Good weather."

Q: "What's that got to do with it?"

A: "It takes fuel to run the heater in cold weather."

Q: "Are you serious?"

A: "Of course, why not?"

Further questioning drew no more information from Mr. Arnow.

New York, October 22. On first word of the Arnow interview, the stock market rose five points. (See "Interview" on page D2.) When the full interview became known, the stock market fell twenty points. (See "Disaster," page A1.)

Silicona, Calif., October 23. Inventor Edwin Storch today backed up the claim of financier Jacob Arnow that the two men are producing a new vehicle named the Star:

Q: "Are you, or aren't you?"

A: "Yes, it's in production. And 'Star' is the name. It fits. In more ways than one."

Q: "Where are you building it?"

A: "I said it's in production. I didn't say we're building it."

Q: "How do you produce it without building it?"

A: "No comment."

Q: "Is this going to be just as uninformative as Arnow's interview?"

A: "Probably."

Q: "Why? The whole country's waiting for the answer! Are you serious, or are you kidding?"

A: "Serious."

Q: "Then why are you stalling?"

A: "You want a serious answer?"

Q: "Yes."

A: "To give Jake Arnow time."

Q: "Time?—For what?"

A: "He's a financier. If you can't deduce what he wants time for, you're not reporters."

Q: "He's—You're saying he's *buying stock?* That doesn't—"

A: "He's assembling control of the public companies we'll need to go into large-scale production. That's *his* special skill, not mine."

Q: "Can he do it?"

A: "He thinks so. That's enough for me."

Q: "What's new about this car?"

A: "He's told you."

Q: "Good gas mileage?"

A: "Excellent mileage."

Q: "The imports get good mileage."

A: "You haven't seen anything yet."

Q: "What's revolutionary about this thing?"

A: "The power plant."

Q: "This 'Star' will beat the imports?"

A: "It will do more than that."

Q: "You're not convincing *us*. You won't convince the public. Where's a model?"

A: "We've got them coming off the line, but the purpose is testing, not sale as yet."

Q: "Where is this line?"

A: "We'll explain that later."

This was all the information Mr. Storch would reveal. There have been no known models, no photographs, and no real explanations. Both Arnow and Storch appear serious. Both have formidable reputations in their fields. The consensus of reporters who heard them is that either they are bluffing for some unknown reason, or are actually onto something so big that they feel no need to explain.

Meanwhile, the Stagpression goes on.

Tokyo, October 23. Asked about the rumors from America, NKF head Setsui Tamizake replied, "It's a nice dream, but it isn't possible. We have the best, and we improve constantly. Even *our* sales are slow."

★ ★ ★

Detroit, October 24. CM today began recalling workers to its "A" car production plant.

New York, October 24. Auto, steel, and rubber shares rose here today from the opening bell without a break. No-one has an explanation.

Silicona, October 25. A caravan of trucks today pulled into the huge Storch LCJ lot, crossed one by one to a loading dock covered by an enormous tent, and backed inside. The truck convoy is being guarded by the state highway patrol.

London, October 26. Observers here are convinced something is astir in the United States. A heavy flow of investment funds to the U.S. is reported.

Detroit, October 27. More workers are being recalled to the "A" production line.

Detroit, October 27. The head of a California truck convoy reached the main CM plant at 4:12 this afternoon under heavy guard.

Detroit, October 30. Representatives of major U.S. banks are reported meeting today in the main CM plant.

New York, November 1. The stock market continued its vertical rise, passing the 400 level.

Detroit, November 3. The "A" line here is being lengthened. It is reported that the truck convoy carried equipment to add to the line at crucial points.

★ ★ ★

New York, November 4. A financial reporter has managed to obtain access to information regarding stock market operations of persons believed acting for financier Jacob Arnow. This information reveals heavy purchases, at recent severely depressed prices, of shares in the giant automaker, CM; in suppliers of parts for CM; in certain chemicals manufacturers; in manufacturers of road-building equipment, tire manufacturers, and related companies; in many almost-bankrupt auto supply firms, and in some actually in bankruptcy. Arnow evidently sold, earlier, large holdings of oil stocks. The result is that he appears to have built up an integrated auto-building empire, in some respects almost comparable to Henry Ford's in the early nineteen-hundreds.

Tokyo, November 17. Giant NKF Auto Industries today reported a strong sales increase in the last month, outside of the U.S. NKF president Tamizake explained, "We have benefited from the American news reports. People hear of an economic upturn coming, and feel they can buy a car now. Naturally, they buy the best car at the best price—ours. Except for the Americans. Out of patriotism, they are hoping CM and Arnow will come through, somehow. Personally, I doubt it."

Detroit, November 18. The first Detroit-built "Star" automobile rolled off the "A" assembly line at the CM main plant here at 10:01 this morning. A dark-green compact front-wheel-drive station wagon, with reclining front and folding rear seats, this car did not look like a revolutionary vehicle to watching reporters. But in the brilliant autumn sunlight, Frank B. Service, president of

CM, walked across the huge freshly surfaced parking lot to the car, removed the cap from the fuel tank, thrust in a flexible measuring rod, and drew it out still dry, show- ing that the tank was empty. He next took from an assis- tant a *one-pint can*, took the top off with a Swiss pocket knife, and handed the can around amongst the reporters. What was in the can looked and smelled like ordinary twenty-weight motor oil. Mr. Service emptied this can into the tank, and slid into the front seat. The car made no starting noise, but merely *slid forward silently*, with a faint crunching sound of occasional dirt particles under the tires. Mr. Service twisted the steering wheel, tied it with a short length of cord, apparently to a grab bar on the passenger's side, and jumped out. At last report, five hours after starting, the "Star" car is still circling silently.

Detroit, November 19. The only noticeable change in the Star vehicle, after twenty-two hours, is that the finish seems to have grown darker in the sunlight, eerily match- ing the dark surface of the newly refinished lot. The car now looks an intense jet-black, unusual in that it is a very flat finish without noticeable reflection. Nothing has been added to the fuel tank since that first pint of what looked like motor oil.

Detroit, November 20. The Star is still circling. The only change since it was started has been an occasional correction in the steering by a smiling workman stationed here for the purpose.

New York, November 21. Inventor Edwin Storch today announced further details of the Star's sales plan. The news conference, attended also by European and Asian reporters, revealed several staggering surprises, including the vehicle's price, announced by Mr. Storch:

A: "We're pricing it from about $5,000. The standard model will be $4,999 before taxes."

Q: "What?"

A: "Five thousand dollars apiece—for the standard vehicle in the A-body style. We have plans for a later Star of our own design, which will probably sell for $8,000 to start.—Later, we hope to lower the price."

Q: "Did you say *five* thousand for the A-body car?—Which is loaded with new technology?"

A: "Right."

Q: "How can you afford it?"

A: "First, volume production. Orders are pouring in from all over the world. Second, a rise in the value of the dollar. Third, a special road-surface program that will proceed at the same time as the car sales."

Q: "Why should the dollar go up?"

A: "Auto exports. Lower oil imports. We expect Star sales to directly cut into oil sales."

Q: "Because the Star uses less fuel! Wait, now—They can just cut oil production, again, and charge the same amount!"

A: "No. We no longer need their oil."

After the shouting died down, Mr. Storch continued:

A: "We no longer need gas for auto fuel. Our own production will handle other uses. Therefore, oil prices are going down. If they want us to buy, they'll have to compete with our own production."

Q: "The road-surface program you mentioned —What's that?"

A: "A special reinforcement and surface treatment. We'll offer it to every city, state, village, county, and town, at a reasonable profit. At first, we expect to suffer a loss on our vehicle sales; but once enough of our vehicles are in use, we expect to sell the surface program all over the country, and, in time, all over the world."

Q: "How do you figure that?"

A: "Cars are owned by adults. Adults vote. Where they don't vote, they still make their desires felt in one way or another."

Q: "Where's the gimmick?"

A: "Long-term, the cars won't run reliably without the road surface treatment. Because what we're selling rests on two related products. First, a greatly improved storage battery. Second, a photoreactive coating capable of being applied by molecular spray, using a special process to form, in effect, a complete layer of photocells on the auto's surface. The car is then constantly absorbing light and charging its battery. But suppose you exceed its capacity?"

Q: "Yes. How does this road treatment help?"

A: "We lay down this same general kind of surface *on the road itself*. Embedded in the surface are thin strips that define the lanes for cars equipped to sense the strips; all Star models come equipped with the sensors."

Q: "You are saying the road becomes, in effect, an *endless series of photocells?*"

A: "Why not? Why waste all that road surface? There are two-, four-, and six-lane highways roasting in the sun with hardly any traffic a good part of the year, or a good part of the day for almost all year. The problem is to accumulate that energy. Another problem is to *transfer* energy throughout the system. Why have people stranded in Montana and overflowing with unused energy in New Mexico? Once there's a continuous road surface from one region to another, the transmission layer helps equalize that available energy. The entire hard-surfaced road net accumulates, stores, and transfers energy to vehicles using the net."

Q: "Won't the traffic wear the surface off? It'll be all over the road."

A: "Star cars sense the location strips, and spend most of the time in readily predictable lanes."

Q: "So—You'll sell the vehicles at $5,000, say. Then, when there are enough sold in any given territory, your customers will vote for an improved road surface locally?"

A: "Now you have it."

Q: "And when adjacent sections are joined, the energy will flow from one section to another?"

A: "Yes."

Q: "What about *trucks?*"

A: "We expect the first Star truck to come off the line in about six months."

Q: "This surfacing material is a paint?"

A: "No, it's a durable surface layer, laid down by a series of precision spray deposition devices. It is a complex layer with an exceedingly durable surface."

Q: "*Durable?*"

A: "Yes. But not everlasting."

Q: "So it has to be replaced, patched, or refinished, from time to time?"

A: "Correct."

Q: "How does this work in the north, with road salt, snow plows, and so on?"

A: "The photocell, storage, and transmission layers work, though of course there's much less energy accumulation than on clear roads in summer. Bear in mind, we intend to be coating the road surface, making the tires, and building the cars. Every part fits together. It can be done a lot easier with unified design of all components."

Q: "Those first Star cars we couldn't find? What were they?"

A: "Conversions of conventional cars, for test purposes."

Q: "That pint of oil, or fuel, in the tank of the first 'A' Star car? What did it need fuel for, anyway?"

A: "The car has a small emergency engine, in addition to our type of storage battery. If we'd needed it, we'd have started the generator."

Q: "Why do you need a generator?"

A: "Some people live on dirt roads. Our layer won't work on a dirt road. There are also going to be places not yet joined up to other parts of the country. How do you charge the battery? You can't rely for sure on the local utility. It may already be overloaded. That's the purpose of the engine. In emergencies, you start it up, and *it* charges the battery."

Q: "So the fuel cost—"

A: "In ideal circumstances, the fuel cost is nil. Eventually the battery will have to be replaced. The car surface is durable, and with reasonable care should last indefinitely. The road surface is also durable, but subject to wear, and will have to be redone at intervals, depending on usage."

Q: "I still don't follow how you charge this battery, unless you run the car's own generator."

A: "If your local utility isn't overloaded, you connect the car to a battery charger overnight. We have a special charger you can buy, if you want."

Q: "This is only till the roads are resurfaced?"

A: "Right."

Q: "The sun shines on the road, but how does the energy get from the road to the car?"

A: "In the right circumstances, at slow speeds, we can recharge the car on the road. We can theoretically do this at high speeds, but there are complications. What we expect is a chain of charging stations on or near the highways, possibly based on an arrangement with the present oil-company filling stations, which will receive the energy from the transmission strips, and quick-charge the battery for a fee. I might also mention our Star-lite conversion."

Q: "What's that?"

A: "Photolayered roof and siding panels for garage and, perhaps, house use."

Q: "Why 'perhaps'?"

A: "Not everyone wants a flat-black house."

Q: "It will charge the battery?"

A: "Right."

Q: "You're not planning to run the electric utilities out of business?"

A: "We expect to cut into their business in some ways, and increase it in other ways. The overall effect for their customers and ours is lower energy costs."

Q: "Resurfacing is where you expect to make the real profit?"

A: "Right. Bear in mind, if you've got a well-made road, our surface layer increases its durability, to lengthen the life of the road."

Q: "Where it works, then, you derive your energy directly from the sun—Which, incidentally, is a star!"

A: "Yes. That's another reason for the name."

★ ★ ★

Oil City, Sultanate of Tazar, November 23. Tazar today slashed its oil price all the way to twenty-one dollars a barrel.

Zurich, November 24. The dollar strengthened dramatically against all major currencies, as word reached here that work is already beginning to convert the gigantic U.S. road net into a nationwide solar-conversion plant.

San Francisco, November 29. Setsui Tamizake, dynamic head of ailing NKF Auto Industries, arrived here today to seek licensing agreements for the deposition-photocell process. A smiling Jacob Arnow met Mr. Tamizake at the airfield.

Honolulu, November 30. Some liquidation of foreign holdings is reported under way here, to help raise money for the licensing fees on the Star photocell process. One property reported to have changed hands was the Interislands Restaurant and Hotel chain, believed sold by Oceanasian Development to Jacob Arnow.

San Francisco, December 3. Setsui Tamizake, dynamic head of ailing NKF Auto Industries, left today for Tokyo, looking somewhat pale, but carrying the necessary licensing agreements for the deposition-photocell process. A genial Jacob Arnow accompanied Mr. Tamizake to the airport.

Silicona, Calif., December 17. Edwin Storch, inventor of the deposition-photocell process, was cornered by reporters on the way to his car in the newly photosurfaced company lot:

Q: "Mr. Storch, will this boom in Star vehicles last?"

A: "We think so, because it's an honest bargain. Meanwhile, we're making the pilot model of a still more durable vehicle with especially useful features."

Q: "If your car is too durable, there go your replacement sales."

A: "I got a little tired of cars wearing out every three years, didn't you? The idea is to give solid value, not plant a suction pump in the customer's wallet."

Q: "You'll cut your bottom line, won't you?"

A: "We haven't forgotten the bottom line. But there's another line you don't want to forget, either."

Q: "What's that?"

A: "The bottom line is the gain *you* get. The top line is *the gain you deliver in return*. If you provide the customer with a buy well worth having, you've taken care of the top line. That doesn't guarantee a profit, but Ford, Edison, Bell, Land, and a host of others have done right by the top line, and everyone was better off because of it. Naturally, the bottom line is important. But there needs to be something on the *top* line first!"

★WAR...★

IDEOLOGICAL DEFEAT
★ ★ ★

Arakal, King of the Wesdem O'Cracy's, got up early on the day of the Soviet ambassador's visit, finished his exercise at the Post, studied the latest plot brought up to date by Colputt's flasher, and then met with the Council.

Easing into the luxurious armchair at the head of the table, with the white-bearded Colputt to his left and broad trusty Slagiron to his right, Arakal once again got stuck in the side by the double-beaked, two-headed bird that adorned the hilt of his sword, the scabbard being guided in the wrong direction by the support for the left arm of the chair.

"This meeting," Arakal began, as he reached down and got the beak of the bird out of his flesh, "will now begin. In case anyone hasn't seen the plot this morning, the Kebeckers are as good as their word, and the Brunswickers are going along with them. The St. Lawrence is watched from the coast in, the armies are ready to move, and Kebeck Fortress is reinforced. I've sent word by flasher that if the Russ make a lodgment anywhere on the south bank of the river, we will help take them. If they try to get Kebeck Fortress, we will cross the river west of the fortress, and hit the Russ from behind."

There was a murmur of approval.

Arakal got the sword situated, and sat back in the chair.

To Colputt's left, Smith, Colputt's shrewd assistant, turned respectfully to Arakal. "By your leave—?"

"Yes, Smith?"

"We've got the night-flasher working."

There was a general stir. Across the table, young Beane, stuck handling the foreign diplomats, looked surprised.

"But I thought that was *impossible!*" He glanced at Arakal. "Beg pardon, sir."

Arakal nodded. "Go ahead. I've said my say."

Smith said, "Old Kotzebuth had us thinking it was impossible, but we decided to try it anyway. It works. Of course, the sun has set, and we have to spend some oil. But it works."

Slagiron's broad face creased in a grim smile. He said nothing, but Arakal had a good idea what he was thinking. The Russ prided themselves on their superior communications.

Further down the table, Casey, Slagiron's chief organizer, growled hopefully, "Will this work in bad weather?"

Smith shook his head. "Fog, snow, or rain blots out the flash."

"The Russ," said Casey, "can talk to each other almost *any* time."

"Well, they're using Old Stuff."

"That doesn't help us any. If we've got a bunch of them cut off, what do they do but yell for help, and here comes one of their damned iron birds, or a rescue force on wheels." He turned to Colputt. "We've got to do something about their long-talkers."

"Radios," nodded Colputt. "We've got a crew working on it, and I think we're finally getting a grip on the thing. Now, don't misunderstand me, I don't say we will *ever* be able to make long-talkers the equal of what the Russ have. But we should be able to do three things: First, we should be able to set up our own long-talkers to help out the flasher network. Second, we should be able to listen in on what the Russ say. Third, we should be able to turn out portable garblers to block their long-talkers. That is, they could still yell for reinforcements, but all that could be heard on the other end would be garble."

"That would all help."

Arakal said, "Anything would be an improvement. But why should we have to take second place? You're as smart as any of their men—probably smarter. Smith here is as shrewd as any they have to offer. Why must they be in front of us?"

Colputt shook his head sadly. "Old Stuff. They have more Old Stuff than we have. Captured radios have been turned over to me, and we've studied them, thinking to make our own, but to no use. We can't begin to work out the way they're made. The trouble is, the Old Soviets got in a fight with the Old O'Cracy's, and the Russ threw more stuff, did more damage, got the edge on the O'Cracy's. I don't say they won. But they did more damage. They have more Old Stuff left over. Long-talkers, iron birds, power sailers. We were knocked off our perch entirely. They had enough left over to use it still. Some of it, even, they may know how to make again. Not the long-talkers. But other things. They threw *us* back so far that I can look at the latest of our old books about radios, and see the words in front of me, and read them, and not know what they mean. That shows how far we were thrown back."

"Then," frowned Arakal, "this special crew you set up—"

"Ah," said Colputt, beaming, "that's different. We go at it now from the other end. We use the *oldest* of the old books—those we *can* understand. And we're working our way forward. The Russ, now, have their stocks of Old Stuff. Very useful. But, when it *runs out*—"

Slagiron looked at Colputt, smiling. "You aim to have a position you can *hold*?"

Colputt nodded, and his eyes glinted.

Arakal glanced at the clock on the wall. "This ambassador of theirs gets here when?"

Beane said, "Shortly before the sun is at full height, sir." He craned to look at the clock. "Another three hours, say."

"What is this one like?"

Beane shook his head. "The same as the rest."

"He is on safe conduct, of course?"

"Yes, sir. Worse luck. But he wouldn't come without it."

"There is always a chance of treachery—*either* way. Have all your precautions ready. Does this one talk English, or—"

Beane brightened a little. "There is *that* difference. This one does talk English. Of course, when he talks—"

"Let your translator take a place amongst the guards. Who knows? He might overhear something."

Beane nodded, smiling.

"Yes, sir. But I think they learned that lesson the last time."

Vassily Smirnov, Ambassador-General, glanced uneasily at Simeon Brusilov, Colony Force Commander, as the helicopter thundered around them.

"Just how safe," said Smirnov, "is a safe conduct from these savages?"

Brusilov said moodily, "Safe enough. As long as you don't look too long at any of their women, sleep with your ears under the covers, or drink anything except water or milk. Watch out for this Arakal. He's smart in streaks."

"What does that mean?"

"He's ignorant in obvious ways, but just overlook that. Where it counts, he's smarter than any of us."

Smirnov frowned. "An odd statement for our own commander to make."

"I say it because I *know*. And I did not enjoy gaining the knowledge."

"And just where *is* he smart?"

"Militarily."

"You flatter yourself. That is *not* what counts. Ideology is what counts in the end. That is why *I* am here."

"It didn't help us much in that last ambush."

"With your technological advantage, I'm surprised the natives dare to ambush your men."

Brusilov shook his head.

"Comrade, kindly get it through your skull that there are *two* technologies on this continent. One is shipped to us packaged and ready to use, but if it goes bad, who is going to fix it? The other is growing up steadily, and knitting the pieces of the continent together, and while it is in every way less impressive than ours, there is much more of it, and it is getting very tricky.

"For instance, there is this sun-signal system. It started in Arakal's sector, and now he's linked up with the descendants of the Canadian survivors. Six months ago, we tried to cut Arakal's zone up the line of the Hudson, preparatory to biting off the whole of the old Northeast United States. The idea was, with that in our hands, we'd have a base suitable for protection of our colonies to the south. Arakal saw the plan in a flash. It was nothing but traps and ambushes, and dead stragglers and small parties yelling for help all the way from the time we hit the Forest.

"But we expected that. What we didn't expect was that an army would come boiling out of Quebec and the old seacoast Provinces, and get to us before we could finish the job. Not too long ago, Arakal would have had to send couriers. Now he uses the sun-signal system. We were lucky to get out of there with a whole skin."

"Certainly the savages' speed of motion is inconsiderable, compared with yours."

"We have the edge there, all right. It's just too bad so much of the road net is centered on the worst zones of lingering radioactivity."

"Is that their camp, there?"

Brusilov looked out, to see a tall steel tower. A gun thrust out and followed the helicopter, but didn't fire.

"That is one of their sun-signal towers. You see, these 'savages' have learned to work steel again."

"You should bomb them—*destroy* them!"

Brusilov looked at the ambassador. "Will *you* increase my shipments of fuel, and bombs, and planes? Will *you* get me more pilots? Do you know what this one trip is costing me in gas, and hence in future freedom of action?" He glanced out. "There is their camp. Try to remember that they are not as stupid as they may seem to you. Backward, yes. Stupid, no."

Arakal shook the hand of Smirnov, smiling gravely but noting the softness of the ambassador's grip. Such was not the grip of the Russ commander. The ambassador was like the rest of their ambassadors, but Brusilov, now, was a good man.

"The great Central Committee," Smirnov began impressively, "sends its greetings to you, despite the fact that your actions have not been of the best."

Brusilov muttered something and removed himself out of earshot, to the far end of the tent. Slagiron excused himself and went over to talk to Brusilov.

"This war," said Smirnov, with the air of an oracle, "costs much money, many lives. It must end."

Arakal smiled pleasantly.

"Then get off the continent."

"This land is ours," said Smirnov, spacing his words, and making his tone deep and impressive.

"Go home," said Arakal brusquely. "*Leave.*"

"Our colonists grow their wheat, plant their trees, speak their tongue, sing their songs. This is our land and belongs to us, just as the land of your tribe belongs to you, so long as we grant it to you."

Arakal gave a low growl of irritation, then looked up as Casey came over. Casey glanced around, apparently for Slagiron.

"Excuse me, Mr. Smirnov," Arakal said. "What is it, Casey? Your chief is over there with Commander Brusilov."

Casey nodded, looked thoughtfully at Smirnov, who was waiting impatiently for the interruption to cease, and then Casey spoke intently to Arakal, seeming somehow to send an additional message along with the spoken words: "Carlo is there."

Arakal's eyes momentarily shut, and he seemed to shiver. Then he drew a deep careful breath.

"I see," he said. "Well, I don't think it's worth bothering your chief with *that*. You can tell him later."

"Yes, sir." Casey smiled, bowed slightly, turned, and left.

Arakal looked at Smirnov blandly.

"Now, Mr. Ambassador, let me explain why you should do as I suggest. The Old O'Cracy's, which is to say the great clan to which we all here belong, once owned *all* the land, that which is good, that which is sick, and that upon which you have planted your colonies. The O'Cracy's once fought at your side long ago, and were mighty warriors, armed by the incomparable wizards who lived at that time. But they grew weary of war, and made fewer magical weapons than the Old Soviets, who in time struck them down. Why, or how this came about, I do not know. That is of the past. Both sides suffered, but that is over. Now, however, the land *was* ours, so it is not stealing when we take it back. It again will be ours, because we are growing stronger much faster than that part of your clan which is over there. This is why you should now get out."

Smirnov looked at Arakal and laughed. "There is not and never was a 'clan' of the O'Cracy's. Your 'knowledge' is a mixture of fables and errors. I suppose that word *O'Cracy* came originally from the word 'dem*ocracy*,' an inferior governmental system which your leaders made much of in the past, before we destroyed them. But never mind that. I will explain to you why you must not only end your rebellion, but must, and will, come to us that your tribe may be lifted by stages into ideological purity and civilized knowledge. And that you may know that my words are indisputable, I will tell you first just who and what I am."

Arakal leaned forward in his seat, as one braces himself into a wind.

Smirnov said, "As you know, the rulers of all the Soviets are known as Party Members, and not just anyone can be a Party Member. Only the child of a Party Member can be a Party Member, except by direct action of the great Central Committee itself. Now, Mr. Arakal, you are sprung out of nothing, and have nothing behind you. But *I* am the child of a Party Member, who was the child of a Party Member, who was the child of a Party Member, and indeed even *I* do not know for how many generations back this may go. You see the difference?"

Arakal's eyes narrowed, and he said nothing.

"You observe," said Smirnov, "that I speak your tongue. You cannot speak my tongue. But I speak yours with ease. It is nothing to me. This is because of my *education.*" He held up his right hand, turned the palm toward Arakal, and made a little thrusting motion of the hand toward Arakal. "Education is to be taught at such an age and in such a way that the knowledge becomes one with the person who is taught. He need make little effort to learn, Mr. Arakal, because he is naturally intelligent, and taught by skilled persons, whose job it is to teach, and to do *nothing else.* Such a thing you have not, but it is mine by right of birth. Those are *two* things we have that you do not have and cannot get without coming to us: One, the Party. Two, Education. But that is not all."

Arakal watched the glint in Smirnov's eyes, and listened to the wasp note in Smirnov's voice.

"Three," said Smirnov, "we have Technology. Let me point out to you, Mr. Arakal—and remember who it is that is pointing it out—that when your ancestors dared to raise their hand against us, the Central Committee gave the word: 'Strip from them all their power and all their technology, that they may never have power again. Because it is only from technology that power comes.' But, in the same order, the Central Committee said, 'See to it that *our* technology is stored, good and plenty, with grease and all the instructions to keep it running.' And so it was done. And our ancestors smashed yours to their knees, and then they kicked them off their knees onto their face, and they smashed your technology, and you can never rebuild it, because you have no Education. You are savages, nothing more, and never can be more, except you come to us to ask for it. Those are *three* reasons, and now there is the fourth, and most important of all."

Arakal pushed his chair back, and took pains to get the swordhead free of the arm of the chair.

"The Party, Education, Technology," said Smirnov, "and then the greatest—Ideology. And it is in this that *I* am an expert. I could have been anything, but I chose this, the most difficult of all—"

Arakal came to his feet.

"It has been interesting to listen to you, Mr. Ambassador."

"I am not through. Sit down."

Behind Arakal, someone drew his breath in sharply.

Arakal didn't move, and there was a sudden hush.

Across the tent, Brusilov came hurrying, his expression harried. Slagiron was right beside him, alert and self-possessed.

Smirnov said irritably, "Sit down, sit down, Arakal."

Brusilov glanced in astonishment at Smirnov.

Smirnov raised his hand and thrust up one finger. "First, the Party." He thrust up another finger. "Second, Education." He thrust up a third finger. "Third, Technology." Each time he put up a finger, he gave his hand a little shake. "And fourth, *Ideology*." He looked at the King of the O'Cracy's. "*Ideology*, Arakal."

Brusilov's jaw fell open.

From behind Arakal came a murmur.

Slagiron's lips tightened and his eyes glinted, but aside from that, there was no play of expression on his face.

Smirnov looked around.

"What's all this? Be seated, the lot of you!"

Brusilov glanced anxiously around.

Arakal could sense his men gathering behind him. Now Brusilov's pilots and guards came running, their hands on their holstered weapons.

Arakal took pains to keep his hands at his sides, though his left hand tilted the scabbard just enough so that he could get his sword out quickly.

The situation got through to Smirnov, who came angrily to his feet.

Brusilov stared at him.

"Mr. Ambassador, what have you—"

"*Bah!*" said Smirnov. "I am trying to teach this savage a minor lesson! *Very* minor! But it is all that is suited to his intelligence! The fools know nothing and so cannot think!"

Slagiron's eyes widened. He glanced at Arakal.

Arakal sensed the opportunity, sucked in his breath and gazed skyward for an instant, imploring guidance. He cleared his throat.

Behind him, there was an ugly murmur, and the clearly perceptible rattle of loosened swords.

Brusilov's men glanced around.

Behind them, more of the O'Cracy's stood ready, their eyes on Arakal, waiting the command.

From above, the words came to Arakal.

He raised his right hand, palm out, and spoke distinctly, and his translator spoke after him in the tongue of the Russ.

"Men of the Russ—go in peace. We have no fight with *you*."

Brusilov exhaled, and glanced at Arakal with suddenly bright eyes. Behind Brusilov, his own men murmured, the sound one of surprise, and relief, and something more.

Arakal looked steadily back at Brusilov, and smiled, admiring the poise and insight of the Russ commander.

Slagiron grinned suddenly, and clapped Brusilov on the shoulder. He said something in his ear, and Brusilov gave his head a little shake, but smiled nevertheless.

Smirnov looked around, his eyes narrowed.

"What's this? Why are they—"

Brusilov abruptly grabbed Smirnov by the arm, and whirled him around.

Arakal shouted, *"You men!* Form an honor guard for the warriors of the Russ!"

All at once, there was a cheer.

Brusilov propelled Smirnov between the lines, and the other Russ hurried along behind. Slagiron and Arakal went to the front of the tent, and watched the Russ climb into their big iron birds.

As they took off, Arakal smiled and waved, and from inside the iron birds, some of the Russ smiled and waved back.

As the helicopter thundered around them, Smirnov spoke furiously.

"You dared to lay your hand on me! And I am a *Party Member of the Fourth Degree!*"

"Mr. Ambassador," said Brusilov shortly, "would you rather have had your head sliced off and rolled around on the floor of that tent?"

"You *touched* me!"

Brusilov opened his mouth and shut it. His gaze seemed to turn inward for an instant, then he took a hard look at Smirnov, his gaze cold and measuring.

Smirnov, staring back, put a hand on the holstered automatic at his side.

Brusilov tensed, then caught himself. For a long moment, he was motionless. Then he gave his head a little shake.

"No," he said. "No, it would be wrong." He looked at Smirnov again, then Brusilov went to a seat across the aisle and sat down, his face set and unresponsive.

Around them, the helicopter thundered, as it carried them above the tower of the O'Cracy's.

Arakal and Slagiron bent intently over the plot.

"So far," said Arakal, "there is no word from the Kebeckers of the Russ fleet entering the river. The Kebeckers say there is no sign of the Russ at all."

"Hm-m-m," said Slagiron "I wonder if they could be going to try the Hudson again—with their main fleet this time."

"In that case, they would be in sight by now. Our lookout on Long Island has seen nothing, and the same word has come in from our boat off the Hook."

"Peculiar. Still, there is a delay in getting word to us."

"True. We get the word quickly from Kebeck Fortress over the flasher, but a runner crosses from Long Island by boat."

Smith cleared his throat apologetically.

"Beg pardon, sir. Just last week, while you were . . . ah . . . working with Carlo, we got the flasher set up across Long Island Sound."

"What? There's a tower there?"

"No, sir, that would be too risky, but the sea is flat, and we can do without towers over that distance. There's still a delay in reports from off the Hook. But from the Sound, in good weather, we get them fast. There was no long delay on this report."

"Good. But now, you see," he said, turning to Slagiron, "that leaves us up in the air. They've sent this new ambassador. This Central Committee is as regular as clockwork. They never send a new ambassador without sending reinforcements, and they never send reinforcements without sending their fleet. Now, we've had the ambassador. Where's the fleet? We want to take that blow on our shield, not on our head."

The door opened briefly, and they heard a rumbling thud, like distant thunder. Arakal looked around, to see Colputt, smiling faintly, hang his coat on a peg and walk over.

"Now they're bombing the conference site," said Colputt.

Arakal smiled. "The more they drop there, the fewer they can dump on our heads. And they bring those things a long distance."

Slagiron shook his head. "This ambassador is their worst yet. If a thing is disastrous, he does it at once. No doubt now his pride has to be soothed."

Colputt added, "*And* their fleet is sighted. We just received word."

"What? *Where?*"

"Penobscot Bay."

Arakal looked at the contoured plot, and the wide deep indentations in the Maine coast.

Colputt went on, "They are landing troops at Bangor. Before the landing, their planes knocked out the flasher tower at Skowhegan."

Slagiron looked at the plot thoughtfully, and glanced at Arakal.

Arakal turned to Smith. "Send word to the Kebeckers. Describe this landing. And tell them *Carlo is ready.*"

Slagiron said, "Will they come?"

"Why not?" said Arakal, looking at the plot, where the markers were already being set down. "Could we ask for more?"

"On the map," said Slagiron, "this will look bad. From Bangor it is only . . . say . . . a hundred and eighty miles to Kebeck Fortress, across the country. The Russ can cut straight for the river, and split us off from the Kebeckers—on the map."

Arakal smiled. "A hundred and eighty miles of *what?* And when the Russ get there, they're on the wrong bank of the river. Meanwhile, their fleet is stuck at Bangor, or coming around by the Gulf, or else it gets there without the troops. Try the Kebeckers, and see what they say."

Brusilov returned the major's salute.

"Sir," said the major, glancing around at the rugged peaks, and swatting at mosquitoes, "that map is either wrong, or we're turned around. There *is* no road. And the sniping is getting worse."

Smirnov spoke up sharply.

"You are a soldier, are you not? You expect to fight in a war, do you not?"

Brusilov spoke coolly, "We aren't lost, Major. Simply assume that the map is right, and cast around for the road. Don't worry. It will be broken up, but it's there."

The major said stubbornly, "The men say this is going to be the Hudson all over again. They don't like it. They are growing hard to manage."

Brusilov smiled soberly and shook his head. "Have them look at this mess of lakes, ponds, and swamps. Did we have anything like this on the march up the Hudson? No." He waved a hand at the cloud of small black flies that, interspersed with occasional mosquitoes, settled on him as soon as he devoted himself to anything else. "So," he said, "it is not the Hudson all over again. This is quite different. Console yourself, my friend. We have variety, at least."

The major looked sullen, but saluted. Then he trudged off up one of the interminable hills over which the road through the heavy forest climbed and plunged.

Brusilov glanced at Smirnov.

"Isn't this far enough? Speaking as a merely military man, devoid of ideological finesse, *I* think this is far enough."

"We must press on," said Smirnov. "Until we are sure the natives are fully committed."

Brusilov shook his head.

"Comrade, in a general way, this plan is not bad; but there are details, and it is the details that will ruin us. Arakal will not react as you expect. You would draw him here by a threat, fall back before him, lure him to the coast, embark, and strike elsewhere. He will not be drawn, however. He *will not take the bait*."

Smirnov smiled in a superior way.

"I know the aboriginal mind. This native leader is without training. He is brave, and has personal presence, but no sense of grand strategy. He is already beaten in the realm of ideas."

"No, he is not." Brusilov frowned and waved away a cloud of the tiny flies. "That is the trouble. He is a master of conflict, in the realm of ideas as elsewhere."

"Look here," said Smirnov, suddenly earnest. "The method by which the fellow's ancestors were beaten was quite simple. We took a little advantage, repeatedly, until we had a big advantage, and at each point the change was too small to stimulate them to action. The records are somewhat confused as to details, but obviously when we had *enough* advantage, *then* we struck. Now, this conflict here is the same thing, except that there is no longer another ideologically able side to oppose our movements. We have now the fruit of the last war, an ideological and technological advantage they can never overcome. Specifically, our speed of movement is faster than theirs. That is enough. It is unbeatable. It is the advantage that will give us everything else."

"I am not sure of it."

Smirnov's earnestness gave out, and he spoke irritably. "You *were* defeated. Your plan was good, but you lacked subtlety. You proceeded straight ahead. 'Cut them up the line of the Hudson!' A good idea. But you were too direct. You should have drawn them elsewhere first."

Brusilov shook his head. "It was their solar flasher that wrecked my plan. They are not aborigines! Aborigines do not *know* of technology. Arakal's people remember what they could do; they know it is possible. They keep thinking, trying to find the way again. It is *that* that distinguishes them from aborigines."

"Well, their solar flasher is what will destroy them now, by decoying their main forces to this place. And it is *our* speed of movement that will then deliver the deciding blow."

"I hope so," said Brusilov. "But where is Arakal?"

Arakal, perspiring in the humid foggy dawn, looked through the precious long-seeing glasses, and noted the lone guard pacing atop the breastworks, on the far side of the canal.

Beside Arakal, Slagiron murmured, "They seem asleep."

Arakal nodded. "They would be flattered to know how many are watching them. They have never had so many of us at once before—though we have traded with them secretly so long they no longer dread us."

Slagiron shut his glass with a snap, and grinned.

"Now, we will find out if all those crisscrossing rivers shown on our maps are obstacles or not. Only let us not be invisibly burned to bits by all the slagged ruins in the vicinity, and we will even see if your plan can work . . . War without blood . . . I doubt it, but it is worth a try."

Arakal glanced around and saluted the Kebecker leader, who beamed and raised his hand. Then Arakal turned to signal to his own cavalry chief.

The cavalryman grinned and took off his hat in a sweeping gesture, then turned and beckoned to the dense woods behind him.

A long line of mounted men in gray emerged from the forest and, at a walk, started down toward the canal. Behind them came teams of oxen dragging long heavy logs, and behind *them* came small groups of infantry, some stripped to their waists, all quiet, and most looking cheerful, as if on some kind of outing.

Atop the breastworks, the sentry halted, turned, and started back. Hypnotized by his routine, he paced methodically, halted again, turned, started back, and suddenly froze. He stared up and down the line of smiling horsemen leisurely approaching the canal, stared at the oxen pulling the logs, looked hard at the infantrymen gaily jumping into the water, and before he could recover, someone called out in his own tongue, making him uncertain for an instant who this army belonged to.

Meanwhile, the infantry swam the canal. In the water, the engineers were taking the ends of the logs as they were rolled down, and pulling them out into the water. The cavalry were swimming their horses across, and soon, if all went well, the guns and catapults could go across on the bridges.

Atop the breastworks, the troops were now banging the stupefied guard on the back, and he himself was starting to grin and laugh, and now shook his head and turned to shout to someone, who climbed up, looked around in amazement, stared in both directions up and down the canal, where the gray uniforms were crossing over, and finally shrugged and spread his hands.

Slagiron murmured his satisfaction, and turned to Arakal.

"You were right. No shots, no advance bombardment, *no attack*, just an *advance*."

"As long as it lasts," said Arakal. "When we hit the garrison at Salisbury, it may be different."

"If we get to Salisbury," said Slagiron, grinning, "we've got the whole colony. They'll have one sweet time getting us out once we get to Salisbury."

"Remember," Arakal warned, "they must be treated like O'Cracy's. They are good hard workers and decent people, and if we treat them right, they will *become* O'Cracy's."

Slagiron nodded. "I have pounded it into the troops. *They* know. I even almost believe it myself now."

Brusilov, half eaten up by bugs, was in a murderous frame of mind. He had three tanks in a bog, half-a-dozen out for repairs, the sniping was continuous and getting worse, and worst of all, the men had no heart for the fight. Smirnov, however, was delighted.

"I would say we are now drawing in the first of Arakal's troops. Would you agree?"

"Hard to say," growled Brusilov.

"All this uproar could not be caused by locals."

"You can't be—" Brusilov frowned at a courier running up the slippery ruts. "What's this?"

The courier, out of breath, saluted and held out a slip of paper.

Brusilov unfolded it, read quickly, and stared at Smirnov.

"What is it?" demanded Smirnov.

Brusilov handed it to him.

Smirnov took it, read it, stiffened, looked up blankly, read it again and, absently fanning at the bugs, stared blankly at the towering hills.

"Impossible. Delaware in the hands of New Brunswick troops. The Army of Quebec on the line of the Nanticoke River. Arakal swinging around to the east of Salisbury. *The whole Maryland-Delaware Colony is lost.* How can it have happened?"

Brusilov said grimly, "I've tried to explain to you not to underestimate Arakal. Well, *now* what do we do?"

Smirnov broke out in a fine perspiration.

"It is *impossible!*" He glanced at Brusilov. "You are the military commander! What is your opinion? This is *your* specialty!"

"Oh, of course. But you are the one with the letter of authority from the Central Committee. Also, *you* have the ideology."

"What would you *advise*?"

"Pull out. Maybe we can still save Carteret, Beaufort, and Florida Colony. We aren't doing any good here."

Smirnov stared into the distance. Suddenly he drew a deep breath.

"It is *impossible* for an unlettered fool who thinks the O'Cracy's fought the Russ with magic wands to win this contest! He has won a chance victory, but he has lost the war!"

Brusilov shook his head wearily. "How do you reason *that*?"

"He has shifted the full strength of this part of the continent to the south, against our colonies. *We* will strike to the north, take Quebec Fortress, open the line of the St. Lawrence, and later strike simultaneously up and down the Hudson to cut off all New England. He has won the Maryland-Delaware Peninsula; but can he hold it, can he pacify it? We will at once warn the other colonies of his atrocities. They must stand in their own defense at once. Meanwhile, *we* will get this burr out of our hide, get this river fortress into our *own* hands!"

"You want the troops back on the ships?"

"*No!* Every last soldier must come *here!* Then send the ships around to come down the St. Lawrence and ferry us across. We will now cut loose from them entirely and march overland!"

Brusilov considered it thoughtfully, and shook his head. "No. Look—"

But Smirnov made an axe-like gesture of the hand, from the shoulder straight out.

"Cut the continent, from the Atlantic to the river line. Wheel south and east, smash all resistance in our path. Cut Arakal loose from his base. Swiftness, speed, decision—and the ignorant tribesman is whipped. In this first fight we will turn our soft soldiers into hardened troops, *veterans*. Then we will see!"

Brusilov stood thinking, his right hand on the flap of his holster. Finally he shrugged, and turned to give the necessary orders.

Arakal reread the message that had come in flashes of light down the line of towers from New England. He looked at Slagiron.

"The Russ are heading for Kebeck Fortress, *overland*." He handed the message to the leader of the Kebeckers, who had just joined them, and whose translator, standing between his chief and Arakal, translated Arakal's comment, then bent over the message and read it in a low voice.

The Kebecker chief glanced at the plot, where the red emblems climbing the green and brown slopes and surrounded by a multitude of small blue markers were now being moved further forward. Then he turned with a slight smile, to give the message back to Arakal.

"*Ça sera un peu difficile pour les Russes*," the Kebecker said, speaking slowly and distinctly, and holding one hand up to silence his translator.

Arakal winced and glanced at the ceiling. It came to him that the Kebecker had somehow learned of the hundreds of hours he, Arakal, had put into a study of the Kebeck tongue, while the depth of winter made campaigning impractical. Arakal had been prepared to forget all about this and rely on the translators, but someone's sense of humor had given away the secret. All winter Slagiron and the others had joked slyly at Arakal's laborious progress, while Arakal, chafing at the depths of linguistic incapacity revealed to him with each day's effort, nevertheless had refused to give up. Determinedly good-natured, he replied, "While you pass the winter in perfumed idleness, *I* am laying the groundwork for the future. If we are going to clout the Russ in the springtime, one of us, at least, ought to understand the Kebeckers' chief. He has shrewd ideas, but the translators are no military geniuses, and now and then they miss the point. And it is up to us to solve it somehow. You know as well as I do that their chief can't speak a word of English—not that he hasn't at least tried."

Slagiron shook his head. "He *did* memorize that greeting when we got Carlo across the border and went up there for a talk."

Arakal nodded, remembering the incident soberly. "That's what I mean."

Colputt turned to Smith. "Did we ever figure out what he said?"

Smith looked helpless. "Don't ask me. Did you see the looks on the faces of the translators?"

308 *Christopher Anvil*

"In my opinion, it wasn't anything," said Casey. "Neither their talk nor our talk. Just *noise*. It *sounded* like something, but nobody could make it out."

Arakal shook his head. "Our translators explained it to me later. He had *our* words and *his* way of speaking. That's why nobody could follow it. But the translators finally figured it out. What he said was just what we thought he *must* be saying, from his expression. He greeted us, praised Carlo, and looked forward to our future cooperation."

"Hm-m-m," said Slagiron slyly, "but will *you* be able to do as well come next spring?"

Everyone had laughed at that as the snow whipped around the winter camp, and the cold set its teeth into the logs of the buildings.

And now, after the victory over the Russ, Arakal stared at the ceiling, and the Kebecker chief smiled and waited.

Slowly, in Arakal's mind, the meaning evolved: "That will be . . . a little difficult . . . for the Russ."

Arakal thought it through again. Unquestionably, that was what it meant. Now, he avoided glancing at the grinning Slagiron, and trusted to the labors of his Kebeck-born translator. It was a somewhat ambitious reply he had in mind, but he thought he could get it out. He drew a deep breath, then spoke slowly and carefully:

"*Carlo et nous, nous ferons beaucoup des difficultés pour les Russes.*"

Across the room, Arakal's translator winced, but the Kebecker translator looked agreeably surprised.

Arakal laboriously went over it again in his head now that it was out. Surely what he had just said had come out as it was supposed to: "Carlo and we, we will make plenty of difficulty for the Russ."

The Kebecker chief glanced at the ceiling for only a moment, then smiled and nodded.

"*Ah, oui. Carlo et nous.*" He bent over the Plot, and speaking clearly and slowly his meaning came across almost as plainly as if he spoke English.

"Carlo—where does he go in these hills? Will the Russ not find him?"

"No," said Arakal carefully, now suspecting that he had already made one mistake in his first answer. "Carlo is back of those hills. The Russ will not find him. But we will show them what he can do."

Brusilov, though by no means charmed with this plan, was still uncertain whether it might not, after all, turn out to be workable.

Smirnov, now that he had set his mind on a definite idea, proved to have at least one outstanding quality —total ruthlessness.

"Hang them!" he commanded when suspected snipers were brought in. "Leave their bodies dangling as a warning to others! Enough delay for these dogs! Forward! We must go forward!"

Under the lash of his tongue, with the reinforcements pouring in from the ships, the army had begun to move again. Through swamps, streams, rivers, up and down mountains, through dense forest, over a track of a road that had long since ceased to be useful, where the pines and oaks and hemlocks grew ten inches through and had to be felled to make way for the tanks and supply trucks. Through endless snipers, who used guns, and longbows that were worse than guns—whose arrows could pin a man to a tree to wait in shock and despair for the next arrow that would finish him.

But they moved.

And with progress and a definite goal, the troops began to look up. Soon the endless hills would have to grow smaller. Arakal's men, on foot and on horseback, could not hope to return from the South in time.

Now Smirnov's troops were in the swing of the work, their superior weapons and numbers making themselves felt. Sensing victory, they became tougher, would not be stopped, would not be overawed or intimidated. The crafty Arakal was at long last outmaneuvered, and they were the ones who would beat him for good.

Before them, the snipers melted away, to content themselves with picking off stragglers that had fallen behind.

Smirnov grimly urged more speed, and now there was nothing but forest and hills and water and bugs to contend with.

They camped one night in a place where two small rivers came together, to flow away in a larger river to the north. They had lost many of the tanks and quite a number of the trucks, but their spirits were high despite their weariness.

Brusilov listened to Smirnov's prediction.

"My friend," said Smirnov, "this march will go down in world history as a major military stroke."

"If," said Brusilov soberly, "it were not that we will rejoin the ships soon, we would be in serious trouble. Our gas, food, and even ammunition is getting low."

"But we *will* rejoin the ships."

"We could have accomplished the same trip by boarding the ships and being carried there without losses," said Brusilov.

"True, but also without victory. We are conquerors now. And the men know it."

"There is truth in what you say. And yet—"

"And yet?"

"It is hard for me to believe that Arakal is beaten."

Smirnov laughed.

"You have been beaten by him, and so you think he can beat anyone. I have seen deeper than he from the beginning, and beaten him ideologically."

"No. He outmaneuvered you at the meeting. He turned the men against you."

"If so, where is the result now? The men are blooded, tough and determined. The effect of Arakal's cleverness is lost. He has been *out-thought*."

But in the morning, when they tried to cross the river, murderous sheets of fire greeted them.

Brusilov, looking down around the edge of a small boulder, and seeing the burning vehicles, the men spread-eagled in the water and other men who rushed into the stream while still others straggled back from it—Brusilov, seeing this, wormed backwards, dropped down a short slanting bank and ran doubled over toward the center of the camp. The heavy firing, he noticed, was all from in front, none from the rear or flanks.

Quickly, he gave the orders to pull back, then try probing toward the east. They *had* to get to the river, but they could never make it going straight ahead.

Meanwhile, the sniping that had let up a little while ago was worse now than it had ever been. The tanks, in this country, were worthless alone. They could sometimes ride the trees down, but only to make a tangled jumble that was worse than what they had had to contend with in the beginning. A way had to be cleared for them, but who could fell trees in this blizzard of bullets and arrows?

Toward ten o'clock, Brusilov, with the speechless Smirnov in tow, broke through toward the east, then swung northward again toward the river. But in the unending fighting, in the dense roadless forest, the tanks and trucks were an unbearable encumbrance.

Smirnov, finding himself alive, recovered his voice.

"Let us send the armor and transport back the way they came. There, the old road is cleared, and they can escape."

"Where to?" demanded Brusilov. "Back to Bangor?"

"Why not?"

"Do you know what will happen to the men? Remember, you had the suspected snipers hanged and left as a warning. What will the people do now?"

"Our men can overawe them with their weapons."

Brusilov laughed, and gave orders to fire all the remaining ammunition of the tanks in the direction of the enemy and then smash the engines. The trucks he had unloaded of whatever was useful, and rolled them into the river.

"It is a waste!" cried Smirnov.

"We need every man we can get," said Brusilov.

Desperately, they fought their way toward the north, and suddenly and unexplainably the opposition gave way.

A lone cavalry captain under a white flag made his way to Brusilov and Smirnov, to invite them to a conference.

"Do they wish to surrender?" wondered Smirnov aloud.

Brusilov looked at Smirnov and shook his head moodily—and accepted the invitation. He gave orders that the march was to continue, conferred with a few trusted officers and went with Smirnov to the conference.

Arakal seated himself across the little table from Smirnov, smiled at Brusilov's look of amazement and turned briefly to Slagiron.

"The pursuit, of course, is being continued?"

"Yes, sir," said Slagiron respectfully.

Arakal faced Smirnov.

"We regret that we have to use harsh measures. But the men are in an ugly mood. They have seen the corpses dangling from the trees. And some of these corpses were badly disfigured. You understand that we must be severe or the men will take matters into their own hands."

Brusilov was nodding moodily. Smirnov said nothing.

"We know, of course," said Arakal, "where the order came from." He looked at Smirnov, and waited.

Smirnov, frowning, said, "So, the message was a hoax?"

"What message?"

"The message from Salisbury."

"A hoax?" said Arakal. "Ah, you think we *decoyed* you here?"

"Yes."

Arakal shook his head. He turned to an officer standing beside a wooden chest. "Show the Ambassador General the flag from Salisbury."

The officer bent, opened the chest, took out a large flag, and handed it to Smirnov.

Smirnov held it, passed the cloth between his fingers, and looked up at Arakal. He tried to speak, swallowed, and tried again.

"So, it is true. You have taken Delaware Colony."

Arakal bowed his head.

"By the Grace of God. We also have Beaufort and Florida Colonies. Carteret is still holding out. We will go down later to Carteret and return the favor the Army of the South is doing for us here."

Brusilov jerked as if a hot wire had touched him.

Smirnov blinked, but it took him a moment longer to respond. "The Army of the South? *Kilburne's Guerillas?*"

Arakal smiled. "General Kilburne commands the Army of the South."

"But . . . how—?"

Suddenly Brusilov clapped his hand to his head, winced, then recovered his composure and drew a deep breath. He spoke sharply to Smirnov, his words indistinguishable to Arakal.

Behind Arakal, an officer cleared his throat.

"General Brusilov suggests to the Ambassador that if what this must mean is true, then the Ambassador can appeal to the devil's grandmother to save the Russ colonies here. It must be, the General says, that the Americans have rebuilt the railroads."

Smirnov looked as if someone had poured a bucket of ice water over his head.

Arakal leaned forward, smiling.

"Is there anything more natural, Mr. Ambassador? What else is there that will run on coal or wood—and we have plenty of that—and exceed the speed of your fastest tanks and trucks run on expensive fuel? What else can easily outpace all your transport ships and all your warships save only those rare few that ride on narrow wings let down under the water? Is there any other way that we can travel a thousand miles in a day, and move an army from place to place faster than you can transport it by ships, and in far greater numbers than you can move it by air, and in any kind of weather? Why would we *not* connect together whatever well-sited roads of steel survived your attack, and why would we *not* salvage all the cars and all the engines that can use wood or coal to pull those cars and put our best men to work making new engines? Why not?"

Smirnov said sharply, *"We can do the same thing!"*

"No, you can't," said Arakal. "Not here. There would be nothing easier for us to sabotage. *You* must rely on tanks and iron birds and trucks. You can rely on nothing you cannot guard at all times."

Smirnov shoved back his chair as if to get up.

Brusilov rested a hand heavily on Smirnov's shoulder, and glanced gravely at Arakal.

"What did you ask us here for? To tell us this?"

"To ask the surrender of your army."

Brusilov shook his head.

"Do not catch the conqueror's sickness of quick conceit. Remember, we are a world empire, while you are only a part of a ruined nation that was once great. Do not press too far. Be generous, and hope that we will be generous in turn. To avoid the trouble of a great effort, our leaders might come to an arrangement with you, *if* you are reasonable."

Arakal waited a moment, then said quietly, "We seek nothing that belongs to the Russ. We ask only that which belongs to the O'Cracy's."

Brusilov's face twitched.

"It must be negotiated."

An officer stepped up beside Arakal, and excused himself. "Sir, news of the Russ fleet."

"Speak up," said Arakal. "Our guests will want to know, too."

The officer cleared his throat. "They have passed Cape Cat and are moving at high speed upriver. Their iron birds are scouring the shoreline."

Brusilov straightened. Smirnov sat up in his chair.

Arakal said quietly, "You see, I am being fair with you. But I can do only so much. The more you fight with us, the more determined and filled with anger my men will become. It would be best to surrender to us and be escorted, without the weapons of your men, to the ships. But to be released in that way, the Russ must agree to make no move against any of the colonies which have become ours. Any colonist who wishes may, of course, go home with you, if you care about that."

Brusilov frowned, and spoke carefully, "If the world-wide might of the Soviets were to be concentrated in this spot—"

Slagiron said quietly, "Then all the world would rise up wherever you pulled out."

Smirnov came to his feet.

"I am the Ambassador of the greatest empire—yes, *empire*—on earth." He tilted his head back, and Arakal leaned slightly forward, waiting. Smirnov, however, for some reason, did not say more.

Brusilov said firmly, "We can accept no condition that would reflect discredit on our nation."

Arakal said, almost regretfully, "Now that the Army of the South is with us, and the Army of Kebeck, and the Army of Brunswick, and the Maine Militia, I would say you are outnumbered better than three to one. We respect your courage. But you must consider these facts."

Brusilov was silent, but Smirnov said, "You forget our Fleet."

"No," said Arakal, smiling, "I have not forgotten that."

Smirnov gave his head a little shake.

"They are *still* savages. They have learned nothing! Let us—"

Brusilov interrupted, and his voice came out in a roar.

"*Enough* name-calling!" He turned to Arakal. "We thank you for your courtesy; but we do *not* give up! And we remind you that if we decide to put forth our strength, you will regret it!'"

Brusilov turned on his heel and went out. Smirnov trailed out after him, then paused at the entrance and looked back.

"I associate myself with everything the Commander has said." He nodded and went out.

Slagiron said exasperatedly, "How do we separate Brusilov from that little worm?"

"We can only send our prayers for that," said Arakal. "We must be very careful now, that in trying to gain all we do not let the whole business slide through our fingers." He glanced at Slagiron. "Let us see how long we can keep them from reaching the St. Lawrence."

Brusilov, so tired by now that each motion took its separate effort of will, stared at the new columns of dust rising parallel to the column of dust raised by his own marching men.

Wearily, he said, "Arakal underestimated his strength to us. That is worse than three to one."

Smirnov peered around.

"It is true. Look, we will be forced into the bend of that big stream."

"Do you think I don't see it? But on this side they are ahead of us in great numbers. We *can't* go straight. We must cross here and hope that we get completely across before they . . . Listen!"

They glanced up.

With a thunderous beat, three helicopters came flying toward them, and swerved suddenly as they took in the situation.

The nearest column of local troops, however, did not break or flee. Instead, they at once swerved to attack Brusilov.

Smirnov cried out, but Brusilov laughed half-hysterically.

"They want to get *close*. They wish to mingle with us to be safe from the bombs." He shouted orders, and his ragged columns broke into a run toward the stream.

The helicopters swerved to attack the oncoming troops.

Under the brilliant sun, the scene seemed to hang suspended, the men, the clouds of dust, the planes—all seemed to exist in a moment that would last forever.

And then the helicopters lit in a blaze as of a hundred suns.

Brusilov, stunned, saw the clouds of smoke where the pilots lost control and the planes crashed, but his mind could furnish no explanation. Then a sort of terror seized him, as if he were in the grip of some supernatural force that step by step undid the gains of the past, and would never let up until it had its way.

Shouting and cursing, he drove his men into the stream, led them out on the other side and pointed to the distance, where a shimmer like steel showed the presence of the great river.

Now the enemy was so close, however, that Brusilov in the wild flight could no longer say whose men were his and whose belonged to the enemy. All were fleeing in a tangled jumble, and behind them came a tightly controlled body of cavalry that with repeated charges harried them till they were all one tormented, running, indistinguishable mass of suffering, seeking the river and salvation.

Brusilov, his mind hazed by fatigue and confusion —and the shock of the unexpected and the unpredictable— gave up trying to reason and just thought of the river, and the ships, and peace and safety.

And at last they were there, after no man knew how long. The sun had climbed up past the zenith and was now hanging in the west, and Brusilov, by pure habit, scarcely aware what he was doing, was ordering the men, placing this one or that one in a better position to fire, organizing a defense to hold off the harrying cavalry and the fast-approaching columns of troops.

From all the ships, warships as well as transports, the boats came in and ferried out load after load of stunned, dazed, dead-tired men, men too drugged with fatigue to do anything but clamber into the boats and fall down one on another. Men who stared stupidly when given an order, and had to be moved from place to place by hand . . . But they were getting them onto the ships.

As the big guns of the ships held off the encroaching enemy, Brusilov wished dazedly for rockets, but those, unfortunately, were reserved for special purposes. Still, the guns held off the pursuit, the last men were loaded into the boats, and now it was Brusilov's turn to accompany them, and—

A glare lit the ships, as if the sun, to the west, had risen and passed in a flash to the east, and multiplied itself a hundred, a thousandfold.

From a point of land upriver, a little cloud of smoke rose up in the air.

A plume of water rose high beside the largest of the ships.

A heavy *Boom* reached Brusilov's ears—a sound as of distant heavy thunder.

Suddenly he was surrounded, horsemen were everywhere, and before he knew what had happened he was caught up; the world spun around him, and he gave it up, and plunged into a deep black quiet that welcomed him into its depths—and long long after, it yielded him up again, refreshed and wondering at the confused impressions that he found in his mind.

Arakal, smiling, was standing beside a round window. "You are awake, General Brusilov?"

"You again," said Brusilov. He sat up, and nodded also to Slagiron. "So, I did not reach the ships?"

"Look around," said Arakal. "Feel the motion underfoot. Of course, you have slept so long that it must seem natural."

Brusilov stared around.

"But why are *you* here?"

"These," said Arakal blandly, "are our ships, taken in return for some little damage you did in Bangor and on the way here."

Brusilov got carefully to his feet. He looked at the bland Arakal and the grinning Slagiron, and peered out the porthole of the cabin. There, riding at anchor, were the other ships of the Fleet.

"How did you do *this?* Are you like those wizards of old you spoke of?"

"Did it seem," said Arakal, "that your ranks became somewhat swollen toward the end of the fight?"

Brusilov shut his eyes and sat down on the edge of the bunk.

"My men," said Arakal, "were rescued along with yours—special corps whose uniforms are really not too much different from your own. They were very tired from catching up and joining you, and so they collapsed almost as soon as they were on board. Therefore, Colputt's big multiplied version of his solar flasher did not blind them as it did your men. And so, when they stood up again they found it easy to overpower your blinded men long enough for the rest of my men to get out here. Oh, it was uncomfortable, and our railroad gun almost wrecked everything by taking a crack at you before you tried to get away, but we still got your fleet. It is ours now, but you need only join us, and it will be yours, too."

Brusilov stared at him.

"I tried to tell that fool Smirnov not to underestimate you militarily. And I wound up doing it myself. He is dead, I suppose?"

"No," said Arakal, "I persuaded my men that your great Central Committee will do things to him that we could not dream of, and then the weight will be on *their* souls, not ours. Moreover, to destroy him would be a gain for your side. We are sending him back to them with an offer of peace, if they return the lands of the O'Cracy's."

"You have already got them," said Brusilov. "All except Carteret. I can't believe *that* will hold out long against you, now that our fleet . . . cannot interfere."

"Why," said Arakal, "there is still the land of the Kebeckers across the sea. And Old Brunswick, from which the New Brunswickers came. All that must be returned to the O'Cracy's. It would be as well to do it. You are stretched too thin holding so much."

Brusilov stared at him a long time, then started to grin. "You are sending Smirnov to carry *that* message to the Central Committee?"

"Yes. We hope they will agree. But in any case, we want them to have him. He is so well-educated, and of such good birth, and knows so much about technology and ideology that it is to our benefit that they have him."

Brusilov grinned.

"And what is your idea about the greatness of . . . yourself, for instance? When your son is King of the O'Cracy's, what will his education be like?"

"We of the O'Cracy's," said Arakal seriously, "believe that only the best man should lead—the best person for the particular job, that is. Not the son of the best man, unless he himself is best. The only way we have found to pick out this best man is to have an election, but that method is not yet perfected. Why not join us, and see if you can help us work out improvements? You have so much experience with Party Members of the fourth generation that you must have done some thinking and have *some* ideas."

"So, you would have me, eh? But then I would be a traitor to my own people."

"Which people? Smirnov—or the Delaware colonists who have joined with us voluntarily?"

"Voluntarily? You *conquered* them!"

"We conquered the troops stationed among them—such of them as woke up in time to fight. We then agreed to keep those like this Smirnov of yours away from them if they would join us. They were very agreeable. They have had much ideology jammed down their throats."

"Ideology," said Brusilov in disgust. "True, it is important. But the fact is that where Charles Martel stopped the advance of the arms of the Arabs, there the advance of Islam ceased. Cromwell defeated the English king, and Puritanism was established. Hitler went down in defeat, and Nazism ended. America overspread the earth, armed with the ideology of democracy and with her know-how and power, and then they took things too easy, and my ancestors got more power than they, and that was too bad for the American dominion. And now this donkey, Smirnov, tells me it is the *ideology* that counts!"

"Well," said Arakal, "it does count. His reasoning has become confused, but the general idea is right."

Brusilov looked doubtful.

Arakal said, "Ideology *counts*. The only catch is—almost always when ideology counts, *it does the counting with a sword.*"

THE STEEL, THE MIST AND THE BLAZING SUN
★ ★ ★

I. The Inheritors

★ 1 ★

The sky was dark, the snow deep, and the wind bitterly cold as the little file of men on snowshoes awkwardly made their way forward. Each clutched with thick mittens the rope that kept him from losing the others when the whirling snow was all there was to see. The leader, at the head of the file, glanced frequently back over his shoulder at the studious-looking man who came next in line, and who looked often at a small gray box he carried in his left hand. This box was attached by a smooth, thick, black cord to a pack on his back, from which projected a shiny antenna. He now called out sharply and, at the head of the file, the leader reached inside his thick fur coat, took out a whistle, and blew a long shrill blast.

The file came to a halt. The men began to help each other unload their packs. The leader, after an intent glance all around, conferred with the man next in line, who gave a final look at the little gray box, and helplessly spread his hands. As the wind died down, both men glanced uneasily around, as if they might be overheard, and lowered their voices.

"I may be a scientist, Comrade," said the studious-looking man, "but still I can't be *sure*. The astronomers are the ones who predict the timing, and they leave themselves a good margin for error."

"I don't want to get too close too soon," said the leader. "Are we at least sure that's the spot, up ahead?"

"What is 'sure'? We carry out the calculations as best we know how, analyze the data, rely on the surviving geodetic satellites to help us fix position accurately, and try to correct any erroneous assumptions that creep into our calculations. Nevertheless, we calculate according to assumptions that may or may not prove valid in any given case. I *think* that's the spot. There is no way I can *know*."

"The last one of these little expeditions," said the leader shortly, "didn't come back. That was how it was discovered that their predicted intensity was wrong."

"Well, I am responsible for the present intensity prediction, and I am here to take the consequences."

The leader blinked, then grinned, and clapped the scientist on the shoulder. "It will give me great pleasure to see you go, too, if your damned calculations are wrong. But at least you are here to listen to my complaints. Would that these higher-ups of ours were a little less remote."

"It is best not to speak of such things."

"And I hope the Americans, at least, got well paid back for this."

"Shh. It wasn't as you think. In any case, they did. But we cannot talk of such matters."

"Who is to hear, in this place?" Nevertheless, the leader glanced around uneasily. After a silence, he said, "Can't you give me some idea when it will start?"

"In all probability, it *will* start, that is all I can say. We are given a time-band that is supposed to represent an extreme limit of possibility. But . . . Look! The snow!"

Ahead of them, the snowfield grew brighter, reflecting a new glow of the clouds overhead. The leader put his whistle to his lips, and blew a succession of short blasts.

Before them, the reflected glow strengthened. The snow shone with a white light. The glow became a glare. Then the snow ahead was one dazzling blaze of blinding light.

At that moment, the leader, turning to check that his men had their instruments in use, chanced to see the expression on the face of the scientist.

Afterward, what the leader remembered most clearly was that expression. He had seen it somewhere before, knew it from the past, and it connected with strong emotions somewhere beneath the surface of his memories. But at first he could not recall where or when he had seen it.

It was only later, back in the barracks, that he remembered. Lying awake in the darkness, in the early morning chill, he could see again his brother's face, long ago, back in the time after the famine and the migration, when a wandering drifter had broken into his parents' cabin while his father was away in the woods. He had smilingly insulted his mother, and with easy slaps knocked the two small children out of his way. He had helped himself comfortably from the table, cuffed their mother when she tried to gather the crying children to her, and then, grinning, had suddenly caught her by the arm.

At that moment, the door with the freshly broken latch had come open behind the intruder. Gun in hand, their father stepped in.

It had been then, and in the moments following, that he had seen the grim exultant expression on his brother's face, and hadn't thought of it since, until, with that merciless blaze pounding down from the sky, he had seen the same expression again, on the face of the scientist.

"Why?" he asked himself, lying in the darkness. What was there about that terrible light and heat and glare that was like the father returning home as the family was in desperate need?

Lying motionless in the dark, he recalled the bits of information that were all he had managed to wring from the scientist:

The Americans had been paid back; but don't talk of it; and it wasn't as you think.

Frowning, he lay in the darkness thinking it over, and for the first time he wondered, what had it been like on the other side of all that had happened? He lay for a time recalling the contradictory accounts of the Americans that were all that he had heard. It was little enough to go on, and, always, it was wisest to say nothing, best to ask no questions, most prudent to offer no comment, as the scientist had warned him.

Thinking of it, he again fell asleep, and his mother was there, comforting him, and his father's deep voice was in the background, reassuring and steady, and everything was all right, and he was sound asleep, no longer thinking about the Americans, and the war, and what had happened back there in the confusion of the past.

★ **2** ★

Thousands of miles away, Calder still lay, the service rifle beneath his hands, turned toward the entrance from the tunnel that led to the old abandoned mine shaft. From the place where he lay, the location of the massive steel door that closed the mineshaft end of the tunnel was easy to see. The odds on anyone coming in through that door were almost nil, but the general had insisted that one place where the Reds excelled was in the gathering of intelligence, and he would take no chance on the assumption that they didn't know what was concealed here.

Calder's assignment had been to guard this entrance, and he lay now in almost the same position he had chosen when that sudden premonition of trouble had struck him, just after he had come down and relieved Minetti, who had complained that this was a damned hard floor, either to stand on, sit on, or lie on, and they should have made it out of wood instead of this damned concrete. Concrete was bad for the arches, gave people rheumatism, and aggravated other unmentionable complaints that Minetti described in full and enthusiastic detail, and then, grinning, he had said, "Enjoy yourself, kid," and started back down the corridor. And nothing had seemed to change here, nothing had seemed to change at all, deep inside the mountain, until the grating noise had sounded at the massive steel door, and the vibration had traveled up the corridor, and the bright steady light had come in through the ring of new holes in the door, and then at last the big section had been tilted out, and now the men came in through the opening, neither in Russian uniforms nor in the American uniforms worn by Calder and Minetti. These men, in their strange gray uniforms, advanced warily up the corridor, led by a tall man with a full white beard, who, frowning, knelt beside Calder as the brilliant white lanterns shone down, felt carefully at Calder's wrist and throat, looked up wonderingly, slowly straightened, and turned to the man with him.

"This is the uniform of the Old O'Cracys themselves. But this body shows no wounds. And it is not decomposed. Yet the air here is breathable. This air should support life, including the life of the organisms of decay. Look up the corridor—there lies another soldier of the O'Cracys. What killed these two men? And why is there no decomposition?"

A look of intense speculation crossed his face. "Could the Old Soviets have attacked this place to kill the defenders without destroying what they defended?"

He turned to an officer whose branch of service was indicated by a small silver disc at the lapel of his uniform jacket.

"Send to Arakal over the flasher our time of entry through that door, and two sentences: 'O'Cracy installation. Seems intact.' Sign it 'Colputt'. Use the code book, and query every half-half until we have confirmation."

He glanced intently up the corridor, took the pad held out to him, and initialed the message.

The communications officer went quickly back down the corridor toward the mine shaft that led up to the outside.

Colputt led the way past the two bodies into the silent interconnecting corridors.

II. The Chiefs

★ 1 ★

Arakal, King of the Wesdem O'Cracys, was in the Plot Room, bent over a model of the territory that once had been the eastern United States. The contoured surface showed rivers, lakes, and oceans in blue; forests in shades of green; and stretches of cultivated land in brown; with light gray for mountaintops, and pale yellow for large towns and cities. The carefully detailed surface was mostly green, with little yellow anywhere. Arakal was now examining a branching narrow black line with tiny crossbars which threaded its way from the northern border southward.

"The southern end of the iron road—Where is it now?"

Beside him, Buffon, the white-haired chief of the Special Operations Staff, said, "Still at Thomasville, sir.

Before they go down into the Peninsula, they want to look over the ground."

"Swamp?"

"Yes, and a certain amount of lingering radioactivity."

Arakal nodded, and straightened. Absently, he adjusted the belt and shoulder strap that held his sword, and his left hand felt warily for the twin-headed, sharp-beaked bird that long had adorned the sword hilt. His groping fingers felt a new hilt designed to fit his hand as the weapon's blade fit the need to cut or pierce.

Arakal was reminded of other improvements since the last campaign against the Russ. He glanced at the model, noting the more numerous blue markers that represented the country's militia, and the large tan markers, bearing Roman numerals from I to IX, that stood for the reinforced divisions of his army, concentrated now in the nest of bays, rivers, and inlets that was the former Russ Maryland-Delaware Colony.

Arakal noted improvements, and also something that remained the same—the overlapping dull gray disks along the model's western edge, that blotted out the blue and green and brown as if the land there had been transformed into the hammered face of the moon.

Just then, a sergeant stepped over, carrying a slip of paper.

"Pardon, sir. New positions for the fleet."

Not far out on the dark-blue surface that represented the ocean, the sergeant moved tiny markers closer, along with a small symbol in white and blue and red—the Old Flag that now flew again from the Slagged Lands of the West to the Atlantic, from the Florida Peninsula to Kebeck and New Brunswick in the north.

As the sergeant left, Arakal glanced again at the gray western border.

"Any news from our expeditions?"

"Not yet, sir," said Buffon. "But settlers trickle in who haven't been able to find a way through."

"Any recently?"

"A hunter, yesterday. His party gave up five or six weeks ago. Last week they made it out to the iron road. While the rest went on south, he came in to collect the bounty for their records."

"Where did they try to get through?"

"West of the Ohio Territory, where we'd heard rumors of a corridor just south of the lake. He said it was even worse there than further south."

"You talked to him yourself?"

"Yes, sir. He seemed reliable."

"Well—It makes sense. The old maps show good-sized cities there. Cities that size nearly always got plastered."

Buffon nodded regretfully.

Arakal considered the model, and shook his head.

"Sooner or later, the Russ will recover from our last fight. Meanwhile, they'll build a bigger fleet. Then they'll be back over here. Unless we can develop our strength, there's no reason why they shouldn't finish with us what they started with the Old O'Cracys."

"At least there are limits, sir. From questioning their men, it seems clear that while they have a good deal of Old Stuff from before the war, it doesn't include the kinds of usable long-range rocket-bombs that did all this damage."

"Even without them," said Arakal, "they have the wherewithal to either beat us, or keep us endlessly fighting off invasions. We can't rely on their making the mistakes they made the last time."

Buffon began to speak, hesitated, and glanced at the small symbols of ships that the sergeant had moved closer to the mainland. "Well, we'll know more soon enough, when Bullinger gets back."

Arakal nodded. He glanced around the Plot Room, noting the roughly dressed engineers and road builders examining freshly prepared contour maps and, across the room, three of his generals bent intently over a large-scale model of the Maryland-Delaware Peninsula. Not far from where Arakal and Buffon stood, intent artisans in paint-spotted overalls were putting the finishing touches on a large model of Western Europe. Arakal thoughtfully considered this new model.

Buffon followed the direction of Arakal's gaze, and looked troubled. "Sir, we might forestall the Russ. But it would be very risky."

"If," said Arakal, "we can't open up a way to the West—"

"You're thinking that, as things stand, we don't have the potential strength the country had before the war?"

Arakal nodded bleakly. "If we can't get through to the West, we'll take things in a different order. But it would be better to recover first what the O'Cracys held on this continent."

Buffon hesitated, then frowning, began to speak. Then with a look of relief, he glanced around at the interrupting sharp rap of approaching heels. He looked up as a young lieutenant, the silver disc of Communications at his lapel, came hurrying across the room to Arakal.

"Sir, a message just in from Mr. Colputt."

"Good." Arakal reached for the folded paper.

★ **2** ★

At the moment that the message was delivered to Arakal, far away around the curve of the Earth, the high official spoken of respectfully as "S-One" stood at his office window, looking into an enclosed courtyard. His face bore a look of deep contentment as he drank in the courtyard's blaze of red and yellow and violet. With a connoisseur's interest, he noted that certain shades of color, seen against dark-green leaves, looked almost fluorescent.

Smiling, he glanced up at the braced overhead structure of steel and glass, partly opened now in early summer, that gave the flowers a head start despite the temperatures that afflicted this part of the world.

His spirit refreshed, S-One turned away, sat down, and glanced at the thick bound stack of typed pages that lay open on the polished walnut surface of his desk. His chiseled features grew set, and his gray eyes acquired a remote considering look as he picked up the report.

His gaze rose to the opposite wall, with its map-like display of the North American continent, its center marked from the Great Lakes to the Gulf of Mexico in overlapping disks of dull gray, its west and east coast regions marked in scattered gray disks overlapped with green, blue, or brown.

Centered on the west coast region was a small symbol—a hammer and sickle within a white star on a blue disk.

S-One frowned at the flag, then opened his thick sheaf of papers, the edge darkened from much handling, to read:

" . . . true insight into their motivations is problematical, as we have as yet no reliable source within the controlling group. We are forced to rely largely on electronic methods, which can be grossly misleading, because of:

1) Poor coverage.

2) Changes of plan. Sudden reversals by Arakal, Slagiron, Colputt, and other leading personages of the present quasi U.S. Government are common.

3) Secretiveness. The present quasi U.S. Government is, in its essentials, an absolute monarchy. In such a government, the true intention may be known only to the monarch.

The effect of such factors is to very seriously hamper our planning. . . ."

S-One shook his head in irritation. He put a hand on the edge of his desk, pulled out a slide inset with numbered pearl-colored push-buttons, and with the ease of long familiarity selected a button well up in the right-hand column.

Across the room, the display lit up to show nine small numbered markers, representing Arakal's army, clustered in the former Maryland-Delaware Colony. The locations of two of these markers differed slightly from their positions on Arakal's Plot. Off the shore, tiny symbols represented Arakal's ships, with no perceptible difference between their location on S-One's display or Arakal's Plot.

S-One glanced at his clock, shoved in the slide with its rows of buttons, and picked up the interoffice phone.

"General Brusilov is here?"

"Yes, sir. He arrived exactly on time."

"Send him in."

The door opened, and a broad bear of a man came in, his expression wary, but his jaw out-thrust.

S-One came to his feet, stepped around the right side of his desk, and held out his hand.

General Brusilov, surprised, gripped the proffered hand.

S-One said gravely, "Please seat yourself, General. I appreciate your punctuality."

Brusilov spoke gruffly. "I believe in being on time, even for my own execution."

S-One sat down. "We are all, in one way or another, 'executed' eventually. In my job, I must sometimes accelerate the date of such executions. That is not so in your case. There are three reasons why your only punishment will be the loss of one day's pay."

Brusilov blinked in surprise.

"The first reason," said S-One, "is the testimony of the former Soviet plenipotentiary, Smirnov. Smirnov returned to us in a state of shock. He took the entire blame for the American disaster on himself. His testimony exonerates you completely.

"The second reason is that you came back to us voluntarily.

"The third reason is the statement of Smirnov that you were friends with the present U.S. leader, Arakal. Is this correct?"

Brusilov gazed briefly out at the flowers, then turned to look S-One in the eyes.

"Arakal, and his officers and men, were nearly always friendly. Not only to me, but to most of my officers and men. That is," Brusilov added dryly, "between fights."

"After you had fought with them, they were still friendly?"

"On all occasions, except in our attack through New England toward Quebec Fortress. Brutal methods were used in that attack. The ill feeling was relieved only by blood."

"They were usually friendly. Yet they fought?"

"They fought like wildcats."

"But afterward, they were friendly?"

"Yes."

"Do you understand their reason?"

Brusilov hesitated, then shook his head.

"How can I be certain? Their reasons seem to me to be questions of temperament, of Arakal's calculation, and of historical policy."

S-One sat back, frowning. He picked up the thick report lying on his desk.

"Take a look at the size of this. Weigh it in your hand. This is an exhaustive strictly secret critique of the U.S.A. as we now see it. But is it right? Are we intellectualizing our opponent's whims or reflexes? You know them."

Brusilov thoughtfully weighed the report in his hand, shook his head, and passed it back to S-One.

S-One said, "Why do you suggest 'historical policy'?"

Brusilov shrugged. "They are Americans, Comrade."

" 'Quasi-Americans' in the words of that paper. That is, they live where the Americans died."

"And are descended from them."

"Perhaps I am descended from a Tatar tribesman. Does that mean I am one?"

Brusilov's right hand, resting on the arm of his chair, lifted, palm out.

"There is a difference between a Frenchman and a Finn. The Poles are one thing, and the English another. The Americans are something else again."

"For the sake of argument, not to correct you, I say that the Americans *were* something else again."

Brusilov's voice was respectful, and his expression very serious.

"They were. And they are again."

"You regard this Arakal—this *King of the O'Cracys* —as an *American*?"

"He is an American, and so is his chief general, Slagiron, and so are all the rest. And it was the historical policy of the Americans, in their own view of things, to bind up the wounds of the suffering, attack tyranny, shoot pirates, twist the lion's tail, and spit in the eyes of those in authority. In a fight, the Americans, Comrade, love to spring a nasty trick on you, and then afterward they clap you on the back. There are no hard feelings, finally."

S-One gestured to the display on the wall behind Brusilov.

"The people you speak of sound like giants. Observe the gray area in the heartland of their country, after some specimen of which, perhaps, your friend Slagiron is named. The only real Americans, if there are any left, are on the *West* Coast. These East Coast people are tribesmen."

Brusilov looked at the map, and nodded absently. His voice was polite, but without hesitation.

"Comrade, the son of a cat is a cat, the son of a Russian is a Russian, and the son of an American is an American. I grant you, as a nation they have had their hat pulled down over their eyes, and they have been chucked under the chin with a sledgehammer. They have also had their ribs smashed. They are crippled, as a nation, just as we are perhaps not quite so vigorous, as a nation, as we were once. But we are both still the same people. I say this not to be argumentative, but because I have spoken with them, and fought with them, and they are not English, French, Canadian, Chinese, or anything else, but Americans. Their ancestors may have been foolish. I do not say they are giants. I say simply that Arakal, Slagiron, and the others *are* Americans. And they do certain things because it is the historical policy of Americans to do these things. The Americans unload forty tons of bombs on you, then they offer your children chewing gum, and make you a loan. These are the Americans all over again. But there is, I admit, a difference."

"What is this difference, then?"

"Now they have the recent experience of a terrible near-total defeat. And, too, they have Arakal."

S-One frowned. "You say Arakal's *calculation* has to do with their attitude?"

"Yes."

"What does this king of the Americans—"

"That is an error."

S-One blinked. His face, which had been friendly, was suddenly expressionless.

Brusilov said, his voice courteous but somehow flat, "Arakal's title is 'king'. But it is not what we mean when we say 'king'. A better word might be 'chief', but that is not right, either. There is the word, 'boss'—the person who runs things, who decides how things are to be done. There is no trace of divine right in this title of 'king'. The office is elective."

S-One glanced at the thick report, then at Brusilov.

"Elective?"

"He told me so, himself. Certain things they have had passed down to them from the survivors of our attack. Arakal is the boss, the chief—Where this word 'king' comes from, who knows? Their present civilization grew up in the ruins of their former civilization. They used what pieces they could find, and that word, perhaps, was all that was ready to hand at the time."

"Then to call their government an absolute monarchy is an error?"

Brusilov thought a moment.

"Call if an elective absolute monarchy governing through a nonhereditary oligarchy. The closest thing I can think of is some form of republic; but I am not sure that is right, either. Frankly, I don't know what it is. But I know it works. I have seen it work."

S-One exasperatedly looked at the report, then out into the garden, and rested his eyes on the glorious colors. After a moment, he turned back to Brusilov.

"How does Arakal calculate this policy of friendship?"

"It is a calculation, I think, that shows him there is no gain in the pointless multiplication or intensification of enmities. With him we have, not festering enmity, but friendship interrupted by conflict. Friendship is what he appears to aim at, by courteous behavior and strictly fair treatment. Of course, friends may fight, because of opposing beliefs or desires. He wants to recover the Land of the O'Cracys. We claimed control of all of it. There is the basis for as much conflict as anyone might wish."

S-One smiled at the expression, "the Land of the O'Cracys."

Brusilov shook his head.

"Do not think that they are foolish because we cannot correctly translate their tongue. The meaning of that expression, 'the Land of the O'Cracy' is emotional: 'the powers, insight, and territory which once were ours.' "

"World dominion?"

"Their idea is simply to free North America, plus England and France."

"Not Germany?"

"They have lost the awareness that West Germany was an ally."

"You mentioned one other factor—temperament."

"That can be explained in a few words: They are friendly."

S-One stared for a moment, then sat back, frowning.

"So, what we are up against is a people heavily armed, friendly, risen out of nuclear disaster, led by an elective absolute monarch ruling through a nonhereditary oligarchy, and whose policy is to courteously smash the opposition, and then nurse the survivors back to health? How do we contend with a thing like that? Is that, at least, the total of it?"

Brusilov stolidly shook his head.

"That is true, as far as it goes. But there is still another factor."

S-One regarded Brusilov with no great warmth.

Brusilov said, a trace of stubbornness in his manner, "It is the temperament of Arakal and his people that they, in general, like us. As Arakal said, approving of our colonists, 'They are good workers.' I heard such comments, myself."

S-One spoke seriously, "I appreciate all such first-hand information. We have had little enough of it. Go ahead."

Brusilov said, "It is historical policy with the Americans to accept—even to invite—immigration. They did not attack our colonists, as nearly any other people would have done. Instead, they moved in by surprise, in force, with no bombardment, and explained in a friendly way that the land the colony was on belongs to the O'Cracys, but that our people could become O'Cracys, and keep everything they had, and the only difference would be that the colonists would no longer have to take orders from *us*. That block of colonists moved from our side to their side with scarcely a sign of complaint."

S-One said exasperatedly, "There is the language problem. How will they solve that?"

"There is much trade between Arakal's own people and our former colonists. They have a school system now, with many small schools. Perhaps they will teach English in the colonists' schools, who knows?"

"This will cause trouble."

"Comrade, there is a noticeable tendency, with Arakal, for things to *not* work out as you expect."

S-One nodded moodily.

"In any case, what we have, then, is an elective monarchy governing through a non-hereditary oligarchy. The monarch is tactically shrewd. Monarch and people are descended from the East Coast survivors who lived through our nuclear bombardment. They have certain characteristic past American traits, including friendliness and a readiness to accept deserving outsiders as new Americans. They also, while fighting our troops in their own territory, have succeeded in gaining several victories, including one very damaging success, which won them all that remained of our seagoing fleet." S-One looked at Brusilov. "Is that correct?"

Brusilov considered it.

"It is largely correct, as far as it goes, but it contains one element of serious error. There is a condescension toward Arakal and his men which is characteristic of all of us, until we have felt their blows. You say he is 'tactically shrewd'. The word 'tactically' denies him status in the spheres of strategy and high policy. That is an error. Arakal is, in my opinion, a great master of conflict, alike in policy, strategy, tactics, and perhaps also in personal combat. One element of his strength is our condescension. In my opinion, he is not our inferior, but very possibly our superior."

S-One looked at Brusilov without expression, and Brusilov looked back with a stubborn yet not disrespectful expression. Finally, S-One gave a grunt, and sat back.

"You are outspoken, General."

"Even unpleasant truths may be serviceable. Lies break under strain."

"Is it true, as Smirnov said, that you regard Arakal as 'a master in the realm of ideas'?"

"As a master of conflict even in the realm of ideas. Yes."

"Do you feel," said S-One, his voice even and smooth, "that our ideology is subject to overthrow by Arakal's superior understanding?"

Brusilov frowned. S-One sat absolutely still, studying the general intently. Finally Brusilov cleared his throat, and looked directly into S-One's eyes.

"I am a military man, Comrade, not a political expert. But I will give you the best answer I know how to give. First, your question seems to presuppose knowledge of a conversation between Arakal, me, and Arakal's chief general, Slagiron. If you have knowledge of that conversation, you will understand that my personal opinion of ideology is low. I fear its teeth—the power of enforcement of those who are devoted to it—but I have a low opinion of ideology itself. It seems to me that first one side, then another, embodies its beliefs in a set ideology, which gains or loses power, depending on the force at the disposal of its followers, and on the shrewdness with which that force is used. As Arakal said, 'Ideology counts. But usually when it counts, it does the counting with a sword.' Considering the force at our disposal, no, I don't think Arakal can overthrow our ideology."

"Does he *wish* to overthrow it?"

"He wants to recover the lands of the O'Cracys. I don't think he wants to overthrow our ideology."

S-One said, "Can we overthrow him?"

"I don't think so. He is too strong at home."

S-One leaned forward, his gaze focused intently on Brusilov.

"And what if Arakal comes over here?"

Brusilov nodded slowly, almost sadly, then suddenly he laughed. "Yes, if Arakal comes over here, we well might beat him."

"Why do you laugh?"

Brusilov shook his head. "Comrade, how do I explain? A boy might laugh at the thought of a red-hot rivet dropped down the neck of an octopus. It is the thought of two such contenders coming together."

S-One nodded, and settled back. He looked at Brusilov and smiled.

"Well, he *is* coming. I am sure of that. And it is, I think, the opportunity of a lifetime. Do you agree?"

Brusilov nodded, and now his expression was somber and foreboding.

III. The Planners

★ 1 ★

The evening of Admiral Bullinger's return, Arakal and his chief lieutenants gathered in the Plot Room. Maps lined the walls, and the model of the East Coast of North America stood near the new model of the West Coast of Europe.

The admiral, short, clean-shaven, with two tufts of hair that stood straight up at the back of his head, put his finger on the new model where it showed a curving body of water that wound back between dominating hills on the big island Arakal and his men knew as "Old Brunswick."

"This," said Admiral Bullinger, "is Glasgow, where the biggest shipyards are located. There are other shipyards, all working overtime, where the Russ are starting to build their new fleet. These yards are all hard to approach.

None appears defended now, except Cherbourg, which was their main Atlantic base. That is, none of the fortifications, which date from way back, seems to be actually armed. But they will be. And this ship-building program is something we can't match. Five years from now, the Russ could be back here with a new fleet, and another invasion army."

Arakal said, "You're sure these shipyards aren't armed *now*?"

Bullinger shook his head. "I'm morally certain, that's all. We entered every one of those ports except Cherbourg. I was careful not to risk the whole fleet at once, and we didn't open fire; still, the situation was pretty tense when we went in, flying the Old Flag. The local people went crazy. The Russ have dominated them all this time, and they could have ended the uproar quickly, by sinking us, *if* they'd been ready. Not a shot was fired."

There was a silence, then broad Slagiron, Arakal's chief general, spoke in a low growl.

"Yellowjackets don't make much trouble in the springtime."

Smith, speaking for the absent Colputt, nodded. "In the summer, when there are more in the nest, look out."

Slagiron's chief organizer, Casey, studied the curving waterway leading into Glasgow.

"Why wait till they arm these places?"

Arakal glanced at Admiral Bullinger.

"Suppose we wrecked every shipyard they're using. How long till they rebuilt them?"

"I think it could take several years."

"And *then* they'd have them so fortified we couldn't touch them?"

"Yes."

"How many local people would we kill in the attack?"

Bullinger hesitated. "That, I can't say. I suppose we could warn them. But it would be risky. We don't know how much rolling artillery the Russ may have."

Casey said, "The right way to do it would be to appear unexpectedly, hit with everything we've got, then either land or get out."

Arakal shook his head.

"Our aim isn't to turn everyone into allies of the Russ. Suppose you were over there, and our fleet sailed in without warning, and killed your brother and father in a surprise attack on a defenseless shipyard. Would you love us for it?"

Slagiron said dryly, "War and love aren't exactly the same."

"It's easier to make enemies than friends."

Admiral Bullinger said, "Once the Russ get all these new ships afloat, it won't make much difference whether the Old Brunswickers love us or not. We'll have another Russ army at our throat."

"There's a question," said Arakal, "whether we'd be better off facing another Russ army in five years, or a Russ army plus the active hatred of Old Brunswick and Old Kebeck a few years later."

Slagiron thoughtfully massaged his jaw, and turned to look at the contour model of the East Coast of America. He glanced back at Arakal.

"It's true that, using a bloodless method *I* didn't think would work, we freed the Russ colonies, and they joined us willingly. But that was a special situation. And, as you remember, there was a bloodbath worse than sticking pigs when the Russ went for Kebeck Fortress the long way. It took killing to win that."

Arakal's voice was ironic. "That's true. We've had no trouble with enlistments from Maine since the Russ went through."

There was a silence as Casey, Slagiron, and Bullinger stared at the walls or ceiling, then nodded ruefully. Bullinger cleared his throat.

"All the same, we'll regret it when the Russ control the seas again."

Arakal nodded. "But you say the people went wild when you entered the harbors?"

"Yes. And the fishermen and coastwise traders we picked up were friendly, too. They all agreed that to get the Russ out of there is going to take an armed force of great power. I could follow most of their reasoning, but they didn't understand our actual situation. I had the impression they all thought we were comparable to the Russ in strength."

"Would you say that the people were ready to throw out the Russ?"

"Yes. If we'll do the main part of the work. They don't think they *can* do it."

"They wouldn't fight on the Russ side?"

"No."

Arakal walked slowly around the new contour model, looking at the harbors, studying the bays and inlets, and the outthrust peninsulas. He turned, briefly, to look back at the more familiar contour model of the East Coast of America. His gaze rested on the flat, gray, slightly glazed markings that formed the western border at the edge of the massive table. He turned back to Admiral Bullinger.

"Did you see any such damage across the ocean as there is here?"

"No, sir. But then, the damage would probably have been further inland, where they would have fought to stop the Russ coming from the east."

Arakal nodded, and again considered the new model. He looked up, to glance from one massive table to the other, and then to Buffon, standing respectfully back from the little group around the tables.

"These two models are to the same scale?"

"Yes, sir."

"Good." Arakal glanced at Bullinger. "You didn't make any try at getting into this—hmm—Mediterranean Sea?"

"No, sir. The entrance is fairly narrow, measured by the range of a coast defense gun, and our information is that the Russ control both sides. Incidentally, a chart of the Mediterranean that we bought from a coastwise trader disagreed with the charts on board the fleet when we captured it."

"Had this coastwise trader ever been there?"

"No, sir. It was just one of a set of charts he had on board."

"How were *your* charts?"

"The ones we used were accurate."

Arakal looked the two models over, frowning. "Despite the shipyards we've captured here, the Russ have a greater capacity for building ships over there?"

"Yes, sir," said Bullinger. "Much greater."

"And yet, so far as we know, the Russ were using *only* the Maryland-Delaware Colony to build warships before?"

"Yes, sir. The yards over there were used before, but as far as we can learn, they were used only to build fishing vessels, freighters—things like that."

"You didn't try to enter the—let's see—the Baltic Sea—to the north?"

"No, sir. We stuck to the coasts of Old Brunswick and Old Kebeck. That is, what they call 'the U.K.' and 'France'."

"What we have here is a bigger puzzle than we had to start with. You saw no Russ ships?"

"No *armed* Russ ships."

Slagiron spoke, his voice a low growl.

"Except for the shipbuilding, everything seems about as we would have expected."

There was a murmur of agreement from Casey; but Smith, Colputt's assistant, was frowning. Arakal nodded to Smith.

"What do you think?"

"That's just it. *Except* for the shipbuilding. And, excuse me, what about their aircraft?"

Slagiron looked startled. "That's right." He glanced at Bullinger.

The Admiral shook his head. "Not a single iron bird."

Arakal said exasperatedly, "Why not build their warships at *home*?"

"These present yards they're using may be bigger," said Admiral Bullinger.

"Then why did they ever build ships over *here*? Thanks to that, we now have three new bombardment ships that should be finished late this summer, on which we can mount very powerful guns, and which will run on coal, not oil. Yet, when they lost these yards, what did they do? Start construction in other yards, again outside *Russland*. Why? Why, in the first place, build on *this* side of the ocean when they could have used the yards over there? There's something here we don't understand."

Admiral Bullinger nodded. "Unfortunately, I can't add anything more."

Arakal said, "How was the Fleet's oil usage?"

"It matched what the Russ volunteers had told us. Counting the stocks in their colonies here, and in two little tankers we captured, I'd say it could last us from three to four years, assuming they don't find some way to blow it up on us."

Arakal looked back at Smith.

"What would *you* say about the way they build their ships?"

"They must," said Smith, "build them where they do for reasons that make sense to *them*, at least. But there must be something wrong in their arrangements. It doesn't make sense to build ships where they're vulnerable to attack. It must be that, for some reason, conditions are even worse elsewhere."

Slagiron said stubbornly, "All this is guesswork. The *facts* are that if we let them use those shipyards, wherever they're located, we lose the only advantage we have."

"Yes," said Admiral Bullinger.

Arakal, examining the indentations in the coastline, glanced at the Admiral, and rested a forefinger on the port Bullinger had called "Cherbourg."

"You think this port, at the end of this peninsula, was their main base?"

"Their main Atlantic base, sir. In the Mediterranean, I suppose, they would have had another main port."

"It's protected against the weather?"

"Yes, sir. For one thing, there's a tremendous breakwater."

"Do they have oil storage there?"

"I think they'd be bound to. Our information is that they do."

"You think the fortifications there *are* armed?"

"That was our information, and it seemed reasonable, since this was their main base."

Arakal glanced around, and Buffon said, "Scale, sir?"

At Arakal's nod, Buffon handed over a small folding measure. Arakal held one end on Cherbourg, and swung the other end successively to Le Havre, Bordeaux, Dover, and Portsmouth. As his men watched intently, Arakal carefully measured the sides and width of the narrower portion of the peninsula, at the end of which was Cherbourg. He glanced at Bullinger.

"Why would they make this their main port?"

"For three reasons, sir. First, as you see, it's in a central location. Second, it's apparently ice-free in winter. Third, it's on a peninsula, which they could seal off in the event of an uprising on the mainland."

Arakal nodded, and glanced at Buffon.

"Do we have a detailed map?"

"Yes, sir. But it's based on information from before the war. Just a moment."

As Buffon unrolled a large map of the peninsula, Arakal, Slagiron, and Casey bent over it. Arakal's gaze settled on the peninsula's eastern coast, and he glanced at Bullinger.

"Have you seen this coast here?"

"Yes, sir. Though we didn't get too close."

"Did you notice any fortifications or batteries?"

"No, sir. They may be there, but we didn't see them."

Arakal studied the map in silence.

"Buffon?"

"Sir?"

"What's the accurate range of those big guns we're planning to mount on the bombardment ships?"

"The last test showed them still accurate at eighteen miles, sir. We won't really know until they're mounted, and the ships are afloat."

"And the total capacity of those Russ troop transports we captured?"

"Thirty-six thousand men, sir, with normal loading."

Arakal straightened.

"If we do nothing, the Russ will recover, and, sooner or later, we'll find ourselves right back where we started. We'll have gained time, but that won't be enough, because we don't know how to use that time to strengthen ourselves beyond Russ interference. We're hemmed in on the west by the slagged lands, and hobbled where we do have control, by the same thing. Everywhere we turn, there's another orange marker to show where the spotter teams have found some more 'lingering radioactivity'."

There was a murmur of agreement, and Arakal went on, "Now, for the time being, we have the power to strike back freely, whenever we choose. But a few years from now, that power expires, since the Russ are building a new fleet. We can gain more time, if we wreck the shipyards. But then we kill our own friends, and possibly turn them against us. Yet, now, these same people cheer us. Meanwhile, though we know the Russ are far stronger overall than we are, we have a clear suggestion, in the way they build ships, that there must be some weakness in their arrangements that they have to make allowance for. It seems to me there is only one thing to do."

Around him, their expressions varying from rapt attention to alert worry, Arakal's lieutenants watched as he put his forefinger on the contoured model's port of Cherbourg.

"Here we have the former main base of the Russ fleet, with guns and stores of fuel. And it is situated on a peninsula, which could be held against superior numbers. All along this east coast, there are beaches. If we land there, we either make it ashore without a fight, or else we're fighting Russ, not O'Cracys. And if enough Russ get drawn in there, how do they hold down the population at the same time? And what will the population do? There *could* be one flame of revolution, to throw the Russ back a thousand miles to their own territory. If not, we might still capture this peninsula, take their fortress port from behind, base our fleet in easy striking distance of their main captured ports and shipyards, cut their sea lanes between Old Brunswick and Old Kebeck, force the Russ in Old Kebeck to fight us in prepared positions, and rattle the Russ in Old Brunswick on their perch. From this base, fighting the Russ, who are the common enemy, we can call on the workers through all the territories of the Old O'Cracys to cut up the Russ from behind, blow up their iron roads, and lag and shift at all the work the Russ call on them to do."

"Yes," said Smith, Colputt's assistant.

Admiral Bullinger nodded his approval. "From our information, there could well be enough stored fuel in Cherbourg for a year's service."

Casey, his face twisted with concern, glanced at Slagiron.

Slagiron, jaw outthrust, growled, "And what if half the men drown on the way ashore, and the rest get sunk in this damned swamp it shows on the map? Or if the Russ have machine guns set up at the edge of the beach? Where do you take cover on a beach? And why attack *here*, of all places? This is nothing less than the Russ citadel! Of all the choices on the whole continent, do we have to run our heads into that? This is the very place they must be best prepared to defend!"

"Against an *uprising*," said Arakal. "But this is a landing from the sea! Why should they prepare against that when they had the only fleet in the world?"

"And what the devil," Slagiron went on, "do we know about landing over a beach? Did you ever try to run on sand? Isn't it enough that the Russ will probably have tanks by the dozens and cannon by the hundreds to slaughter us as we come in? How do we unload so much as a single one-pounder off a boat onto a beach? Why not, for the love of heaven, land, at least, in a *port*? There we could walk off onto a dock. Anyone who wants to swim ashore with forty pounds on his back, and a rifle in one hand, is welcome to it!"

Arakal, smiling, said, "What do I have generals for, except to help me work out these details? What you are talking about is why it will be hard. What I am talking about is why it is worthwhile. Do we want to do what the Russ expect? Or do we want to hit them where they don't expect it, and where, if they lose, they have to fight us with one foot in a hole? Look at the lay of the land. Do you see any other port so useful to us, that we could expect to hold against the Russ the way we could hold this one?"

"We have to take it first. And we don't know the first thing about landing on a beach."

"What do you think we're going to practice between now and the time we go over there? If we land in that port, and it *is* defended, then we lose not only ships, but also we wreck the port. If we land on this beach, right here, north of this small river, we are at the rear of the port, and we should also be inside the Russ defenses of the peninsula toward the mainland."

Slagiron bent beside Arakal, over the map.

"Yes, but—Let's see, here . . . I can foresee one sweet mess trying it. All right, if you want to do this, let's take time, and do it *right*. This year, hit those shipyards, so we end that for now. By next spring, we could have troops trained to go in over a beach, and we could have rafts, or *something*, to bring in the artillery. That way, we can try it, at least, the way it ought to be done."

"Yes," said Arakal, "if we can just get the Russ to go to sleep till then. By next year, when we're satisfied we know how to do it, the Russ could have guns defending every target we want to reach, their troops at a fever pitch, and half the continent hating us because of the stories and pictures of the unarmed people we slaughtered in attacks on defenseless ports. And who has the bigger productive power—us, or the Russ? Why should the passage of time favor us, once we get past the time when those bombardment ships come into our hands?"

Slagiron, his hand to his chin, eyes narrowed, glanced at Arakal. "You want to try it as soon as the new bombardment ships are ready?"

"We need to be *ready* to try it then."

Slagiron studied the model.

"If it works . . ."

Then he turned to Casey.

"We're going to need a beach to practice on, and we've got to find some way to float in the guns . . ."

★ **2** ★

S-One shook his head, and put the report down carefully on his desk. His window was partly open on the inner court, and he could hear the rain pouring down on its glass roof. From somewhere came a gurgle of water flowing through gutters and downspouts, to be fed downward into the underground filter tanks and cisterns. The murmur of flowing water was usually a cheerful sound for S-One, but today it fit into a general gloom and sense of disappointment. S-One picked up the interoffice phone.

"Is General Brusilov here?"

"He is waiting, sir."

"Send him in."

The door opened, and Brusilov, big, bearlike, cleareyed, came in, and nodded respectfully to S-One.

S-One said solicitously, "You look well, General. Sit down."

"Thank you," said Brusilov, a look of wariness crossing his face.

S-One said, "I am disappointed in your hero."

Brusilov looked blank. "Sir?"

"Arakal proposes to land his troops in *Normandy.*"

Brusilov frowned in puzzlement.

"Yes," said S-One, settling back, and watching Brusilov alertly, "we now have information on Arakal's plans."

Brusilov's face cleared. "From the ships?"

S-One smiled. "He gained and lost when he captured those ships. It is a great loss to us in power, but a gain in information. What is sad is the mystery stripped away when your opponent reveals his imbecility in all its obscure convolutions."

"Arakal is not stupid."

"They are having practice landings now. Think of it. They plan to come ashore on the old Utah Beach, strike inland behind Cherbourg, and capture the narrow part of the peninsula. They will do this with no more than thirty-five thousand men."

"What is stupid about this?"

"We can sink his whole fleet in the bay, and slaughter his landing force. I am embarrassed for this Arakal. His general, Slagiron, sees the difficulties. Arakal will not be moved."

Brusilov leaned forward.

"Comrade, there is a difference between ignorance and stupidity. Arakal is profoundly ignorant of conditions here. Even, doubtless, he has been misled."

S-One smiled in satisfaction. "To the degree that we could misinform his Admiral Bullinger, Arakal has been misled."

"What do you propose to do?"

S-One shrugged.

"An elaborate deception plan has been prepared. It seems a shame to waste it on such a donkey."

"Comrade," said General Brusilov, his expression worried, "invariably Arakal is underestimated—I have done it myself—and invariably, a rude awakening follows. Whether it will be the same here, on our own ground, I do not know. But take no unnecessary chances. *Arakal does not always do as you expect.*"

S-One's eyes narrowed, and for a moment he studied Brusilov thoughtfully. Then he nodded.

"Very well. An excess of subtlety is always dangerous, and I was about to say that we should expect to destroy this fellow and his fleet in the bay and on the beach. And I think, still, it is what will happen. But, just in case, we will continue with the deception plan. Who knows? He might show flickers of sense even yet."

Brusilov said earnestly, "When he appears stupid, that is the time to take extra precautions."

"He appears extremely stupid now," said S-One with feeling.

Both men turned at the sound of a rap on the door.

S-One's second-in-command apologized for interrupting, and stepped in, frowning. S-One spoke half-jokingly, "What is it, S-Two? You do not look happy."

"Arakal, sir. A second coded message has arrived for him, from his chief scientist, Colputt."

S-One looked interested. "What is it about?"

"We don't know," said S-Two indignantly. "Arakal decodes the message himself, and explains nothing to the others. And the others don't dare ask him, though amongst themselves they are consumed with curiosity. And now he has left by rail, and we have no way to know what is happening!"

IV. The Unknown and the Known

★ 1 ★

Arakal followed the white-bearded Colputt along the corridor, noting the number of interconnecting passages. They were now well beyond the end of the electrical cables that stretched down the mine shaft from the clearing, and were relying on Colputt's mantle lantern, which lit the corridors brightly as he led the way around a corner, and pushed open the door of a metal staircase that led them down and around, and down and around, seemingly endlessly, through a succession of landings blocked by heavy doors that must be shoved back, until they pushed open one last door, and the brilliant light of Colputt's lantern was swallowed up in an enormous room, its rough ceiling supported by massive pillars of uncut rock.

As Arakal peered into the gloom, he could see, beside the nearest of the pillars, a huge shadowy frame resting on coil springs. Within the frame was what appeared to be a metal box roughly the size of a large room.

"That's what you wanted me to see?"

"That's the lead-lined protective case around it."

As they walked forward, Arakal soon began to feel dwarfed by his surroundings. Only very slowly did the position of the pillar seem to change, while the frame, as he came closer, loomed higher and higher. It seemed a long time before he was at its base, looking up.

Colputt handed Arakal his lantern, glanced up at a raised metal ladder on the side of the frame, reached up, got hold of the lowest rung, swung himself up onto an awkwardly located platform to the side, knelt, and reached down. Arakal handed up the lantern, and climbed carefully up. As he stepped off at the top, Arakal crouched, squinting up into the glare and the shadows, sprang up, and pulled himself rapidly onto the ladder. He climbed up in the sudden dimness as the lantern passed beyond the top edge of the frame.

As Arakal reached the top, Colputt held the lantern up high.

"Look at the size of this."

Arakal had the impression he was on the deck of a ship. The flat surface stretched into the shadows, with a straight dark line down its center, and strongly braced metal arms reaching out from the surface to either side, bearing massive counterweights.

"This top opens?"

"Down the center. Each side of the deck swings back and up—like opening gates."

Colputt lifted a hatch in the deck, and led the way down an enclosed ladder into a confined metal booth with a narrow door. They stepped out on a metal walk, several feet above a billowing gray cushion-like surface. Some fifteen feet away, reflecting the lantern light in a few bright points, was a low, wide, smoothly curving metallic form with a broad dome rising toward its center.

Arakal moved further along the walk, to find a better angle of vision. A second set of reflections, further away, shone back at him.

Arakal glanced at Colputt.

"Two of them?"

"Yes."

"What are they?"

"If I'm not mistaken, they are two samples of the Old O'Cracys' 'ground-effect machines'. If so, they can cross solid ground, quicksand, swamps, beaches, rivers, and even stretches of ocean. So long as it's fairly level, it's all the same to a ground-effect machine."

"They *fly*?"

"Not exactly. They ride above the surface on a cushion of air. They use the air the way a wagon uses wheels."

"What do they use for power?"

"I hardly dare say it," said Colputt, "but from a list we found in an office upstairs, I think these use a form of atomic engine. Incidentally, they aren't as big inside as they look. Only the center part seems usable."

"What was the list you found?"

"Fuel requirements. It listed amongst other things, 'platform couriers'. There were apparently eighteen 'platform couriers', plus two more for spares. We think these are the two spares. Beside each of these 'platform couriers' was a little number that referred to a note, 'See Nuclear Fuels Section'. The list was all we've found, so far."

"Are these in as good shape as everything else seems to be in here?"

"We don't know yet. If you care to go a little closer, I'll show you the problem."

They dropped from the walk, plunged through the cushioning material, and climbed out on the curving metal surface. Colputt stepped forward, and held the lantern so that the light shone through a transparent section of smooth upcurving dome. They leaned forward.

Inside was a sort of padded armchair before a wide curving covered panel. Everything they could see had a sleekly finished appearance, with no working machinery in sight. Arakal straightened, frowning, and looked around. The outside surface was smooth, with no visible joins or openings. Even the transparent window seemed of one piece with the metallic sections that adjoined it. Arakal ran his hand across the join, and felt only a smooth unvarying surface. He glanced at Colputt.

"I begin to see your problem."

Colputt nodded. "If there's a handle, hinge, latch, catch, or even so much as a pinhole here, anywhere, we haven't been able to find it."

"Could they have entered from underneath?"

"I suppose it's not impossible. But we've pushed underneath, and found no opening, and I don't see why they should have done it that way. And that is by no means all we don't see. The trouble is that our technology is nowhere near as advanced as theirs was. We'll just have to hope that somewhere in this collection of shafts and tunnels, we'll find something to help clear up the problems we can't work out on our own."

When they went back up to the surface, Arakal and Colputt found a quiet place amongst the oaks and evergreens, overlooking the new clearing where a rough shed had been built over the entrance for the mine shaft. Beside the shed, a massive steam-crawler ran the generator that supplied light and power to the crews working underground.

Arakal looked down into the clearing for a moment, then turned to Colputt.

"How long, do you suppose, before you'll be through here?"

"Well—first, we need a better way to ventilate the tunnels. Second, there are the questions raised by those dead but undecomposed bodies. Third, there are the ground-effect machines. Fourth, there's the problem of what this installation was, and how it fit in with the O'Cracys' plans. We may never find that out, and yet it could be important. Finally, there are your standing orders in case of a discovery like this, that we be very careful not to spread the news, since it might find its way to the Russ. That limits the people I can have here to a specially selected group."

"Nevertheless," said Arakal, "let's stick to it. I'm sure the Russ have ways of learning our arrangements that would surprise us."

"Well, then, there also are the details of the things in there. There are books, instruction manuals, tools, equipment, even several workshops and a sizable laboratory." Colputt shook his head. "There's no way to predict how long it might take."

Arakal nodded. "Don't rush the work. This is just what we've hoped to find. It wasn't wrecked in the war, or stripped afterward. Take your time, and do it right. By the way, Bullinger is back with the Fleet. I suppose Smith explained our plans to you."

Colputt looked faintly guilty. "He offered to explain them. I was too busy."

"In that case, I'll explain them, myself. The main thing, though we don't know, is that there may be survivors of the Old Soviets' attack, somewhere to the west. If we could find a way, I would link up with them. We haven't been able to get through."

Colputt's gaze grew remote. "Some *could* have survived. Who knows? But is it so important?"

"It is to the survivors—and to us, if they have any of the Old O'Cracys' technology still in use."

"In time, we should get through."

" 'In time' may not be soon enough. If you study the old records, you find many centers of technology to the West. But it's three thousand miles from one coast to the other. The Russ are not a great deal further away from our West Coast than we are. While we are locked up on the East Coast, *they* could take over the west. They could, perhaps, even turn the remains of the Old O'Cracys' technology against us."

Colputt's eyes narrowed. "But since we can't get through—"

"Then we aim to cross the Atlantic, and free Old Brunswick, and, if possible Old Kebeck."

"What if the Russ are too strong?"

"It all depends on details." Briefly, Arakal described his plan, and Colputt, looking worried, said, "I am no general. But there is a serious risk from the Russ technology. In the first place, they may well have a spy network with transmitters planted in one of their former colonies. They could then get wind of your practice landings, and report them. Second, they may have ways to detect the approach of your ships. They could then shift their troops by the iron road, to meet you where you landed."

Arakal nodded. "It won't be easy. Now, what do you think of their building their war-ships, first over here, then where they are building them now? Why not build them at home? Why should they do it this way?"

"There are only two reasons I can think of."

"What?"

"Ice and enemies. If their home shipyards are iced in, they might prefer to build elsewhere. They might have preferred to build here, instead of across the ocean, because they could control their own colonists better than foreigners."

"*Would* their shipyards be iced in?"

"In winter, perhaps. I don't see any reason why it should be worse than before the war. There's certainly been no great climatic changes, or we'd have felt it here."

"The one certain thing is that they aren't stupid. They must have *some* reason."

Colputt nodded. "There has to be a reason. But it's hard to imagine what it could be."

★ 2 ★

S-One looked up at the strongly reinforced barrier of glass and steel above the dim courtyard. It looked as if it had been heavily dusted with flour. He shook his head, turned, and sat down at his desk.

"No word of Arakal?"

"He is back with the ships. They had another practice landing, this time at night."

"How did it go?"

"A disaster."

S-One smiled, and sat back.

"What happened?"

"Confusion amongst the units. There was bad weather, some of the troops reached the wrong beach, the

arrangements for getting artillery ashore didn't work—
Slagiron and Casey had an argument with Arakal—Just
about everything went wrong."

S-One leaned forward, smiling.

"What about the argument?"

S-Two smiled, leafed through a sheaf of papers, separated one section from the rest, and handed it to S-One.
S-One sat back comfortably and read:

Slagiron: "But it can't be done! And I'll be damned
if I'll be responsible for landing men straight into the
meat grinder!"

Arakal: "What about you, Casey?"

Casey: "After tonight, sir, I'll resign before I go on with
this. We've got a hundred and fifty men missing, right
now, just from the storm alone. We can't—"

Arakal: "Are you saying that I don't care about those
men?"

Slagiron: "A devil of a lot of good it does them
whether—"

Arakal: "I was speaking to Casey."

Casey: "I don't say you don't care, sir, but that doesn't
help them a bit. They're missing, possibly dead."

Arakal: "I see I am subject to criticism because I stayed
on the ship instead of leading that landing. Well, that
wasn't my idea. I'm going on the next landing."

Slagiron: "That won't *help*! It isn't—"

Casey: "Then *you* might be killed! That water is vicious!
And in the dark—"

Arakal: "I want the next practice landing scheduled for
tonight. Officers only. There's no army on earth better
than ours, and if they can't do this, it's because we're
giving them the wrong orders. The only way to fix that
is to find out what's wrong for ourselves."

Slagiron: "But, even if we finally learn how to do it on *this* beach—"

Arakal: "Do we have any better beach?"

Slagiron: "It can *still* be a disaster on another beach!"

Arakal: "When those bombardment ships are ready, *we've* got to be ready. If we put it off any longer, it will be too late. This is the only chance we may ever have!"

Slagiron: "Sir, there isn't any time limit. We don't *have* to go now!"

Arakal: "The Russ aren't fools. Bullinger's visit has warned them that their shipyards, ports, and seacoast are vulnerable. One thing we know the Russ can do is make cannon. Another thing they can do is to calculate, and bring force to bear on obvious weak points. When we have beat them, it's been by surprise, and because they underestimated us. If we try to outcalculate them, and match force to force, *they* will win. We have to surprise them. We have to be stronger than they realize. We have to strike at a place they don't expect us to hit. We can't count on time to favor us, because time may be on their side. While we argue, they build. We have to appear off that coast before they think it's possible!"

Slagiron: "Buffon was saying—"

Arakal: "Buffon thinks we have land enough already. That we can develop what we have and defy the world. If we could get through that barrier of radioactive slag, he might be right. But we can't. So we don't know what's on the other side."

Casey: "In time, sir, the radioactivity should die down, and then—"

Arakal: "That's part of the problem."

Casey: "How—"

Arakal: "When that happens, what will we find on the other side? *We* are blocked from going through. But the other side is open to the Russ, coming from the West."

Slagiron: "You don't think they could be colonizing—"

Arakal: "How do we know what they're doing? It's easy for us to imagine that we are big, because we can all remember when we had practically nothing. But all we are is the half-alive head and right arm of the O'Cracy, with the rest of the body unconscious, dead, or smashed. Most of our memory is gone—the Russ even correct us as to what we call ourselves. We can't match the Russ until we recover the lands of the O'Cracy. And since we can't go West, we'll go east. But we have got to get there before the Russ expect us."

Slagiron: "About this practice landing tonight—"

Arakal: "I'm open to suggestions."

Slagiron: "Some of the officers who are going to end up going out are completely beat. It would be almost murder to put them through it again tonight."

Arakal: "Can you get together officer volunteers for one boat?"

Slagiron: "I'll volunteer myself. But it's going to be a worse mess than anything you can think of."

Casey: "I'll volunteer. But aside from possibly killing the lot of us—"

Arakal: "I am now murdering you personally?"

Casey: "I didn't say that."

Arakal: "I've explained my reasoning. But I am very close to the end of all explanations."

Slagiron: "Excuse me, sir. Casey—"

Casey: "To go out there tonight—"

Slagiron: "Casey! Who in hell do you think you are? Do you realize that for the last ten minutes you've been laying down conditions, questioning the judgment of your superiors, and generally inviting trouble? You think you're protecting the men, and you've done more complaining than any fifty of them, and half of that in the wrong tone of voice. Go out there and get the volunteers! No officers below the rank of colonel, except by special permission. And if you drown six hours from now, you can thank me you lived that long. *Not another word! Get out!* . . . The damned fool!"

Arakal: "How did you know?"

Slagiron: "I was there when Cotter said we had to give up. I remember how that went. He had almost exactly the same tone in his voice, and you told him almost the same thing—that you'd come to the end of explanations."

Arakal: "What's wrong with Casey?"

Slagiron: "His younger brother's missing. And, farcical as it may seem, Casey promised his mother he'd protect his brother."

Arakal: "It was my mistake not to be out there with the rest."

Slagiron: "Sir, you were worn out."

Arakal: "The water would have woken me up. But Casey had better come to an understanding with his mother, or get a guarantee from Almighty God for his brother. We can't make the training soft. And we can't be crying over a hundred and fifty men missing when the units are all mixed up. The wonder is we don't have a thousand missing."

Slagiron: "I think we ought to do this practice landing in daylight."

Arakal: "Good. Then we'll do it twice."

S-One lowered the papers and glanced at his deputy. "How did all this turn out? The officers in the boat?"

"They went out twice, sir, and got wrecked on the beach each time, the second time at night. They came back in an indescribable frame of mind. But it was very popular with the men."

"With—" S-One blinked. "What was that?"

"The men, sir. The ordinary soldiers were delighted."

"I see. And the losses? The men who were missing?"

"Most turned up the next day, sir. Some had got lost on the beach; others were still in the wrong units."

"There is an aspect to this that is difficult for me to grasp. What are the relations now between Arakal, Slagiron, and Casey?"

"Back to normal, sir. Casey apologized."

"I see. . . . Well, there is still one thing, at least."

"What is that, sir?"

"Arakal recognizes that they need surprise." S-One smiled. "Though he is blockheaded, he *does* recognize that. But—" S-One handed his deputy the papers. "—they can't surprise us, *whatever* they do."

V. The Invasion

★ 1 ★

Arakal clung with aching hands to the rail of the *Panther* as the bombardment ship wallowed through seas that dropped away like canyons, then heaved themselves up like mountains rising to the sky. Arakal's gut was sore, his head ached, and his senses swam. There was nothing stable in any direction. The ship, massively reinforced to sustain the shock of its big guns, shuddered to the crash of uncountable tons of sea water.

"Sir!" called a voice, and Arakal turned from the slanting walls of gray water to see Admiral Bullinger clinging to the rail with one hand, his expression concerned.

Arakal managed to nod, and the Admiral leaned closer.

"We've found a spy device—built into the ship."

"A—*What*?"

"Spy device, sir. A listening device."

Arakal's attention was abruptly riveted on Bullinger.

"Is it effective? Can they hear anything with it?"

Bullinger leaned closer in the wind.

"It's a long-talker, a radio, sir. We've traced the connections. It's possible the Russ have overheard everything we've said on board since we captured the ships."

Arakal clung to the rail.

Bullinger, who had silently debated with himself how to tell his chief this terrible news, saw in surprise a brief look of grim exaltation as Arakal leaned closer.

"It's in working order?"

"Yes, sir."

"They could use it at this distance?"

"Can't be certain. But they could have arrangements to relay it. There are still satellites up there."

"Where does it pick up conversations *from*?"

"Your cabin, mine, the bridge—it's apparently connected to every cabin we use."

"If they picked up the signal, they know our plans?"

"Yes . . . If. There's still some hope, sir, that they didn't. But we don't know."

Arakal clung to the rail and watched the gray water climb up against the sky.

Bullinger said, "Shall we rip it out?"

"No. Leave it. You haven't disabled it?"

"No, sir."

"When was it found?"

"Late yesterday."

"In this storm?"

"Yes, sir."

"How?"

"There was a file case in the radio room, and it wasn't properly secured. It fell over, and split the paneling. There was wiring behind the panel."

"Who saw it?"

"The radio officer. He got curious, traced it, realized what it was, and showed it to the ship's captain. The captain took me out into the storm and told me. We've been very careful with the damned thing. We haven't said a word aloud where *it* could overhear."

"Who knows about it now?"

"You, me, the captain, the radio officer, and the three radio ratings. They've been working all day and all last night to trace it."

Arakal looked briefly over the rail, down into a sickening chasm of spray and spume and huge moving surfaces of gray water.

Bullinger now saw with astonishment that Arakal was smiling. "Sir—what do we do?"

"Swear them all to secrecy. Cover up the damage. Hide it, that is, and say nothing. Could the Russ know we've found it?"

"Not unless they can recognize the sound of prybars in this storm. Should we warn the other ships?"

"No. But tell me at once if *they* report finding anything."

Bullinger nodded, waited for a favorable tilt of the ship, and let go the rail.

Arakal looked around at the sea where the sky should be, and his face paled. Sickeningly, the sea rose. The ship plunged. Arakal's insides churned.

But if he could just live through it, this storm was bound to end, sometime.

★ **2** ★

S-One shook his head, careful to keep his bearing courteous. He reminded himself that in the formal hierarchy of the State, the man across the big table was his superior.

"No," said S-One, "I see no danger from this so-called invasion."

Across the table, his gaze intent, the tall, lean, faintly studious man formally identified in the table of organization as "G-One," for "Head of Government," and also known as "P-One," for "Chairman of the Central Committee of the Party"—this individual looked intently into S-One's eyes, until S-One felt the impact like a bright light glaring directly onto the retinas of his eyes, to explode across the back of his brain. But S-One neither flinched nor looked away.

Across the table, G-One broke the contact, and glanced around at the others seated at the table. No one ventured an opinion. G-One said, "General Brusilov?"

"Sir?"

"What is your opinion?"

Brusilov did not hesitate.

"I think it represents a great danger, and a great opportunity."

"Why?"

"It is a danger, because Arakal is a master of conflict. It represents an opportunity, because, if we can make peace with the Americans—a real peace—we should be able to overcome some serious problems."

G-One frowned, and glanced at S-One.

"Your reply?"

"I repeat what I have already said. Neither Arakal, his army, nor his disastrous plan, represent any danger to us."

G-One glanced at Brusilov.

Brusilov, some strain evident in his voice, said, "I don't want to seem insubordinate—"

G-One nodded. "We are well aware, General, that our defeat in America, and the loss of our fleet and our colonies there, was no fault of yours. We know that the fault lay in one who, contrary to your warning, underestimated this same opponent our colleague here—" G-One glanced briefly across the table "—tells us is no danger to us now. This precedent requires some attention on our part. Let us hear your honest opinion."

Brusilov waited a moment, then spoke in a careful voice.

"I have, speaking of my own experience, found Arakal to be honest and steadfast in friendship, and totally unpredictable in war. He is without conceit, free of serious delusion, and profound in his understanding of conflict. His blows dislocate the mind, as well as overwhelming physical resistance. His army is not to be judged by its numbers alone. His spirit actuates this army."

S-One spoke sharply. "What is the meaning of this statement: 'His spirit actuates this army'?"

G-One's eyes glinted, but he glanced curiously at Brusilov.

Before Brusilov could speak, S-One went on:

"The General speaks as one mentally dominated by another."

Brusilov's voice was suddenly flat. "I am warning you of what I have experienced myself. I will say frankly that from the information you have given me, I, too, would think Arakal has no chance. But I have been asked for my opinion, and I will state it:

"Arakal is dangerous. So is his army. Don't laugh at him because he speaks of the Wesdem O'Cracy, and before his army appeals to God for aid. Don't smile when you measure him against his ancestors. A part of the risk is that it is so hard to take such seeming backwardness seriously."

"I smile at him" said S-One, "when I consider his plan. Of all the places in Western Europe where he might land, and do us damage, he selects the one spot where no popular enthusiasm can help him, where we can destroy him as if he were a nut in a nutcracker."

Across the table, G-One said thoughtfully, "What is your plan?"

S-One controlled his voice.

"In deference to the General's warning, I am holding in reserve a carefully worked out deception plan, in the event Arakal should actually set foot alive on the continent, and survive the first day, which I do not expect."

G-One nodded. "This is prudent."

S-One waited a moment, to be sure that his voice was level.

"If, however, things work out as now seems probable, Arakal and the larger part of his force should be too badly mauled in the landing attempt to cause us any serious trouble."

"What are the specifics?"

"Arakal intends to land by moonlight at the full tide on a beach southeast of Cherbourg, on the east coast of the Cherbourg Peninsula. This is the old World War II beach known as 'Utah'. The Americans successfully landed there in 1944. In World War II, however, they came from Britain. Arakal is coming all the way across the Atlantic in one bound. They have already passed through a severe storm. They will arrive weak and none too fit for combat."

Brusilov spoke politely but definitely.

"Excuse me, Comrade, but those troops are tough. And we know they are well trained. This is not the first storm they have experienced."

S-One waited a moment before speaking. His candid belief was that he was surrounded by a pack of fools. This belief might find its way into his voice and manner if he was not careful. He cleared his throat, and spoke politely.

"Have you ever been seasick, General?"

Brusilov said gruffly, "More than once."

"I think you are as tough as Arakal or his men. How combat-worthy did you feel after you had just been seasick?"

"I was as weak as a kitten."

There was a murmur, and a sense of relaxation around the table. Even G-One, across the table, looked relieved.

S-One said quietly, "Arakal's invasion force, which we estimate at not over thirty-five thousand men, should arrive off the old Utah Beach in time for him to put his men ashore somewhere around dead *low* tide—not high tide—since we managed to insinuate into Admiral Bullinger's possession faulty tide tables for the region. The Admiral, despite his rank, is inexperienced, and so are his men."

"So," said G-One, "the troops will arrive at low tide? What is the practical significance of this?"

"The beach is very flat. Their landing boats will run aground far out."

"Their walk inland will be longer?"

"Yes, and exposed to our fire all the way. We will allow the attack to proceed until Arakal is well committed. We will then open fire on the ships with our very powerful camouflaged guns. We will destroy the men by fire from machinegun nests at the base of the cliffs. The fortifications of the peninsula were planned to stand a siege, and could be held with ten thousand men, such is the degree of automatic control. Actually, we have forty thousand men on hand, ready for anything."

"So, even if he should break through locally, you should still smash him in the end?"

"Even if there were *no* up-to-date fortifications, as is the case elsewhere, we should be able to smash him here. We can hit him when part of his men are ashore and part are still on the ships. The important thing is, we know *where* he is coming, and we are ready. It would be a different matter if we had to guess which place he would strike. We do not have to guess."

There was a murmur of approval, and, across the table, G-One nodded grudgingly, and glanced at Brusilov.

"General? What do you say of this?"

"So far, so good," said Brusilov. "But where is our main reserve?"

S-One barely held back a sarcastic reply. Before he could find an answer suitably polite, there was a rap, the door opened, and an apologetic voice spoke urgently from the doorway. S-One recognized his own deputy, and watched in astonishment as S-Two crossed the room rapidly toward him.

"Sir, excuse me! This won't wait!"

He thrust out a slim sheaf of papers, and S-One recognized the usual form of translated comments received by way of hidden electronic devices on the ships. Searching his deputy's face, he recognized an urgent look of warning.

S-One's calculation suddenly vanished. His voice came out harsh and cold. "This is a report of *what*? Speak up, S-Two."

His deputy's voice was low. "Of a meeting of Arakal and his generals on board the bombardment ship *Panther*. On page four, sir—"

S-One spoke sharply. "Don't try to spare me. Speak up! What's wrong?"

"Arakal, sir! The attack is not going in against the Cherbourg Peninsula, after all!"

S-One felt as if the earth moved under him. The blood roared in his ears.

"What? *Where*, then?"

"Le Havre, sir."

S-One swore, heard the uproar around the table, and then Brusilov's voice, patient but grimly persistent:

"Where is our main reserve in France?"

S-One drew a deep breath. "Metz."

"Then it can't help us. He'll get ashore. What do we have between Le Havre and Paris?"

S-One thought carefully.

"Nothing."

Brusilov nodded moodily.

"We have just been outmaneuvered."

S-One's deputy was still right there, his expression still urgent.

Across the table, G-One spoke dryly.

"Is there more?"

S-One looked back at his deputy. His voice was harsh, strained, and he made no attempt to conceal it.

"Tell us frankly. There is no way to break news like this gently."

"Sir, Arakal gave instructions that, and I quote: 'the signals for the uprising should be sent'. We already have word of coded signals that, so far, have not been possible to interpret."

Across the table, G-One held his hand palm-out for quiet. His eyes were unreadable as he looked at S-One.

S-One turned to his deputy, and held up the sheaf of papers.

"You have read this? Or did someone else summarize it to you?"

"Both. After the summary, while the information was being verified, I read it."

"What explanation did Arakal give, that he had changed the landing site?"

"That, in war, misdirection is the key to victory; that it would be suicide to attack the main Soviet base in Western Europe when that base was warned in advance of the attack; and that, since the plans and preparations had been made in the vicinity of our former colonies, we were certain to have been warned of the practice landings, and the target; and so we would be waiting in the peninsula. This fact, that we had been misled, would clear the road to Paris, and the seizure of Paris would in turn strike a heavy blow to our prestige. The uprisings would maintain the split in our forces, which, united, would doubtless be more numerous than theirs. Beyond that, he said, it was impossible to predict, since everything depended on particulars. But with the fleet, with a mobile army, operating in a country where the transportation system could be cut, on signal, by the guerrillas . . ."

"The guerrillas?"

"I believe he said, 'the local patriots', but the real meaning was guerrillas. In such a situation, with part of our troops locked up in Normandy, and another force trapped in Britain, there would be bound to be opportunities."

There was a silence. Across the table, G-One turned to Marshal of the Armed Forces Vasilevsky, who had said nothing so far, and even now sat dourly staring at the far wall, his clasped hands resting on the table top.

"Well, Marshal?" said G-One.

Vasilevsky turned his head to look at G-One. It was as if he aimed a gun. His voice was a rumble, as of artillery in the distance.

"You want me now to make war on a map?"

G-One grappled with the comment, and, without a word, turned to Brusilov.

Vasilevsky went on. "The next thing, we soil our pants with fear of this American. He is still on his ship, isn't he? Let everyone stand to his guns where he is, and start the reserves from Metz toward Paris in the morning. If he lands at Le Havre, so be it. Let's see how much artillery he brought with him."

Brusilov said at once, "I agree."

G-One exhaled, and glanced quizzically across the table.

S-One, hearing the Marshal's rough voice, felt the pressure fall away. Brusilov, too, he noted, had not panicked. Good. But an uprising in Europe would make far more than military problems. He shook his head.

"We can undoubtedly beat *Arakal*, just as a large cup of water can extinguish a match. The trouble is, the cup of water cannot necessarily extinguish the blaze that the match may cause when it is dropped into a pile of dry wood."

Vasilevsky grunted. "The French are not happy with us, eh? Well, I'm not sure the Germans are, either. Or the Dutch, or the Italians."

"That's the point."

Vasilevsky was silent a moment, then he shrugged. His voice was stolid, fatalistic.

"I have given my advice."

Across the table, G-One said, "If the Marshal's advice does not appeal to you, S-One, what do *you* suggest?"

S-One saw the wedge driven between himself and the Marshal, but ignored it. He turned to his deputy.

"What is Arakal's immediate plan?"

"Some of his ships will drop anchor off the Normandy peninsula. The rest will continue toward Le Havre. A few boats will set out toward the Normandy beaches, and make sounds to deceive us. Tomorrow, his fleet will enter Le Havre, and the troops will entrain for Paris."

"*When*, tomorrow?"

"He was evidently illustrating what he said with a detailed map, or a blackboard. We assume there was a diagram showing the relationship of the different parts of the attack, and the times. There was a good deal of confusion at first, and the analysis of the conversation is not yet complete. We have the expression 'at dawn' repeated several times, but we do not know with certainty what it refers to."

S-One looked across the table, and saw from the bland expression of his superior that this reverse was not without its incidental benefits from the viewpoint of G-One, the Head of Government.

S-One spoke with a humility much more real than the restraint he had imitated before.

"I believe," said S-One, "that it is still possible to forestall Arakal militarily, thanks to the reports of this conference of his. If not, we will at once activate the deception plan. The aim of the deception plan is to deflect the force of any popular uprising. If the deception plan should fail—which does not seem possible to me—but if it should, then we must seek a military solution. In preparation for that, our military forces have already been drawn back to mutually supporting positions. This is the reason why our Reserve France is back at Metz."

Marshal Vasilevsky spoke up.

"Where is our Benelux Reserve?"

"Liege."

"And the Forward Reserve Germany?"

"Trier."

"Where is our Main Reserve Germany?"

"Muhlhausen."

The Marshal nodded.

S-One continued, "I will have to give the orders at once if we are to lose no time. My intention is to move the troops in the Cherbourg Peninsula by rail to Rouen. Depending on the speed of Arakal's movements, we may be able to forestall him at Le Havre. At the very least, we can block his way to Paris."

G-One looked questioningly at Marshal Vasilevsky.

The Marshal grunted. "Who can say? We may get beat. On the other hand, while he tries to fool us, maybe we can catch him with half his men still on their boats. At least, we will find out what there is to this guerrilla business."

G-One looked surprised.

"You approve?"

"I am not in charge. I neither approve nor disapprove. It is not what I would do. I have already told you what I would do. But it may work. These things are not decided on a map, but on the ground."

G-One said, "General Brusilov?"

"I would use Marshal Vasilevsky's plan. But I am not familiar with all the factors, and this present plan may work."

G-One nodded, and turned to S-One.

"Very well. Proceed. The matter is entirely in your hands."

S-One came to his feet, bowed, and left the room.

VI. Blows in the Dark

★ 1 ★

The sea moved in long slow swells, beneath a moonlit fog that hid the beaches, the bluffs, the other boats, and the ships that were the source of the heavy rumble of anchor chains heard far out in the bay.

Through the fog, like fuzzy images of beetles crawling across a surface of dark and slightly rippled satin, came long, low, open boats, the men laboring steadily at the oars, the officers crouched tensely at the bows, peering into the fog.

Wrapped in a cloak, one hand gripping the boat's wet gunnel, the other cupping a large watch whose luminous dial showed two minutes before 3:00 A.M., Arakal spoke in a low voice to the trumpeter crouched close behind him.

"We should be almost there. Stay right with me. And when we get out, keep that flag case up out of the water."

"Yes, sir."

Arakal snapped the inner cover shut over the watch face, pressed shut the outer cover that fitted down onto the hopefully waterproof gasket, slid the watch into its oilskin pouch, and methodically checked its fastenings. He counted silently as he checked watch, sword belt, map case, canteen, bandage box, cartridge box, and the bulky leather case for his long-seeing glasses. He eased his sword's fastenings around, and gathered up the edges of his cloak, as either sword or cloak could trip him getting out of the boat. Then he waited, and he continued to silently count:

. . . ninety-nine . . . one   hundred . . . one   hundred and one . . .

There was a clash of oars, and the helmsman's voice, low and patient, guided the oarsmen back into unison.

Arakal mentally rehearsed what to do when the boat hit the sand. As he thought over the possible complications and their answers, he was still silently counting:

. . . two   hundred   sixty-one . . . two   hundred   sixty-two . . . two hundred sixty-three . . .

Behind him, the huddled trumpeter shifted the flag case uneasily.

Arakal peered ahead, to see through the fog the glimmer of open water still in front of them.

The rhythmic splash and pull of the oars continued. Absently, he counted:

. . . three hundred and six . . . three hundred and seven . . . three hundred and eight . . .

Still, ahead, he could occasionally glimpse the water.

The rhythmic splash, and the gurgle of water past the boat, went on.

Tired from the storm, with the drifting fog around him, Arakal's eyes went almost shut.

There was a hiss of the hull scraping over sand. The boat slowed. The helmsman growled, "Stow—"

Arakal was suddenly wide awake. "Not yet. There's water in front of us. We've hit a bar."

The men fitted their oars back between the pegs. There was a scrape and thump as the helmsman unshipped the rudder. Again, he gave his low chant. With a faint grinding sound, the boat slid unevenly forward.

Arakal peered around in the fog as they glided ahead once again, and again time stretched out.

Where was the beach?

★ 2 ★

S-One tensely watched the display.

By now, at last, the laden troop trains were finally passing through Rouen. Position indicators for the ships showed a swerve in course, as the bulk of Arakal's Fleet swung past Normandy, and approached Le Havre. Left behind, several ships still lingered off the east coast of the Normandy peninsula. Reports from a small scout force left at the old Utah Beach told of the sounds of anchor chains, of faint rumblings and thuddings, even of the sounds of oars—but nothing whatever had yet appeared on the beach.

The wall opposite S-One's desk now showed a detailed representation of Normandy, the Bay of the Seine, and the railroad lines connecting Cherbourg to Rouen, and Rouen to Le Havre. On the display, blue lights in the bay showed the approach of Arakal's fleet to Le Havre, while on land short bright-red bars moved steadily along a black line, representing S-One's troop trains, which soon would be approaching Le Havre. The display suggested a close race, which should soon be decided, one way or another.

S-One felt the throb of a more rapid pulse, and a faint sense of shortness of breath.

Brusilov, across the desk, sat with his chair turned, watched the lighted wall, and said nothing.

Methodically, S-One thought over his dispositions. Le Havre, for all practical purposes, was defenseless. But he had over forty thousand men on the way, and by dawn the first troops should be close to the port. Surely they would be in time to smash Arakal's beachhead. But even in the event of military failure, the deception teams were already warned and ready, and could act in Normandy, Le Havre, or elsewhere. If, somehow, Arakal should see through the deception plan, then S-One would hand the whole situation over to Marshal Vasilevsky, who had already tacitly approved the location of the troops.

Testing the connection of these arrangements, S-One found no flaw. Yet, as time passed, it was becoming increasingly hard for him to breathe.

Across the desk, Brusilov's head turned, as from the east a line of light passed slowly across the map, leaving it lighter. The glowing markers on the map darkened by contrast. The change represented the coming of daylight in France.

S-One stared at the display.

There was an urgent rap on the door.

S-One called, "Come in!" and the door opened, to admit his deputy.

"Sir," cried S-Two, "we have reports that Arakal has landed. *In Normandy!*"

★ 3 ★

Arakal, and the other men from the first boats to reach shore, had climbed to a kind of shelving terrace partway up the slope above the beach. By some miracle, they had all reached the same beach, and Arakal was now crouched with Slagiron under the hastily erected tent. They had a map spread out before them, and a small portable lamp trailed a thread of smoke as it cast its flickering shadows over the map. Around them, the tent slatted in a rising wind, and Slagiron, one big forefinger on the map, shook his head.

"Nothing matches."

Arakal noted the small blue Xs that marked the positions of the ships anchored off the coast. He slid a marker along the edge of the scale, clamped it at his estimate of the distance the small boats should have traveled, considering the time that had passed, held the pin at the end of the scale to the nearest blue X, and swung the scale around.

"The tide must still have been going *out*. So, we were coming in against the tide. And, on top of that, there must be a current out there."

"Bullinger claimed to have accurate tide tables."

"They must have been like those maps of the Mediterranean he told us about. We're going to have to bring the bulk of the men ashore at dead low tide."

"Ashore. But *where*?"

Arakal lifted an edge of the map to get the flickering light more directly on it.

"Look. Back of this other beach, over here, where it isn't so steep. The distances match, if we make allowances for a current."

Slagiron swore under his breath. "This puts us on the wrong side of the river. On top of that, there's the marsh, and we're on the wrong side of it, too."

"But everything fits. That second bar we hit would have been about here. And we finally landed here. And now, we should be—" He put his finger on the map, back of the beach "—here."

Slagiron peered at the map. "We can't reach Cherbourg from here. And we could get bottled up in this hole."

"But at least," said Arakal, "we're on *land*."

"There is that," said Slagiron with feeling. "All right. Do we try to get to the right beach? Or do we use this one?"

"If we try to get to the right beach from here, we'll have a mess like that fourth practice landing. There won't be any unit not mixed up with some other unit. Just keep them coming in. And give your account to Bullinger on paper, so if their spy system still works, we don't tell the Russ about this."

★ **4** ★

S-One gripped the arms of his chair, looked back at the display, then at his deputy.

"*Normandy?*"

"Yes, sir."

S-One glanced up.

Off Le Havre, on the display, the ships were now swinging away, moving further out into the bay. And now a blue marker had appeared on the Normandy coast.

For the second time in two days, S-One felt the world step aside, to go on without him. He kept his voice calm, as he turned to his deputy.

"Activate the deception plan."

S-Two said, a trace of anguish in his voice, "Sir, the scout team on the spot reports that the coast defense system is still undamaged. There has been no bombardment or actual penetration of the defenses."

"And?"

"We can open fire on Arakal's ships, turn the troops around in Le Havre and start them back toward Normandy."

"That will take time. How many of the enemy are already ashore?"

This time, S-Two's voice was clearly anguished: "We don't know."

"A hundred? Five thousand? Twenty thousand?"

"We can't be sure! There may have been more deception. I would guess between three and twelve thousand. But we don't *know*."

"And how many men do we still have in the Citadel?"

"Very few, sir. But until there is heavy damage, the guns can be worked by automatic control. It is a very efficient system, designed and built before the war."

S-One hesitated, and glanced at the display. Suddenly he sat straight.

"But that is not Utah Beach!"

"No, sir. They completely avoided Utah Beach."

S-One sat very still.

"In short, we have received from them nothing but misleading information?"

S-Two nodded.

S-One glanced briefly at Brusilov, who sat stolidly, saying nothing.

S-One looked back at his deputy.

"What they have done is nothing less than to use *our* electronic information system to lead us around by the nose." He glanced at Brusilov. "What would you do, General?"

"Roughly as your deputy suggests."

"How do you think it would work out?"

Brusilov considered the map, and shrugged.

"Who can say? No matter what we do, it could turn into an ugly mess before it's over."

S-One considered it, narrow-eyed. He turned to his deputy.

"Order the last of our troops out of the citadel. Reroute the units at Le Havre to Metz. Activate the deception plan, at once."

S-Two stiffened, gave a slight bow, and hurried out.

S-One looked at Brusilov.

"As a purely military solution, I suppose my deputy's idea has its merits. But I see now that we have to aim at more than military victory. Arakal has acted on a different level entirely." S-One paused, frowning, then looked at Brusilov curiously. "*This* is what you meant, when you spoke of Arakal's blows 'dislocating the mind'?"

Brusilov nodded. "This is a sample of it. And if you will excuse me for giving too much advice, I think the situation is now so dangerous that it would be better at once to hand over command to the Marshal. In my experience, the riskiest way to fight Arakal is with subtlety. In a plain straightforward fight, we can wrestle him to a standstill. He is tough, but so are we, and our weapons are better. But when the bright ideas begin to flow, look out. He has the edge, there."

S-One nodded. "I can well believe it, General. And if it were a question of a fight, I would do exactly as you suggest. But I have discarded that idea. I am not planning to fight Arakal."

Brusilov blinked. He glanced at the display. Then he looked again at S-One.

"Arakal is ashore in France, with the world's only battle fleet, and thirty-five thousand men at his back, and France by your own reckoning is a tinder box awaiting the match. *And you are not going to fight him?*"

S-One smiled. "That is correct, General."

"Then, if I may ask, Comrade, what *are* you going to do?"

"The deception plan, that I spoke of, is already in action."

VII. The Welcoming Party

★ 1 ★

Arakal, by his own estimate, had four thousand men ashore, a number of machine guns, half-a-dozen small rocket launchers, and two one-pounder cannon. The sea, so calm last night, was now rough; the tide had come in, and a triple line of bright-yellow marker buoys bobbed on the churning waters of the bay. Each buoy was held by a long slender cord, its far end attached to some artillery piece that now rested on the bottom, where its raft had overturned. From his height above the beach, Arakal could look to north or south along the shore, and see the painted snouts of Russ big guns looking out to sea from turrets disguised to match the surrounding rock of the bluffs.

In both directions, Arakal could make out little groups of his men looking up at the guns, wondering perhaps how quickly the sand and rock they had fed into the snouts of the guns could be cleared out from inside if enemy gunners were in there. So far, nothing had happened. But Arakal had word of more Russ guns, these still out of his reach to north and south, but probably well able to smash ships landing troops here.

Slagiron had gone out to Bullinger, the troops already ashore were moving inland rapidly, the weather was still getting worse, fewer and fewer reinforcements were reaching the beach, and Arakal, looking down at the surf, at the sand and pebbles below, at the men staggering ashore from an overturned boat, and seeing in his mind the map and what was further inland, groped for the next unpleasant surprise.

Just then, a strongly built sergeant ran down a path from behind a clump of small trees bending in the wind. He raised his hand in a quick salute.

"Sir, we've found a way into one of the turrets!"

"Good! Where?"

"Just above here. It's a kind of vent shaft or escape hatch, planted around with brush. A steel ladder runs part way down the shaft. At the bottom of the ladder, there's a room cut in the cliff. From there, you can fire the gun."

"Any sign of the Russ?"

"No, sir. The place was empty."

"Let's get a look at this."

★ 2 ★

S-Two bowed very slightly. "The deception plan is activated, sir."

S-One sighed in relief. "Good."

★ 3 ★

Arakal squirmed feet-first under the upraised rock, found the ladder, eased down into the vertical shaft, and then, from below him, the sergeant called, "The gear-wheel, sir! Watch out, or you'll get caught in it."

Arakal freed his sword from the ladder rungs, twisted sidewise, and pulled his cloak loose from the geared mechanism that raised the rock at the top of the shaft. He paused to consider this mechanism, which was free of rust, and freshly greased. Then he made his way down the ladder, to step carefully off the last rung into a sort of wide recessed archway, where the sergeant pushed open a heavy door, and then Arakal found himself amongst several of his men, in a dimly lit room perhaps forty feet across.

To the right, at the far end of the room was the gun. The breech, the massive wheeled mounting, and the tracks for the wheels, took up most of that end of the room.

To the left, in the middle of the rear wall, was an open door into what appeared to be a kind of large dumb-waiter. Several low massive tables stood nearby, and a low, heavy, wheeled cart.

Directly across from Arakal, on the opposite wall, was a detailed map of the shorefront, and, above the map, several dark grilled openings. From the high ceiling, two shiny brass tubes reached down, bearing near the lower end of each, a pair of outthrust handgrips and a set of eyepieces. Through one of these, a frowning corporal with five campaign stripes was now looking, his hands tense on the grips. Beside each of the tubes padded headsets hung down on thick black wires.

Arakal glanced across the room at the gun, to see another dangling headset, its cord hanging from an overhead bar that appeared to pivot in unison with the traverse of the gun.

Arakal's glance met the gaze of one of his soldiers, standing to the side of the gun, with a look of baffled curiosity.

Arakal took hold of the free set of handgrips, and pulled down. The shiny tube with its eyepieces slid easily down, and suddenly he was looking out at two separate views of a ship riding at anchor on a rough gray sea. He twisted the handgrips, and the images separated further. He twisted in the opposite direction, and the images merged. With a sense of shock, he recognized one of his bombardment ships, a faint slender cross superimposed on its center. As he moved the grips, changing numerals came into view below the view of the ship. With each turn of the tube or twist of the grips, came a low heavy rumble from across the room.

He tore his gaze from the eyepieces.

Across the room, the gun was now more elevated than when he had first seen it. The bar holding the upper end of the dangling headphones had swung slightly to the left.

Outside the room, in the shaft, the ladder rattled.

Near the gun, a soldier cleared his throat.

"Sir, this gun follows every move you make with that tube."

Carefully, Arakal turned the handles until he saw nothing but an unfocused view of a large-numbered buoy floating in otherwise empty water. He stepped over to the gun, examined the mechanism intently, then straightened, frowning.

At the other tube, the corporal said soberly, "This scope also controls that gun, sir. But the scope you used overrode it. There's a red button on the handle of each of these scopes."

Arakal nodded. "Don't touch it, or we could get a nasty shock. The barrel is plugged with pebbles and dirt."

"It looks as if one man could aim and fire this thing."

Arakal nodded. As he looked around, it also appeared to him that a part of the gun that he hadn't understood was an automatic loading mechanism.

From the doorway leading to the shaft, a voice called out, "Sir, we've got a funny kind of prisoner up there. You might want to see him."

Arakal went up the ladder, crawled out at the top, and found two men and a bemused corporal standing beside a slight dark figure with a large moustache, face smeared with charcoal, wearing a camouflage suit, leather boots, and a narrow red-white-and-blue armband.

The corporal said, "Listen to him a minute, sir."

Arakal nodded to the slight mustached figure, to be rewarded by a quick grin displaying a mouthful of stained teeth. The figure spoke briefly and rapidly, in French. After a moment's uncertainty, Arakal pieced together what he had said:

"Moi, je suis Pierrot. J'ai detruit les russes."

Arakal took a hard look at the slight figure. The two sentences rang in Arakal's head. "I am Pierrot. I have destroyed the Russ." Arakal thought of the gun, and of his bombardment ship in its sights. With an effort, he framed in French the question, "How did you do that?"

"It was very simple," came the answer, and, listening intently, Arakal followed as the words poured out. "Follow me and I will reveal to you the means. I am Pierrot. It is I who command the Striking Force for Independence. The Russ here are no more. You will join me in the march on Paris."

Arakal glanced around.

His men were streaming up the path from the beach, and heading inland. Dark clouds were rushing past low overhead. The trees swayed in the wind.

Arakal spoke slowly as he groped for the words:

"When you say the Russ are destroyed *here*, do you mean on this beach?"

Pierrot made a wide sweep of the hand.

"Throughout the Normandy Citadel."

"And Cherbourg?"

"Cherbourg is mine."

"You say you have destroyed all the Russ in this peninsula?"

"It is as true as that I stand before you."

Arakal strained to get the slight figure into focus.

"You *personally* destroyed them?"

Pierrot looked startled.

"Personally? But no. I am the brain of the Striking Force for Independence. I am the spirit which controls the Striking Force for Independence. The Striking Force for Independence is, as it were, my body, and in that sense, yés, I destroyed the Russ personally. But not with my own hands. No. And those of them who are not destroyed physically are destroyed militarily. They are in desperate flight, the Russ. It is I, Pierrot, who tell you this. Throughout the Normandy Citadel, from Cherbourg to Saint Lo, from the Bay of the Seine to the Bay of Biscay, the Russ are dead or in flight."

Arakal glanced from Pierrot to the corporal, at whose collar was the small blue diamond-shaped emblem signifying that he could speak the tongue of the Kebeckers.

"Do you understand this?"

"Yes, sir. That is, I understand the words."

"You don't believe him?"

"Not the way he tells it."

"Why?"

The corporal smiled, man-to-man. "Just look at him, sir. I'll believe he's beat the Russ when I see a mouse chase a panther up a tree."

Arakal turned intently to Pierrot.

"Do you have means of transportation?"

"Everything the Russ have not fled in belongs to me. Have you need of transportation for your troops?"

"Yes."

"I, Pierrot, can provide it."

"Good. And you say you can prove the Russ are beaten here?"

"Follow me and I will show you."

"How far?"

"Down this ladder and down a hallway."

"That ladder goes down to a room, not a hallway."

"It goes to a room and then to a hallway. I know the Russ fortifications here as I know my own hand. I saw to it that the Russ could not fire upon our allies as you approached. It is I, Pierrot, who have struck the sword from the hand of the Russ in their Normandy Citadel."

"Show me."

The corporal said earnestly, "Let a few of us go along, sir. Don't trust yourself to this hero."

Arakal nodded. He glanced around, to see a colonel crouched with a captain at the head of the path from the beach, frowning over a map. It was, if anything, even darker than it had been. Not far away, thunder rumbled, as a patter of rain swept along through the trees. Arakal turned back, to see that the corporal had already got half-a-dozen men together.

Arakal turned to Pierrot. "Lead the way."

Pierrot inclined his head, slid under the inclined cover, and swung easily onto the ladder. Arakal followed, then the corporal and his men. Below Arakal, Pierrot stepped off the ladder, and pushed into the room.

Arakal and the rest filed in.

Pierrot reached out, took hold of the ladder, lifted, and pulled down. The ladder ran down with a clicking noise, to come to a sudden stop. Pierrot stepped onto the ladder and climbed quickly down.

Arakal followed. Pierrot stepped off, and pushed open a heavy sliding door that led into a wide dimly lighted corridor, which ran in a long gradual zigzag past another door like the one they had just stepped through.

"These doors to the right," said Pierrot, "each lead up to a shaft coming down from a gun. Each gun had a commander and a crew of five. The gun could be aimed, fired, and reloaded by power, under the control of one man. Or, if the power should be lost during an attack, the guns could be worked by hand. Both methods were practiced on a regular schedule. All this fortification was planned in advance, before the occupation that followed the Russ attack on America, and the American abandonment of Europe. When, several months ago, your fleet stood well off the shore, and examined this coast, these guns were registered on a few of your ships. But whoever commanded the ships was wary, stayed well out, and the Russ did not fire. That silent confrontation was our notice that once again America was interested in Europe, and if Europe wished to free herself, Europe must prepare to help the Americans when they returned. We have kept a watch ever since, especially along this coast. Last night, when your ships anchored in the bay, the Russ sentinels were overpowered, and our plan was put in action throughout the Citadel."

To their left were double doors, and Pierrot pushed them open.

"The mess hall for this unit of coast artillery is just down this hall."

Arakal glanced back.

Behind him, his men looked suspiciously around, their guns at the ready.

Pierrot shoved open a second set of double doors, and gave a sort of solemn bow, his expression grave.

Arakal stopped abruptly. Ahead was a large room, where at tables and on benches, green-uniformed men sprawled unmoving. The smell of vomit was overpowering. As Arakal slowly turned his head, he saw men outstretched on the floor, men who had fallen over backwards from benches and lay partly on the floor. Here and there others had dropped to the floor while carrying trays. The eyes of most of the men were open, and their expressions fixed.

Pierrot said, "Underground, here, there is protection against nearly everything—except a poisoned air supply. We considered poisoning the food, but that involves too many uncertainties. This was quick."

Arakal stepped aside, to let his men come in.

Pierrot said quietly, "Other situations in other places required other measures. Most of the Russ fled. You may, since we are nearby, care to see one more point of interest down here—the obstacle store room."

He led the way back down the hall, took out a set of keys, and opened a wide sliding door. He led the way along a corridor that seemed to run straight back into the cliff. He slid open another door.

Arakal looked into a chamber that extended back for possibly a hundred feet, and that appeared to be forty feet or so deep, vertically.

This chamber extended to the right, buttressed at intervals by thick pillars. From the ceiling dangled large hooks on chains that hung down from traveling hoists. The room was packed with stacked pyramids of welded iron, some painted a dark red, others the color of wet sand. The sharp points and edges glittered like oiled blades.

Pierrot said, "There are enough obstacles packed in these storerooms to block this whole sector of beach. These devices would force you to come at high tide and risk having the bottoms of your landing boats ripped out, or else to come at low tide and cross a wide flat beach on foot under fire." He pointed to sliding doors in the back wall of the chamber. "Back there they have elevators, to carry these obstacles up to the loading point. From there, they go down on tracked transporters to the beach. They also had mines with multiples trip-wires to plant amongst the obstacles."

Arakal said carefully, "Did they also have aircraft?"

"Aircraft? No. It is rumored that they had a helicopter stored here somewhere. We have never seen it."

Arakal cast a last look at the stacked obstacles, and stepped back.

Pierrot said, "Now, you need transport?"

"We do. The sooner we can get ashore in Cherbourg, the better."

The next few hours passed in a blur, compounded of thunder and lightning, pouring rain, countermanded orders, missing units, and bad tempers—to end finally with the men who had started inland from the beach settled instead on flatcars moving through a tunnel lighted at intervals, dropping deeper and deeper, then crawling upward to settle finally into a steady run at some twenty to twenty-five miles an hour, with a cool wind in their faces, and an occasional glowing white light that appeared out of the darkness, allowing them a brief glimpse of a white concrete pillar and curved brackets supporting conduits of varied sizes, and then passed and faded swiftly to a dot behind them, while, far ahead, another dim white glow appeared.

At last, a brighter glow appeared ahead, the repeated click of the wheels on the tracks came at more and more widely spaced intervals, and then a long lighted platform pulled into view as the track leveled out. The train moved past this platform slowly, passed through a dimly lighted place where the tunnel widened, and swung around to the right where the light reflected from a dizzying pattern of tracks, and then again they were moving at twenty-five miles an hour down a tunnel lit at intervals, and then a second lighted platform pulled into view. The train of flatcars slowed and stopped.

Pierrot let go the lever in the lead flatcar, swung off a low stool, and waved to the beaming camouflage-suited men who appeared on the platform, carrying rifles and submachine guns. Here and there amongst the rapid exchange of comments that passed, Arakal caught a word or two. Then Pierrot turned to him, and spoke a little more slowly:

"This is East Fort, near St. Pierre Eglise. From here, you can contact your ships by radio. They will have to enter Cherbourg Harbor, and it would be prudent to send our pilots to bring the ships in. I trust you have interpreters?"

"Yes, we have interpreters."

"Then we must waste no time. The sooner we are on the track of the Russ, the less chance that they might recover and give serious resistance."

That same afternoon, Arakal stood on a dock in the brilliant sunlight that had followed the storm, as the main body of his troops marched in to the cheers of a crowd wild with enthusiasm.

VIII. The Tiger in the Trap

★ 1 ★

S-One rose slowly behind his desk as G-One entered, then found himself waiting, as if to see whether armed troops might follow the Head of Government.

G-One smiled ironically, "The execution squad? Not yet, at any rate."

"You must admit, this is unusual."

"My motives were of the most common. I wished to find some place to talk undisturbed. And largely unobserved."

"Everything you say here will be recorded."

"I am not unaware of the fact. But the records are in whose custody?"

"To tell the truth, I don't know."

"You astound me. If I had your job, that is one of the first things I would find out."

407

"Then you would not have my job. One of the first things we learn is complete trust in the organization."

"Even after you are the head of it?"

"Those who judge our trust are capable judges of character. If we did not *truly* trust, we would be unlikely to be considered for the job."

"And if I ask you to find out?"

"You are the head of the government. I will certainly obey."

"You don't say 'comply with your request'? You say 'obey'?"

S-One shrugged. "You have the authority. If you impressed me as incompetent, or dangerous to the security of the state, then my thoughts might follow a different track. But I have problems enough to do my job without seeking to obstruct you in the performance of yours."

"Shall we, then, come to the point at once?"

"And why not?"

"Very well. The military are uneasy about the situation that has come about."

S-One nodded.

"From a military viewpoint, we have a disaster on our hands."

"That bad?"

"From a military viewpoint, yes."

"And from a political viewpoint?"

"It should soon be equally bad."

G-One looked at him soberly.

"Frankness is often a great virtue. But it cannot stand alone."

"I am not attempting to cover failure. I said 'disaster', not 'failure'."

"I have to admit, to me they are certainly very close to synonymous."

"In my position, I must look beyond disaster."

"You assert a primacy of your position?"

S-One shook his head.

"I take it for granted that there can be no conflict of authority between you and me. It is a very simple situation. If you dislike me, you can remove me. But I must do my job to the best of my ability. Any explanation you want, within the limits of what is permissible, you will have."

G-One's frown had grown longer as S-One spoke.

"Comrade, what is this now if it is not a conflict of authority? You say that you will obey what I suggest within the limits of what is agreeable. This is a conflict of authority."

"Then my meaning is not clear. I am saying, you can remove me at any time. But while I am in charge, I have no choice except to do my duty to the best of my ability."

"While you are here, you will do as you choose?"

"Let me make an example. The house is on fire. You send for the firemen. The head fireman is directing the pumps and hoses when you say to him, 'I have greater authority than you. I order you to direct the stream of water not where you are directing it, but over there, where my judgment tells me that you should be directing it.' What do you expect him to do?"

"You tell me."

"If he is competent, he will say, 'Either let me do my job or replace me.' He will not obey you, because he has been trained for the job, and is therefore more competent in it than you, not having had the training, may realize."

"Then you assert an expert knowledge that I cannot appreciate."

"What I am asserting is that I have reasons for my actions, even if those reasons are not yet evident."

"And these reasons are based on expertise?"

"Yes."

"Could a military man understand your reasoning?"

"It would depend on the military man. It would, however, run counter to his training."

"I repeat that the military are profoundly uneasy."

"I am not surprised. We have had already a military disaster—our ousting from France."

G-One stared at him. "I was not aware that we had been driven out as yet."

S-One smiled. "We are on the run. Next will follow the political disaster. France will rise up. Next, Arakal will attack us more deeply, as the nations of Europe rise against us."

"I will have to tell you that this plan, assuming that it *is* your plan, does not fill me with confidence."

"You doubtless wonder," said S-One, "how we can prosper from being overthrown."

"Yes." G-One was watching him alertly.

"The answer," said S-One, "is that, of course, none of these things will happen. The head of the firefighters must sometimes permit the fire to run on its way, in a direction which does no damage, in order to protect that which is truly valuable."

"That sounds very good. What is your actual plan?"

"If I should reveal it to you, would you tell the military?"

"That is a question of my own discretion."

"In that case, I must respectfully decline to explain. Because the military, by their actions, might nullify the effect of the plan."

"In that case," said G-One, his face darkening, "I will regretfully have to point out to you that it is my responsibility to see that the state survives this invasion. A state cannot have two heads. You will either tell me the nature of your plan, or I will have no choice but to relieve you of authority."

S-One nodded. His voice was calm, unconcerned. "Certainly you have that authority."

G-One blinked.

S-One looked out at the garden and smiled. "Isn't is beautiful? Such floods of color."

G-One did not move.

S-One said, "What you have said is very true: 'A state cannot have two heads.' But it *can* have a head, a heart, a liver, a spinal cord—There is no conflict in such different and separate organs which complement and reinforce each other. Just so, the state can have a number of organs, which may function on different levels. I have said that you can remove me, and you can. I will offer no resistance. But let me point out what you doubtless already know. I *could* resist."

"I am aware of it."

"Yes," said S-One. "Power in a state always resides somewhere, and it does not always reside in the obvious place. You, for instance, possess the formal authority, according to the table of organization of the state. I defer to that authority. It is largely in that deference that the true power of your position resides. If you set me aside, as you can, you must then deal with another head of my department. You may set him aside—" S-One looked directly into G-One's eyes, and smiled "—if you wish. But there are circumstances in which your wish might not be truly effective. However, if you agree to say nothing to the military, I will at once explain the deception plan to you. Believe me when I say that I have no desire to take over the formal authority of your office. There can be no such competition between us. The head must always delegate certain functions because of a simple lack of time, if nothing else. Now, do you agree to say nothing to the military?"

Arakal, who detested wild celebrations, was able to see the victory party coming even before Pierrot, who had been insisting on pursuit of the Russ, suddenly announced that "the people demand a celebration."

By dint of heaping praise on Pierrot, several mayors, Slagiron, Casey and his own three dumbfounded corps commanders, and after giving a brief speech in halting French on "le liberation de la belle France," Arakal was able to make himself progressively less conspicuous; he pretended a trip to the men's room, found a side door unattended, slipped out, crossed the alley to a small white-painted hotel, and went up the steep narrow stairs to his room on the fourth floor. The guard outside the door snapped to attention—he was one of Arakal's men —and Arakal looked at him thoughtfully.

"Would you like to go to that party?"

"Well—yes, sir, I would. But—"

Arakal wrote rapidly on a small pad, tore off the paper, and wrote again on the sheet beneath.

"This first note releases you from guard duty this evening. The second is for General Slagiron. You'll find him at the head table, surrounded by Old Kebeck mayors in civilian clothes, and guerrillas in camouflage suits."

The guard looked thoughtful.

"Thank you, sir. But I'll be back after I give this to General Slagiron."

Arakal, putting his key in the lock, looked up in surprise.

"You can stay."

"I'm not too crazy about these guerrillas. And I'd lock that door, if I were you, sir, till General Slagiron gets here."

The guard was gone before Arakal could make any reply. He stepped into the room, turned the key in the lock, and paced the floor until a knock sounded, and Slagiron's deep voice broke in on his thoughts.

Arakal opened the door. Slagiron, one hand to his head, smelling powerfully of wine, stepped in.

"Thanks for getting me out of there. My God! What if we should have to fight tomorrow?"

"According to Pierrot, the Russ are on the run."

Slagiron shut the door, and through the crack of the closing door Arakal could see the guard take his place outside.

"Pierrot," growled Slagiron. He glanced at Arakal. "I'll have to give you credit for the way the landing worked out. *I* thought we'd have a fight."

"Pierrot hasn't explained why we haven't?"

Slagiron thrust out his lower lip, and put his right hand on his chest. " 'I am Pierrot. It is I, Pierrot, who have enabled you, our allies, to come ashore unharmed. It is I, Pierrot, whom the Russ fear as a nightmare.' About that time he got going faster than the translator, so I don't know the details."

Arakal soberly described the big guns set into the rock face, the sighting and aiming arrangements, the obstacle storeroom, and the mess hall with its unmoving occupants.

Slagiron listened soberly.

"We seem to owe him something. But yet—"

Arakal said exasperatedly, "Do you believe his story?"

"No."

"Then what did happen?"

Slagiron said, as if trying the words to test their sound, "You tricked the Russ out of here. The rest is pure fakery."

Arakal said, "How do we account for those dead bodies?"

"Prisoners of the Russ put to death to fool us."

"They were in Russ uniform."

"More trickery."

Arakal shook his head. "It's getting too elaborate. It begins to suggest an organization as big as their army. And where's the gain?"

Slagiron thought it over and shrugged.

"Maybe Pierrot is real. But he seems fake to me."

"Where's Bullinger?"

"The last I knew, well out in the bay. He was planning to keep the bulk of the ships out of Cherbourg Harbor until he had a clearer picture."

Arakal nodded. "The catch in all this is, we're relying on someone else. If it works, all right. But—" Arakal glanced toward the door. "Our guard, out there, doesn't like the guerrillas. Since Pierrot showed up, I've had a corporal, two sergeants, and a private, warn me offhand to keep an eye on him, or let them stand between me and him, or let them go along, just in case."

"He's helped us."

"Yes."

Slagiron massaged his chin. "Suppose this *is* a trick? How the devil does it work? And what can he do to gain by it?"

"*If* the Fleet had come into the harbor, conceivably he might have captured it."

"Knowing Bullinger, that, at least, isn't likely."

"Suppose there's something they're holding back?"

"But what?"

"I don't understand why the Russ used iron birds against us at home but don't seem to have them over here."

"Of all the Old Stuff from before the war, what is there that's trickier to use or harder to maintain? Beside that, they eat fuel like starving rats in a grain bin. The Russ would get more value here out of iron roads, the same as we do at home."

Arakal thought it over, then shook his head. "There's still something out of focus."

Slagiron said, "It's been too easy. We expected a fight. Instead, we've had the whole thing tossed in our lap, and we don't believe it. We're sure there's a catch somewhere. Meanwhile, we're full of at least four different kinds of wine. It may all seem different tomorrow."

★ **3** ★

The next day, Arakal's men found themselves up early, many still asleep on their feet, as Pierrot warned through bullhorns in the hands of shouting translators, "We must pursue the Russ! Never, never must we give them a chance to make a stand! All France is aflame! The Russ bases throughout all Europe are under attack! Now is our chance! We must pursue them!"

Meanwhile, Arakal, stung by the experiences of the day before, had been the first up, and had delivered his message to rudely awakened generals and colonels: Each unit must be kept together. Each must be fit for combat anytime. No unnecessary reliance must be placed on the guerrillas. This picnic could end any time, possibly in some form of ambush or betrayal. But until that happened, the guerrillas must be treated with strict courtesy.

Out in the harbor, supply ships had been unloading all night, and now the admiral's flag was flying from the bombardment ship, *Panther*, whose huge guns were exciting the admiration of an enthusiastic throng. As the unloading went on, Arakal insisted to Pierrot that the supplies must go with the troops. During the delay caused by the loading of supplies, Arakal boarded a launch sent in by Admiral Bullinger, and went out to the flagship, where now the men were drilling at the guns, which swung slowly around, aimed out to sea, and fired a salvo whose crash rattled the harbor.

Arakal, smiling, met the admiral in a cabin with a bare stripped look that told of ripped-out listening devices. Bullinger was uneasy.

"I brought *Panther* in here as soon as I could. I thought you might want something visible as a token of strength."

"I'm also happy with the supplies. I don't care to depend on somebody else for food and ammunition."

"If you pursue very far, you're bound to depend on them, at least for food."

"The longer we can put that off, the better. Have you any word from Colputt?"

"A signal for you, sir. As you asked, I decoded it myself. Just a moment."

Bullinger stepped outside, and came back with a sealed envelope. Arakal pulled out the slip of paper to read: "Both platforms work. Power supply as we thought. We are sending for *Alligator*, which is just finished. Will be there as soon as possible, but can't predict time.— Colputt."

Arakal thoughtfully considered the message. *Alligator* would be their new vehicle-carrying ship.

From back toward the stern of the *Panther* came a heavy crash, a shock felt thought the deckplates underfoot as well as heard.

Bullinger said mildly, "The crews need drill at the guns. And there's no harm letting it be known that we have teeth."

Arakal nodded, and folded Colputt's message into his pocket.

"When do you think *Alligator* will be ready to make the trip across?"

"Impossible to predict. We haven't made a ship of that design before. It might do anything."

"We still have this question of supplies. You remember, at the start, we considered various possibilities. If the landing failed. If we had a half-success. If we had a success in landing, but got stopped at Cherbourg. If we had full success. If the populace then rose up and threw out the Russ. But what we actually have here didn't occur to us."

Bullinger nodded.

"Yes, sir. I remember."

"We are obviously going to need to be supplied now. Can you do it?"

"I have the arrangements set up. That was taken care of before we started. It's something I can cancel, but that otherwise will take place as arranged. But what happens in Cherbourg? Will they, perhaps, eat up the supplies themselves? Or throw them in the sea? Or sell them for what the traffic will bear? I can bring the supplies to the dock. There it ends."

"I'll make arrangements for them to be sent on."

"If these guerrillas control delivery, they've got their hand at your throat."

Arakal nodded, and Bullinger growled, "It would have been a lot more convenient for us if we had fought the Russ for this place and it was *ours*. This business is a mess."

Bullinger's remark occurred to Arakal in the launch. It occurred to him again as he climbed onto the dock to find Slagiron waiting, and, behind Slagiron, Arakal's three corps commanders, all in evident ill humor, and two of the three apparently in none too robust health.

Arakal nodded to Slagiron, returned the salute of his officers, and said at once, "Who has an outfit we can trust to unload supplies and ship them to us by the iron road?"

Burckhardt, the burly commander of I Corps, queasily eyed the slosh of water against a nearby pier, and said nothing.

Beside Burckhardt, Simons, the well-built, pugnacious, and often profane commander of II Corps kept his mouth shut.

Arakal looked at Cesti, the slender and thoughtful III Corps commander. Cesti's right eye was half-closed, and his head was oddly tilted toward his half-closed eye. His face, like Burckhardt's, was unusually pale. Cesti met Arakal's gaze dully; other than that, he made no response.

Slagiron looked around at the corps commanders, gave a grunt, glanced at Arakal, and said, "I'd say the Beaver or Groundmole Divisions could do it, sir."

Simons, his three divisions named respectively, "Lightningbolt," "King Snake," and "Panther," nodded agreeably.

Burckhardt said, "If we get into a spot where—" He swallowed and paused a moment before going on "—where we have to dig in, we'll miss the First Division."

Arakal nodded thoughtfully. The First Division, the "Groundmoles," had yet to be thrown out of any place they had decided to hold.

Cesti said fretfully, "We may have to cross rivers."

Cesti's Beavers specialized in river crossings.

Arakal glanced at Slagiron, who, eyes slitted, gnawed briefly on his lip. "That's true. In that case, I'd say the King Snakes could do it."

Simons stared at Slagiron as if Slagiron had slapped him. He turned to Arakal.

"Sir, Second Corps is the shock troops of the Army."

"That's true," said Arakal. "But the Russ are supposed to be already on the run. And I think the King Snakes could handle this better than anyone else. If they controlled the trains, as well as the loading, it would be better yet."

Slagiron nodded. "But can we convince Pierrot?"

"We can find out."

Simons turned back to Slagiron. "Damn it, sir, we're supposed to be here to *fight*. Without the Fifth Division, I'm cut almost to half-strength."

"Two-thirds strength," corrected Slagiron.

"There's only sixteen to seventeen percent difference between half-strength and two-thirds strength. On top of that, the artillery synchro units are with the King Snakes."

Slagiron frowned. "Nevertheless—"

"And," said Simons, "if there should be a stab in the back, the Russ may end up with those units."

Arakal and Slagiron glanced at each other.

Arakal said, "Let those units stay with the Second Corps."

"Good," said Simons. "And, since it shouldn't take much to do this job, maybe we should leave a battalion on this end to handle it."

Arakal looked at Simons' expression of obedient helpfulness. Since each of Arakal's divisions were composed of three regiments, and each regiment counted three battalions, what Simons was suggesting was that roughly *one-ninth* of the King Snake Division should be left to do the job.

Arakal shook his head. "If our supplies should get cut off, it would be like slitting the throat of the whole army. We have to have a strong force here to prevent that. We can't fight the Russ while we're worried about what's going on behind our backs."

Simons looked stubbornly unconvinced, but held his peace.

Arakal glanced at Slagiron.

"Where's Pierrot?"

"I've been trying to find him. He disappeared after that early-morning harangue."

"In that case, let's get hold of the mayor. He shouldn't be any more hung over than anyone else around here."

"I don't know about that. I saw him put down almost half a bottle of that rotgut in one long pull."

Burckhardt, as Slagiron mentioned the Mayor's half-bottle, glanced desperately around. He stumbled over to the side of the pier, and bent over the edge. Cesti went in a hurry to the other side of the pier.

Slagiron shook his head. "Five days of seasickness, and then a damned drinking party. Let's hunt up the mayor."

The mayor, just outside his office, showed himself delighted that Arakal planned to leave troops in the city. He spoke enthusiastically in his own tongue:

"But that is magnificent! And would it be possible to leave someone to protect the guns?"

"Guns?" said Arakal, as Slagiron looked on with the elaborately unconcerned expression of one who understands nothing that is being said.

"The fixed artillery of the Russ," said the mayor, "in the fortifications around the city, and commanding the harbor. If bad elements should get control of them—"

"*No one* has control of those guns?"

"The Pierrot had suggested that I put my constabulary in charge. In the flush of enthusiasm, I agreed. But this is not practical. They are too few in number, and who, then, will do *their* work?"

"You are agreeable that my men control the defenses?"

"But, of course! That is understood. These fortifications are in the Military Zone. They are outside the jurisdiction of any civil authority in Normandy. It is natural that you control them, until they are one day turned over to the central government in Paris." He looked shrewdly at Arakal, and said, "I realize it is an extra care. But if *I* had ships which were to enter that harbor—"

Arakal bowed.

"We will do everything we can, regardless of the difficulties."

On the way back, Slagiron listened in astonishment. "This changes the whole picture."

"Let's hope Cesti and Burckhardt are still alive."

Back on the pier, the two generals, sick and miserable, listened dully.

"We could," said Burckhardt, "end up split into fragments."

Cesti was frowning. "On the other hand, this gives us a foothold. The wonder is Pierrot hasn't taken over."

"He wants to chase the Russ," said Burckhardt, "and that's the way to use your strength. What good do the men do back here?"

Slagiron glanced questioningly at Arakal.

Arakal said, "Just suppose that we're entangled with the Russ, and for some reason our supplies don't get through. Pierrot and his men melt into the scenery. They speak the language and know the country. What do *we* do?"

Slagiron glanced at Burckhardt, who said, "We fall back to the coast."

"With no established base here," said Arakal, "how can Bullinger even stay on this side of the ocean? Worse yet, suppose anyone but us takes over the guns?"

"Yes," said Burckhardt, frowning, "but we'll miss every man we leave here, once we're up against the Russ."

Arakal nodded. "That's undoubtedly true." He glanced out at the *Panther*, riding on the sparkling waters of the harbor. He thought back on the coast defense gun, moving as he moved the aiming device.

"Well," said Arakal, "we can't hope to equal the strength of the Russ on their own side of the water. But we have a fleet, and we should soon have a base." He glanced at Burckhardt.

"We're going to need your Groundmoles with us, when we attack the Russ. And I think we'll need your Third Division. Together with Simon's Fourth, they'll keep the Russ on the run if anyone can. But pull your Second Division out of the loading plan. We're going to need them here."

"But, sir—My God! We can't—"

Slagiron said quietly, "You have your orders, General."

Burckhardt swallowed, shut his eyes, and swallowed again.

Slagiron took a fresh look at Burckhardt, and seemed surprised to find him still standing there. Slagiron's dark brows came together.

Arakal had turned to Cesti.

"Your Seventh Division is already loaded?"

"Yes, sir," said Cesti, nervously. "Well, it's loading."

Arakal, frowning, considered that Cesti's Seventh Division was named "Nutcracker," for its stubbornness at blasting opposition loose from tough positions. The Seventh had more and heavier artillery than any other division except Cesti's Ninth, known as the "Sledgehammer Division" for the size and power of its guns.

Arakal was vaguely aware of Slagiron speaking to someone, somewhere, but the words didn't reach him. He was balancing whether to leave behind the Seventh Division or the Ninth Division.

Cesti, through some feat of telepathy, said urgently, "Sir, I think the Russ were more wary of the Ninth than of any other unit."

"What I'm thinking of is the Russ tanks," said Arakal.

"Yes, sir," said Cesti, looking relieved.

"But," said Arakal, "the Seventh can also take care of tanks, especially since Colputt got those explosive rockets worked out. And if there is anything that can get bogged down, in bad weather, it's the Ninth Division."

"Yes, sir," said Cesti, "but—"

"And it was raining yesterday," said Arakal.

"Sir," said Cesti, "our information is that the Russ are particularly strong over here in artillery."

"We're getting into that part of the year where we can expect bad weather. And there's one other reason to leave the Ninth here. They're artillerymen. We need artillerymen to handle these guns; if anything should go wrong with the power loading and aiming arrangements, we have no one else so well equipped to work out what to do. Moreover, if the Russ armor should attack and break through the defenses, we've got no other unit so well equipped to stop them."

Cesti nodded moodily. "I'll pull them out of the loading pattern, sir."

"The only question," said Arakal, "is whether that's enough." He turned to Slagiron, to find him, jaw outthrust, eyes narrowed, just returning the salute of a pale and shaken Burckhardt. Arakal glanced back at Cesti, returned Cesti's salute, and turned back to Slagiron, who was running a handkerchief around the inside of his collar, his eyes still narrowed.

Arakal shook his head.

"Sir?" said Slagiron.

"I'm tempted to leave Burckhardt's Third Division here, too. It would put more teeth in the defense, if we needed it."

Slagiron's jaws clamped with a look of grim pleasure, but then he shook his head.

"I don't think we'd better do it. We've got each of these divisions overstrength, for us. There are three more men in each squad, and we used to have nine-man squads. When we take one division out of each corps, that reduces our strength by a third, which brings us back not much below the strength, in men, that we had to begin with. We have one-third fewer formations, but each formation we have is one-third stronger. So if we stop there, it's not so bad as it seems."

Arakal nodded. "The overall effect is as if we had detached one division, instead of three. Well, it should keep anyone from overrunning the defenses here on the spur of the moment."

Slagiron smiled. "It should do that, all right. And it leaves us enough strength to do something with. But, of course, Burckhardt is right about one thing."

Arakal nodded. "We'll miss every man we leave behind."

IX. The Judo Master

★ 1 ★

S-One turned from the brilliant colors of the enclosed court to his deputy, who said respectfully, "Sir, news of the enemy's latest dispositions." He laid the sheaf of papers on S-One's desk.

S-One glanced from the papers to the display on the opposite wall. He sat back, frowning. The fortified narrow part of the Normandy peninsula was now colored blue. Blue oblongs were moving toward Paris along the narrow lines that represented railroad tracks. Along distant extensions of these railroad tracks, red oblongs were drawing back toward the northeastern part of France.

"Hm," said S-One. "I have to admit, S-Two, that this barbarian has a nasty habit of changing his mind. When did he decide to occupy the Citadel?"

S-Two looked embarrassed. "We don't have any word on that yet, sir. The last we knew, he regarded the Citadel as definitely in Pierrot's province."

"What this means, of course, is that the Americans now have a solid foothold here. How are we going to dislodge them from those fortifications? They can be supplied by their Fleet, from outside. Where is Arakal himself?"

"With the trains, sir."

"We are sure of that?"

"Yes, sir."

"That is something, at least. You realize, we will have to make a stand somewhere in France."

"Yes, sir."

"Are we prepared?"

"Yes, sir. There is no problem in that."

"Good. Now, you perhaps are aware of a certain disagreement between myself and the Head of Government?"

"Yes, sir."

"I must, of course, accept his decision. But it would be unfortunate if his decision caused any rupture in our deception plan. It would be a help to me, and, I think, a service to the state, if unexpected actions on his part could be avoided, or at least moderated by foreknowledge."

"Certainly, sir. Our latest information is of a meeting between the Head of Government and Marshal Vasilevsky, General Kolbukhin, and General Brusilov. The former plenipotentiary to our occupation forces in America, Smirnov, has also been briefly called in, to answer questions. The tone of the meeting is one of intense concern. Serious reservations have been expressed about our actions so far."

"*Our* actions? Whose actions?"

"The actions carried out under your direction, sir."

"I see. And what are their conclusions so far?"

"The marshal is confident that he can beat Arakal, and any combination of Arakal and guerrillas. He still thinks it would have been best to have fought Arakal shortly after he arrived."

"What does Brusilov say?"

"That you tried it, and were outmaneuvered."

S-One nodded soberly. "And Kolbukhin?"

"Kolbukhin is in favor of letting Arakal penetrate deeply, so that he can be cut off and exterminated. The danger, he says, is not in Arakal winning the fight, but in his getting away, to come back later and harass us with blows here and there unpredictably."

"And what is the conclusion of the Head of Government?"

"He has expressed no actual conclusion. Our impression is that he is taking care to prepare everything in the event that the deception plan fails. As he does not know what the deception plan actually is, he is under something of a handicap in forming his own plans."

"If I had told him, he might have told Brusilov, or the Marshal. They might then have decided whether or not to intrude. Do they know yet that Arakal has occupied the Normandy Citadel?"

"Yes, sir."

"What is their response to that?"

"The Marshal and General Kolbukhin consider that Arakal is a military amateur to leave so large a proportion of his men behind. General Brusilov is not sure. The other two joke at Brusilov's expense, saying that Arakal could slip on a cowflop and land in a pile of manure, and Brusilov would suspect there was some clever plan behind it."

"And how does Brusilov respond to that?"

"He admits there is some truth in the charge, but says it is an outlook based on experience."

S-One nodded. "Are we receiving reports from the Citadel?"

S-Two hesitated. "Yes and no. We are receiving *transmissions*."

"Ah, yes. There is a translator shortage?"

"Yes, sir. We have switched more men from the U.K. Sector. But there is still trouble with the accent of Arakal's men, and their particular choice of words. Their outlook also is sometimes difficult to grasp."

"Well, that will clear up. What about Arakal himself?"

"We are almost constantly in touch, now that he is on the train."

"Good. Bring me word of any important decisions as they are made."

★ **2** ★

As the clack of the train signaled the passage of the miles, Arakal studied the map, with Pierrot at his elbow, and Slagiron across the table. Outside the window, the green countryside fled past. Arakal caught glimpses of rushing streams, shady glens, and once, in the distance, high on a hill, ruined fortifications from long ago. Pierrot, meanwhile, overflowed with words in his own tongue.

"All France is aflame," he said. "The Soviets are in flight, and we pursue them mercilessly. They flee before us, and we must not flag. Always, always, we must pursue them!"

Arakal said, "Who is this 'we' the Russ are running from?"

"The partisans. The men of the Striking Force for Independence. The guerrilla heroes of the nation."

Slagiron studied Pierrot curiously. Unable to understand Pierrot's words, he was considering Pierrot's manner and gestures.

Arakal said, "So far, so good, then. But where are the Russ reserves?"

Pierrot put his hand on the map, forefinger outstretched. "Here, near Metz."

"How strong are they?"

"In physical size they are large important forces."

"Tanks?"

"They have nearly a hundred tanks."

"What about their artillery?"

Slagiron, recognizing the word, "artillerie", looked attentive.

Pierrot, for his part, looked thoughtful. Then he shrugged.

"I am afraid that the great Napoleon taught them a lesson at Friedland—a lesson about artillery—that they have learned only too well. Their artillery is strong and mobile. It is a terrible thing to face their artillery. We must fight in such a way as to avoid that."

Slagiron said, "What does he say?"

"That the Russ have strong reserves near Metz. Amongst other things, these reserves include nearly a hundred tanks, and strong artillery. He says we need to fight in such a way that we keep away from their artillery."

"How do we achieve that?"

Arakal turned to Pierrot.

"Have you thought of some practical means to avoid their artillery?"

Pierrot said, "My men strike unexpectedly and are gone. *Pouf!* You must do likewise. Speed, decision, the quick blow, and then away! It will not do to trade blows with an opponent made of iron."

Arakal explained this to Slagiron.

Slagiron listened without enthusiasm.

Arakal said to Pierrot, "What is the size of the Russ artillery force? How many guns, of what caliber?"

"Many guns, of all sizes."

Arakal paused, then went on.

"Any airplanes?"

Pierrot shook his head. "Their aircraft usually crash, or cause other troubles. The most recent of these aircraft that I know of flew, but when it came down to land, the wheels would not lower. These aircraft are great eaters of fuel, hard to maintain, and only of odd types left over from the past. They are not practical."

"Are the tanks new?"

"In my belief, they too are left over from the past. But they are maintained in excellent condition."

"And the guns—the artillery?"

"Some are old, some new. All are well maintained and terrible to face."

Arakal summarized for Slagiron, then looked thoughtfully at the map.

"Why pursue the Russ? They're almost out of the country."

"If we do not throw them back, they will advance."

"Why not negotiate with them? After all, they have men in Old Brunswick who are cut off from the mainland. We can allow these men to cross—we could even ferry them across—in return for the Russ going completely back over the border."

"You do not understand their way of thinking. They are masters of all Europe. They will not leave willingly. Either from here or from England."

"Then we had better plan some way to slow them up when they come back. Because what we have here right now isn't going to stop them. Especially if we have to get out of the way every time they bring up the artillery."

"Surely when your main forces come over, then we can deal with the Soviets on at least an equal basis."

Arakal said noncommittally, "What I am talking about is now."

There was a rap on the compartment door.

Arakal called, "Come in."

A corporal of Arakal's army stepped inside, holding a yellow envelope.

"Sir, a message for General Pierrot." The messenger noticeably split the name into two words: "Pier" and "rot." This, at least, was an improvement over the usual pronunciation, "Pure rot."

Arakal, pronouncing carefully, said, "Let General Pierrot have the message, then."

"Yes, sir." The corporal handed Pierrot the message. Pierrot tore it open, read rapidly, then looked up. "This is serious. The enemy is advancing toward the Meuse. He has already passed Gravelotte."

Arakal glanced at the map.

Pierrot said, "We must stop him." He scribbled rapidly on the back of the message, sealed it, and handed it back to Arakal's corporal.

Arakal said, "Give that to General Pierrot's communications officer."

Arakal pronounced "Pierrot" carefully, so that the corporal would again have the advantage of hearing the correct pronunciation. The corporal saluted and went out.

Pierrot said, "Are we one on this? Will you join me in driving back the enemy?"

"We're willing to try," said Arakal. "But I'm not sure it will work."

Pierrot stood up. "We can only try. But we *must* try."

★ 3 ★

S-One glanced from the report to the display. Arakal's troop trains were now beyond Paris, on the railroad line to Reims. The symbols on the display were lit, signifying that it was now night for Arakal and his men, just as it was night here, for S-One. It was night, and S-One was tired. It was well past time for bed. But S-One looked at the softly glowing blue outline around the Normandy Citadel. He glanced from the display to the latest report, to read:

" . . . word from the scene, as well as indications from electronic sources, indicate that Arakal had left behind three divisions, or one-third of his force, to hold the Citadel. These troops now appear to be the 2nd, 5th, and 9th Divisions, known respectively as the Hammerclaw, King Snake, and Sledgehammer Divisions. The 9th, or Sledgehammer Division, is particularly strong in artillery, and might be considered as the heavy artillery of Arakal's army. While it is too early to provide details,

indications from the scene suggest that all these
troops are being intelligently used to occupy the
fortifications. Although Arakal's Divisions are
smaller than our own, these units appear to be
about thirty percent overstrength; such is the state
of automatic control of the Citadel's weapons that
there seems little doubt that these troops can man
the entire perimeter, while maintaining strong
reserves in the interior. It must be emphasized that
our experience with these units in America has
been unfortunate. The Sledgehammer Division, in
particular, is capable of delivering the heaviest sort
of blow. The troops in Brusilov's army customarily
referred to this division as 'The Scrap Man', from
the effect of its heavy artillery on our armored
units. It must further be noted that the terrain
within the Citadel is ideal for defense, and unfavor-
able for armor. . . ."

S-One glanced up from the report, and delivered himself of a low oath. "The Scrap Man." Who could have
expected Arakal to leave this powerhouse behind him?
Somewhere in the report, a similar paean of praise
appeared for the "King Snake" Division. S-One had no
trouble remembering it: " . . . this division appears to
serve as a general repository for the most adventurous
spirits of Arakal's army. Its name is derived from the
zoology of America, where the most dangerous com-
monly known reptile is the rattlesnake; the king snake
kills rattlesnakes . . . "

S-One exhaled a deep breath. The Hammerclaw Division, he had read in here somewhere, was known for its
ability to rip out stubborn opposition. The report

acknowledged the division's toughness, but considered it only average for Arakal's troops. S-One did not know if this was good or bad, since the report conceded that the Hammerclaw Division was "extremely tough, resourceful, and efficient." If that was the average for the army as a whole, what were the two other divisions in the Citadel like?

S-One sat back, scowling. Brusilov had warned him that "dislocation" followed from the blows of this barbarian. S-One was aware that he was now suffering from a particularly bad case of dislocation. He had no doubt that if he turned the Marshal loose on Arakal, the Marshal would smash him, and then, one way or another, batter his way into the Citadel, provided only that enough troops were put at his disposal. But it would be done at the price of a casualty list S-One did not wish to contemplate, and it might well lead to a continental upheaval even the Marshal would be unable to put down. Meanwhile, Arakal's fleet was loose, and the United Kingdom might well settle accounts with the comparatively small force of troops stationed there, who could be reinforced only by droplets sneaked across in the teeth of a blockade. The Marshal could do nothing about that, and the ultimate outcome was unpredictable. And all this mess followed from Arakal's control of the Citadel. Without that, his fleet would have no nearby base from which it could maintain a blockade. Without that, these divisions left behind in the Citadel would be with Arakal, where, however tough, they could be gotten at. *Pierrot* should control those guns!

How the devil had this oversight come about?

S-One shook his head. Somehow, those divisions were going to have to be manipulated out of that fortress, before they wrecked everything.

Frowning, S-One sat back, looked at the display, and picked up the interoffice phone.

"S-Two?"

"Sir?"

"We will have to accelerate the attack on Arakal and Pierrot. We will also need to reinforce it."

There was a brief silence, then S-Two's response, obedient but startled:

"Yes, sir. I'll be right in."

★ **4** ★

Arakal came awake to a scream of metal on metal, the blast of a whistle, a sudden jolt, and then, as a deafening roar died away, there came the crash of breaking glass, the whine of bullets, and a white glare that lit the inside of the compartment, to show Slagiron stretched out on the opposite seat, automatic in hand, sighting into the glare outside. Arakal barely glimpsed this as he rolled off the bench onto the floor of the compartment. The floor bucked beneath him, there was a sense of the world turning over, and then he was struck as by a heavy club.

Arakal came to in motionless quiet, to hear the tinkle of glass, and then a distant hammer of machine-gun fire. Around him, there was a faint gray light. Slagiron was gone, and the door into the corridor open. From somewhere came a remote sound of shouting. An instant later, there was a fresh hammer of gunfire.

Carefully, Arakal rolled to his feet.

Outside, the corridor was empty. The air was thick with an unfamiliar pungent smell, and the smell of burnt wood. Arakal eased open the door of the compartment across the way, and, staying well back, looked out the broken window. Abruptly, he caught his breath.

Down below, facing toward the railroad car, Slagiron, Casey, Pierrot, and several other officers stood with raised hands before four olive-uniformed men cradling what Arakal's men called "bullet-eaters," from their appetite for ammunition, and what others called "tommy-guns." The helmets of the four men below were easily enough recognizable as Russ. Arakal loosened his sword, and looked up.

Both sections of glass in the window were broken, with shards and splinters adhering around a cracked and charred wooden frame, and in a fragile line of shattered blackened wood and glittering splinters across the center.

Arakal freed himself of his cumbersome cloak, quietly drew his sword, studied the men below intently, and drew a deep breath. Suddenly he was through the window, conscious of a burning scrape across his chest and arms. He yelled, and his voice came out high-pitched, an unnatural scream that seemed to come from everywhere at once, as if it had no single point of origin. Then he was living in fractions of seconds, both hands gripping the sword hilt, his mind a maze of angles, inertia, and vulnerable points, of the soft unresisting parts of the bodies that had to be struck, and the hard metal that was to be avoided. Before his gaze, the living soldiers of the enemy dissolved in a butchery so sudden that only the last managed to turn and fire. Then Arakal, his gaze suddenly watery, his ears ringing, could hear Slagiron's voice shouting orders, could hear the sudden sharp crack of an O'Cracy rifle, and he fell into blackness with a sense of harsh gratification that was finally translated into a stinging sharp pain, a sense of fire burning across his chest, a soreness and a weakness, and a male voice saying, "That's the last of the stitches. Move that light back before we upset it."

Arakal opened his eyes, to meet a hard blue gaze that studied him alertly. He was lying on his back on a flat padded table under a dark canvas tent on which drummed a steady heavy rain. The tent was lit by small globular lights that gave an intense white glow. One of these, as he watched, began to turn dark. A thin stream of smoke wavered up. A slim girlish hand reached out from behind Arakal's head, as if to adjust the lamp—and then hesitated. Absently, the surgeon reached over and adjusted the light. Arakal glanced at the surgeon. His voice was a whisper, and he had to try again.

"Can I get up?"

"How do you feel?"

"I don't know."

"I've just dug one bullet and a shell fragment out of you, and God alone knows how many splinters of glass. You've lost a good deal of blood, and you have bruises all over your body. If you want to try to get up, I can't stop you; but take it slow."

Arakal rested his hands on the side of the cot, tried to swing his feet over the edge, and the room faded out. He was vaguely conscious of the thud of his head falling back against the pad. He came to, looking up at the canvas. The surgeon shook his head.

"Better get some rest."

"Where are we?"

"That I don't know. Somewhere in Old Kebeck, about a mile from the iron road."

"What happened?"

The surgeon looked at him, frowning. "You've forgotten?"

"I remember going to sleep, waking up when the train was stopped, and jumping through a window to fight some Russ. After that, I must have passed out. What's the situation?"

The surgeon shook his head. "I'll get someone who can give you a better account than I can."

Arakal lay back, and a cool, soft hand rested on his forehead, and remained there a moment. He looked up at a vision of milk-white skin, blue eyes, and soft golden hair. This vision smiled down at him, then the ruby-red lips parted, and a sweet, soothing voice spoke softly, in the accents of Old Kebeck. Arakal's mind belatedly translated the words, so that at first they were a strange and incomprehensible murmur in a delightful voice, and then they came across clearly, the meaning obscuring the voice:

"Qu'un sang impur abreuve nos sillons."

"Let an impure blood soak our furrows."

The sound of rain grew briefly louder, and Slagiron stepped in, looked gravely toward Arakal, and raised his hand in salute. Arakal saw the movement, out of the corner of his eye, but his gaze was fixed intently on the blue and gold vision above him. Like everyone else in his army, Arakal felt protective toward the nurses. But this girl was not one of them. He saw her blink in momentary confusion, then smile. The smile was delightful. But this was no one he had seen before.

Arakal said, "Is anyone else waiting for the surgeon?"

She shook her head, and spoke clearly, but with a slight and pleasant accent. "No, sir."

"Good." Arakal glanced at Slagiron. "What's the situation?"

Slagiron said, "We're in rolling low hills. There's a forest in the distance, across a river. We're dug in amongst the hills, overlooking the river and the iron road. The iron road crosses the river not far from here. Near that bridge, on the side away from us, there's a second bridge that carries a highway across the river."

"Where are the Russ?"

"They've got a bridgehead that takes in this end of both bridges, and the last we saw before the rain started, they were bringing up reinforcements on the other side of the river."

"How deep is the Russ bridgehead?"

"I'd say about six hundred yards."

"Much artillery?"

"Not on this side. It's practically hub-to-hub across the river."

"Are we all here?"

"Except for the men we left back around Cherbourg."

"None of our trains were shunted onto any other track?"

"No, sir."

"Where's Pierrot?"

"Gone."

"Gone where?"

"That's something we don't know. His whole outfit ran for it while we were fighting the Russ."

Arakal glanced absently at the girl, then looked back at Slagiron. "This leaves us with the iron road solidly blocked with trains reaching back how far?"

"We sent the trains back."

"Good. Now, what happened? The Russ blew up the tracks? Then hit us?"

"It's the only thing that seems to make sense, but it doesn't make sense. Our information from Pierrot on the location of the Russ was wrong, and the way we walked into that trap, we should have been hurt a lot worse. The first thing I knew, there was an explosion. I have a vague memory of taking a shot at something—at someone with his arm back to sling something. The next thing I knew, the train was stopped, and I jumped down, to see what was going on. It was just getting light. Casey came out, in as much of a daze as I was, and the natural thing happened. Some Russ with bullet-eaters turned up, and surprised us. I was damning myself for being so stupid when, from down the line of cars I heard someone shout, "We have your leaders. Come out with your hands raised." Just then, you came through the window, landed almost on the back of the first Russ soldier, finished him, and tore into the rest. At practically the same time, down the line, all hell broke loose. Right then, Pierrot took to his heels. It was all over in a minute. The Russ had some machine-guns back from the tracks, but they weren't dug in, and our men picked off their gunners. That was all there was to it. As nearly as I can figure it, they blocked the track, then blew up the embankment beside the track, using a charge too weak to really damage the train. Well, maybe somehow that was somebody's mistake. But then they've got artillery enough near here. Why not bombard the train when it was stopped? Next, why tell men to come out, when they're still armed? Why not at least dig in the machine-guns, and then, when we're stopped, just open fire?"

"Or," said Arakal, "let us start to cross the river, then blow up the bridge when we're on it?"

Slagiron nodded. "They could have done any number of things. This business makes no sense. It was planned. But it was planned wrong."

Arakal said, "Ease me up, if you can. The last time I tried, I passed out."

Slagiron put an arm behind Arakal's back, and lifted carefully.

This time, with only a dizzy throb in the head, Arakal found himself sitting on the table, his feet over the edge. He sat still a moment, listening to the pouring rain. He hurt all over, and his left leg throbbed painfully. But he felt no overpowering weakness. He had felt worse than this on the ship. He glanced around, to see the nurse watching him. He cleared his throat.

"My uniform?"

She looked around, and handed him a pile of crumpled, badly torn, wet and bloody garments. The left leg of the trousers had been cut off, and the remnants included in the pile.

As Arakal, partly supported by Slagiron, put on the remains of his uniform, he saw his sword in its scabbard in the corner of the tent, and buckled it on.

Slagiron said, "We'll have a fresh uniform for you, sir."

Arakal nodded his thanks, then realized with a shock that he had been overlooking something. He glanced at Slagiron, and, briefly, his voice was harsh.

"How many killed?"

"We lost three killed, twenty-seven wounded. Mostly when their machine-guns opened up."

Arakal blinked. "And how many of the Russ?"

"I'd say around thirty or forty. Some may just have been wounded, and gotten away, or been picked up by their own people, afterward. It was all over quick, and they never had men enough there to win it, anyway."

Arakal was thinking back to that brief moment when he had seen the Russ holding his officers captive. He shook his head.

"We will still have to bury the dead."

Slagiron nodded. "But not just now."

Arakal pulled open the flap of the tent. The rain was coming down so hard that at a glance it seemed a good question whether there was more air outside, or more water. "No," he said, "we can't dig in that." He shut the tent flap. "There's a command tent near here?"

Slagiron permitted himself a faint smile.

"We're with the First Division, sir."

"Ah," said Arakal. He glanced at the girl. "You can take care of these lamps?"

She nodded.

Arakal turned to Slagiron. "I don't dare try to run. Go ahead if you want. I'll be right behind you."

"No, I'll go with you, sir. Watch your step."

★ 5 ★

S-One rested his eyes on the garden, then looked back at the report. Lack of sleep the night before did nothing to improve his mood now. He tossed the report onto the desk, and sat back, frowning. The situation summarized in the report was by no means the worst that it might be. But there were touches in it that did nothing to ease his sense of discomfort:

" . . . this moment the enemy commander tore his way out through the broken window of the railway car, sword in hand, and, moving with indescribable rapidity, killed four of our men armed with submachine guns. It is believed that one shot was let off, but it is not certain if anyone was hit . . . "

S-One considered first the words, "the enemy commander tore his way out the window of the railway car, sword in hand . . . " Here, he told himself, were four men armed with submachine guns. Supposedly, they all must have had their backs to the train. That was a serious error in itself. But there were *four* of them. With this *sword*, he dispatched four men armed with subma-chine guns?

One bullet only, from any of those guns, would stop and perhaps kill him. And right there was another miscal-culation. Considering the special orders given, how had it come about that Arakal was in physical danger in an operation designed to shock, not kill him? It could only be that he was traveling near the head of the train, when any sensible commander would be further back. No word of this important fact had been reported in advance.

Next, there was the behavior of the enemy troops. Stunned, caught at the earliest light of dawn in the sights of machine guns supposedly dug in, from inside of the wrecked train they had opened fire with such murderous accuracy that it was all over in a few minutes. What did the report say? " . . . accuracy of fire was such as to sug-gest that the weapons were equipped with special sights for night fighting . . . "

Now, here were these barbarians, clearly less advanced than their opponents, who had stopped them for the administration of a swift bloody nose, followed by quick withdrawal. But their opponents, reporting the disastrous outcome, attributed superior technological skills to the barbarians to explain away what had hap-pened.

S-One shook his head, put the report in his desk, and took out a slightly slimmer report, which omitted all mention of the special instructions, and treated only the strictly military aspects of the clash. He called in General

Brusilov, handed him this second report, and sat back to watch him read it.

When, at last, he saw Brusilov's eyes widen, then narrow, S-One said, "You didn't tell me Arakal had supernatural powers."

Brusilov looked up, frowning, then his face cleared. "Oh, you mean his prowess as a fighter? That isn't what bothers me. What bothers me is the depth of this bridgehead, and that apparently it's Arakal who has the high ground. They're underestimating him again. Let them either give up the bridgehead, or else expand it. But whatever they do, do it *quick*. This isn't going to work."

"But that he should jump out this window, and kill four men before they can react—"

Brusilov shook his head. "It doesn't matter to me if he can bite steel-jacketed bullets in half with his teeth. Pump two or three shots into him in the right place, and that's all over with. You make a man desperate enough, and if he's in good physical shape, you'll be surprised what he can do. That's neither here nor there. But these dispositions are an invitation to ruin. That *matters*."

"What's wrong with them?"

"That bridgehead isn't deep enough. Arakal can put the bridges under a murderous fire. *We* can't reinforce the men on his side of the river without running a gauntlet."

"You think he might destroy the bridges, and capture the men on that side of the river?"

"No, that is what I might have been afraid of once. But I've had experience of him. That is *not* it."

"Well, then, what?"

"What if he does *not* destroy the bridges?"

"Then we can reinforce."

"We can?"

"Why not? We have the bridges. And we have artillery such that not only can Arakal be placed under fire where he is, and his own artillery smothered, but if he attempts to attack the bridgehead, we can intervene in that fight, too, with our artillery fire." S-One sat back, thinking over the arrangements, and finding that everything seemed to hold together. "You see," he said, "Arakal must be made to feel his lack of the so-called Sledgehammer Division, by opposing to him an overwhelming force of artillery, and placing him at a disadvantage. Then he will send for that division. *That* will remove it from Cherbourg and the Normandy Citadel."

Brusilov sat still a moment, then looked at S-One.

"We are now making our dispositions in order to lead *him* to undo *his* dispositions, previously arrived at?"

"Yes," said S-One. "In judo, the opponent is placed off-balance. In seeking to recover his balance, he is led to make the misstep that we aim at, and that enables us to further put him off-balance."

"Is the marshal in command of our troops at that river?"

S-One looked startled. "Of course not."

Brusilov shook his head.

"Possibly I am mistaken. But I have already seen the result of one such clever plan. That is why I am here now, instead of in America."

S-One smiled, and Brusilov stiffened at the peculiar snakelike quality of the smile.

S-One said, "That is not the only provision we have made."

★ 6 ★

Arakal, in a deep exhausted sleep, breathing the cool fresh air somehow led into the bunker by the craft of the Groundmole Division, turned restlessly as his hearing, somewhat blunted by too much exposure to loud and continuous sounds, nevertheless detected a rustle, as of silk, that was alien to his surroundings.

The cool air brought to his nostrils a faint delicious perfume.

Arakal was suddenly wide awake.

In the darkness, something came closer.

X. The Battle

★ 1 ★

Arakal, partly upright on the cot, heard the rustle of cloth, and then another sound—a faint creaking from several directions around him. He was able to identify this second sound, but the sliding murmur of cloth and the perfume were something else. Carefully, he folded back the blankets, groped along the frame of the cot, felt the hard curve of wire he was searching for, unhooked it, held it out to the side and up, and squeezed the handles.

In the flicker of the spark-light, against the background of fitted logs that formed the walls of the bunker, stood a girl, her skin milk-white, her hair golden, her figure accentuated by the clinging brief dark net that she wore, her face frozen in shock as she blinked around at the dozen or so men, their faces in shadow, some of whom sat up on cots or peered out of bedrolls on the floor, some halfway to their feet, two partway to her, their hands gripping weapons unrecognizable in the brief light.

Arakal squeezed the handles again, saw the girl's look change to horror, recognized her face, and said, "I think this is supposed to be a nurse. But how did she get in here?"

In a cot to Arakal's left, the division commander, a burly muscular man with head shaped in flat planes suggestive of a gun turret, stared at the girl, then bawled, "Guards!"

From above came a thud, a shout, a sound of boots.

To Arakal's right, someone lighted a lamp, and its intense white light lit up the girl, the room of watching men, and the startled guard who appeared at the door.

"Sir!" the guard saluted.

His commanding officer said dryly, "*You're* the one who let this in?"

"I—sir, I let a nurse in here about five minutes ago." He stared at the paralyzed girl. "She said she was here to give the chief some medicine. I said this was the right place, and to go down and light the lamp in the hall before going in. She sure wasn't dressed like that when I saw her."

"There are some clothes on the floor over there. See if there's a weapon with them."

The girl looked up, startled, but said nothing. She bowed her head, clasped her arms across her breasts.

"No weapons here, sir," said the guard. "A couple of pill boxes, and a brown bottle. That's—"

From outside came a muffled crash. The room jumped. The light flickered. The girl shut her eyes.

The guard raised his voice. "Nothing in the line of a weapon, sir. Unless it's on the girl herself."

"Give her those clothes to put on, and take her to the chief of nurses to be searched. Now get out of here." He turned to Arakal, and gave a fleeting smile. "Sorry to interfere with medical treatment, sir."

Arakal, listening to the crash and roar, nodded with an absent smile. As the guard led the girl out of the room, he and his officers got up, and hurriedly reached for their clothes.

The bombardment abruptly ended.

Arakal was trying to ignore the soreness of his left leg as he dressed. Around him, the room was alternately light and dark as men stepped in front of the lamp, then stepped aside, and their huge shadows leaped across the walls and ceiling. There were the sounds of cloth, leather, the stamping of boots, the snapping of holster flaps—and all sounded loud in the sudden quiet.

In the hall outside, someone lit the lamp.

Arakal adjusted the shoulder strap that supported his sword, and then they went up the stairs, stumbled on a loose step, and pushed past a heavy hanging made of overlapping metal scales sewn onto a leather backing. The air outside was fresh and chill, the wind blowing from them toward the Russ. The sky was dark, with no stars in sight. Around them, in the quiet, there was a faint stir and creak as men and officers tried to guess what might happen next.

The silence stretched out.

Then there was a squelching of boots in mud, the stamp of feet on wood, and a shadowy figure approached, paused, and a deep voice said, "General Mason?"

Beside Arakal, the division commander said, "Here."

"Corporal Givens, sir, from Watch. We've got word from all the listening posts. There isn't a damned thing moving over there, sir."

"The Russ are quiet?"

"Like a graveyard."

Mason turned to Arakal. "Shall we send *them* a little something, sir?"

"Save it until we can see them," said Arakal. "If they want to waste ammunition, that's their business."

"Right. They always were a little prodigal of it."

Nothing further developing, they went back to bed, though a few muttered exclamations preceded the sleep.

The bunker jumped.

A muffled crash and roar reached them, slightly louder now and then as something struck nearby. An acrid odor came down the vent shaft. Across the room, a protesting voice said, "I liked the way we got woken up the *last* time."

Arakal lay still, waiting.

Mason swore.

The bombardment stopped.

A little later, there was a sound of feet on the steps, a bang, and a low curse.

Mason's voice said, "Watch?"

"Sir. Givens. Same damned thing as the last time."

"All right. Watch it on those steps. The second slab from the bottom is loose."

"I already found it, sir."

There was the sound of feet retreating up the steps, and Mason turned to Arakal. "If you want, sir, we can wait half an hour and open up the sky. I have the impression they don't appreciate our guns yet."

"Let them waste their own ammunition. We have to bring ours further."

There was another sound of approaching feet on the steps, and, this time, a dim light. A lantern appeared, casting its glow on the floor and the smooth log walls. The lantern lit the uniform of an officer whose face was unrecognizable in the shadow cast upward by the rain-shield of the lantern. A male voice said, "Wait right there. I'll check."

To Arakal's left, General Mason spoke sharply.

"We're all awake here. Who is it?"

"Rabeck, sir, Colonel, B Regiment. And the chief of nurses, sir. I offered to bring her over."

"Sorry, Rabeck. I didn't recognize your voice."

"We're all a little deaf tonight, sir."

"What does the chief of nurses have for us?"

A slender, dark-haired woman, her facial expression severe, stepped into the edge of the lantern light. "Possibly what I say should be said only to the king."

Arakal said, "There's no time for that. Just go ahead."

"The girl claims you arranged for a meeting with her."

"When did I do this?"

"After the surgeon left, when your wounds had been dressed."

"I suppose I had the chance, when the surgeon went out to get General Slagiron. I'm afraid I didn't think of it. What else?"

"There's a considerable amount, which I don't want to repeat."

"What's the substance of it?"

"She claims that you assaulted her, to condense a long detailed account."

"What else?"

"That is the substance of it."

"Now, Chief Nurse, perhaps you can explain something to me."

"Sir?"

"Where did this girl come from? I never saw her before. If I'm not mistaken, it's your responsibility to have trustworthy nurses."

"I—she volunteered in Cherbourg. She said she was from Old Brunswick, in Cherbourg for a visit. I thought we would need extra nurses, and gladly took her on. She worked hard. She seems capable."

"You think a nurse is capable who tells a story that a wounded man just out from under the anesthetic, unable to sit up, was chasing her around the tent?"

"Well, I—She didn't say *that*."

"The *details* were different?"

"Well . . . men . . . everybody knows—"

"Take her over to Jinks," said Arakal shortly, "and find out what's behind this. Tell Jinks not to destroy her looks if he can avoid it. As for you, Chief Nurse, if any more volunteer nurses show up, report the matter, and see to it there is some part of their uniform that at least shows us they are not our own people."

The chief nurse said stubbornly, "I don't think Captain Jinks should be allowed—"

Arakal sat up, vaguely conscious of the sudden silence, where before there had been low murmurs, and an occasional ribald comment.

Arakal's voice grated. "Captain Jinks has the ability to listen to a liar, and not be angry. Where I or one of my officers might forget ourselves, and later regret it, the captain shakes his head and cautiously increases the pain. She is much safer telling lies to him than to me. Now get out of here. And if that pretty liar is not delivered by you to Captain Jinks, *you* will answer for it with your head!"

The chief nurse drew in her breath. "Yes, sir."

General Mason said, "Light her way, Rabeck."

"Yes, sir."

Arakal settled back. His leg throbbed, his head was swimming. His muscles were sore, and he felt as if he had been gone over with coarse sandpaper, all over his chest and back. But in the mind of the chief nurse, he was a man, men were unreliable, and that concluded the matter.

To the right of his cot, over near the wall, someone was laughing in a low voice about the chief nurse being an old maid, and delivering unutterable comments about this fact, and the reason for it, and suddenly the accumulated exhaustion outweighed Arakal's irritation, and he was falling into a darkness that swallowed him, removing the blonde girl, the chief nurse, the Russ, and all else around him, so that there was nothing left but the soft deep blackness.

There was a roar, a heavy smash, an explosion that lifted, then dropped him. There was, interlaced with this, a faint whine, somehow muffled, that grew slowly louder like an approaching mosquito, then blew up in his face. Arakal opened his eyes in the darkness.

The bombardment ended.

Mason's voice said quietly, "Sir?"

Arakal growled, "What?"

"We can teach these people something."

"We'll use our own method when we do it, not theirs."

Someone murmured to a snarling neighbor, "Don't move around, just keep your eyes shut, and you can go right back to sleep."

Arakal, with the same thought, was lying back on the cot. He felt himself begin to drift off.

The bunker shook to a heavy crash.

Arakal sat up carefully.

Now everything was quiet.

There came the sound of footsteps running down into the bunker.

General Mason snarled, "Watch?"

"Yes, sir. Givens. It's the same thing again. Except I got thrown about fifteen feet by that last one. I wasn't expecting that one."

"You hurt?"

"No, sir. There was stuff whining past pretty close, that's all."

"The bastards think they're cute. Good luck going back."

"Thank you, sir."

"Watch that step."

There was a thud, and Givens snarled, "Damn it! Yes, sir."

Arakal lay back, felt the room seem to swirl around him, and then there was a heavy crash, a whine, a sound as of fast trains thundering closer on an iron road built in the sky, and then there was a crash that shook the earth—and then there was silence. The silence stretched out, and then vanished in a bombardment heavier than what had gone before. At last, that came to an end.

Arakal rolled over and went back to sleep.

During the night, which seemed to go on forever, he came awake from time to time, conscious of noise and shock, and then fell asleep again. Eventually he woke with someone shaking him gently.

"Four-thirty, sir."

Arakal came wide awake. His leg hurt, and he was sore more or less everywhere. But he felt as if he had had part of a night's rest. He remembered with pleasure that he was with the First Division.

"Where," he asked, "is the washroom?"

"Out the door and to your right, sir."

Arakal gathered his clothes together, and limped off to get washed. Behind him, in order of rank, the other officers were being woken up. In the washroom, the incredible luxury of a bucket of hot water and soap, with fresh towels, was waiting. In the Groundmole Division, no one had to wash out of a helmet.

Arakal had a hot breakfast, and thirty minutes later, he, Slagiron, and Casey were in the headquarters bunker, hunched over a map with the three corps commanders.

★ **2** ★

S-One, still a little sleepy, but with a good breakfast inside of him, entered his suite of offices the back way, walked down the hall past a guard who snapped to attention, and entered his own office. The window was up, to admit the pleasant morning air of the courtyard. The desk and all the furniture had been dusted, and the room had been cleaned till it shone. S-One settled comfortably into his chair, then looked with foreboding at the display across the room.

So far, nothing seemed to have happened. The bridge-head appeared as it had been, the position on the near side of the river looked the same, and the position held by Arakal and his men seemed as it had the last time he had seen it. The only sign of motion was a train, symbolized by a blue rectangle, that backed away down the black line representing the track.

S-One caught himself breathing a sigh of relief. It came to him that the mental domination that had been inflicted on Brusilov had, to no small degree, also begun to affect him. Frowning, S-One considered this, then remembered that he had invited Brusilov to be here this morning. He glanced at the clock on the wall. A little after seven-thirty. He glanced at the display, where the small figures read "0531." He had that advantage. He had a longer time to sleep. And, he thought, smiling slightly, he had slept better.

He glanced across the room again at the display, and, at that moment, S-Two informed him that General Brusilov had arrived.

"Send him in," said S-One.

Brusilov, looking as if he had slept badly, came in.

S-One smiled, "Now, General, we will see how this Arakal of yours performs against a force superior in artillery."

Brusilov looked at the display, and winced.

S-One frowned. "What's wrong?"

"The bridgehead still isn't deep enough."

"That's a minor point. The main thing is the artillery. There is a dis—" S-One paused, staring at the display. He had been about to say that there was a disproportion between the artillery on both sides such that any minor element in the positions of the two forces was completely outweighed, and besides, the position of the forces in the bridgehead, and behind the river, struck him as superior to Arakal's position. But before he could complete the sentence, the display lit up dazzlingly.

Brusilov said, "How is this controlled?"

S-One, leaning forward, watched the flashes amongst the artillery positions on the near or easternmost side of the river. Evidently, Arakal's artillery was firing, firing with a murderous incredible rapidity, and these flashes represented the result of the firing. Suddenly, he saw the point of Brusilov's question, and called in S-Two.

"Sir?"

"How is this display controlled? For instance, we see flashes of light. They represent explosions, isn't that correct?"

S-Two blinked at the display.

"Yes, sir."

"All right. Now, how is this done? Do we have people attached to the various units, who report the attack? Obviously—"

S-Two shook his head.

"No, sir. That was true in the case of the Normandy Citadel. Our agents reported what happened, and it was shown on the display as a change of color, representing a change in the occupying power. But it is not true here. In the height of battle, those arrangements for reporting the outcome of the fight could easily be hit."

"That is my point. How do we know that this picture is accurate? What method is used?"

"This particular display is controlled by a remnant of what used to be known as the Satellite Battle Reporting System. The details are highly technical. But the idea is that satellites overhead detect heat and light, or other electromagnetic impulses, report them by what is left of the communications network to the Battle Reporting Computer, which interprets the data furnished to it, and shows it on this display."

S-One glanced at the display, then at Brusilov. Brusilov was looking wide-eyed at the display.

S-One turned to S-Two. "This is from before the war?"

"Yes, sir."

"Do the Americans have any such system as this?"

"To the best of our knowledge, the ground part of their system was completely destroyed. The satellite part may still be functional. As far as we know, Arakal has no access to any such system as this. But the Americans were a capable technological people, and of course realized the force of the attack that their system might be subject to. We can never be sure that, somewhere, there may not be a ground display station, heavily protected, that is still functional. We have often felt concern lest Arakal stumble on some formidable weapon left over from that war, and still functional, and it could happen."

"But Arakal, so far as we know, could not have any such device as this with him?"

"No, sir."

S-One nodded, and turned, frowning, to look back at the display.

Brusilov tore his gaze from the screen. "What if there should be a heavy overcast. Will this still work?"

S-Two replied, "There is a sort of mist-like appearance on the surface of the display; through this the visual representation appears more or less blurred. This is to indicate some decline in reliability. A legend appears to the side of the display to explain the cause of the blurring."

"What we see now, when the display is clear, is an actual visual representation of what is happening?"

"In effect, sir. But it is actually a computer reconstruction of signals picked up by satellite. It is therefore theoretically subject to error in the satellite detection, the transmission, or the computer reconstruction."

"But these errors are infrequent?"

"So far as we know, very infrequent."

After S-Two had left the room, Brusilov stared at the display, which now showed many flashes on both sides of the river. After a moment, Brusilov looked up, frowning.

"Who is in charge?"

"General Andronov."

"Andronov? I don't know him."

"He is one of ours," said S-One. "He is a security officer."

Brusilov stared at S-One, then looked back at the display. "He is getting beaten. We have underestimated Arakal's artillery."

"Surely," said S-One, "it is too early to know that."

"It is altogether too early to know it. But now that we understand that this display is not just a stylized representation, already we can see the outlines. Look at the fire of the two sides. Who is being hit the heaviest?"

The display showed an almost continuous overlapping series of flashes on the eastern side of the display, across the river from Arakal's army. On the side of Arakal's army, the number of flashes was dwindling. And now, as they watched, the flashes began to shift, very slowly but clearly, increasingly hitting the bridgehead. These flashes, the visible signs of hits by Arakal's artillery, continued heavy, while the opposing artillery fire became lighter and lighter; though never dying out entirely, it was clearly dominated by Arakal's artillery. Now a sort of blue shading began to move forward, against the northern edge of the bridgehead, which was outlined in red. As if it were a lump of sugar dissolving in warm water, the red swirled, faded, and dissolved, and the blue moved in. The intense flashing was now almost all on the west side of the river, in the bridgehead. Now, as they watched, a red shading began to move across the bridge, flowing into the bridgehead.

"Ah," said S-One, in a tone of relief, "at last. Reinforcements."

Brusilov straightened. His right hand gripped the edge of his chair. A flash appeared on the railroad bridge, where some of the red shading was coming across. A flash appeared on the highway bridge, where a heavier shading of red was crossing into the bridgehead. The flashes increased in intensity. Still, the red shading came on. Time passed. Now the flashes striking Arakal's position increased. Abruptly, the fire on the bridges and into the bridgehead ceased, there was a brief delay, then suddenly the east bank of the river lit up in bright flashes, not uniformly spaced, but rapid retreating flashes centered on the same or nearly the same points.

S-One stared. Brusilov came halfway up out of his chair.

The brilliant display ended, leaving an impression of blackness on certain points of the screen, by contrast. Now, again, the flashes lit the two bridges, and began walking across the bridgehead. Brusilov came to his feet.

"This is murder. You must end it."

"I don't understand."

"What we are watching is the destruction of our army."

"That is too strong a statement. There are very heavy forces not in this fight."

"Comrade, there is such a thing as inertia in warfare. You may not believe it, and I don't claim to understand it; but if you let Andronov's army be smashed by Arakal, then the only hope is to unite our reserves, put the Marshal in charge, and turn the whole control over to him. There is a psychic element in war—"

"You mean psychological."

"I don't know what word is right. But if Arakal wins this as he is winning it, strength will flow from us to him—or something will happen that will have the same effect. He will become the champion. We will hesitate to strike. He will act. Our position will dissolve. He is a kind man, and I am sure there will be no vengeance. But if you want to hold the position you have now, I tell you everything is now in the balance. This battle has got to be turned over to someone who understands war. The Marshal is our best, and he has the—"

S-One, watching the display, felt a sudden quickening of the pulse, a tightness of breath. The blue shading had bitten into the northern flank of the bridgehead, all the way to the railroad bridge. Now what? To his astonishment, the blue moved out on the bridge, preceded by flashes that crossed to the other side, and then the blue was on the other side, too. Now what? This was suicide, wasn't it? How had they gotten across so soon? On the highway bridge, the red was still crossing from east to west, while on the railroad bridge, the blue was crossing from west to east. S-One suddenly found himself unable to think, to draw conclusions from what he was seeing.

Brusilov, seeing the expression on S-One's face, turned, looked at the display, swore, and turned back to S-One.

"My God, man! Don't stand there! Send for the Marshal!"

S-One was thinking, "Is this panic? I can't think. So this is what panic is?" He drew a deep breath, and blanked his face. Above all, he had to maintain an appearance of control. One who gave that up, who was seen to lose control—how could such a person ever live down the knowledge in the minds of others that he *had* lost control? Abruptly S-One could think again. He made a gesture of the hand. "This has all been allowed for in the plan."

Brusilov stared at him.

S-One said, "But what I don't understand is, why do they cross the river? They are in as bad a position as we. In a worse position! Their bridgehead has *no* depth. Why do they cross?"

Brusilov looked at the display, where the red shade was falling back, crowding now at the west end of the highway bridge. It was a rapid movement for the scale of the display and they could see it happen like a flow of molasses across a tilted plate, a streaming motion that continued with no visible rational object except to coalesce at the west end of the bridge.

Brusilov spoke in disgust. "Do you think this display gives any real idea what those men are going through? All this shows us is certain geometrical aspects of what is happening. Do you think that is all there is to war?"

"Why do our men crowd at the end of the bridge?"

"Because word has no doubt reached them that the enemy has gotten to the other side of the river. Their retreat is being cut off. They feel trapped."

S-One nodded, understanding the point.

Brusilov shook his head.

"For the last time, Comrade! Will you call the Marshal?"

S-One sat down. He shook his head. "There is no need for panic, General. All this has been allowed for, in the plan."

Brusilov made no motion. His face became expressionless, as if the nerves controlling the facial muscles had been switched off. Then he looked alert, as if he were listening.

S-One frowned, and sat up. Now he heard it, too.

Outside, there was a tramping, a shot, a fusillade of shots, a yell.

The interoffice phone buzzed. S-One picked it up, and his deputy's voice rang in his ear:

"Sir! Troops are forcing their way in!"

"Under whose command?"

"I don't know yet!"

On S-One's desk, the outside phone rang. S-One scooped it up. "Hello?"

The Head of Government's voice said, "Any resistance will be futile."

S-One looked up, to see General Brusilov holding a pistol in his hand, holding it very steadily so that S-One could almost look down the barrel.

S-One shook his head, and spoke into the phone. "Don't be silly. Of course there will be no resistance. Do as you will." He rested the phone on the table, setting it down without hanging it up. "S-Two?"

"Sir?"

"Signal the guard detachments that there is to be no further resistance. They will lay down their arms if the army units demand it."

"Sir, the corridor is mined. We can very easily leave. I can disembarrass you of your problem, if you say the word."

"No. General Brusilov is doubtless acting on valid orders. Turn on the public address system. They can hear my voice form this phone, can't they, if you connect it in the circuit?"

"If you say so, sir."

"Turn it on."

"It is on, sir."

S-One spoke carefully.

"This is S-One speaking. General Brusilov and I are coming out down the main corridor. Stay where you are. General Brusilov and I are coming out together."

S-One glanced at the blank-faced Brusilov. "Well, let's go. What are we waiting for?" As Brusilov began to put the gun away, S-One said, "No, keep that in your hand. It explains the situation, so the troops can feel easy."

At the door, S-One paused, and looked back.

"I will miss the flowers," he said.

XI. The Pursuit

★ 1 ★

Arakal and Slagiron were with the Fourth Division that night. They had just finished eating, and were in their tent, studying a map by the light of an ill-trimmed lamp with a tendency to smoke. Arakal had turned down the wick, and was waiting to let the mantle burn clean, when a voice spoke from outside.

"Pardon, sir. There's a Captain Jinks out here. He wants to talk to you."

"Send him in," said Arakal.

The tent flap came open. A burly middle-aged man with a tired sad expression let himself in, peered around in the gloom, and saluted Arakal. Arakal returned the salute.

"Have a seat, Captain. What did you find out?"

Jinks sat down, and sighed. "She's a spy, sir. And a novice tripjack artist. On top of that, she brought a plant, and left it in the bunker with you and General Morgan and the rest. Her final story to me, before she cracked, was that she's a French girl—an Old Kebeck girl—struck with hero-worship for you, and that she lied to the chief nurse in order to come with us. That's a lie, like what went before. She's Russ. She belongs to some outfit that supplies spies to some other outfit called 'S'. She's scared of 'S'. This outfit she belongs to is called the 'Professional Assistance Corps'. If 'S' wants a nurse to plant somewhere, or a bricklayer, or a clerk, they go to this Professional Assistance Corps. Everyone in it is trained to do two jobs—the one they're supposed to be expert at, and spying. She is a qualified nurse, and has worked at a hospital in Old Kebeck, here. I got the story out of her without marring her looks, but I'm afraid her spirits are a little dented."

"What was the plan?"

"She only had instructions, and we have to guess at the plan behind them. Her instructions were first to locate you, after getting in using as a mask her occupation of nurse. After you were wounded, her being sent to the right surgeon's tent was pure luck. She had this device to plant in your quarters."

"This was the plant you mentioned?"

"Yes, sir. It's about the size of a man's thumb, with a sticky claylike stuff on the outside. It looks like a lump of clay or dirt. She stuck it to the corner of the wall just inside the room where you were sleeping. It contains fine wires and little things like tiny beads. We don't know what it is. Neither does she. She just did as she was told."

"All right. What next?"

"Next was the tripjack stunt. If possible, she was to get you to make love to her. They instructed her in about forty different alternative approaches to work that. Nobody told her what the idea was. She was just supposed to be mad with hero-worship of you. But except under torture, she was only to *admit* that to you. To everyone else, *you* were responsible, *you* made the arrangements, you took the initiative. Her explanation to you was to be that she was too embarrassed to admit her passion to anyone else. Meanwhile, she was to keep her eyes open, and learn all she could about our arrangements and plans. She wouldn't try to pass that on until 'S' got in touch with her. That covers her instructions. We can guess at parts of the plan, and, just in case, the doctors are checking her over right now, to find out whether possibly she was given some disease she was supposed to pass on during all this love-making."

"If so, she didn't know about it?"

"No, sir. She just did what they told her."

"How did she get in this Professional Assistance Corps?"

"They selected her, and told her how patriotic it was when she expressed some doubts. She was too afraid to object."

Arakal nodded.

Captain Jinks said, "To avoid marking her, I stuck to straight pain, sir. I told her in advance that I was under orders not to mark her, and that I would also avoid deliberately breaking her spirit. I also told her that there was more pain in the world, and she could experience more of it, than she had any idea of. It was a mistake to tell her all that. Looking at her, I thought she would break easy. She didn't. I should have let her worry about her looks. It would have broken her down quicker, and been easier on both of us."

Arakal nodded moodily. "If she hadn't been here as a spy, it wouldn't have happened. Now the problem is, what to do with her."

Slagiron moved uneasily, "Sir, while we deliberate on that, time is passing. There are a great many different ways to get rid of a spy, and if you want me to, I'll take care of it personally. But right now, we have more important things to think of."

Arakal glanced at Jinks. "When will the doctors be through with her?"

Jinks shook his head. "Maybe they know, sir. I don't."

"Do *you* have any idea what to do with her?"

Jinks frowned. "She's beautiful. She has brains and will. The trouble is that she just happens to be on the wrong side, and the wrong orders were given to her. She *is* a capable nurse . . . I think I'd ship her back to them."

"Are you sure she finally gave the facts—the whole truth?"

Jinks sat back, frowning. "All the *facts*. As to her motives, I can't be certain. She resisted longer than I would have thought possible. There had to be a strong motive. I didn't get that out of her."

Arakal nodded. "Well, when the doctors are through, let me know." Arakal got up, and walked the few steps to the front of the tent, and held back the flap. "Watch that tent rope."

"Yes, sir. Thank you. Good night, sir."

"Good night, Jinks. Thank you."

Arakal carefully shut the flap.

Slagiron cautiously turned up the lamp, and growled, "Now that we've got shock-resistant mantles, we need smokeproof wicks."

Arakal nodded. "Now, let's see." He looked at the map. "There are enough rivers in this place."

"Yes. And we ought to be able to knock the living daylights out of them at every crossing. But what if the Russ have another army around somewhere?"

"They're bound to," said Arakal. "This isn't their main force. Not only that, we can't hope they'll all be mishandled."

"No," said Slagiron. "But where are the rest? And what are they doing now? Not knowing that, we could get caught with blown bridges behind us, and our supplies cut off."

Arakal frowned at the map. "Let's suppose the worst case—"

★ 2 ★

S-One, with General Brusilov beside him, was escorted down the corridor to a big double door with armed guards to right and to left. The lieutenant in charge of the escort went inside, then came out to say to Brusilov, "If you stay right with him, sir, we will remain outside."

Brusilov gave a grunt of assent, and went in with S-One.

Inside, at the big table, flanked by Marshal Vasilevsky and General Kolbukhin, sat the Head of Government. He spoke shortly.

"Come in. Sit directly opposite us."

S-One did as told, without a word. Brusilov glanced questioningly at the Head of Government, and at his nod sat down beside S-One.

The Head of Government, habitually spoken of as "G-One," as a monarch is spoken of as "the king," leaned forward, his eyes narrowed.

"Your precious Andronov is defeated. Reserve France is running from Arakal. There are uprisings in France, Germany, and Poland. We have word of sabotage through all western Europe. The U.K. is in open rebellion. The Americans own the Normandy Citadel. Their fleet has cut our communications to the U.K. All this has followed from your plan." His voice sharpened. "Can you give me one reason why I should not have you torn to bits with red-hot pincers?"

S-One blinked, frowned, then spoke, his voice suddenly calm, with undertones of power.

"That you can speak this way follows from the fact that you are not yet dead, as you would already be if I had chosen to have you killed, and as you will be if I choose now to raise my hand against you. Your only guarantee of safety is my continued good will, which is, I think an excellent reason not to have me torn to pieces with red-hot pincers. A second reason is that neither you nor anyone else in this room has the faintest conception of the S Plan for dealing with Arakal; modesty is a more appropriate attitude for the ignorant than menace. In the third place, your own power, even if I permit you to lay hand on me, is only to burn a corpse, not cause me so much as ten seconds' pain."

G-One's eyes seemed as if lit from within.

"We can test that."

"Think," said S-One coldly. "Do you really wish to test what I have said?" His voice rose very slightly as he spoke, to convey a threat that made the Marshal look up, and G-One pause, halfway to his feet.

S-One spoke again, this time quietly, like a parent to a foolish child:

"Sit down."

G-One, his expression alert and baffled, sat down. Then he shook his head.

"You have gained a minute with your bluff. Go ahead. Talk."

S-One said quietly, "There is no bluff. Don't make the error of laughing at a bear on land because he seems clumsy in water."

"Meaning what?"

"If you judge the S Plan by its *military* results, you sneer at the bear because he is not a fish. That is a premature judgment. You can judge a creature accurately only in his own element. That applies also to you and me. If you judge me as helpless because as a general I seem ineffectual, you risk a sudden discovery of just what my element is."

G-One looked away a moment, then looked back, directly into S-One's eyes.

"All this is a clever net of words. If you expect to tie me up in it, you are mistaken. Just incidentally, you are the person who, not long ago, professed loyalty to the so-called 'formal power' of my position. We will find out about those red-hot tongs and your power to resist."

S-One said patiently, "Think back, and you will recall what I said. That loyalty is to the person in your position who is fitted by ability to be in that position. It is not a personal loyalty to you. It is loyalty to G-One. If you demonstrate the wrong trait, you cease to command my loyalty. Just so, I must manifest the traits of S-One. Why do you think we use these silly appellations? Because there is a possible difference between the position and the traits it requires, and the individual in that position. Only so long as you manifest the proper traits can you command my loyalty, because that loyalty is not to you personally, but to G-One."

G-One said, "I think I will test what strength is behind this logic."

S-One said coldly, "Do you wish to die suddenly, or would you like it to be long and drawn-out, so that I can explain to you what happened, and why it must be that way?"

Brusilov, listening uneasily, and seeing the Head of Government draw back again, cleared his throat. "May I speak?"

G-One turned slightly, his expression angry and baffled. "Go ahead. But quickly."

"I don't like to say this. But while we sit here, stalemated, Arakal is in action. After the soldiers came, and when S-One was leaving his office, he looked back and said, 'I will miss the flowers.' If S-One could still control events, would he have said that?"

Across the table, G-One's face cleared, and he turned toward the door.

S-One spoke flatly, "I said that because I expected to be rudely dismissed, not assassinated."

G-One, partly risen, as if to call out to the troops on the far side of the door, sat down again. A look of astonishment washed across his face.

"What you say now is that if I say, 'You're fired,' you will offer no resistance?"

S-One's face slowly suffused with color. He leaned forward. "How many times do I have to say it to you? If you dismiss me, I am dismissed. We have been all over this! What did we talk about the other day?"

"I thought there were threats in your words. You said that my real power—"

"The real power of your position."

"You said that it depended on *your* loyalty!"

"That is true."

"Then what power—"

"It is a statement of fact. There is no threat, because that loyalty is assured. *To G-One*."

"But it is up to you to decide!"

Across the table, Marshal Vasilevsky glanced at General Brusilov and shook his head ever so slightly, then settled back with a glazed expression, eyes half-shut, like a student in an over-heated classroom.

S-One said, "This is no personal matter that I may warp to my advantage in a struggle for power. It is a question like that of the blacksmith who judges the readiness of the iron by the color of its glow. But I will say it plainly: You may dismiss me. That is a question purely up to your pleasure. You may do this as long as you hold the position of G-One. If I should decide that you are unfit to *be* G-One, I may remove you. But those selected to fill the position of S-One are not chosen for their fitness to fill the role of Attila the Hun. Neither are they selected for their capacity to lick boots. I will defer to the formal power of your position. In *that* lies your safety. Just incidentally, if I am dismissed, there is no assurance that whoever follows me will be any more to your taste."

"Your deputy will succeed you?"

"Not likely. An S-Two is selected for different reasons than an S-One."

"Then we are still in this asinine stalemate!"

"You may end it at any time."

"Only to have the same thing with someone else."

S-One frowned. "One moment. The crux is not a personal matter. It is simply a question of the S Plan for dealing with Arakal."

G-One looked away, and swallowed.

S-One leaned forward, and spoke earnestly. "I mean no offense to anyone at this table. But I can explain that plan only to the Head of Government, personally, and to no one else. I will talk about it, very generally, if you wish, in the presence of others, but I will only explain the plan itself to you *if* you promise not to reveal it to anyone else. The reason for this is that this S Plan is not a military plan. But it depends on the actions of military people. For the military to understand the plan would be a complicating factor the effects of which I cannot predict."

G-One slammed his fist down on the table. He got up, walked the length of the room, walked back, spun his chair around, and sat down, astride the chair. His voice was intense.

"Let us talk about this S Plan generally, then. If it works, will it recover everything we have lost to Arakal so far?"

"Everything but the Normandy Citadel, and whatever depends on it, such as the blockade of the Channel."

"What will happen to Arakal?"

"He will no longer be of any concern."

"And America? Will we regain America?"

"We did not have complete control of America. The plan is a method to penetrate America, just as we penetrated Europe, but more slowly. Finally, we should have complete control."

"And the Fleet?"

"*We* will not control the Fleet. The Americans will control it. But we will control the Americans."

G-One looked at S-One wonderingly. "It encompasses all that?"

"Yes. But let me point out that it is a plan only. It depends on the reactions of people, and we do not understand completely the reactions of Arakal or of his men. The bullfighter's dominance in the ring depends on his practical understanding of the psychology of the bull. We believe this plan will work, but this is a different breed of bull. There are obvious risks."

Marshal Vasilevsky's eyes came wide-open, and he laughed. "We could get gored, eh?"

S-One said, very seriously, "We could."

G-One said, "Has the plan failed *yet*?"

"In the case of the Normandy Citadel, yes. No, otherwise."

"What about Andronov's retreat?"

"No, that is not failure."

"And the uprisings?"

"They were anticipated, let me say, and do not represent a failure of the plan."

"In your opinion, does the plan underestimate our opponent?"

S-One thought a moment.

"It may. *I* underestimated him."

"If so, are we in danger?"

"It depends on unknowns. Arakal and his men are in very great danger. We are in some danger. There are opportunities and risks for both sides. In my opinion, the opportunities for us are far greater, and the risks far less. I may be mistaken."

Across the big table, G-One stood up, swung his chair around, and sat down again. He exhaled sharply. "This is of interest, but too general to rely on. And we cannot continue in this deadlock forever."

S-One shrugged. "The initiative is with you."

"That is not my meaning."

"Then what is your meaning?"

"I hesitate to say, lest more time pass in talk."

Marshal Vasilevsky moved slightly in his seat. His voice was quiet, and his tone noncommittal. "I take my orders from the Head of Government. The last time I looked, my men were outside the door."

S-One smiled, and said nothing.

The Marshal spoke again, quietly. "All this is a political matter, and I make no claim to understand politics. But I understand guns. If you want to stop Arakal, we can stop him."

G-One, the Head of Government, said exasperatedly, "This situation has got to be simplified." He looked at S-One. "What if we all here swear not to repeat this plan. Tell all of us. There are enough of us here of expert judgment to gauge the worth of the plan."

S-One shook his head. "An S Plan cannot be revealed to the military. The military may aid in carrying it out. They cannot sit in judgment over it. Only you can hear it."

"Let me convene the whole Central Committee, then."

"They are not properly constituted to sit in judgment on it."

G-One clenched his fists. His voice was even and conversational as he turned to the Marshal. "The difficulty is that we need the S organization. We can smash it, yes. But if we smash it, we smash an instrument useful, and perhaps essential, to us." He glanced at Brusilov, his voice wondering. "Is there any way Arakal could be creating discord among us? All this upheaval comes about in response to *his* arrival."

Brusilov shook his head, then paused, frowning. Then he shook his head more definitely. "No. He has no means to do that, at least."

The Marshal said, "He is skillful, and I think he has been lucky. The strain he puts on our arrangements shows up our weak points. That puts us all in a bad humor."

"That is sensible," said G-One. He looked across the table, frowning. Abruptly he said, "All right. I will listen to this plan of yours."

★ 3 ★

Arakal lowered the long-seeing glasses. Ahead of him, the Russ, under a heavy bombardment, were crossing the last of the series of rivers on the way to what he knew as "Allemain," what the Old Kebeckers called "Allemagne," and what the maps of the Old O'Cracy called "Germany." Whatever they called it, Arakal didn't want to go there. He turned to Slagiron.

"Call up the troop trains. Once the Russ are well over that river, we'll head back."

Slagiron nodded. "The sooner we get out of this place, the better."

★ 4 ★

G-One was sitting on the edge of the desk, staring at S-One, who had sat down in an ornate green-and-gilt armchair and was leaning forward as he talked. To G-One's astonishment, the S Plan seemed possible, and its description short and to the point.

S-One now made a gesture of the hand as if tossing aside a crumpled paper, and said, "That is the plan. While I do not insist that it will work, I assure you that it is practical, and it well *may* work."

"The trouble is that if it does not, we may be ruined."

"We had to deal with this Arakal in *some* way. If he had been stupid, or unlucky, we would already have finished him. We could not count on that. The plan allows for his military success."

"You have certainly revealed to me more of the workings of your organization than I expected. Implicit in such a plan as this are many things."

"I can speak plainly to you because you are G-One. It is possible to select and train an S-One. To select a Head of Government is much harder, if it is possible at all. So many factors are unpredictable. Even this Arakal sees the problem. It was in Brusilov's report. My problem is simpler. I need only recognize one who has been selected."

G-One shook his head. "No one *selected* me. I am here because the complacent people who preceded me made serious mistakes. But that is neither here nor there. We have two problems. The first is the Americans. The second is the relationship of your organization and the government. I will tell you right now that it came very close, several times, to your not living to explain this plan. I tell you that no capable person is going to tolerate your elbow constantly in his ribs. Also, I want to be able to sleep at night. For now, we must settle with Arakal. But let us think ahead a little. You have got to give me more room."

S-One sighed.

"Some time soon, I must explain something else to you. It has to do with the last big war, and the Americans.

You will not believe me. But I will show you the documents. If necessary, I will show you the realities."

G-One shook his head. "Not now. We must reassure the Marshal and the others."

"No, but soon. Then you will understand why S is as it is."

"How long will it take?"

"It is a long story."

"I will give you a long time to tell it. Now, let's go out."

★ 5 ★

Arakal was with the Seventh Division that night, had eaten and talked with the men, had looked over some of the artillery that the division was so plentifully supplied with, and had checked to be sure that their supplies were getting through. As the men were settling down to finish cleaning and oiling their guns, Arakal and Slagiron were bent over their maps. There were a number of these maps, all more or less unsatisfactory, and as they came up against the limitations of one map, they tried another. At length, Slagiron growled, "Well, it *seems* practical."

"On the map," said Arakal.

"On *these* maps, anyway."

"All right, now. Suppose—" He put his outstretched forefinger on the map "—that they erupt out of this forest, and come down on us from the northeast?"

"Then," said Slagiron, smiling, "we'll hit them while they're crossing the river here—What's this one? The Aisne."

"And if, instead, they march along to the north of it, headed for the ocean?"

"Then we march parallel to them on the south. It looks as if we have the better road, and two good bridges over this next river. What's this one? The Oise? But now, suppose they stay north of the Oise where it comes in from the west, here, and then they swing around to come south, still on the far side, and get between us and Cherbourg. *Then* what do we do?"

"If we find out in time, we can go back and stop them before they cross the Seine, here. Or, we can try to hit them from behind, if we have supplies enough built up."

"Suppose they're on the way right now, and we don't find out in time?"

"Then we could put our trains on the iron road headed south, here, and turn east, here. Meanwhile, we yell for Admiral Bullinger. Or there are other possibilities."

"None of them very boring," said Slagiron, looking at the map.

"No."

One by one, Arakal and Slagiron tried out the possibilities. Suppose the Russ turned up here? Or there? What if the tracks were cut, or a bridge blown? What were the possible effects of these canals, paralleling or joining these sections of rivers? Suppose they took up a position here, or here? How would the supply trains reach them? How long to go between these two points on foot? How long by rail?

When they were through, Arakal said, "We have an idea, at least," and Slagiron nodded. "The reality may be something else." Before they could say anything further, outside there was a sound of hoofbeats.

Then there were two shots from a rifle, followed by the blast of a whistle.

★ 6 ★

As S-One looked on, the Head of Government, seated again between Marshal Vasilevsky and General Kolbukhin, spoke quietly.

"I will say frankly that I would not have believed it possible, but I am reassured about this plan. I have agreed not to describe it, but I want to give some idea why it now seems a reasonable plan to me. First, our colleagues in S have put far more of their resources into it than I had realized. Second, it does truly allow for success on Arakal's part, and we can win, regardless. Third—"

An urgent knock sounded on the door of the room.

G-One paused, an odd expression on his face.

"Come in."

The door came open, and S-Two hurried in, carrying a sheaf of papers in one hand. He bent urgently by S-One.

G-One looked on coldly.

Across the table, S-Two straightened, nodded abstractedly, and headed back for the door.

As the door shut behind him, G-One looked at S-One, and said ironically, "Now what?"

S-One was glancing rapidly through the sheaf of papers that his deputy had brought in. He looked up with an exasperated expression.

"Arakal has broken off pursuit of Andronov, and has fallen back behind the Aisne. He is taking up what appears to be a formidable *defensive* position."

General Kolbukhin, in a low voice, swore.

The Marshal grinned. "The fellow has more sense than I gave him credit for." He looked at Brusilov. "I begin to understand your viewpoint. He is not so easy to lead around by the nose."

General Kolbukhin said angrily, "What the devil are we doing with our *other* armies? While he was chasing Andronov, we could have come in behind him, cut off his supplies, and cracked him like a nut."

The Marshal grinned. "Now, now, that is not *subtle*. This plan, now, is subtle. The only thing is, this Arakal, he is no more subtle than we are. That is what is causing all this trouble."

"All right," said Kolbukhin to S-One. "Run away from him, lure him into Central Europe if you want. But then, when you've got him there, then *cut him off*. What is the point of having an advantage if we don't use it?"

G-One spoke angrily to the Marshal. "You are right, this plan *is* subtle. And there is more to it than you think."

Brusilov said carefully, "Arakal is very quick to scent a trap. He is not likely to take the bait, however subtle the plan, if it puts him at a disadvantage."

The Marshal growled, "But do we *have* to be subtle to put him at a disadvantage?"

S-One and G-One glanced at each other across the table. G-One cleared his throat. "I have examined this plan. It is not perfect. But it offers us more, if it succeeds, than a strictly military solution to the problem. The reason is that a strictly military solution to the overall problem of which Arakal is a part—a strictly *military* solution of that problem—is probably beyond our strength."

The Marshal frowned. "What is this overall problem?"

"The problem of America."

"If our ancestors had been just a little more thorough, that problem would not exist."

S-One spoke up, his voice carefully neutral. "There were reasons for their actions. There were limitations then, too, to solely military solutions."

The Marshal was silent a moment, then said, "I am not political. But I would like to ask whether your plan cannot be frustrated by Arakal, using purely military means?"

S-One thought a moment, frowning, and turned to Brusilov, as if to ask a question. Instead, he suddenly turned back to face the Marshal.

"In the short run, yes. In the long run, he must find a non-military answer."

General Kolbukhin said, "Why? Isn't the problem solved if Arakal and his men are trapped and killed, and if we smash the defenders of the Normandy Citadel, and recapture it?"

"No, because, among other things, all conflict has two parts, gain and loss. Breaking into the Citadel could be a very expensive procedure."

Marshal Vasilevsky nodded. "But it can be done."

"We *think* it can be done. Let me, though I am not a military man, point out that Arakal has heavy artillery under his control there, in addition to our automatic cannon. Our opinion that we can retake the Citadel may be mistaken."

General Kolbukhin glanced at the Head of Government. G-One was listening, a slight frown on his face. General Kolbukhin looked back across the table at S-One. "*Our* artillery is heavier yet."

"Their mobile artillery reserve is heavier than our mobile artillery reserve."

Kolbukhin leaned forward, his eyes glittering. "That is false."

S-One looked at him mildly, and waited.

Kolbukhin, confident that in this, at least, he had the Head of S at a disadvantage, said challengingly, "Name even one gun they can put into that battle that is bigger than ours."

"I can think of a number," said S-One quietly.

"What size?"

S-One spoke in a low voice, so that it was necessary to listen closely to hear him. "And when I name it, you will name one of ours that is larger, is that it?"

Kolbukhin, who had the known details of Arakal's army memorized, smiled. "Yes, I will."

S-One's voice was almost humble.

"Well, then, perhaps I have been mistaken, but in any case I will be glad to hear your answer."

"Go ahead. *What* guns? Name the largest they have. Let's get on with this."

"I am thinking of their 355-millimeter guns."

The general sat back, blank-faced.

"We are talking about mobile artillery?"

"That is correct. My information is that, in good weather, these guns can be moved at over thirty kilometers per hour, and can be fired while in motion. They can hit any spot on the battlefield, while out of range of our own weapons. They carry enormous quantities of ammunition with them at all times. They are invulnerable to infantry attack."

Kolbukhin stared.

"What," said S-One, "do we have that is bigger?"

"If what you say is accurate, then I have to admit, we would have a bloody experience trying to break through that. But I also cannot conceive of it. When did they develop such guns?"

S-One said earnestly, with no trace of superiority in his manner, "The guns I am speaking of *are* their mobile artillery in this case, General, though it is natural to overlook them, because they are not part of Arakal's *army*.

These are the naval guns on his new bombardment ships. But that will make slight difference to us if we have to come up against them. Let me mention that they are not necessarily the worst we may have to face. We happen to know that Arakal has at least one railroad gun that is, if our estimate is correct, a 530–millimeter gun. What do we oppose to that?"

"We could build—"

"We are talking about *now*."

Kolbukhin nodded glumly. "I see your point."

The Marshal spoke up, his voice quiet, but nonetheless assured.

"Your point is that it would be expensive—that we would pay a steep price in men and equipment to recover the Citadel?"

S-One spread his hands. "I suppose it can be done. But is it worth the price?"

"There is a point we had better face now," said the Marshal. "In my opinion, we undoubtedly still have the military force to defeat Arakal, and to recover the Citadel. Arakal has got, or can take, England, if he lives, and if they will have him. He still has his fleet. And we will still have this problem of America that you speak of, afterward. This is not a good situation. But there are worse situations. If we fritter away our troops, if we fumble around, if we try only to draw Arakal into errors, and place ourselves at a disadvantage in doing it—then we can lose our clear advantage in strength. Meanwhile, Arakal is making a name for himself. I begin to be impressed by his good sense, myself. When this process goes far enough, all of us are going to feel that he is the superior. We will feel fear, even awe. Unless this S Plan allows for this, we had better face the fact that there are worse things than paying a stiff price to win back our control in a more limited space than what we had before. We had better face the fact that we are risking the loss of everything we have." The Marshal noted a change in Brusilov's expression, and said at once, "What is it? You don't agree?"

Brusilov shook his head. "I agree, except for one thing. Arakal would never put us in the position you mention. He would never try to conquer us. All the territory he wants is *the land of the O'Cracy*. He interprets that as 'Old Kebeck', and 'Old Brunswick'. France and England —That is, France and the United Kingdom. Even, he would have an alliance with us. But first, we must disgorge France and England. I have talked to him on the subject until my head swam. There is no enmity, no desire for revenge. He is exasperated by what happened in the past, does not understand it—who does? But he has more friendship for us than enmity."

"How can he feel friendship? After all, we killed his forebears."

Brusilov shook his head. "Who is 'we'? Did you? Did I? Is there anyone who really knows what happened? Did *we* come out of it undented? This friendship I speak of is not solely a matter of reasoning or policy, but also an emotional response. We can get along together. He likes us. There is no ill will. I mention this because, if we think otherwise, we are calculating on a false basis. He is not a conqueror or a marauder."

When Brusilov stopped speaking, there was a silence. The Marshal nodded his head, eyes slightly narrowed. His face cleared, and his expression smoothed out. "Well, in that case—But, of course, we still want to win."

Kolbukhin, frowning, said, "France and England. Well, how are they vital to us? But we must have something in return."

S-One stared blankly from Kolbukhin to the Marshal. For an instant, the muscles at his jaw clenched, and his face reddened slightly. Then he glanced at the Head of Government, who looked at Brusilov, and said, "If this is true, the sensible thing to do appears to me to be to simply hold out of the battle the forces which now are not yet in the battle, and meanwhile let the fight proceed, and see if the S Plan will work."

Brusilov spoke carefully. "That may be. As I don't know the plan, I can't judge."

S-One nodded in relief.

But when, a little later, he was back in his office, looking out at the garden, S-One suddenly turned to S-Two.

"We have," said S-One to his deputy, "a different and worse situation on our hands than I realized."

"How is that, sir?"

"I have fallen into the same hole as that blockhead, Smirnov, who succeeded in losing our colonies in America to this damned elective king. I have underestimated him!"

"In thinking he would advance—"

"No," said S-One, furious, "*that* was bad enough. This is worse!"

"I've had no word—"

"I've been thinking of him as a military opponent. It is worse than that. You should have heard the Marshal, and this General Kolbukhin—"

S-Two smiled modestly. "I did hear them, sir."

"Then you know what I had to sit through! I might have expected it from Brusilov. But from the Marshal! Then suddenly it struck me!"

"What is it, sir?"

"It is an illusion to think this is just a military war. That would be trouble enough. But it is worse than that."

"How—"

"Arakal is fighting us *politically*!"

S-Two's eyes narrowed. "By sending back Smirnov, and Brusilov, to bring his viewpoint to us?"

"Yes. For one thing. And in his approach to our colonists. In his refusal to use any more bloodshed than necessary. In retreating back into France, so *we* must be the aggressors." S-One's eyes flashed in anger. "But he will find it hard to fight us politically *here*. He will not take the bait, eh? If necessary, we will take the baited hook, and ram it through his jaw!"

★ 7 ★

Arakal, surrounded in the firelight by his troops, looked at Pierrot, who was talking earnestly, and so fast that the translators could not keep up. At length, there came a pause, and one of the translators summarized:

"What he says, sir, is that he has been harassing the Russ, and when we stopped chasing them, he was left alone to carry on the fight by himself. He's mad about it. He figures we betrayed him, deserted him in combat, ran out on him, turned yellow. He would have been finished by the Russ, he says, but somebody by the name of—Stalheim, I think it was—hit the Russ from another direction, and got him loose. Now he wants to know are we going to lurk back here, and leave it to him to carry the war to the Russ? Or are we going to—ah—take our courage in both hands, and *fight*? I think I've got the substance of it, sir."

There were angry murmurs from Arakal's men as the translator gave his summary, then Arakal asked, "Did he mention at any point where he's been since the Russ attacked and he disappeared?"

"He says he's been fighting the Russ, sir. Harassing them, that is."

"Did he say where?"

"No, sir."

Arakal glanced around at Slagiron.

"General, could you step into that tent, and get me one of those maps?"

Slagiron nodded. "Yes, sir." A moment later, he handed Arakal a worn map. Arakal turned to Pierrot, and spoke to the translator.

"Ask him if he can show me on this map where he and his men were located, so that we can get a clearer picture of how the battle developed. Tell him I'd also like to know more about Stalheim, and how Stalheim helped him get free of the Russ."

The translator spoke and was interrupted by Pierrot. The translator turned to Arakal.

"He says, sir, that you can speak his tongue. Why does he have to speak through someone else?"

"I don't speak it that fast. There seems to be a misunderstanding, and I want to be sure it's cleared up, not made worse. Here's the map."

Pierrot examined the map, turned it around, studied it in silence, nodded, and began to speak volubly, pointing to the map, then to himself, then gesturing at people nowhere in sight. His face lit in a beaming smile as he talked, his features twisted as he pantomimed sighting a gun, then made a gesture as if heaving a grenade. His camouflage suit, smearing with mud and what appeared to be crusts of blood, gave off a smell of sweat, wine, and horse dung as he talked, more and more expansively, tapping the map first here, then there, and holding his raised forefinger up for attention as he poured words at the translator.

At length there came a pause, and the translator turned to Arakal.

"What it seems to come down to, sir, is that they sniped and bushwhacked, caved in the skulls of Russ stragglers, and managed to mine some roads in the rear of the Russ retreat."

"*Where?*"

As Arakal looked from the translator to Pierrot, from somewhere behind them a booming voice shouted what sounded like: "Pierrot! *Vo ist air? Vo ist air?* Pierrot?"

Arakal looked around, to see a big roughly dressed man with a large moustache push his way forward, and spot Pierrot. Pierrot turned, and his face lit up.

After several rapid exchanges that were all gabble to Arakal, Pierrot turned and unleashed a stream of words at the translator. The translator said, "This is Stalheim, sir. He's evidently chief of something called the Free German Legion."

Pierrot let loose another burst of words.

The translator said, "According to Pierrot, Stalheim reports that the Russ are coming, sir, and Stalheim says we'll have them on top of us in another four or five hours at the outside."

★ 8 ★

It was another two days before Arakal had his next chance to get more than twenty minutes rest at one time.

The Russ attack, this time, started with more tanks than Arakal had seen together ever before, and the tanks were well handled, and capable of surviving all but a direct hit from the heaviest guns he had with him, or from one of his none too numerous tank-killer rockets. In this battle, Arakal and his men had all the troubles they had expected in the preceding battle, and they had these troubles despite the fact that the Russ were advancing against a position Arakal and Slagiron had selected in advance. An especially unpleasant surprise was that the Russ proved skillful at infiltrating, in numbers, at night. Arakal's troops, overconfident at first, put forth all their craft and skill, and stopped the Russ advance; but their advantage in position was offset by numbers and equipment, until the night sky was suddenly lit by a tremendous flash. The ground jumped underfoot, and there was a deafening roar. Pierrot appeared, saying, "Now is the chance! Stalheim did that, and he and I will make their retreat a hell! But you will have to smash in their front!"

Arakal was already giving the orders, not for a frontal attack, but for an attack by troops he had been shifting to the right ever since dusk. The Russ, dazed, their minds on what had happened in their rear, were pushed to their own right as their left was driven back. Now Arakal was able to duplicate his first victory, with the addition that, this time, the Russ were split, and a sizable force pinned back against the river, where they resisted stubbornly despite murderous artillery fire.

Once again, the Russ retreat cost them dearly—But once again, Arakal, sensing the risk from other Russ troops, broke off the pursuit, and moved back to take up a position of his own choosing.

And now, he had scarcely gotten his troops in position, and they had scarcely gotten a good hot meal, and fresh ammunition, when word came from Arakal's own scouts that the Russ were on the way back, this time led by a large body of cavalry.

Slagiron swore, and Arakal, unwilling to trust his own frayed nerves, let a grunt answer for him. Pierrot soon turned up. "This is the way to defeat! When you have them on the run, *pursue* them! The casualties you inflict then cost you little. They are running. They cannot run and fight both. This way, you are fighting the same battle over and over again. Fight their retreating back!"

Arakal gave his orders to dig in. The men were already digging in with a will.

Again the Russ attacked, and, for ferocity, this was the worst of the three battles, but the quickest, as for the first time the attackers showed signs of being short of men, and their troops, thrown in as they appeared on the field, soon showed a sullen tendency to dive to the ground and stay there. For the first time, some of the infantry began to surrender without a serious fight. The will of their general was plain enough; but now as they were thrown for the third time against troops well dug in and skillfully supporting each other, on a field dominated by murderous artillery that could not be got at and wouldn't be silenced, the troops that were supposed to attack were thinking of what had happened the last two times.

Arakal now received word, through Pierrot, from Stalheim.

"The Russ reserves are on the march," said Pierrot.

"Headed where?" asked Arakal.

"Toward Saarbrücken."

Arakal glanced at the map.

"They can have it."

"The population has risen up," said Pierrot. "This is territory that formerly belonged to the Western Democracies."

"What, part of the land of the O'Cracy?"

Pierrot put his hand on the map. "You see, the border was here."

As Arakal questioned him, Pierrot briefly explained the past history of the region.

Arakal turned to Slagiron. "Am I right in thinking this batch of Russ here is pretty well worn down?"

"They seem at least too worn down for now to hit us again."

Pierrot said, "The populace will be slaughtered by the Russ if they are left to their own devices. Stalheim will do what he can, but he lacks the strength to stand up to the Russ."

Slagiron said, "So do we, if they put forth their strength."

"But you have fought and won—"

Arakal looked thoughtfully at the map, and growled off-handedly, "If they'd always fight us with their left hand only, we could win more often. But, if we can get this present batch permanently out of the fight, maybe we *could* advance. Not that it wouldn't be more sensible to stay here."

"Perhaps *your* men don't mind standing still," said Pierrot exasperatedly, "but mine wish to drive these tyrants far away."

"If we drive them far enough away, we'll have one sweet time to get our supplies. But—" he looked at the map "—perhaps we can return the favor for Stalheim."

Early the next morning, Arakal's army smashed through the demoralized enemy, sent the remnants fleeing in front of them, repaired the railroad, and brought

up the troop trains. Late that same afternoon, they were
in the wooded hills near Saarbrücken. Early that evening,
their outposts clashed with the approaching Russ. Stalheim attacked them from the east, Pierrot from the west,
and the startled Russ pulled back. The next day, there
was no sign of them.

Arakal's men entered Saarbrücken to the cheers of a
delirious populace.

The day following, the Russ blew up the railway
beyond Saarbrücken.

Arakal attacked. The Russ retreated. Arakal pursued,
and the Russ fled before him. Arakal halted, thinking to
pull back. The Russ attacked. Arakal, noting their weakness in tanks, maneuvered against them. The Russ with-
drew in good order, fell back, and now Arakal's railroad
gangs had the track repaired, and supplies got through.
Arakal pursued the Russ. The Russ fled. Pierrot and Stalheim were ecstatic.

Welcomed with frenzied excitement by a population
only a very few of the translators could talk to, Arakal
and his army drove the Russ back, unable to bring them
to a stand, unable to gain any decisive advantage, but
still pushing them back.

And now two more guerrilla armies joined in the fight,
the troops of Echevik and Koljuberowski. Koljuberowski,
after a fashion, spoke English. Echevik could be talked
to only through consultation between his interpreter and
one of the ablest of Arakal's interpreters.

With this new increase in the numbers of their opponents, the Russ retreated faster. Arakal dubiously eyed
his new allies, who rarely dug themselves in regardless
of the situation, who often fled on the approach of the
Russ, who specialized in raids against their opponent's

flank and rear, and who followed each raid with drinking parties to which they dutifully invited Arakal and all his senior officers, who desired nothing so much as a night's rest. The Russ retaliated after these raids by night bombardment of the enemy camp, the general location of the target being as clear at night as a lighthouse, since all the partisan bands delighted in big bonfires over which to burn their meat, and help ward off the increasing chill of the season. Already, they had seen snow.

As they advanced, two more partisan armies appeared, and then, one day, there even arrived a representative from Old Brunswick—which he called "the U.K."—to tell of the fighting there against the Russ, and to harangue Arakal on the need to push the Russ armies back beyond their own frontiers.

Arakal now received word from Admiral Bullinger, who was forcing the Kiel Canal to enter the Baltic Sea, in case Arakal should need help, or some means of evacuation.

It was not long after that, in a rolling country now well covered with snow, that Arakal and his men, fortunately possessed of heavy winter clothes brought to them in supply ships from home, and then all the way from Cherbourg, woke up in a blizzard. The temperature dropped twenty degrees overnight, and in the following days worked lower still.

One day, they drove the Russ out of a fortified outpost above the banks of a frozen river that Arakal could not identify on the map, and which was of slight interest to the partisans, who assured him that the only worthwhile feature of the geography was "the backs of the fleeing enemy." That same afternoon, the partisans found a little community of Russ farmers, and before Arakal knew what was happening, the partisans had massacred most of them. When Arakal, his silent men with leveled guns beside him, demanded to know the reason, Koljuberowski smilingly wiped the blood off his knife, and answered, "You should see what their soldiers did to us. We have much to make up. We are starting now."

"Those were farmers."

"So? They might have children, and the State will take the boys to make soldiers. We just kill them before they are born. They are more easy to kill that way, hey?" He laughed. "What do you say about that?"

Arakal said shortly, "We will take our share of the prisoners," sent his men to rescue the remaining Russ, and then gave short precise orders that spun his own troops around, and brought them back to the fortified outpost the Russ had just been driven out of. Around this outpost, Arakal selected the most dominating ground on the near side of the river, and announced a halt. His men at once began to dig in. The Russ delivered a short sharp attack, were driven off, and pulled back across the river as the snow swirled down.

★ **9** ★

S-One settled back in his chair, smiling. He no longer looked out the window to feast his eyes. Now he looked at the display that showed the position of Arakal's army.

Across the desk from him, Brusilov looked at the display, and nodded slowly. His expression was almost sad, as at the passing of a legend.

XII. The S Plan

★ 1 ★

Arakal, the next morning, stood on the firing step in the captured Russ blockhouse, and peered east through long-seeing glasses across the frozen river and the snow-capped plain. The sun again today was hidden by dark clouds. But the snow had stopped, and whenever the fitful wind died away, it was possible to seek out the winter-camouflaged Russ tanks.

Behind Arakal, keeping warm by pacing the floor of the narrow concrete-walled room, Slagiron exhaled a cloud of frozen breath, and banged his mittened hands together.

"Any motion?"

The wind swirled fresh clouds of snow across Arakal's field of vision. He lowered the glasses.

"Not from the Russ."

498

"What about our *friends*?"

"Koljuberowski's putting some men across the ice where the river bank is low."

"How many?"

"A section."

"What do they have with them?"

"A leech-bomb slinger on skids."

There was a little silence as Slagiron grappled with the question that had already baffled Arakal.

"What," said Slagiron, "do they expect to accomplish?"

Arakal exhaled.

"They seem to be crawling toward the spot where the forwardmost Russ tank was yesterday."

"Ah, where it was *yesterday*."

Arakal, feeling under pressure to support an ally, even an ally like these allies, strained to find something favorable to say. In the resulting quiet, he could hear the chink of picks and the scrape of shovels as his men labored to improve their bunkers and firing positions.

Slagiron grunted in disgust.

Arakal glanced at a little stud in the thick tube that joined the two halves of his long-seeing glasses, then he stepped down, and handed the glasses to Slagiron.

"See what you think."

Slagiron, his broad build made broader by his thick fur coat, climbed up on the firing step, bent at the slit, and raised the glasses.

Arakal pulled off his leather mittens with their separate trigger finger, pulled off the woolen mittens underneath, and blew into his cupped hands. With stiff fingers, he readjusted the cumbersome straps and belts that held his sword, pistol, ammunition, and the bulky case for the long-seeing glasses.

At the slit, Slagiron growled, "Where did the Russ move that closest tank?"

"Well back, and to your left. Low in front of that lone clump of evergreens."

"Hm . . . If this wind will . . . There . . . I see him . . . Well, now, what have we here?"

There was a gathering pound of approaching hoofbeats and Slagiron's voice became ironical. "Marshal General Catmeat and his Gorilla Guard."

Arakal absently made the correction: "Koljuberowski."

The hoofbeats faded, as the horsemen passed the blockhouse.

"His bomb team," said Slagiron, "is still crawling toward the tank that isn't there. The Russ are taking a few shots at them, so *he's* coming back . . . Now—what's this?"

The fading hoofbeats seemed to return.

Arakal listened intently. "He's going out again?"

"No . . . this is Parrot and *his* gang."

"Pierrot," said Arakal absently. "What? Koljuberowski comes in and Pierrot goes out?"

"It's Parrot's *turn*," said Slagiron. "Next, Slitneck will go out and take a rush at them."

Arakal groped mentally. "Echevik," he said.

"Then finally," growled Slagiron, still bent at the firing slit, "after they've all been beat one at a time, the whole crew will get together around the fire, break out the rotten cheese and wormwood, and invite *us* over. Stallburger will give a speech." Slagiron's voice suddenly changed tone, like a drill that bites through wood into metal. "Unless, that is, they can find a few more unarmed Russ farmers and their children to—"

Arakal's voice grated. "Stalheim."

Slagiron was silent. Finally, he straightened, and yanked back a large knob at the end of a thick metal rod. At the far end of the slit, under a curving metal plate that served to ward off wet snow and freezing rain, the metal cover shut with a clap. Slagiron glanced at the firing slit's inner door on its dented and rusty slides, thought better of trying to close it, and stepped down. He handed the glasses to Arakal.

Arakal checked the little stud, then slid the glasses into their case.

Slagiron blew into his cupped hands.

"If we've got one man who wants to go any deeper into Russland, I don't know who he is. But the Russ retreat to draw us on, and we advance because the partisans want to attack. And ninety percent of the time, the partisans are frankly worthless."

Before Arakal could reply, there came from outside the muffled challenge of a sentry.

Arakal and Slagiron glanced around.

Through the doorless archway from an adjoining larger room came the sound of the heavy outer door creaking open, to admit wind and a stamping of feet, and then to shut again with a heavy thud. There was an approaching tramp of boots and rattle of metal.

"Nuts," came Casey's voice. "If we went over the ice by day a few at a time, the same thing would happen to us. What do they expect? Why can't they either forget it, or else attack *together*?"

The voice of Smith, the acting chief technician, was irritable. "Anything with even *two* heads can't function normally. This so-called army has *seven* heads."

Beane, whose patience and language capabilities stuck him with the diplomatic jobs, said dryly, "Don't forget Burke-Johnson."

Smith growled. "Right. *Eight* heads. And all the heads speak different tongues."

As they came in, Casey saw Arakal, and said at once, "Sir, Koljuberowski wants us to back him up in an attack. He claims the Russ have dug in, have no fuel for their tanks, and once we get past them there's nothing from here to Moscow that can stop us."

Arakal nodded. "Nothing but snow, wind, frostbite, stragglers, ambushes, rear attacks, and broken supply lines. This is far enough."

Slagiron looked relieved, and blew into his cupped hands.

Arakal glanced at Smith. "Any word from the Fleet?"

Smith nodded. "They're through into the Baltic. And they're up to their necks in Dane and Swede partisans who want the Fleet to take them to Russland by way of Finland."

Arakal nodded moodily. "Let's see. Finland is—"

"Well, you remember, sir, the Baltic Sea is shaped roughly like a curved 'Y'. The lower part of Finland is between the two raised arms of the 'Y'."

Arakal nodded. "And the Fleet is now near the bottom of the curved leg of the Y, which stands on Denmark."

"Yes, sir."

"What does Admiral Bullinger say?"

"He says it's five hundred miles to Finland and five hundred miles back; the Fleet is still battered up from that Russ fort that hung on at the upper end of the Kiel Canal; he doesn't know the coast and neither does anyone else he can talk to without two sets of interpreters; he doesn't like the look of the Baltic if there should be a storm; and moreover he has it on good authority it can ice over solid around Finland."

"He doesn't want to do it?"

"No, sir."

"Then this latest batch of partisans can get to Russland on foot."

"Yes, sir. But the admiral wants to pass it on, for whatever it's worth, if anything, that the partisan chiefs claim they can go in through Finland, hit the Russ by surprise, and make the other half of a pincer with us coming up from the south, and together we can shear off the whole Baltic coast, and maybe the Russ people will join us and revolt."

Arakal exhaled carefully, and glanced at the archway, above and behind Casey's head.

Slagiron growled. "It *might* have worked. The Russ people *might* have joined us."

Casey said tonelessly, "Before they evened up the score with those Russ settlers."

Arakal decided he could now trust his voice.

"Signal Bullinger that we may halt here for the winter. Our plans are uncertain. But we aren't going further."

Casey said uneasily, "Who is 'we', sir? Koljuberowski, Echevik and the rest are yelling their heads off that they want to kill Russ."

"If we advance," said Arakal, very reasonably, "what will the Russ do?"

"Retreat, to draw us on." Casey frowned. "From what we got out of those Russ farmers we saved from the partisans, this isn't a bad spot. That is to say, you can at least recognize the weather here as *weather*. They've evidently got worse places than this for us to advance into."

"Then," said Arakal, "suppose we stay here. Then what?"

"The Russ will attack us. Then, when we counterattack, *then* they'll retreat."

Arakal nodded. "If Koljuberowski and Stalheim want to 'kill Russ', all they have to do is just stand still and fight."

Casey nodded without conviction. "That's just common sense, sir. *That* will never convince them."

Smith finished setting down on his pad Arakal's message to Admiral Bullinger, and handed pad and pencil to Arakal.

Arakal read the message, initialed it, handed it back, and glanced at Casey. "From here to the other end of Russland must be five thousand miles. It's snow from one end to the other, and it's cold enough to freeze quicksilver. We had that much on good authority, before we talked to those Russ farmers."

Casey nodded glumly. Slagiron growled his agreement.

Beane said hesitantly, "There's still Koljuberowski, sir. And Echevik. And the rest of the partisans. They hate the Russ. And from the stories they tell, sir, I don't think you can blame them."

Again Arakal didn't trust himself to say anything.

Slagiron spoke with an edge to his voice. "Now the Russ can tell stories."

"Yes, sir," said Beane. "But the point is, if we *don't* advance, we'll end up quarreling amongst ourselves. Koljuberowski, Echevik, Stalheim, Rindovin, Alazar, and Pierrot have one thing in common. They all want to fight Russ."

Arakal said, "Let them dig in here and they can *fight* Russ."

"I know it, sir. But they want to fight them *going forward*."

Arakal shook his head.

"I think we've paid back the debt we owed these partisans for their help. They can go on, if they want. We've gone far enough."

"Then, sir, what do we do next?"

Arakal glanced at Casey.

"Suppose we should just leave? What do you think would happen?"

Casey said, "If we just pull out?"

Arakal nodded.

"I'd think the Russ would retake everything from here to Normandy."

Arakal glanced at Slagiron, who rubbed his chin thoughtfully.

"I don't know."

Casey looked surprised. He took off his heavy mittens, and blew on his hands.

"Sir," said Casey, looking at Slagiron, "Pierrot and Koljuberowski and the rest may be brave, but they can't face the Russ army. They aren't equipped for that."

Slagiron looked at him.

"Neither are we equipped for it."

Casey looked startled. "We've beat them before. Here and at home."

"In our own country, yes. At the end of *their* supply line, not ours. But as for beating them here—This business here isn't as it looks. They're only using part of their strength."

Casey paused, frowning. "There's truth in that. Yet—"

"They retreat to draw us on. They haven't truly put forth their strength except when we dug in."

Arakal said, "The Russ retreat—but it's all calculated."

Reluctantly, Casey nodded.

Slagiron growled, "What puzzles me is how sparing they are lately with ammunition. What they specialize in now is *night bombardments*. It almost seems as if they just aim to ruin our sleep."

Casey said hesitantly, "Of course, with the uprisings —the confusion—"

"They *should* have used their strength to end it quick while they had control. Why let us get this far?"

"But if they thought there were more coming behind us—"

Slagiron shook his head.

"Whatever anyone else here may think, the Russ *know* the shape we're in."

Arakal could see in his mind's eye this continent's cities—huge by his own standards, and their system of iron roads. The Russ had been masters of all this, but they retreated. Somewhere here, there was an illogicality, a something that didn't fit. In short, a trap.

As they stood grappling with uncertainties, behind them there was a brief howl of wind, the heavy slam of the outside door, the stamp of feet, and then a voice, somewhat high-pitched, and artificially cheerful, called out:

"What ho, chaps! Arakal, my dear fellow! Are you here?"

Slagiron grunted, glanced up at the slit, and held out his hand. "Just in case—"

Arakal, eyes narrowed, handed him the glasses.

Slagiron climbed on the firing step.

Casey glanced around, and swore under his breath.

Smith grunted, and blew on his hands.

A tall pale figure in furs was suddenly framed in the archway. Slagiron's voice, from where he stood behind Arakal on the firing step, had an ironical tone.

"Hullo, Burke-Johnson."

Burke-Johnson cast a penetrating look at Slagiron.

"Er, how are you, my dear general? Actually, I'm delighted to see you." He glanced around. "But, Arakal. It's to you that I really *must* speak."

Everyone in the room, save Arakal and Slagiron—who had a concrete wall behind him—contrived somehow to back, side-step, or otherwise ease further away from the newcomer.

Arakal reminded himself that Burke-Johnson, supposedly the emissary from Old Brunswick, this same Burke-Johnson had been detected by Smith's monitoring team in the act of reporting Arakal's movements to the Russ, and reporting them in the Russ tongue. Ever since, they had been feeding Burke-Johnson false information, which he duly reported to the Russ. Yet, unless Burke-Johnson were stupid, which clearly he was not, he had long since realized he was unmasked—a fact which he determinedly ignored.

Arakal coerced his voice into a passable imitation of friendliness.

"What is it, Major?"

Burke-Johnson straightened.

"My dear fellow, I'm really quite dished at the way you've been treating Koljuberowski."

Arakal groped for the meaning of the word "dished."

Beane, the language specialist, cast a fishy look at Burke-Johnson.

There was a screech of metal as Slagiron shoved back the cover at the end of the slit, and turned his back on the proceedings.

Arakal said, very seriously, "What did I do wrong this time?"

Burke-Johnson's gaze slid away, and, eyes averted, he spoke rapidly, with an exaggerated emphasis:

"You Americans have simply *got* to realize that the people here are *not* about to trade the Russian yoke for your own. You simply *must* understand that wars are *not* won by the outsider telling the chap on the spot what he *can* and what he *cannot* do. You must get cracking, dear boy. Kol feels that the Russian front here is simply a hollow *shell*. And he should *know*. Smash it, Arakal. *Smash* it!"

Arakal studied Burke-Johnson's averted gaze, and listened closely to Burke-Johnson's emphatic but somehow empty voice. The effect was of an insincerity so plain that Arakal could not accept even the insincerity as genuine.

Again there was the thud of the heavy outer door.

One of Smith's men came in, cast a wary glance at Burke-Johnson, tugged at Smith's sleeve, and pulled him back out of earshot.

Arakal looked thoughtfully at Burke-Johnson.

"To go straight into Russland from here is a five-thousand-mile hike. They can retreat whenever they feel like it, cut in behind us, starve us, pick us off—and meanwhile we'll have to light fires under our guns to work the actions. That's exactly what the Russ want. Why should we do it?"

Burke-Johnson hesitated. For an instant, the effect of masks behind masks vanished. "What do you propose?"

"Go in through Finland, swing around in an arc, and cut all their communications in succession. We should be able to disjoint them—*and* we'll be marching south, not north."

Burke-Johnson blinked rapidly. "I don't believe Kol would agree to this, my dear fellow."

Arakal said, "Let Koljuberowski and the rest of the partisans take them from the front, while we hit them from the rear."

"Well, I might pass along the suggestion, I suppose, but—"

Slagiron tossed words over his back from the firing step. "Good idea. Go talk to Clabberjaw, and see what he says. Then let us know."

Burke-Johnson's face showed a brief struggle. Then, his gaze avoiding everyone's eyes, he nodded, and said loudly, "Cheerio, chaps." He turned, and strode out. The outside door shut heavily behind him.

There was a silence, then a dull clap as the cover dropped shut over the firing slit. Slagiron stepped down, and handed Arakal the glasses. "I wonder who *really* sent him. Does *he* know?"

"What did you see out there?"

"Snow."

Smith came back in, blowing on his hands, his expression intent and serious. He had a sheaf of thin yellow papers tucked tightly under one arm. He glanced at Arakal, and cleared his throat.

"Sir—"

Arakal, bemusedly considering the puzzle of Burke-Johnson, glanced around.

"What is it, Smith?"

"If what I have here is right, another one of these 'allies' is a Russ spy."

In the quiet, they could hear through the wind the chink and scrape of the picks and shovels outside.

Arakal kept his voice level.

"Who is it this time?"

"Koljuberowski."

Arakal kept his mouth shut.

Casey turned to stare at Smith, started to speak, but didn't.

Beane's eyes widened. "I can't believe that—"

Slagiron spoke as if the words exploded from him.

"Then think again! Nothing could have hurt us more than what he did!"

Casey looked at Smith, and said tightly, "What about his troops?"

"It's impossible to say."

Slagiron said, "His officers were all with him in it. Some of the men lagged. And, you remember, one wouldn't go along."

Casey exhaled with a hiss.

"I saw it. They threw him in the pit with the settlers."

Arakal said, "We'd better double the guards." He took out his signal whistle and blew two short penetrating blasts.

Slagiron drew out his big automatic of Old Army design.

Beyond the arch, the outside door creaked open.

A low voice was speaking warningly:

" . . . eyes wide-open. Otherwise, old Cut-Your-Throat may creep up and sling *us* in a hole." The guard stepped inside, shut the door, exhaled a cloud of frozen breath, and brought his gun to present arms.

"*Sir!*"

Casey stared. "What's this, Corporal? You've got a buddy out there."

"Yes, sir. Sergeant doubled us all around, and handed out extra belts."

Slagiron growled, "Good!"

Casey spoke at the same time, so that his voice over-lapped with Slagiron's. "Why?"

"Don't trust old Cat-Jabber, sir."

"That business with the Russ farmers?"

"That about put the cap on it, sir."

Arakal said, "The guards are doubled up *all around*?"

"Yes, sir."

"Good. That's all."

The guard stepped back outside.

Arakal turned to Smith, who was holding the yellow sheets of paper. "You're sure of this?"

"As sure as we can be."

Casey said, "I still can't believe it! Koljuberowski—" He paused abruptly.

Slagiron had begun to speak, but stopped at the look on Casey's face.

Arakal said patiently, "Nothing could stiffen Russ resistance the way Koljuberowski did. Not just their army. Their people."

Slagiron nodded. "We're part of the outfit credited with that."

Casey was nodding unhappily as from the closed outside door came the sound of new voices raised in argument.

Slagiron glanced toward the archway.

"Well, well. Speak of the devil. There's Catmeat himself."

Beane said abruptly, "This may not mean anything, sir. But Koljuberowski has a sleevegun."

Arakal's eyes narrowed.

Slagiron nodded. "It's crooked. What else would he use?"

Arakal glanced at Smith, and spoke in a low voice.

"What *proof* have we Koljuberowski is working for the Russ?"

"Every night since he joined us, at roughly the same time, there's been a—a kind of powerful *squawk*—on the frequency Burke-Johnson uses for his reports."

Arakal nodded.

Smith said, "The night before last, we recorded this squawk, but still couldn't make anything of it. Several hours ago, one of my men got it slowed down, and it turned into words. It was Koljuberowski, reporting that slaughter of the farmers, and what we planned to do next."

"Koljuberowski's own voice?"

"Yes, sir."

"What you have there is the report on this?"

"Yes, sir." Smith held the yellow sheets out to Arakal.

From outside, they could hear the suddenly loud voice of the guard.

"Sergeant of the Guard! Post One! *Armed allies!*"

Casey reached inside his coat.

Arakal spoke quietly as he took the yellow sheets from Smith, then absently loosened his sword.

"Keep your guns out of sight. Beane, take a look. If Koljuberowski's there, tell him I'd like to see him, alone. Try not to let anyone else in. But, if they shove past you—Why then, let them come."

Beane went out through the archway.

Slagiron glanced at Casey, then at Arakal.

"When he pushes his way in, why not tell him Casey and I left after Burp-Jaw went out."

Arakal nodded. He was vaguely conscious of Casey and Slagiron going out the archway toward the inner door that led to the ice-coated wreck of the lookout tower. But his attention was momentarily riveted on the yellow sheets.

" . . . voice has been identified by every member of the intelligence section as that of the officer known to us as Casimir Patrick Koljuberowski. . . . Speaking the Russ tongue fluently, Koljuberowski first related the events surrounding the massacre, then detailed our plans as at that time communicated to him . . . Koljuberowski then acknowledged receipt of orders already passed to him from the Russ in some way not specified. . . . The translation of Koljuberowski's report follows . . . "

Arakal glanced rapidly over the yellow sheets, then folded them, reached inside his coat, and shoved them well down in a pocket of his woolen shirt. As the voices from the door became suddenly louder, he slid the glasses out of their leather case, and handed them to Smith.

"See what you can see through that slit, why don't you?"

Smith nodded, and, holding the glasses gingerly, stepped up on the firing step.

Some part of Arakal's mind now belatedly succeeded in translating Burp-Jaw to Burke-Johnson. Arakal's attempts to correct such mispronunciations had met with such ill success that he had at last been driven to the conclusion that his men must see something in these allies that he didn't see. Uneasily, Arakal considered now just what this something might be.

From the other room came Beane's voice, raised in argument, the foreign words incomprehensible to Arakal.

At the slit, Smith reported, "Nothing moving that I can see, sir."

From the outside door, the guard called loudly.

"General Ratpack Jolliboozski and three armed guards, sir!"

Arakal forced himself to breathe evenly as Koljuberowski, followed by three of his guards with crisscrossed bandoliers over their heavy wool coats, shoved young Beane out of the way, and walked with rolling gait toward Arakal. From somewhere outside, as they approached, came a muffled sound of shots.

Koljuberowski, a large plump man perhaps in his middle thirties, glanced alertly around as he came in. His voice was high-pitched, but his pronunciation was very clear.

"Slagiron? Where is Slagiron?"

Smith shut the firing slit cover with a clap, and stepped down.

Arakal noted the free way Koljuberowski's guards handled their guns as they glanced around.

"Slagiron," said Arakal to Koljuberowski, "left after Burke-Johnson went out."

Koljuberowski cast a last brief glance around, nodded, and smiled.

Smith held out the glasses, and Arakal took them.

Koljuberowski spoke to his guards in a tongue Arakal neither understood nor recognized. Then Koljuberowski banged his mittened hands together, and when his hands separated, the right mitten stayed in his left hand. He seemed to snap his right wrist and forearm.

Arakal, holding the field glasses partly raised, had his right forefinger on the little black stud. He tilted the glasses as he pressed the stud.

The glasses jumped in his hands.

Koljuberowski staggered backward.

Behind Koljuberowski, a grinning guard had just raised his gun toward Smith.

There was a deafening crash and whine.

Koljuberowski's guards jerked and grimaced.

The roar died away.

The guards were partly atop the sprawled Koljuberow-ski, as, at the outside doorway and the door to the tower, Beane, Slagiron, Casey, and Arakal's two guards lowered their guns.

Arakal bent beside Koljuberowski, then straightened, gripping by the barrel a little silver pistol with no trigger guard, which he held out to Beane.

"Watch out. It's still loaded."

Slagiron bent over Koljuberowski, and methodically undid the thick fur coat. Casey crouched to help.

Arakal glanced at the outside door. The two guards had already gone back to their post.

From the floor, there was a rustle of papers. Slagiron said, "Here's something for you, Beane. Looks like Russ lettering to me."

Arakal peered briefly through his long-seeing glasses, then unscrewed the tube from the thick joint between the two halves of the glasses, and methodically cleaned and reloaded the firing mechanism.

Beane looked up from the papers, and turned to Ara-kal. "Sir, this is urgent. Shall I read it aloud?"

"Go ahead."

Beane's voice shook slightly as he read:

"Operational Plan, Summary:
1) If possible, Arakal is to be induced to pursue deep into our base territory.
2) Once he and his men are beyond reach of help or reinforcements, all partisan groups will leave them. Softening and conversion will be facilitated by climatic conditions in the interior.

3) Alternatively, if Arakal rejects the partisan plan, or if his men refuse to accept it, or if Arakal's invasion force appears for whatever reason to be escaping control, Arakal and all his line officers down to and including the rank of full colonel are to be executed. This may be best accomplished by requesting an audience with Arakal first, and then giving word that Arakal has sent for the others. Immediately following completion of this action, the strike codeword should be transmitted to the Combat Forces S-Control, to simplify concealment of what has been done by attributing it to the heavy attack which will follow.

4) No attempt is to be made in any case to convert or train Arakal, Slagiron, Casey, or present line officers down to and including the rank of full colonel. If the partisan plan is carried out, these officers are to become casualties or prisoners.

5) The technicians, including Smith, are to be converted and trained. If Kotzebuth or Colputt are present, they are to be converted, if possible, and if not, coerced. The chief translator and diplomat, Beane, is to be given special treatment, as he is suitable as our replacement for Arakal, and is of a type amenable to control.

6) In future operations, Arakal's troops are to be drawn as much as possible into cruelty toward our base population. This will be facilitated by accounts of the people's past cruelty toward Arakal's allies, and especially by our clandestine seizing and appropriate treatment of Arakal's stragglers. This must be carried out in circumstances where the actions can only be attributed to the populace. Once the appropriate attitude is established amongst Arakal's troops, it will be necessary merely to approve the attitude as entirely proper.

7) It must be remembered that Arakal and his men represent a special opportunity, that of extending indirect control to the American continent. Attainment of this goal requires great delicacy until Arakal and his men are sufficiently worn down. Even then, training of the survivors must proceed with due allowance for their prejudices. The relationship must remain masked and thoroughly rationalized at all times.

8) Alternatively, it must be remembered, Arakal and his men constitute a special and peculiar danger. Although politically naïve and technologically backward, they possess a temporary advantage resting on five factors:

a) Arakal, although a savage, is a skillful tactician, while his men are energetic warriors.

b) Kotzebuth, Colputt, and the other technicians have created a workable, though largely primitive, technology.

c) Past underestimation of these opponents has resulted in their surprise seizure of the only effective ocean-going fleet remaining on this planet; control of this fleet gives them command of the sea.

d) Possible discoveries of usable technological devices developed before the destruction of the U.S. introduce an element of technological uncertainty. Certain devices have been rumored to exist which could seriously alter the realities of the situation.

e) The populace of the Extended Zone is disaffected. The possibility therefore cannot be eliminated of a miscarrying of the present operation, with serious results. In the extreme, this could defer realization of the extension of our control to the American continent, and even force control of the Extended Zone back to the indirect mode.

9) At all times, therefore, the greatest care is necessary. The clearest picture of the real elements of this situation must be borne in mind, and all romanticism must be avoided.

10) This instruction must be reviewed repeatedly, and followed to the letter. Any questions may be directed to Control on the usual frequency."

Beane looked up, his face pale. "That's the end, sir. There's also a separate message. Part of it reads: 'The reports of Burke-Johnson do not conform to Arakal's recent movements. He has, therefore, been unmasked, and his usefulness in this operation is at an end. In the next engagement, he is to feign wounds, and be sent back.'"

Arakal said, "Read the beginning of that first set of papers over again."

Beane read: "1) If possible, Arakal is to be induced to pursue deep into our base territory. 2) Once he and his men are beyond reach of help or reinforcements, all partisan groups will leave them. Softening and conversion will be facilitated by climatic conditions in the interior."

Arakal said, " '*All* partisan groups.' "

Beane nodded. "Yes, sir."

There was a silence.

Slagiron said, "Exactly what we thought. Only worse. It isn't just the *Russ* luring us on. The partisans are part of it."

"Is there," said Arakal, "anything to show who sent these orders?"

"The letter 'S' is at the bottom. But I don't know if it corresponds to a signature, or if it means something else?"

Casey said wonderingly, "They're *escorting* us into the interior of Russland?"

Beane nodded. His voice had an undertone of anger. "And they've already worked out who they think will go along with them afterward."

Arakal said to Slagiron, "We'd better spread the word about these partisans."

Slagiron nodded. "I'll get the corps commanders."

Arakal turned to Beane. "See if there's any word from Colputt."

Beane handed Arakal the papers, and went out, following Slagiron and Casey.

Arakal carefully, point by point, thought over the captured plan. Then he considered what to do. He stamped his feet, and blew on his hands. Who, he asked himself, was "S"? It was the same "S," apparently, that had sent the nurse as a spy. He looked up at the howl of the wind as the door opened.

Slagiron came in, frowning. "Three of Catmeat's partisans tried to jump our guards earlier, and got killed. But *now* everything seems perfectly normal out there. Damned peculiar."

Casey and Beane came in, and Arakal said, "Any word from Colputt?"

"No, sir," said Beane. "Admiral Bullinger hasn't heard from him, either."

"The last Bullinger heard, Colputt had both platforms loaded?"

"Yes, sir. That was before Bullinger entered the Baltic. The admiral has had his hands full for a while. Colputt *may* have signaled, and not been picked up."

Arakal nodded, and turned to Slagiron, but just then, beyond the archway, the outside door opened up.

There was a murmur of voices, and the three corps commanders, heavily dressed, with general's stars on their helmets, exhaling frosty breath, strode into the room. Greetings and comments died on their lips at the sight of the bodies. They halted, and raised their right hands in sharp salute.

Behind them, there was a heavy thud as Beane closed the outer door.

Arakal said, "These so-called 'partisans' just tried to kill us. Beane, translate the papers we found on them."

Beane read in a slow clear voice. His words fell into the quiet like small stones dropped in a deep pool. At the end, the generals, their expressions profoundly serious, glanced at Arakal.

Arakal said, "Speaking for myself, I think the slur on our ambassador and technicians is just the Russ estimate of who amongst us is the most *reasonable*. That far, I think their judgment was not too bad."

The generals glanced at Beane, and smiled.

Arakal said to Beane, "Could we get Burke-Johnson here by himself?"

"I think so, sir. Everything seems normal out there. But what line do I take if these partisans want to know what's going on?"

"Just say I sent you to get Burke-Johnson, and later there may be a meeting of our colonels, but you aren't sure. If they want to know more, that's all you've been told."

Beane nodded, and went out.

Arakal turned to Slagiron.

"Can we handle all these partisans?"

"If we can split them up."

There was a murmur of agreement from the three generals.

"What," said Arakal, "are they actually worth, as fighters?"

Slagiron passed his hand across his chin, and glanced at Casey, who frowned, began to speak, and changed his mind.

The generals remained silent.

Slagiron shook his head. "In the light of what we know about them now, it's anyone's guess."

In the uneasy quiet, Burckhardt said, "We *have* had a chance to watch them."

Simons said shortly, "They can kill women and babies."

Slagiron was frowning. "Still, to play this part, I think they would *have* to be well trained."

The last of the three corps commanders, Cesti, said quietly, "They've struck me since they first turned up as being well trained. But a lot of their men have a wooden quality. I think they don't care."

Casey frowned. "Because they're just playing a part?"

Cesti shook his head. "I think it's deeper than that. They'll do as they're told, but their heart isn't in it."

Simons growled, "What do we do with this bastard, Burke-Johnson?"

Arakal said, "We question him."

"I mean, afterward."

Cesti shook his head. "He wasn't there when they had the massacre."

"He wasn't?"

"He cleared out till the mess was over."

"Then," said Simons, frowning, "maybe he isn't what he seems to be. Whatever *that* may be."

Casey glanced at Arakal. "Sir, possibly when Johnson comes in, we should be spread out a little more?"

Arakal nodded agreeably, and, glancing calculatingly around at the archway, the walls of the room, and each other, they all spread out.

As if on signal, the outer door opened, to admit the howl of the wind, a sound of footsteps, the heavy thud of the door, then an agonized voice.

"Oh, God—" came Burke-Johnson's voice, and then he cut himself off.

Arakal, watching alertly, saw the Old Brunswick major halt, astonished relief washing across his face as he glanced from the heap on the floor to Arakal and Slagiron.

Abruptly, Burke-Johnson came forward, his right forefinger to his lips. He knelt by the bodies, and working with a sort of frenzied silent concentration, he jerked the boots form Koljuberowski, glanced at both of them intently, dropped one, held the other in his hand, and forced the blade of a small pocket knife in where the outer layer of the sole appeared slightly separated from the boot with a faint popping sound. He twisted the sole sharply, whirled it around and around, pivoting it on the heel, and then the heel and sole were in one of his hands, and in the other was the rest of the boot, with a wide glinting threaded cylinder where the heel had been.

As Arakal and his generals looked on blankly, Burke-Johnson held the boot upside-down, so that they could see, nested inside the open-ended cylinder in the heel, a maze of fine wires and what looked like bright-colored beads.

Carefully, Burke-Johnson reached in with the knife blade, and cut something inside the cylinder.

Then, quickly, he checked the boots of Koljuberowski's guards, pulled off one, and did with it as he had done with the first boot. He examined the butts of the guards' guns, and Koljuberowski's holster, then stood and carefully looked around at the walls of the room. He glanced alertly at the floor, then looked up intently at the ceiling, to study a small round depression. He drew a large shiny revolver with a ring at the bottom of the grip, and aimed carefully at the ceiling.

There was a deafening bang, a shower of particles, and a little canister fell onto the floor, one side torn apart in a shambles of tiny broken bits and pieces.

Burke-Johnson knelt by the bodies, felt of them rapidly, and then straightened. He cleared his throat.

"Those—" he nodded at the boot heels and the little canister "—are transmitters. Everything you say in their range is heard elsewhere, until they are broken, as they are now." He glanced at the bodies of Koljuberowski and one of his guards. "There lie respectively the second and first in command of the Reception Group."

Arakal glanced from Koljuberowski to the guard, frowning. Burke-Johnson gave a little laugh.

"The corporal of Kol's guard was in effect the *actual* commander. Kol was merely the acting *military* commander. All of these organized partisan groups are tools of 'S'—'S' for 'Security'. Those tanks across the river are Ground Force operated—but their commander is watched by and can be overruled by the attached representative of 'S'. 'S' sees all, hears all, knows all, and commands nearly all—at least in theory."

Arakal looked at Burke-Johnson.

"And you?"

The major's eyes glinted. "I am nothing. I've done them a certain amount of damage, and I may do them a good deal more before I'm through. There have been others like me before, and there will be others again, after they get me. In occasional moments of lightheartedness, I think of myself as 'Triple-S'."

Arakal watched Burke-Johnson intently.

Burke-Johnson looked him in the eye, and smiled. It was an easy and contagious smile, free of care.

" 'S', you see, is 'Security'. 'Triple-S' stands for 'Spontaneous Sabotage of Security'. Such trifling little matters as an adjustment of Pierrot's orders regarding Normandy."

Arakal blinked. "Is there an organization?"

Burke-Johnson smiled, and glanced around.

"I've said more than I should have, already. Incidentally, don't trust anything I or anyone else over here tells you. 'S' makes a specialty of spreading false information. Work everything out for yourself. You can't trust anyone else. And you can't *always* trust yourself."

"All these so-called partisans are Russ?"

Burke-Johnson looked startled.

"They're 'S', not Russian."

"What's the difference?"

" 'S' is an organization that provides security. 'S' is for spying, sabotage, and secret control of people and governments. 'S' is *the control apparatus*."

Arakal frowned. "But 'S' isn't Russ?"

"The highest levels presumably are mostly Russian. But 'S' is an organization which extends through all Europe and parts of Asia. Obviously, to function, it must include those of the races ruled by it."

"And those uprisings when we landed?"

"You were greeted with genuine delight by the populace. 'S' itself simply stayed underground and notified the Reception Group."

"The 'partisans'?"

"Exactly."

"Why weren't we warned?"

"By whom?"

"By the people."

"Who knew?"

Arakal stared at Burke-Johnson.

Burke-Johnson looked at him earnestly.

"False information is a specialty of 'S'. For a year or more, these so-called 'partisans' have been known to be sabotaging selected Russian installations. It was all done for perfectly false reasons—but the damage itself was real. The populace truly believed that the partisans were backed by the U.S."

"Backed by *what*?"

"The U.S." Burke-Johnson shook his head. "I find it impossible to remember that the U.S. is no more. As much as anyone else, I suppose, I'm a victim of false information."

Arakal groped for the meaning of the faintly familiar expression. "You mean, America?"

Burke-Johnson nodded. "You see, 'S' is shrewd. They permit old motion pictures showing U.S. troops in action. Their own forces, once they've been on the American continent, are kept out of Europe. They occasionally report 'negotiations with the U.S.' The idea put across is that the U.S. could free Europe, but has made a deal, and won't. This is more demoralizing than to reveal that the U.S. has been destroyed."

There was a silence, and Slagiron glanced questioningly at Arakal. Arakal nodded, and Slagiron turned to Burke-Johnson. "What would happen if we were to bring reinforcements, punch into Russ territory through Finland, and swing south and east?"

"Land in Finland by sea? Then enter Russia?"

"Yes."

"If you weren't frozen, drowned, or sunk in mud to your elbows, you might end up the latest victims of the American nuclear counterattack. I've heard it said that certain tracts of that territory are uninhabitable."

Arakal's voice was faintly husky.

"That is where the Old O'Cracys struck back?"

Burke-Johnson looked momentarily blank. "The—Of course, 'the O'Cracys'. The Western Dem*ocracies*." He hesitated, then nodded. "Yes, that is one place where the O'Cracys hit back. Hard."

There was a silence in the room. Burke-Johnson looked around.

Broad Slagiron, his lips a severe line, stood unmoving, his face twisted with emotion.

Casey's eyes glistened.

Against the wall, Cesti stood motionless, his fists clenched.

Beside Cesti, profane Simons stood straight, smiling, tears running down both cheeks.

Burke-Johnson hesitated, cleared his throat, and spoke carefully.

"The main thing is, *don't* attack deeper into Russia. It's all a trap."

There was a silence that stretched out, then a sound in the room as of a faint sigh.

Arakal's officers were all smiling, and looking with grudging approval at the major.

Arakal said, "We have our plans, but invading thousands of miles of snow and ice that the O'Cracys never owned is no part of them. Now, tell us—why were you so obviously a fake?"

"Why, of course, to make you suspicious. I hoped if you became suspicious of *me*, you'd become suspicious of the lot of us."

Arakal smiled. "Well, it helped. And what do you suggest we do now?"

"Slip away as soon as possible, and take to your ships. You can't win here until you beat S. And you can't beat S. They will only falsify your actions to the populace, and profit by your efforts. Their control here is subterranean, and it is too all-inclusive to overcome. It has to be riddled first from within. Leave that to me. If I last long enough, who knows?"

Arakal shook his head.

"We came here to free Old Brunswick and Old Kebeck. We aim to do it."

Burke-Johnson's expression showed an internal struggle. " 'Old Brunswick'—oh, yes, the U.K.—*Britain*. And 'Old Kebeck', of course, is *France*. Well, you *have* freed them, as much as you can. But you can't fight S. It's like a fog or a mist, Arakal. *Your* strength here is purely military, and is limited by what you can transport in your captured ships. You have no really secure base here— nothing reliably solid to fall back on. The 'Russ', as you call them, are not crude swaggering overlords, who can be met on the field of battle, overthrown and ended. Their influence is pervasive, and exercised covertly, *through* S. You can't fight with the weapons in your possession. Your steel is sharp, you see, but it can't cut the mist."

Arakal, frowning, thought a moment. "Has most of the damage in Europe from the war with the O'Cracys been repaired?"

Burke-Johnson blinked.

"In Western Europe?"

"Yes."

"From all the reports I've read, little physical damage was actually done. The Soviet penetration was primarily a *political* and later an economic penetration by—excuse me for the repetition—the establishment of the apparatus of S throughout Europe."

Slagiron leaned forward.

"Then the cities we see, and the iron roads—they were all here *before the war*?"

"Why, of course."

Arakal took a deep careful breath. He spoke dryly.

"They are well kept up."

Burke-Johnson glanced from Arakal to Slagiron and back again.

"You're saying something. But I don't follow."

"With such resources as the Russ have here, *why haven't they long since overcome us*?"

"But the resources *here* are needed for the people *here*. How are they to attack you with the cities and railroads *on this continent*?"

Arakal started to say something, but caught himself. Instead, he said, "Perhaps your idea of slipping away from here is not so bad, after all. *If* we can do it."

Burke-Johnson looked relieved. "We must try to keep S occupied. If you withdraw now, they will expect future attacks from you, and will have to prepare to meet them. I should think the most effective strategy would be one of repeated widely separated threats and pinpricks. That would give us—the opponents of S—the opportunity to do a good deal of damage."

Arakal nodded. "We'll see how soon we can leave." He glanced at Beane. "Read that Russ comment, in the papers we found on Koljuberowski, to the effect that Major Burke-Johnson had been exposed, and should be withdrawn."

Beane read aloud from the yellow sheets.

Burke-Johnson nodded.

"Interesting. Now—If you can leave before S sends down new orders, you will have an advantage."

Arakal nodded. "We'll try. Good luck."

"Good luck."

When the major had gone out, Arakal glanced at his officers.

"The sooner we're far from here, the better."

Slagiron said grimly, "Speaking for myself, I can't wait to get out of this place."

Casey was apologetic. "Excuse me, sir, but how is this different from defeat?"

Arakal said, "Let them follow us too closely, and they'll find out the difference."

XIII. The Wizards' Legacy

★ 1 ★

S-One looked over the summary, then glanced at the display, where Arakal and the partisans were on one side of the river, the defending force was on the other side, and, moving up well to the rear was a powerful body of troops, symbolized by a red rectangle. The weather conditions were clearly enough indicated: Snow and wind. The temperature had already dropped sharply, and it was sure to drop again. The only disappointment was that Arakal had yet to call for the troops in the Normandy Citadel. That, however, was something that would, eventually, prove possible to clear up one way or another.

There was a rap on the door, and S-One called, "Come in."

S-Two, looking dazed, stepped in carrying a thin sheaf of papers.

"Arakal has found the S-Plan."

S-One involuntarily jumped to his feet.

"*What?*"

"Neither Arakal nor his senior officers wanted to advance any further. Koljuberowski gave instructions to remove Arakal, preliminary to changing the command of Arakal's forces."

".What happened?"

"Arakal and his men killed Koljuberowski, his S officer, and two guards. They found the plan summary on Koljuberowski's body."

"What carelessness! How the devil did all that happen?"

"They may also have killed Burke-Johnson."

"*How did it happen?*"

"*We don't know.* There was only one fixed and two personnel sensors in the room where this happened, and none in the room outside. It was just a detached fort, and we never gave it full treatment. Apparently, Arakal or one of his men spotted the sensors. We heard Burke-Johnson cry out. Next, the sensors were destroyed."

"Where are we now?"

"Arakal is planning, as far as we can judge, to fall back again."

S-One looked at the display.

"It would not be impossible for him to reach those ships, and escape."

"Yes. I'm afraid the Plan is wrecked."

S-One brought his fist down on the desk. "The trouble is, they weren't softened up *in advance*. Always, S work should precede the military blow! The stick breaks easier *after* the rot eats its fibers. But, for lack of anything better—" He paused as S-Two stared at the display. Frowning, S-One looked around.

On the display, little blue symbols were already starting toward the west.

S-Two said, "Shall I call the Marshal?"

S-One measured distances on the display.

"No. It is too late for that. Call the Head of Government. We can't do what I had hoped. But we may still be able to achieve something of importance. Then, later, we will make up for this. It will be a more roundabout procedure, but the result should be the same."

S-Two hurried out.

★ 2 ★

Admiral Bullinger, short, clean-shaven, with two tufts of hair that stuck straight up at the back of his head, stood beside Arakal and Slagiron, leaning over the charts of the Baltic. He rapped his finger beside a little peninsula.

"Depth eight fathoms on this older chart, when you get it translated out of their heathen reckoning, while this new updated chart *also* shows eight fathoms. Plenty of water. But just to be on the safe side, we put a boat over for soundings before we went in through the fog. These charts were more detailed than the ones we'd found on the ship, but we wanted to be careful. Well, the place is a deathtrap. If the wind blew hard enough, the rocks would stick out on the surface. Next, observe this lighthouse inked in here by hand, and also the blot of ink over there. The blot of ink is to cover up the *false* location of the lighthouse, as it was shown on this chart.

"Both of these detailed charts, the 'partisans' turned over to us. You see, they're both nicely printed. And they reinforce each other. And the details that we could *easily* check were accurate. It was the things we would have taken for granted that would have sunk us."

"How about their suggestion of going in through Finland?"

The admiral's eyes glinted. "Since we didn't do it, we can't know just where the teeth were in the idea. But, to begin with, it would have been wrong. What need do we have to invade Russland? It would draw us aside from our purpose, which is to free the land of the *O'Cracys*. Next there's the possibility that, on the way, these charts would show some additional little defect we hadn't discovered yet. Then, since we were to transport these armed 'partisans', and there were a great number of them, and they would have had to be distributed all over the ships to carry them all—What do you suppose might have happened before we got them unloaded?"

Slagiron smiled and nodded.

Bullinger shook his head.

"You have to admire their preparations. If we didn't put our foot through in one place, there was another loose board somewhere else. And I don't know as we're out of it yet."

Arakal straightened. "There are enough pieces missing in this puzzle."

Slagiron cleared his throat. "On top of everything else, there's the fact that, with no fight, we were able to get away from our own set of 'partisans'. Why?"

Bullinger looked puzzled.

"If you got out quietly—"

"There was no way we could get out without their knowing it. They *let* us go."

Bullinger stared fixedly at the chart, then nodded.

"I've seen a spider catch a good many flies—and then cut a bumblebee loose from the web."

Slagiron shook his head.

"Don't forget, the Russ themselves were just across the river. We could have had one sweet time to get out of there alive."

"At what price for them?"

Slagiron smiled. "Oh, they would have paid a good price. But it might have *ended* us."

Arakal said exasperatedly, "How do we know how to fight them, when we don't understand them? Their plans have levels, one hidden by the other, the way an onion has layers."

Bullinger said thoughtfully, "After we had the partisan leaders locked up, we got some farmers in here one at a time, showed them these lying charts, explained how we'd been deceived by Otto and Yudrik, and said we wanted to learn the truth. You understand, our interpreters were none too good. But, little by little, it got across.

"This 'S' is an all-embracing control system. You can call it whatever you want, but that's what it is. It aims to control *everything*. Go to worship, and the priest is either an agent of S, or else an agent of S is watching him and possibly also telling him what to do. Serve in the army, and the general's orderly is an agent of S, watching *him*, and from time to time either he or some other agent is giving the general orders. S aims to run *everything*, and to run everything, S has to *know* everything. Spies are everywhere. Have a date tonight with the girl down the road, and the local agent of S knows it by tomorrow morning, and has a good estimate, by the day after, of how things went. It may help S manipulate you—and her.

"Apparently, the only way not to tangle with S is to stick to the basics of your trade, and care nothing whatever about rising. Stay flat to the ground. If you try to rise, S controls your success, and it finally dawns on you that, without S, you go nowhere. The natural thing then is to try to rise *with* S. But, to do that, you have to spy, betray, prove your loyalty to S, care only for what S cares for—and then you've lost all freedom of thought, and scarcely exist as a person. *Not* to succeed means you're shoved down and miserable. But, in this mess, *to* succeed means you have to sell your soul."

Arakal, frowning, looked out the round window at the gray waters of the bay.

Slagiron said, his voice a growl, "Well, we're sworn to free Old Brunswick and Old Kebeck. But this thing has no handle on it!"

Arakal, still looking out, said exasperatedly, "Have we freed Old Brunswick and Old Kebeck?"

"They acted like it when we got there. And the same in Allemain."

"But what have we done that would stop S?"

Slagiron and Bullinger glanced at each other. Arakal tore his gaze from the quiet waters and looked at them.

Slagiron said, "It seems to me that we have done exactly nothing."

Bullinger nodded. "So far, it's a draw. They have us running in circles. We have some military victories. But they must still be far more powerful everywhere but in Normandy."

Slagiron shook his head. "As for S, we've killed or captured a few underlings, who must be easy enough to replace. That's all."

Into the thick silence as they looked at each other, came the quick rap of heels approaching on the deck. There was a knock at the door.

Bullinger glanced at Arakal, who nodded, and Bullinger called, "Come in!"

The cabin door opened, and Smith, the acting chief of Arakal's technicians, stepped inside.

"Sir, we've had word from Colputt!"

Slagiron straightened.

Arakal said, "Where is he?"

"The guide-ships are bringing him in through the channel. He should be here early tonight. He says he has one platform with him, assembled and ready to use, and the other partly disassembled."

Arakal smiled. "Good!" He glanced at Bullinger. "Everything may depend on Colputt."

Bullinger nodded, but with no great show of conviction. "I don't see how we're going to fight an enemy who vanishes into thin air. No matter what we do, he'll just reappear after we leave."

Arakal nodded. "It's all different from what we expected. But I'm glad Colputt's here."

★ 3 ★

The Head of Government was seated at a small metal table in a room where the light came in through high barred windows, below which were walls lined with file cases. A gooseneck lamp cast the only artificial light in the room directly on the file G-One was reading.

"Is this," he asked, his voice low, with a faint tremor, "supposed to be accepted as the truth?"

"It is the truth," said S-One, "as far as I know it. And it fits in reasonably with what I do know, of my own personal knowledge. So far as I can judge, there is nothing of misinformation about it."

"Does the present generation of Americans know this?"

"Not as far as I know. But, it is not impossible that they may suspect something of the kind. It would be possible, even, to provisionally deduce something of this character, from the pattern of the nuclear attack against the Americans. And, you have to remember, they were very careless with nearly every form of internal compartmentation. The information is doubtless there to be found, somewhere." S-One paused, then said, frowning, "Just as other things are there to be found, if only they look. And they are looking."

"What do you have in mind?"

"Our information from within Arakal's army is negligible. From within his government, little better. I had thought to have someone inserted into his personal entourage, but that was crudely handled, and came to nothing. But when he took over our colonies, he gave us the first opportunity to penetrate his organization. We are at least started. Now, as regards Colputt, we have received very curious information, which to me can mean only one thing. Colputt has discovered some possibly formidable device, of characteristics I personally cannot imagine."

"What type of device?"

"Are you through reading that?"

"For now."

"Then," said S-One, his voice perfectly matter-of-fact, "you see the deeper reason for the S organization?"

"What do you mean?"

"We are not just a mechanism for the government's political purposes."

The Head of Government looked at him blankly, then suddenly stared off down a narrow aisle between the rows of file cases. He gave a low exclamation.

S-One said, "You are now in possession of a piece of information that must go no further. Now, let me show you this factor whose details I cannot grasp." He held out a thin folder labeled, "Activities of Chief of American Technological Service Colputt." Apologetically, S-One said, "The title is ours. He is only called, amongst the Americans, 'Chief Mechanic Colputt'. We need some better handle than that to hold him by."

"You receive these reports regularly?"

"That thin folder is a summary of all the hard information in the whole file. I call your attention particularly to the last entries."

The Head of Government skimmed the folder quickly, then read the last part slowly and carefully.

"So, Colputt sent for Arakal. The communications were personally deciphered by Arakal. Arakal's men were consumed with curiosity. Arakal went away, evidently to see what Colputt had found. He returned and apparently said nothing. Now, what does all this mean?"

"I cannot measure it. It fits in with other information I have, but it is still incomplete. But, in light of this, I think it would be wise to do nothing that might hurt Arakal personally. I have sent out a directive to that effect. We have had repeated indications that Arakal does not wish us ill, and might be inclined to cooperate with us. If anything should happen to him, how do we know who might come to power? He is, of course, extremely dangerous politically."

"Better that," said the Head of Government, "than the unknown risks suggested by this development?"

"Yes. But I cannot explain all the reasons, and there are bound to be those in the organization who are over-zealous. Ordinarily, when instructions are given that someone is to be removed as a factor in the situation, it is a matter of pride to carry out these instructions. Some bullheaded individual may still try it. There is little I can do about that. Except one thing."

"What is that?"

S-One's smile showed bright even teeth. "If anyone as much as expresses doubt about the new directive, I will make an example of him that will not very soon be forgotten."

"I will do the same."

"You see the situation?"

"I see the part you have shown me."

S-One said earnestly, "I do not misinform you. When I give you no information, it is for a reason. If I misdirect you, it is for a reason. Bear in mind, I am part of a survival apparatus. One must take human nature into account, if one wishes his measures to succeed. And these measures *must* succeed."

"Your measures have not succeeded with Arakal."

"I have not been able to penetrate his organization. I do not understand him, and so have been unable to dominate him. But that may yet come. Who can say? But let me complete the point I am making that I am not misinforming you *when I say to you* that I am not misinforming you."

S-One spoke very earnestly, and G-One smiled. "If you say you are not lying, then, *at that moment*, you are *not* lying."

S-One looked at his face intently, and then laughed.

"Exactly."

The Head of Government smiled somewhat sadly. "It must be pleasant to have simple comradeship, as in Arakal's army, for instance."

"Yes, but then, look where it leads. And there are legends which suggest that all this may have happened more than once."

"Each time somewhat differently?"

"I would suppose so."

"It is difficult to think or plan on such a long-range basis. The specifics could change considerably beyond what was expected."

"Very true. And, in this case, do you see how the specifics *might* fit together?"

"Hm. . . . Dare we hope?"

"Who knows? I have had the pursuit delayed, to be sure errors did not enter in at the last moment. Of course, we cannot break it off entirely. But the final engagement could be short."

"Yes. Now, let's see. . . . The next move is, I think, fairly obvious." G-One frowned. "Unless the *specifics* are different from what we expect."

"We will have to wait and see. It should not be long."

"The preparations had better be made now. We want nothing to go wrong at the last minute."

★ 4 ★

Colputt, chief of Arakal's technicians, was still somewhat greenish from the ocean crossing as he sat at the table, stroked his white beard, and listened to Arakal's brief summary of their experiences.

At the end, Colputt nodded. "We had our mysteries, too. And if things had turned out just a little bit differently, we wouldn't have got here."

Bullinger nodded. "I knew you must be having trouble, or we'd have heard from you."

Colputt shook his head.

"From your account, and the old books, we knew the Atlantic wasn't nice to cross. What we didn't know was that it had changed since the books were written."

Bullinger looked doubtful. "We didn't notice anything like that. Perhaps, due to lack of experience—"

"Our lack of experience wouldn't move icebergs, or change the temperature of air and water."

"What happened?"

"We ran into freezing rain, then dense fog, and we were creeping through the fog when a wall of ice loomed up in front of us. We changed direction just in time—and lost the radio mast over the side. Like everything else, it was heavy with ice. The ice had accumulated *fast*."

"You must have gotten too far north."

Colputt said, "The ice was too far south. When we came out of this, suddenly it was *warm*—almost hot—too warm by far for where we were. This wasn't like a change in the weather. It was as if we were in a tub, and someone dumped in some ice, then equalized the temperature by pouring in some hot water. I don't know of anything like that in the old records. Yes—after an unusually cold stretch of weather, the icebergs might be further south than usual. This was different."

Bullinger, frowning, glanced around at young Markel, his fleet navigator, standing against the cabin wall behind him.

"What was it you were trying to tell me the other day?"

"Sir—Oh, about the weather?"

"Yes."

"Something the people here said. That after the war with the O'Cracys, it seemed that the weather changed. Sometimes the weather seems too cold, sometimes too hot. And the sun isn't right."

Bullinger shook his head. "Weather never seems right. The normal situation *is* abnormal."

Colputt nodded. "But what we ran into wasn't *weather*."

"What was it, then?"

"I don't know."

Arakal glanced at Slagiron.

"You remember what the farmers told us about the weather in Russland?"

Slagiron said dryly, "Who could forget it? It was one reason not to go deeper in Russland."

Arakal glanced at Colputt.

"They told us it was said that there was solid ice and snowbanks from one coast to the other, and sometimes the sun would shine through hotter than the hottest summer, turn the ice to water, burn through the vegetation under the snow, turn the ground black—and then it would start to snow again."

Slagiron said, "All we actually experienced, where we were, was snow and cold. In the winter, it must be worse than Kebeck Fortress in January."

Colputt frowned. "But, further in the interior, *sometimes for a while*, it was hotter than the hottest summer?"

Slagiron nodded. "That's the way they put it."

Arakal said, "The impression we got was that, for a little while, the place turned into an oven, and that in that place it was a *lot* hotter than the hottest summer."

"I don't see," said Colputt, "how hot weather could be restricted to *certain places* in the middle of winter."

There was a silence as they thought it over. Then Slagiron cleared his throat, and glanced at Arakal.

"How many puzzles does *this* make?"

Arakal said, "First, there was the question why they didn't wipe us out soon after we got here. Our whole picture was wrong. We didn't realize what we were up against."

"But," said Colputt, "*could* they have wiped you out?"

Slagiron nodded soberly. "They could have done it with a thousand men at the right places. You never saw a bigger mess."

"Instead," said Arakal, "we were welcomed. They wined us, dined us, rushed us over the iron roads straight for Russland. All these 'partisans' we've told you about joined us on the way. If they weren't shaking our hands or kissing us, they were giving us bouquets of flowers and bottles of wine."

"But," objected Colputt, "it wasn't the Russ who were doing this?"

"No, but the Russ didn't stop it."

Colputt frowned.

Arakal said, "In fact, they had us surrounded with their own people, and they were rushing us straight into a trap. They got us out of Old Kebeck fast, and without actually putting forth their full strength. They were pulling us straight forward, to freeze us into submission."

"Well," said Colputt, "I would say that's no puzzle. It was extremely shrewd tactics on their part."

"Oh," said Slagiron, "it's no puzzle *now*. Now we've got other puzzles. But it was a puzzle *then*. There was one puzzle after another. The final puzzle was—why did they let us get away?"

Admiral Bullinger said thoughtfully, "I think they just wanted to avoid casualties. At no expense to themselves, they've got us all back on the coast."

"But this is a peculiar way to wage war. This is not how they do it on the other side of the ocean."

Colputt frowned. "There does seem to be something else behind all this. Something out of sight."

Slagiron nodded. "We're still groping in the dark."

Arakal said, "Now we have the question of 'S'. Why do they rule through S? *Do* the Russ rule S? Or does it rule them? What do they plan to do next, now that we seem to know what they were doing before? And, this last puzzle—what's wrong with the weather here?"

Slagiron spoke hesitantly.

"We've all seen what we've seen—and there's no reason I can think of why the Russ farmers would lie to us. But, *could* their weather be so much changed here? What is there that could change it? The sun shines from the sky. The wind blows as it will. What *could* change the weather?"

Colputt shook his head. "In the old days, maybe they could have told you. But I don't know. We have books from that time, but we're short on understanding."

There was a silence, and Arakal decided to change the subject.

"What of the platforms?"

Colputt's look of gloom vanished.

"There, at least, is something we have the Russ don't. And it's positive proof that, whatever the Russ may say now, our ancestors were as able as theirs."

Around the table, everyone leaned closer.

Arakal said, "Are the platforms ready?"

"One is ready now. The other will be before the day is out."

Bullinger, listening closely, glanced from Arakal to Colputt. His curiosity showed on his face, but he said nothing.

Arakal was looking at Colputt. "Inside the tunnels—the bodies on the floor, above the platforms?"

"Started to deteriorate after we'd been in there a while. We gave them a decent burial. Kotzebuth thinks what happened was that when the Russ attacked, some radiation like that of light, but finer, must have penetrated the whole mountain, and killed *everything*, including the organisms of decay."

The room was silent with the listening of Bullinger, Beane, Slagiron, and Markel, all of whose faces were now carefully blank and noncommittal, but who somehow gave the impression that their consciousness was concentrated in their ears.

Arakal said, "But the machines themselves—"

"Well, as you remember, they were sealed off on a lower level, in a room lined with lead, and set on big coil springs, with an arrangement of cylinders to damp the shock. The machines looked all right when we first found them, but when you left, we still couldn't be sure. When we finally got into them, we found no sign of damage. The machines perform—" Colputt hesitated, as if groping for words, then concluded "—beyond our expectations."

"And the fuel—?"

A muscle twitched at Colputt's jaw.

"The arrangement of fuel is as we hoped."

Arakal sat back.

"Our crews?"

Colputt nodded. "Our crews are trained."

Arakal let his breath out slowly.

"If this is so—Then we want to be careful that this doesn't give us delusions of greatness. Yet, I would like to give the Russ a taste of what the O'Cracys used to be. Are we *sure* the platforms weren't hurt in the crossing?"

"As sure as we can be. We kept constant watch on both of them. But if we'd hit that wall of ice, we'd have been sunk in a flash."

Arakal nodded soberly, and turned to the intently listening Slagiron and Bullinger.

"Tomorrow, perhaps, we may see what the Old O'Cracys could do."

★ 5 ★

Dawn—if it could be called that—was a lighter grayness, somewhere to the south of east, as the huge door at the bow of Colputt's ship began slowly to lower. Lower and lower it came, until at last it reached out like a bridge, and then the end sank in the shallow water. From the deep shadows within came a low whine that climbed higher and higher, accompanied by a sound like a rising wind.

Slowly, something moved out from the shadows onto the lowered drawbridge.

Slagiron, watching, caught his breath.

Wide, dark, smoothly curving, with a dome at the center, it glided slowly down the drawbridge, crossed the water in a whirl of mist, and now behind it there came another.

As Slagiron and Bullinger stood paralyzed, there was a sudden change of pitch, the first of the two devices tilted slightly forward, and suddenly climbed into the sky so fast that it dwindled as they watched. An instant later, the second followed.

Bullinger stared up at high twin reflections of the sun, which was itself still below the horizon, then the reflections winked out. He looked east to Russland, and grinned.

Beside him, Slagiron shut his jaws with a click.

Bullinger exhaled. "Now we know."

"The devil," said Slagiron. "Maybe *you* know. What was it?"

★ 6 ★

S-One read the report with wide eyes. He sat up, glanced at S-Two, who was standing by the desk. S-One cleared his throat.

S-Two said, "What will they do with this?"

"I will have to speak to the Head of Government. We must act at once."

★ 7 ★

Arakal, standing as if paralyzed in the eerier silence, stared out the wide curving window. Though he could see nothing now but blowing mist, he had the impression that he was up among the stars, looking down on the slowly turning ball of Earth.

Beside him, Colputt smiled.

Arakal exhaled carefully.

"What was it you said—the machines perform 'beyond our expectations'?"

Colputt nodded. "I didn't now how much you wanted me to mention. And there was no way to describe *this*. It surpasses our wildest imaginings. There is no mountain in the world we couldn't fly over, and no place on the surface of the Earth that we couldn't reach. And we can outrace the sun to get there!"

Arakal felt the universe seem to swim around him. With an effort, he kept silent until he could trust his voice.

"How does it work?"

Colputt shook his head.

"The levers and switches I can show you—and what happens when I work them. *How* it does what it does is beyond me."

"But—I thought you said, back when we found it, that this looked like a 'ground effect machine'."

"It seemed so, to start with. It seemed to match that description closer than anything else. But when we had enough skill to maneuver it, and had it out where there was plenty of room, I tried it one day at full power, and you see what happened."

Colputt leaned forward, to tap a button on the slanting control board. Around them, the solid upper wall of the cabin vanished. As if through thin clouds, the stars shone in. Colputt tapped the button again, and the wall was solid.

"How do I explain such things?"

"Could we go still higher?"

"I'm sure we *could*. Whether it might kill us to do it I don't know."

Arakal shook his head.

"I see now why the Russ make such mistakes when they get their machines in action. Such devices are like strong drink. Better that we go lower, and look around as we'd planned to. And be careful we don't smash into the other platform, and wreck both of them."

As they dropped down, the streaming snowflakes were beginning to glow like fireflies.

Ahead of them, there was a growing brilliance.

XIV. The Conference

★ 1 ★

The sun was sinking out of sight toward the west as the first of the two platforms came back into view of the fleet, slowed with a sudden roar, and glided into the interior of Colputt's ship. A moment later, the second followed.

Bullinger was waiting as Arakal and Colputt climbed up the ladder of the flagship. A heavy concussion, followed by a second, half-deafened them.

Bullinger's lips drew back in a grin.

"A little trouble from your old friends."

Arakal nodded. "They've got more tanks on the way. We saw them."

"If you can spot them for us, we'll take care of them before they get here."

"They're still a long way off. If you have time, why don't you come below. We think we have some answers."

Bullinger nodded, ran up a ladder, spoke with an officer on the deck above, then came back, to guide Arakal and Colputt to a different cabin than they had used the last time. Bullinger shut the door, and glanced around.

"Now, none of our 'allies' have ever been in here—so *maybe* it's all right. And I've had the whole place checked, inside and out. Strange to say, where we were talking the last time, there was a listening device beside the leg of the table, close under the top. There was another in one of the light fixtures. I *think* we got them all, but they may have been cleverer than we are. For that matter, they could have built some more in here when they made the ship. We've checked. But don't tell me anything aloud that you don't want to risk their finding out."

Arakal smiled. "If they can hear this, they can do what they want with it. I think we begin to *understand* them."

"Could you—fly over—?"

Arakal nodded.

"I suppose," said Bullinger hesitantly, "the snow, fog, and so on, blotted out a good deal of it?"

"From direct observation. But we've underestimated the Old O'Cracys far worse than we ever knew. The platform has devices to *see through fog.*"

"*What*?"

"As I say, we've underestimated the Old O'Cracys."

Bullinger frowned at the repetition. Then he stiffened. "The Russ are ruined, too?"

"We didn't try to see *all* of Russland, although with the platform that's not so impossible as it sounds. But most of what we *did* see was like the country well north of Kebeck Fortress in the depth of winter."

"But I thought this Central Committee of theirs meets in Moscow? That's their capital, isn't it?"

Arakal glanced at Colputt.

Colputt said, "There were three fair-sized zones of heat radiation which may mean underground dwellings. The locations correspond on our maps to places called Leningrad, Moscow, and Kiev. Further south and to the east, it looks heavily settled."

Bullinger sat back, blank-faced. "What this must mean is that the Old Soviets got clubbed in that war almost as bad as the Old O'Cracys! But they won! We've always known they won!"

Arakal said dryly, "If two men fight, and one gets shot in the head while the other gets shot in the stomach, who won?"

Colputt said, "They *destroyed* the Old O'Cracys. We have no memory—no continuity of thought descending from that time. They have their Central Committee, their 'S', apparently some underground centers, and the districts to the south—which may have been completely untouched by the war."

Bullinger nodded. "They *won*—but they almost didn't survive it. But that isn't the picture we've had. It always seemed—"

In the corridor, brisk footsteps came to a halt. There was a rap on the door.

Arakal nodded to Bullinger's questioning glance. Bullinger called, "Come in."

The door opened, and Slagiron stepped inside, frowning. He turned to Arakal.

"Catmeat's old gang has been trying to break through. They make better enemies than they did friends, but we're too well dug in; and on top of that, there's the fire from the ships. Fifteen minutes ago, a message came through. They want a 'conference'."

Arakal nodded. "They've got more tanks coming. If they can have us tied up talking when the tanks get here—"

Slagiron put his hand on the doorknob, then hesitated, "Could you see much of Russland?"

Arakal told him what he had told Bullinger, and a look of amazement spread over Slagiron's face.

"No wonder we couldn't understand them! Their position is completely different than we thought!"

Arakal said, "We still don't want to underestimate them. For all we know, they may have something in mind we haven't spotted yet."

Slagiron nodded grimly. "We'll keep our eyes open. I'll let them know what they can do with their conference."

As he turned to go out, there was a sound of rapidly approaching footsteps, then an urgent rap on the door.

Bullinger called, "Come in!"

Beane stepped inside, nodded to Slagiron, and glanced at Arakal.

"Sir, I think we're about to be treated to some new trick. We've just had a message from what purports to be the chairman of their Central Committee. A 'Mikhael Zhtutin' is coming to see us as their 'plenipotentiary'. He is, quote, authorized to deal with all the matters of mutual disagreement between us, end-quote. They—the Central Committee—want a truce in the fighting while he's here."

Arakal thought a moment, then nodded.

"All right. We'll risk it." He glanced at Slagiron. "Tell Koljuberowski's people we'll agree to a cease-fire, but we don't want any conference with them, since Zhtutin will be here. We'll put the platforms up, to see what's coming."

When Beane and Slagiron had gone out, Arakal turned to Bullinger.

"What chance is there of small boats sneaking up on us in the fog, to board?"

"I've already warned the captains. We'll make it hot for them if they try it."

Colputt came to his feet. "I'll get the platforms up."

Arakal nodded. "This conference may be useful. Or it could turn out to be pure poison."

★ 2 ★

It was morning when Slagiron's deputy, Casey, sent word that the plenipotentiary had arrived. Arakal headed for the conference room.

Mikhael Zhtutin turned out to be a lean, somber man, well above average height, neat, slightly stooped, and dressed in a heavy fur coat and large fur hat with flaps for the back of the head and the ears. With him came an interpreter, also wearing fur hat and fur coat.

Arakal, Slagiron, and Beane stood at the end of the table as Zhtutin was escorted in.

Zhtutin cast a penetrating glance at each of the three men, and his gaze settled on Arakal.

Zhtutin spoke in a low, courteous voice. His interpreter turned to Arakal, and adopted the air of a schoolmaster addressing children caught marking the walls.

"You are the tribal chief known as Arakal?"

Zhtutin, just removing his fur hat, froze. Frowning, he asked the interpreter a question.

554   *Christopher Anvil*

Behind Arakal, one of his own interpreters leaned forward and spoke in a low voice.

"Mr. Zhtutin asks if the question was courteously put. The interpreter replies that he used the proper tone for the occasion."

Arakal said, "Politely say to the Russ plenipotentiary that we use that tone of voice to dogs that steal food from the table."

Arakal's interpreter thought a moment, then spoke politely.

Zhtutin spoke agitatedly to his interpreter. The interpreter looked intently from Arakal's interpreter to Arakal, looked at Arakal and said, his voice exaggeratedly polite, "It is *you* who call yourself Arakal?" The interpreter raised one arm as if to point.

Zhtutin's face went blank. His hand flashed for the open front of his coat. There was a deafening explosion. The interpreter slammed against the bulkhead.

Arakal, Slagiron, and Beane, guns in hand, straightened from behind the table.

At the far end of the table, Zhtutin, his expression angry and exasperated, slid a large shiny revolver back inside his coat.

The interpreter, partly hidden by the table, lay on the deck.

At the door, Bullinger, backed up by half-a-dozen armed men, looked in. He glanced at Zhtutin, then at Arakal.

Arakal said, "Get some men in here to clean up the place, and take out the interpreter. Watch out when you move him. He probably had a sleeve gun."

Bullinger called in several sailors, who carefully bent over the interpreter, put a small shiny pistol on the table, carried out the body, then methodically cleaned the room's floor and walls, the deck, part of the table nearby, and Zhtutin's coat.

Slagiron, Beane, and Arakal watched the proceedings in silence. Zhtutin, glum and apparently embarrassed, waited silently, and gave a nod of thanks to the sailors as they went out. Arakal sent one of his own interpreters to the far end of the table. Zhtutin, his lips compressed, nodded his thanks to Arakal, glanced back at the interpreter Arakal was lending him, smiled ruefully, and spoke to the interpreter, who grinned and said something in return.

Behind Arakal, his interpreter leaned forward. "Mr. Zhtutin said, 'Don't worry, we don't always treat our interpreters that way.' Our man said, 'That's all right. It's all in the line of duty.' "

Arakal and Slagiron, smiling, glanced at the Russ Plenipotentiary, who looked questioning, and reached for the chair, still in its place at the table. Arakal nodded, and they all sat down.

Zhtutin spoke in a regretful tone, and the interpreter translated. "I regret that incident. I will explain the background if you wish, but it is related to a change of view within our own councils which has, whether everyone realizes it or not, been settled."

Arakal said courteously, "We ask to hear only what you wish to tell us."

Zhtutin's face cleared. He said, with a slight air of apology, "I should perhaps mention that the name which I am using is a cover for my actual identity, but that I am fully empowered to speak for the Central Committee."

Arakal smiled. "It is your message which interests us. You are welcome here under whatever name you choose to use."

Zhtutin smiled and relaxed, then looked serious.

"Is it *safe* to talk here?"

"We have removed every listening device *we* could find."

"Of *ours*?"

"Yes."

"Can *you* speak freely?"

Arakal answered without hesitation. "Yes."

Zhtutin looked searchingly at Arakal, as if not certain whether Arakal's answer was a reply to him, or might possibly be meant to convince someone else who might be listening.

Arakal added, his voice courteous, "We have no 'S'."

Zhtutin smiled briefly

"Then I will speak plainly. Power abides with those who use it well. The foolish and the indolent lose it. And also eventually the arrogant and the presumptuous. The Central Committee authorizes me to tell you that we will grant you your independence, and the independence of what you call Old Brunswick and what we call the U.K. In return, there are certain things you must do for us."

Arakal waited a moment, then spoke carefully and distinctly.

"We are sworn to free Old Brunswick *and Old Kebeck*. Can you turn over to us all information on S in those two countries?"

Zhtutin looked fixedly at Arakal, then he slowly nodded. He appeared to select his words with care.

"We, in our turn, demand that you use what means you possess to correct—in good time and very judiciously —certain *errors* made in the past. Are you familiar with that of which I speak?"

Arakal kept his gaze fixed on Zhtutin. "We can make no promises, except that we will do what we can to relieve you of the curse which has settled on you, and we aim to do it once we understand the situation and the method clearly."

Zhtutin's eyes seemed momentarily very bright.

"You understand, it is necessary to use *great care*."

"That is becoming more and more clear to us."

Zhtutin sat still a moment, then sighed and sat back.

"You will have the agent lists for the U.K. and France as soon as they can be gotten here. I must go back to my vehicle, and radio our agreement at once. Of course—" he smiled faintly "—The cousins may already know of it. We will take great care with those lists."

"If you need guards—"

Zhtutin shook his head. "There are a few who still do not understand. That is all."

★ 3 ★

Slagiron sat looking at the door by which the plenipotentiary had gone out.

"There must be something to this Central Committee, after all. But what was that you said about a *curse*?"

Arakal said, "There are some things that have to be seen to be believed. Let's find out if Colputt's back. If so, there's something we want to check and you might like to see it."

★ 4 ★

The ground dropped away rapidly as Slagiron, his jaws clenched, hands gripping the edge of the control panel, stared out through the wide curving window where the landscape shrank and the horizon dropped and the whole earth seemed to tilt and then vanish, to leave only blowing mist.

Arakal relaxed with an effort, and looked around.

Colputt was bent beside his pilot, who nodded, glanced up briefly, and tapped a spot on the angled plate where a view of the snow-covered landscape rolled back toward them.

Slagiron exhaled carefully, observed his hands still clamped on the edge of the control panel, and let go.

Colputt cleared his throat.

"A few moments more." He glanced at Arakal. "I'm afraid the Russ may be counting on us to do something we can't do."

Arakal shook his head.

"I think they know exactly what they're doing. And we made no promise that we can't keep."

"Then," said Colputt ruefully, "there must be something you see that I don't."

Arakal looked through the wide window at the glow toward which they were rushing.

"I don't think the problem Zhtutin *mentioned* is his most pressing problem. They have long since adapted to that. I think the pressing difficulty is one he didn't want to mention aloud—that somehow *they have to control* S. And the immediate value of this agreement to him is, he is using *us* to do it. The thought that we might also be able to clear this up—this terrific problem that we have just seen for the first time—that is a useful pretext, and if we can do it some day, it's a bonus, thrown in free."

Colputt looked puzzled. "To control S? Why?"

Slagiron glanced at Colputt.

"How would you like to have S for a subordinate? They have to use S to keep a hold on the army, and to keep the populace too tied in knots to rise up. But it's the nature of organizations to take over more and more, and since *this* organization is secret, how do you know all it's doing, in order to control it? When there's an enemy to concentrate on, that must focus the attention of S more or less where they want it. But we were knocked so flat so long it must have become a question when S would take *them* over. And whatever anyone may say, S isn't equipped to govern. S can spy, thwart, and suppress—*but it can't lead.*"

Colputt blinked. "Then if we eliminate the networks of S in Old Brunswick and Old Kebeck—what we are doing for them is to prune back an overgrown organization?"

Slagiron nodded. "After that, S ought to be so busy trying to rebuild its networks that they will be able to get it loose from *them*."

Colputt stroked his long white beard, then shook his head.

"Such things are as far beyond my understanding as the Old O'Cracy's calculating machines."

"What *I* don't see," said Slagiron, glancing at Arakal, "is this 'curse' you spoke of. Zhtutin knew what you meant. But—"

Colputt said, "Look out there."

As Slagiron turned, the increasing brightness outside lit their faces, lit the edges of the window, lit the snowflakes whirling back, and glowed on the ceiling overhead. The brilliance grew to a blaze; then the substance of the window itself seemed to darken to shade out the glare.

Below, the dazzle of the snow came to a sudden end, and beyond it an arc of land lay dark and steaming beneath clouds of brilliantly lit vapor rushing in the wind.

The pilot swung them out of the dazzling light, dropped fast, and shot through the blowing mist. Suddenly they were racing along above the dark earth, with high snowbanks to either side. Ahead, blowing snow was spreading across a charred band of earth as the pilot dropped still lower.

Slagiron leaned forward, and as they raced along in a channel between high banks of snow, he gave a low exclamation. "It's getting dark!"

Colputt said, "As we go up, look at the sun."

They were rising in the dimness through thick blowing snow. Then suddenly snow and mist were gone. Through the curving window shone a field of stars.

Slagiron looked around. "There's no sun! But it was daylight!"

Ahead of them, swinging into the center of the curving window as they turned, there was a thin fiery arc at the edge of a grayness shot through with tiny brilliant specks.

For a long moment, they stared at it in silence, as it moved across the slowly turning window.

"My God!" said Slagiron. "Is *that* the sun?"

Colputt said, "Yes. There's curse enough for anyone. Now watch."

He tapped the control that turned the opaque upper walls and ceiling transparent.

They looked up and around, at dazzling arcs and disks of glaring brilliance, hanging amongst the stars as if the sun, blotted out where it belonged, had sprung to new locations in space.

"But—" Slagiron paused. "Zhtutin said there had been 'certain errors'. *Errors*? That the sun itself had been blotted out? Or somehow *refocused*?"

Colputt tapped the control, and again the upper hull was opaque.

Arakal cleared his throat.

"I *think* that's what Zhtutin meant."

Slagiron looked at him.

"*Who made the errors*?"

Arakal said, "Until Zhtutin used that way of expressing it, I thought the Old O'Cracys must have done this. I still think so. Who else could have done it, if Zhtutin wants *us* to undo it?"

Colputt said, "There is quite a gap in our records. But it must be."

"But—*How did they do it*?"

"Consider this platform," said Colputt. "Is it surprising that people who could make such things as this could go into the space between the Earth and the sun?"

"No," said Slagiron. "But, having got there—to screen out the sun itself? That's impossible!"

Colputt shook his head. "What is impossible if you possess the means to bring it about? The Old O'Cracys possessed substances very light and thin, yet very strong, and they possessed the means to silver these substances so that they would reflect light. Right there we have the basis of what would be needed. Now—would a shield made from those thin substances *last*? I don't know. And could the shields be exactly positioned to do the work? Again I don't know. Apparently whatever it is has been put in orbit around the sun, and keeps precise pace with the Earth. More than that. The sum total of whatever has been put up seems to be very carefully designed to deliver just as much extra heat, carefully focused, in some places, as it withholds in others. The sum total, over a period of time, apparently remains the same as if there were no interference with the sun. The complications are mind-staggering. But the Old O'Cracys may very well have had the means to do it."

"The depth of that snow didn't look like the delivery of as much heat as had been withheld."

"The depth there. But go a little further, and we find a place with *no* snow Anyway, the total amount of heat delivered must not have changed."

"Why?"

"At the rim of the Baltic," said Colputt, "they say the weather fluctuates. But in Old Kebeck, you heard no complaint of a change in the weather. If there were a serious change here, in the amount of heat received, it would have been bound to affect the weather in Old Kebeck."

Slagiron nodded. "Yes, that's reasonable."

Arakal said, "That means, then, that whatever was done was done very carefully."

Colputt nodded. "And with great skill."

Arakal looked out at the mist again streaming past as they headed back.

"If it was done with such care, would it have been a war? And yet . . . what else *could* it have been but a war?"

Colputt shook his head. "I don't know."

Slagiron was frowning. "If anyone won, it was the Old Soviets. But, if the O'Cracys had such means as these—"

Arakal said, "The details can change everything. To understand this, we need to know *exactly how it happened.*"

Slagiron nodded.

"We'll have to try to find out."

★ 5 ★

Zhtutin, visibly wary, settled into the seat at the end of the table. He spoke briefly and sharply.

Arakal's translator cleared his throat.

"Mr. Zhtutin says, 'You have lists. What more do you want?' "

"There is a question of our doing what we can do, as soon as we understand the situation, and know how to do it."

Zhtutin looked directly at Arakal.

"What of that?"

"You spoke of an 'accident'."

Zhtutin's gaze briefly wavered, then he looked directly at Arakal.

"You object to my choice of words?"

"I spoke of a 'curse'. You made no objection."

"What objection is required?"

"Our word is then pledged only to deal with a 'curse' resulting from an 'accident'?"

Zhtutin frowned.

"What is it you want?"

"The facts we don't have."

"That is your problem."

Arakal leaned forward.

"Mr. Plenipotentiary, in my opinion, *very possibly there was no war*. If so, you have never won in fair combat, because there was no combat. There was, as you say, an 'accident'. I want to know about that accident."

Zhtutin shoved back his chair, started to get up, paused with one hand on the table, looking toward the door, then slowly sat down, turning, and looked directly at Arakal.

"You say there was no war! You see your own country in ruins! It was, once, greater than these European nations you admire. You see the hell in the Soviet Union—and *you* tell *me* there was no war! Are you insane?"

"We merely have no S," said Arakal, his voice quiet, "to tell us what to think, and so we *can* think. Perhaps later, if we develop further, we will have an S of our own, and be as unable to think then as you think we are now. But as for now, if you want us to end the problem, we need to understand the problem. And to do that, it would help for you to tell us about the accident."

"And if I refuse?"

"We will keep our word. You are here under our safe-conduct, and can leave anytime. But neither we nor you know *when* we will have the facts, or when we will know whether in fact the curse we spoke of is in reality a blessing."

Zhtutin, scowling, looked sharply at Arakal, then frowned, and turned away.

"I am only the plenipotentiary, not the Central Committee."

Arakal nodded.

Zhtutin sat back, frowning. Finally, he shrugged, and looked back at Arakal.

"I can show you something, if you will go where I tell you. Let us go in your spacecraft."

XV. All Secrets Revealed

★ 1 ★

The ground dropped away, and Zhtutin bent over the plate where the image of the landscape below unrolled. He spoke quietly, and the interpreter translated.

"Follow this river," said the interpreter. "Now go east."

Time passed as, on the plate, the ground flowed back.

Slagiron spoke to Arakal in a low voice. "What if we suddenly come in range of some Russ anti-rocket station left over from before the—ah—'accident'."

"If it doesn't bother our guest to be blown up," said Arakal, "why should it bother us?"

Slagiron grinned, and at that moment Zhtutin spoke excitedly.

The translator bent by the pilot, and they veered sharply toward the north.

A few moments later, Zhtutin spoke again.

"Stop," said the translator.

They hovered, and Arakal and Slagiron stepped over to the plate—then they both jerked back.

On the plate, superimposed on the image of the flat snow-covered plain, was a stylized skull.

Arakal looked out the curving window beyond the control panel, to see nothing but blowing snow.

The translator listened to the plenipotentiary, then said, "We must go down to see anything, but be careful. There were tall buildings here once."

The pilot looked again at the symbol on the plate, and turned in his seat.

Colputt was frowning. "Go down, but go slow. I think that is just for what this place *used* to be."

The pilot turned back to his controls.

Colputt tapped a switch on the control panel, and abruptly the opaque wall was transparent. They moved slowly through blowing snow, and, off to their right, there appeared a vague arch of white.

Zhtutin, frowning, stared at it, then nodded.

"That way. But *carefully*."

The arch of white slowly resolved into a huge, bent, snow-covered metal frame, supporting what appeared to be a number of gigantic slanting snow-heaped slats.

Zhtutin murmured, and the translator bent close.

"I had no idea the heat could have been that intense . . . Yes, but there it is. That is where the error began—that frame . . . It held up those panels, which were flat. The panels—No, that can come later. Now, you have seen it. We must go elsewhere. First, we must go higher. But *carefully*. If there is another of those frames, bent less completely—good."

As Zhtutin gave directions, Slagiron glanced at Colputt, then at Arakal. Arakal kept his mouth shut. Colputt's look of intense thought was, all by itself, an invitation to say nothing.

Zhtutin bent intently over the plate.

"We must be near . . . Slow, slow—There, the light!"

Outside, a dimness became a white glow, and then a glare.

Colputt tapped the control. The hull, save for the wide-curving window in front, was again opaque.

Zhtutin straightened.

"Go through once, quickly. I think the light is most intense near the edges."

Outside, the glowing snowflakes gave way to a drizzle that coalesced into drops on the curving window, to run back in glittering streams, and then the mist became a shining fog that suddenly vanished as they emerged into a dazzling brilliance that slitted their eyes even as the glass of the window darkened.

Below them, stretching out into the distance, was a bright green field of tall grass moving in long ripples toward the center, while at the edge it quivered and trembled in the focus of a light that seemed to brighten and darken, to strengthen, to fold on itself, as first one then another part of the field felt the compounded blaze hammering down from the sky.

Along the edge, there loomed through the smoke and mist heavy snowbanks that sent sudden sheets and streams of water draining down, trailing clouds of vapor that vanished in the blaze of light.

As the window darkened further, they could see the flames that ran along the stalks, as the focused brilliance of the shafts of light ate their way forward from the far edge of the field.

Colputt spoke sharply to the pilot, and suddenly the drizzle was running again along the curving window, and they were out of the glare.

Zhtutin spoke heavily.

"There is the curse."

Arakal didn't speak.

Colputt said carefully, "The light?"

"The *weed*."

Colputt frowned, but said nothing.

Zhtutin waited a moment. When he spoke, his voice was controlled and quiet. He spoke briefly, waiting while the interpreter translated one sentence after another.

"The first place we saw, just now, was the Experimental Station. If the fool who ran it had possessed a sense of duty, we would not now be in this situation. I have the story direct from the original records. At that Station, an attempt was being made to develop hardier types of hay and feed grains, for use where the summers are short. Nothing could have been more harmless! But the donkey who ran this station did not notify his superiors when one of the many varieties of hay being tested, for some reason not known, fell or was removed from its covered tray, and took root in a field nearby. As it soon proved difficult to control, recourse was had to machines which were being developed here, to cultivate the field. These machines were of an experimental type, large and powerful, which ground the dirt finely. They were used to grind up the experimental plant, in order to kill it."

Arakal, frowning, glanced at Colputt, who said, "And then—?"

Zhtutin made a weary gesture of the hand.

"The machines used to cultivate the field were almost ready for their first trials. These machines were experimented with in different types of soil all over the country.

What none of the agricultural scientists realized was that during the trials, fine bits of this plant, stuck here and there in the insides of the machines, were sown in a great many different places."

Colputt put his hand to his chin.

Zhtutin went on. "And it took root. No one in the other districts recognized at first that this plant was new. Since no word of the accident had been given, there was no warning."

Outside, as the pilot turned, glowing mist blew back across the curving window.

"It was," Zhtutin went on, "merely a *grass*. There seemed to be no cause for alarm."

Colputt, frowning, said, "And when it went to seed—"

"It has no seeds. It forms a husk, and within the husk there is nothing. But it is extremely hardy, and vigorous. In each field where it was found, naturally the attempt was made to control it. In some cases, it was chopped up, in the attempt to kill it. Ordinary grass is hard to destroy, but, if you pull it up, and chop it up, most of it, at least, dies. Any bit of this weed, in contact with the soil, is capable of forming a root, and starting a new plant. In the places where it was let grow, it gave a wonderful yield—of *hay*."

Colputt looked sober. "It crowded out the other plants?"

"Nothing could compete with it. Wheat, rye, oats, corn, barley—*anything* was strangled by it. And it grew *fast*."

"How long before anyone realized—"

Zhtutin shook his head.

"It was a query from the Americans, studying their satellite pictures, that finally made it known. The Americans noticed places where the vegetation seemed to absorb light more fully than the plants they knew of. As it evidently was being very widely planted, they assumed it was a new food plant, and asked for information. But it was the opposite of a food plant. It yielded no grain, and destroyed the plants that did. We could use it to feed animals—that was all. Unless it could be killed, we could never make up for the grain that would be lost."

"It absorbed light more fully?"

"It utilized light more fully. It grew faster. It was said later that it utilized water and carbon dioxide better. It was a very efficient plant. It began to grow as soon as the snow cover melted enough to give it light, and it did not stop till it was covered again the next winter. And then something else was discovered."

Colputt looked uneasily out the window toward the glow.

The translator leaned forward as the plenipotentiary spoke in a lower voice.

"The fields cleared the previous year, at great pains, the following spring grew up in clumps of this plant. For reasons that were never found, because there was not time, parts of the root break off in the soil and become dormant. They can live over until another year. Only when the soil had been sifted, or the root cooked by intense heat, could the soil be trusted."

Colputt's eyes widened. He glanced at Arakal.

Arakal said, "This change of weather is to *fence off and destroy the weed*?"

Zhtutin nodded. "But this was not the only trouble. As our side contended with this, and was being kicked to pieces by it, the Americans had their own accident. And no one knows how *that* happened." He glanced intently at Colputt. "Unless, perhaps, you have found the records?"

Colputt shook his head.

Zhtutin said, "At that time, experiments were being carried out that I personally do not understand. It seems that substances are released naturally in the human body, and that by manipulations involving the structures which control heredity in microorganisms, a microorganism can be so made over that *it* produces the natural human substance. Further, and more surprising, it may be possible to induce the microorganism to release the substance in response to other substances present in the human system, in varying amounts in health or illness. If, then, this microorganism is used to infect a human being, symptoms may be relieved—or a cure may follow—caused by the substance released by the microorganism. Of course, this work required great skill, special apparatus, and *caution*."

Zhtutin glanced at Colputt, who nodded, his expression grave, and Zhtutin sighed and gestured wearily with his hand. "Many were working on such things; they had, as I understand it, great theoretical as well as practical significance. The accident could have happened anywhere. As it was, it happened in an American laboratory, and the result was the release of a quantity of specially altered microorganisms. I assume most died at once. It would seem that they would be ill adapted to act as germ organisms, because of the changes in their structure; but it may be that the scientists had found a way to avoid this, while trying to adapt the organisms for medical use. In any case, America soon had a wave of what was called 'Killer Flu'. Our information is that it was not actually a form of influenza at all. What appears to have been done was to create a form of microorganism capable of excreting—"

The interpreter paused, and after several puzzled exchanged with Zhtutin, the interpreter turned to Colputt.

"I'm not certain how to translate these words, sir. It seems that the body has something in it like sugar, and another substance that makes it possible to get more use out of this substance that is like sugar."

Colputt nodded. "Just call what is like sugar 'glucose', and what makes it easier to use the glucose, 'insulin'."

The translator nodded, and Zhtutin, looking relieved, went on. Arakal, trying to piece together the sense of what was said, found the discussion as confusing as a foreign language.

"Then," said Colputt finally, "the insulin was somehow synthesized by the microorganisms, and released in the body? And the idea was to have a trouble-free source of insulin for diabetics? But what was the insulin formed from?"

Zhtutin shrugged. "Who could say, now? In any case, the work was not finished. The organisms were released prematurely. The control of their responses was incomplete. They invaded non-diabetic individuals. The results were severe."

Colputt stared. "*Insulin shock*?"

"Yes. Which damaged the central nervous systems of the persons infected."

"When did this happen?"

"When our troubles with the strangleweed were well developed, and it had become a question whether we could limit its spread."

Colputt looked out the window. He glanced at Arakal, then at Slagiron. The he looked back at Zhtutin.

"What then?"

Zhtutin turned to Arakal.

"You see the situation?"

"I see it."

"The weed was kicking our ribs in. If it spread beyond our borders, it might never be stopped. The trained germs were slaughtering the Americans. At any moment, these germs, which despite a ban on travel were spreading erratically and unpredictably, might be carried across the oceans to exterminate the rest of the human race. *What could we do?*"

Colputt nodded slowly.

Arakal said, "What happened?"

Zhtutin looked out the window toward the glow, brightening as the pilot swung closer.

"We," said Zhtutin, "took care of the germs for the Americans. They, in turn, took care of the strangleweed for us."

As the luminous drops blew back along the curved window, there was silence.

The silence stretched out.

At last, Zhtutin turned as if to speak, but changed his mind.

Arakal felt the urge to say something, but forced himself to wait.

Zhtutin finally shrugged, and looked at Arakal.

"You said perhaps there was no war. In such a situation as that, who is to say?"

Arakal nodded. "But the grass back there is strangleweed?"

"Yes. It is the largest remaining patch of strangleweed that we know of."

"Are any of the germs left?"

"To our knowledge, no."

Colputt suddenly looked alert. "What is the incubation period?"

Zhtutin smiled faintly, and shook his head.

"If you are thinking you might have caught it when you discovered this vehicle, ease your mind. The time since then has been too great. It acts rapidly."

Arakal glanced at Zhtutin, thought a moment, noted Colputt's look of relief, and turned back to Zhtutin. "The idea is to freeze what weed isn't being burned?"

"Yes. And it is a very complex problem. The weed recurs, world climatic change must if possible be limited, and there is danger if the weed should be spread by minute pieces carried in runoff water. The problem involves complications I do not understand well enough to mention. But, even today, the planet is ringed by satellites, and if, anywhere, a particular characteristic absorption of light should be detected, an intolerable rise in temperature will follow very quickly at that location."

"And this mechanism *runs itself*?"

"There is the difficulty we hope you will take an interest in. We do not know if the array of mechanisms which is fighting the weed is programmed to stop when the weed is destroyed. We assume that the technicians died on returning to Earth—because of the germs. The mechanisms have shown great delicacy of control, and apparently little wear or deterioration. But if you will imagine that you were in our situation, you will understand our viewpoint. This matter is of interest to us."

Arakal said, "What is of interest to us—what we are here to do—is to free Old Brunswick, Old Kebeck, and those other parts of Europe that were part of the land of the O'Cracys. If we can do that, our minds and strength will not be concentrated on fighting to free them. We would then have more time to think of other interests."

"That is understood." Zhtutin looked at him curiously. "Yet you asked for the agent lists only for France and the United Kingdom."

"Too little food and drink," said Arakal dryly, "causes hunger and thirst. Too much at once creates other complaints."

Zhtutin looked at him, and a brief grin crossed his face. He nodded toward the glare outside. "And that?"

"We will do all we can, when we understand the mechanism—and we will do it with great care. But it may be that all that has already been allowed for." Arakal hesitated, feeling the impulse to say more. The thought passed through his mind that if what Zhtutin had said was what had happened, most of the bad feeling between the Russ and the O'Cracys might disappear. But then Arakal considered S, and said nothing.

Zhtutin glanced at Arakal, began to speak, and cleared his throat instead.

Arakal, glancing at Zhtutin's face, seemed to see mirrored there his own thought of a moment before. Involuntarily, he smiled.

Zhtutin made an apologetic gesture, and spoke briefly.

The interpreter looked puzzled, but translated dutifully:

"*It goes on.*"

Arakal nodded.

Outside, the glare faded away as they headed back.

XVI. S vs. Space

★ 1 ★

S-One came to his feet as the Head of Government entered the room, unsmiling and tired. Then both sighed, and, as if unaware of the pause, greeted each other, and took their seats. Each glanced slightly around, as if to check that there was no one else in the room—at least, no one physically present in the room.

S-One said, "A rough trip?"

The Head of Government shrugged. "That is temporary. What I cannot say is whether it will be worth it in the long run."

"We have, at least, exposed every doubtful, reluctant, or questionable member of the organization, in France and the U.K."

"If not, we are truly in trouble."

"Once the local fanatics finish their vengeance on these waverers, the rest will be more reliable. What is your impression of Arakal?"

G-One frowned. "He seems trustworthy. But I think Brusilov is right about him."

"In what way?"

"He is, I think, a master of conflict. Though he does not seem to mean us ill, I think we can expect—surprises."

S-One looked thoughtful. "It may well be. Yet he will have great trouble to win against us, in the long run. And, in fact, from what Brusilov says, he does not wish to beat us. There is a serious flaw. How can he win if he doest not wish to beat us? Because, assuredly, we intend to overcome him. In one way or another."

G-One shivered slightly, and rubbed his hands as if they were cold. "Not once was he discourteous. There was good will evident both on his part and on the part of his men. Yet he did not give way. And he did not ask too much because of their new technological advantage."

"We have, in effect, ceded military control of Western Europe."

"He is well aware we retain indirect control of very large regions, through S. I don't know—" G-One paused, frowning.

S-One leaned forward, and spoke sympathetically. "Something troubles you?"

G-One looked blankly across the room, stared at the Head of Security for a moment as if he were a stranger. "I don't know. If we win—Are we certain—?" Again he paused, frowning. "There was a difference in talking there and in talking here."

"Some of what was said there," said S-One, watching the Head of Government's face with all his attention, "was overheard."

"No doubt."

"With further development, in time, it will be as it is here. And all will be overheard."

G-One's face showed merely a faint expression of annoyance, such as appears on the face of a person who momentarily cannot remember a familiar name. S-One frowned.

The Head of Government suddenly leaned forward, "Listen, I understand the point you explained to me about the S organization. It is logical. But there is a danger."

"There would be a danger if we should fail."

"There is, at least theoretically, a danger if you succeed."

"Ah?" said the Head of Security, his tone silky.

G-One looked at him with eyes that came suddenly to a hard bright focus. "Spare me that tone. And give me the benefit of your thought. You *can* think, can you not? Not all your thoughts are supplied by the local commissary of thoughts? Why do you think that you personally are still in charge of the S organization?"

"I was selected," said S-One seriously. "And you have chosen not to disapprove of the selection." He said, somewhat sadly, "No, not all my thoughts come, at the special low price, from the nearest special commissary. But for the subject you wish to discuss, I can make no promises. I will do my best, but who knows?"

G-One smiled; for the first time a natural expression appeared to replace the look of strain. "Good. I will tell you one reason why you are still here: I could talk to you; there was a meeting of the minds. Now, I want your opinion on this."

S-One settled back slowly, as if bracing himself. "Proceed. But remember," he added dryly, "it will be recorded."

"Good. Now, stand back from all this at a distance, in your mind. Grant that what we believe on certain subjects is a great advance over what went before. Give full credit to our doctrines and beliefs. And our methods."

S-One said, smiling, "I do that readily. I am with you so far. Continue."

"Very well. Now, cast your mental gaze back over all history. All the long life of humankind. There have been many beliefs. Many doctrines. Many methods."

"I am still with you."

"Most of which have been superseded."

"Ah."

"Some of which have been wrong beliefs, doctrines, and methods."

"No doubt."

"Some, though true, could be improved."

"Yes."

"Can we be certain that ours, though a great advance over what preceded them, are the final development in beliefs, doctrines, and methods?"

"They will be," said S-One very seriously, "if we succeed."

"Bear in mind that this is a theoretical discussion."

S-One smiled. "I have not yet accused you of doctrinal deviations."

G-One nodded, his expression remote. "Not yet. But stay with me. If we succeed in gaining control, yes, we can succeed in making our beliefs, doctrines, and methods the last ones in the series to emerge or develop. That is clear."

"Then they are the ultimate development."

"But does that follow because they are necessarily superior, or does it follow because we have arrested the process at that point?"

"Does it matter?"

"Theoretically?"

"That is the wrong expression. You mean 'hypothetically'."

"Whichever you prefer."

S-One shook his head. "I cannot see beyond the point at which I stop reasoning on the question. There is a barred gate in my mental processes. On the gate there is a sign. It says, 'Danger. Keep Out. To Enter is Strictly Forbidden.' "

"That is why this discussion is only hypothetical."

"Dangerous animals in the realm of thought roam beyond that gate." S-One frowned. "Surely you did not discuss—with Arakal, for instance—"

G-One made a gesture of irritation. "What would the answer mean, if I discussed it with him? He is completely outside of this frame of reference."

"I am constrained to stop thinking, and to say that our methods and ways of approach are the best. And if not—" S-One held up his hand as if he foresaw an interruption "—if not, still, for the reason I described to you, we *must* win, and impose an end to the process of competing technological advances. It can go only so far. No further. And we must finally control it."

"In which case, it we *are* wrong—that is, if we hypothetically *were* wrong—we would freeze humankind at a level of technological development below its ultimate potentialities."

"Ah, but we foresee a further process of development, according to our own doctrine."

"Yet, if for the purposes of argument we assume that that doctrine might be improved by the slightest amount—"

"I am up against the gate."

"—then it follows that we are blocking a progress that might continue further."

"To possibly end mankind itself, by technological disaster. We have already had one sample of it. That came close enough to show what can happen."

"There is that. But suppose there is a way to resolve that problem? *Arakal may find it.*"

S-One sat bolt upright. "This is why we must penetrate and control his organization!"

"Wait a minute, my friend. If we control his organization, what chance is there then that he will find it?"

"You do not, of course, mean Arakal personally?"

"How should I know? The point is that our reasoning is valid, so long as we accept certain lines of argument. Grant those lines of argument, and all else follows strictly. But if, hypothetically, those lines of argument should be mistaken—Why, then our whole structure of argument becomes an obstruction of progress. And if that were so, there would exist a very serious danger, aside from rivalry with any other system of beliefs and doctrines."

"You have gotten ahead of me. It seems to me that your thought has branched, and that you are making two points at once."

"You see the first, but you do not see the second?"

"There is danger in this."

"That is certainly true. First, if Arakal finds a success-ful resolution to the underlying problem which is a justi=fication for the present development of S, he will proceed, while we are left in the dust, frozen in a method which, while superior to what went before, still is capable of improvement, and perhaps much improvement. That is a serious and unhappy possibility, but there is a worse one."

S-One frowned, then shrugged. "Go ahead."

"Looking out of that spaceship at the tremendous technological effects—"

"Which nearly ended the human race."

"Yes. A catastrophe. Which reminded me of other, but *natural* catastrophes. If for the sake of safety we stop the progression of technological methods, and freeze it in the present state, what do we do if there should be a need, brought on not by human actions but by nature, for the very strengths whose development we are blocking?"

S-One looked at him bleakly. "If, say, the radiation of the sun should change in intensity?"

"Yes. Exactly."

S-One shook his head. "How do I answer that? Life presents these alternatives. A wooden house is warm, but it may catch fire. A stone house is fireproof, but it is cold. Yes, I see at least the second risk you speak of. But I will still proceed as rapidly as possible to penetrate Arakal's organization and bring it under control."

"Working from France, England, and our former col-onies?"

"Yes. We have a broad foundation. He has escaped us here, but his very victory will be turned against him."

"Let us hope we do not destroy something we may someday need."

S-One looked at the Head of Government and said sympathetically, "You are tired."

"There is no doubt of that."

"Come and take a look at the flowers. They are refreshing."

"What, flowers, still, in this season?"

"One can have flowers in all seasons. You just have to pick the right kinds, and protect them. The colors, the contrast, and the individuality rest the mind, and delight the senses. They are something to take care of, that reciprocates with beauty, that never makes harsh demands."

The Head of Government looked at him quizzically, and then smiled, very briefly. "Did you know that Arakal has a torturer?"

"He has several. There is only one he really trusts. I can give you the reports on that. They are very carefully watched, and used only with great restraint. There is no weakness there."

"Such contrasts amaze me."

S-One looked surprised. "Contrast? Where is the contrast? Any sensible ruler has torturers. Now, let us take a look at the flowers."

★ 2 ★

Arakal, headed home through rough seas on board Admiral Bullinger's flagship, was listening to Buffon question one of his numerous prisoners:

"You say you joined S because your daughter was sick, and needed money for treatment. S helped, and you were grateful; but you later came to think that S was responsible for the trouble in the first place. What did you mean by that?"

"If every day is gray," said the prisoner, "how long will it be before people become dispirited? And if people are kept dispirited, how long before they become impoverished. The presence of S had the effect of unending bad weather."

Arakal thought back over the prisoner's explanation of how he had joined S in despair, of his relief at having money from S to care for his family, of his resulting loyalty, his rise in the S organization, his gradual disillusionment, and his eventual conviction that S was the cause of the trouble that drove people to despair.

Arakal stayed to hear the prisoner add, "But it isn't the *people* in S who cause most of the trouble. It's S itself—the organization—that does the damage. In S, people are like cells in the body of a snake. They may not be evil themselves, but they have become part of an evil thing."

Arakal slipped out of the room, and made his way slowly and carefully along the corridor toward the cabin where Slagiron and Colputt were studying records and photographs of conditions in Europe.

As the weather was growing progressively more foul, it took nearly five minutes before Arakal swung open the door of the cabin, to see Slagiron and Colputt at a table heavily loaded with papers.

Slagiron glanced around.

"Getting worse out there, isn't it?"

Arakal got the door shut.

"Coming up that ladder, it seemed like it." He glanced at the papers on the table, kept from sliding off by sections of a kind of low fence snapped up into position around the edge of the table. "What have you found out?"

Colputt said, "It's almost unbelievable, but the photos and descriptions from before the war show that the physical arrangements then match the arrangements now almost exactly. In every way we can check, Europe has stood still."

Arakal said, "Since S took over."

Slagiron nodded. "It's as if Europe has been pickled in brine."

Arakal slid into a chair bolted in place before the table. "You remember Burke-Johnson saying that not much damage had been done in Western Europe during the war; that S had already taken over?"

"Yes. He didn't seem to think anything of their standing still all this time."

"The Russ must have set S up deliberately to stop progress."

"But why?"

There was a silence, and then Arakal, frowning, said, "What did progress do to them the *last* time?"

Slagiron nodded slowly.

Colputt said, "Yes. Strangleweed and trained germs."

They glanced at each other.

From outside came the howl of the wind, and the crash of water against the ship.

"They must," said Colputt, "have decided to freeze technology where it was. In S, they have an organization first to spy, next to penetrate, then to take control, and finally to smother progress entirely."

Slagiron gripped the table as the ship heeled.

"But it won't work if they just stop progress in their own territory. They have to stop it *everywhere*."

Arakal nodded. "They have to control us, sooner or later."

"Sooner," said Slagiron. "And how do we keep them out? They build their listening devices in when they build a ship, and they plant the things all over. Our troops have found scores of them in Normandy. They slipped that nurse in on us on practically no notice. And the so-called partisans were a collection of fake outfits from the beginning. Just think of the time, men, money, and resources they must tie up in S. And, where we're concerned, they're only getting started. Once they get going, they can pour their spies and agents at us through Old Kebeck and Old Brunswick."

"Hopefully," said Arakal, "we'll have the means to detect that. We have a good number of former agents who don't like the idea that S turned them over to us."

"Some of those will serve both sides."

"Some. Not all. We may learn more about S than S expects."

Slagiron nodded.

"But now that we see how they work, how likely is it that their colonies, when we captured them, weren't already riddled? We're wide open to them."

"What we need," said Arakal, "is some narrow place where they can only come through a few at a time. We could watch *that*. Also, we need some way to cut the ground out from under S itself."

"How do we get at S? We may bring some of its men around to our viewpoint. We may manage to cut off a part of it. But the main organization is out of our reach."

Arakal said dryly, "The answer isn't exactly obvious." Then he added stubbornly, "But it should be there somewhere."

"As for a narrow place," said Slagiron, "is there any place on Earth that fits that description?"

Colputt said, "We'd better find an answer now, if there is one. Because the problem will just get worse. If S is meant to stop progress, then S *has* to either destroy us or control us."

Arakal was frowning. "S is meant to stop progress. *Why*?"

Slagiron shrugged. "We've just answered that. Progress is dangerous. Look at what happened." He paused. "That is, what we *think* happened. I'm assuming we've been told the truth."

Colputt said, "It sounded true to me. Anyway, the point is true. Progress is dangerous. Progress is *bound* to be dangerous. And the further we progress, the more dangerous it is likely to be."

"Nevertheless," said Arakal, "to the degree that we can eliminate the danger, we destroy the justification for S to exist."

Colputt shook his head.

"Progress *is* dangerous. Inevitably, if we progress, we will again reach the point where we can create—among other things—strangleweed and trained germs."

"Let's just suppose," said Arakal, his expression remote, "that there is some way to protect the world from the errors of progress. Look at the resources S uses up. How will it justify the expense if the danger *isn't there*?"

Slagiron began to speak, but, seeing Arakal's expression, hesitated. He glanced across the table to see that Colputt was also looking into the remote distance.

"But," said Arakal, "is that enough? Like a habit, S might continue, just because they are used to doing things that way. And it will still be useful to them as a spy organization. We need to lead them to create an organization that will compete with S by drawing on the same resources S uses."

Slagiron shook his head, but said nothing, and waited.

Arakal's gaze refocused, and his expression seemed to show a momentary surprise, as if he hadn't expected to find himself here. He glanced at Colputt, who said, "I see the *idea*. But there are contradictions. To begin with, we need to have progress, without danger. But the two go hand-in-hand."

Arakal said, "We need to have progress—without danger to *Earth*."

"True," said Colputt. Then his eyes widened. "I see. There *is* a distinction there."

Slagiron frowned. "Without danger to Earth. How?"

Arakal said, "A powerhouse is useful, and dangerous, so we are careful where we put it. We can't get rid of the danger itself. But we can keep the *consequences* of the danger from being so dangerous."

"Yes," said Colputt. "It would be hard, expensive, and inconvenient. But possibly it could be done, at that."

Slagiron glanced at Colputt. "What do you have in mind?"

"The Old O'Cracys' atomic reactor," said Colputt, "had to be a certain size, in order to work. If its fuel were put in too concentrated, and in too small a space, it would not be a reactor, but a bomb. There had to be room for internal shields, or moderators. Just possibly, a technology, too, has to have a certain size, or it will also be a bomb and not a reactor. There has to be space for internal shielding to moderate certain effects—to slow them down and prevent them from penetrating the whole mass as soon as they are created."

Slagiron frowned. "Where do we get this space?"

Before Colputt could answer, the ship and the sea together created a roll and lunge that stopped the conversation. Then Colputt said, "We can look on Earth as 'the world', or we can look on it as the nursery of the human race, with the real world out beyond it. There are satellites, and other planets, and resources in space, and, with the platforms, we have what seems to be a practical means to travel in space. If we can rebuild the technology, by combining what we have ourselves with the frozen skills of the Old Kebeckers and Old Brunswickers, why can't we use *space* to protect Earth? Why couldn't foreseeably dangerous experiments be carried out *far from Earth*?"

Arakal nodded.

"It would be difficult," said Colputt. "But, having seen the alternatives, I think we have to try it."

Arakal said, "If we can eliminate the danger to Earth, while maintaining progress, S as it is now becomes a plain waste of resources. Could it survive that?"

"Better yet," said Slagiron suddenly, "if we move out into space, just how well situated is S—which rejects progress—to follow? There's your narrow place! And to try to overcome that handicap, the Russ will have to use men and resources that would otherwise go to S!"

Colputt said, suddenly cautious, "Of course, this is just an idea. The one thing we can be reasonably sure of is that space will be a very—" He groped for words "—A very unwelcoming environment."

Arakal and Slagiron, both gripping the table as the storm shook the ship, glanced around.

Outside the thin walls, they could hear the wind howl, and the sea smash across the tilted deck. Through Arakal's mind passed a brief vision of humanity's experiences on a planet whose environment was enlivened by such things as volcanoes, earthquakes, sharks, viruses, snakes, and hurricanes.

Despite the queasiness caused by the motions of the ship, he suddenly laughed and turned to Colputt.

"Let's not underestimate our nursery. If space isn't very welcoming, should that scare us away? How have we been raised?"

Colputt glanced around as the ship rolled far over, then he managed a faint smile.

"We have had the problem before, haven't we?"

Inside, as the storm beat on the ship, they thought over the frail, insubstantial idea that had come to them, like a ray of light through dense clouds.

Outside, the storm raged, its freezing wind and drowning depths held away by the ship, each and every part of which had begun as a frail, insubstantial idea.

Severely tried, but still on course, the fleet made its way through the storm toward home.

★OR★
PEACE

PHILOSOPHER'S STONE
★ ★ ★

Dave Blackmer was an interstellar courier, paid to deliver the almost microscopically-reduced electronic message banks which, on arrival at the branch offices of Terran corporations, yielded up confidential instructions and technical data from the home offices and giant laboratories back on Earth. Since the banks were theoretically stealable, certain key messages were given to Dave in deep hypnosis, and passed on by him in the same state when he reached the planet of destination. For Dave, the job itself was routine. Most of the travel was done in fast commercial spacers, the monotony varied by rare moments when hair-trigger reflexes and hidden weapons made a shambles of a highjacker's attempt at the message banks. Between such moments, he had time to consider a peculiar effect of his job that the company recruiter had warned him about before he took the job.

"Now, don't ask me to explain it," the recruiter had said, "but Einstein's theory predicts it, and our experience proves it. The faster you go, the slower the passage of time. At the speeds you'll be traveling, you've got to take this into account. Are you willing to do it?"

"What's it involve?"

"Well, suppose you're married. You go out on the fastest ship available, make two or three subspace jumps, travel at top velocities, deliver the banks, load up for return, and in six weeks total you're back to report to the head office. The calendar in the office says one year and two months have elapsed since you left."

"You mean I'm a year two months older than when I left, and it only seemed like six weeks to me?"

"No, you're only six weeks older. The people *here* are a year two months older. They've lived that long while you were away for six weeks of *your* time."

Dave shrugged. "What does it matter when I live the rest of the fourteen months? I haven't lost anything."

"No, but remember, we said, 'Suppose you're married.' You've been away six weeks, as far as you're concerned. But that was a year and two months on Earth. You're married, and the little woman is conscious of having cooled her heels in solitary neglect for four hundred and twenty-five days and nights. You see what I mean?"

Dave nodded. "That's not so good."

The recruiter said, "In this business, marriage isn't worth it, believe me. But there are compensations, if you're interested in making money."

"High pay?"

"The pay is terrible. You'd do a lot better running a desk in an automatic factory."

"How much?"

"Thirty-five thousand a year, to start."

Dave turned as if to leave.

"Of course," added the recruiter, "you collect that thirty-five thousand at least half-a-dozen times a year."

Dave turned and stared back at him. The recruiter grinned. "We call it the 'accordion effect.' On Earth, time is stretched out like an accordion pulled wide. At high velocity, time is shortened like an accordion squeezed shut. On the company's books, you get paid by the calendar year. But throughout most of the calendar year, you're making subspace jumps and traveling at ultrahigh velocity in the course of your work. You experience the passage of, say five to six weeks, between the time you leave and the time you get back. Meanwhile, on Earth, the calendar year has elapsed, because of the higher rate of flow of time on a slow-moving object. So after five to six weeks' work, you get a year's pay. Nice, huh?"

And that had been Dave's introduction to the "accordion effect." Other delightful aspects had shown up later. Though Dave was earning at least two hundred thousand a year, from his viewpoint, the government saw this as a mere thirty-five thousand a year, repeated six times; the government was thus content to go after his paychecks with a moderately loose net, rather than with the harpoons, axes, and big knives they would otherwise have used. Conversely, though from Dave's viewpoint only a year had passed on the job, from the viewpoint of his bank, the interest on his money had been compounding, piling up, and reproducing itself for half-a-dozen years.

At first, Dave's only worry was that some technological development would eliminate his job. Then he began to notice other results of the accordion effect: the apparently accelerated aging of Earthbound acquaintances; the stepping up, from Dave's viewpoint, of social and technological changes; the perceptible shift of position and power among the peaceable but still strenuously competing nations on the home planet. These, and the sudden emergence of totally unexpected developments, kept Dave constantly aware of the difference in viewpoint that his job brought about.

And now there was a new change. For the first few years—from his viewpoint—Dave had traveled in the fastest American and Soviet ships. Of late, however, his trips more and more often were made in spacers like the *Imperial Banner*, the *Unicorn*, the *Lion*, and the *Duke of Richmond*. He was currently aboard the *Queen of Space*, which was hurtling him from Transpluto Terminal to Aurora Shuttle-Drop with a time-lead of twelve hours fifty-seven minutes over the next fastest transportation. Some idea of life on the *Queen* could be deduced in advance from the first lines of the shipping company's brochure:

"With three grades of accommodation: magnate class, luxury class, and first class, the new liner *Queen of Space* fulfills your fondest expectations . . . "

But Dave had been unable to foresee all of it. With one hand behind him on the silver doorknob of the first-class lounge, he stepped into the corridor and glanced to his left to see, strolling toward him down the corridor, two elegantly-dressed young men, a little above medium height. They were spare, well-knit, and groomed to perfection. Dave, who seldom noticed clothes, became oppressively aware of their perfectly-tailored jackets, knife-creased trousers, and black shoes polished to mirror brightness. They favored Dave with a brief flick of a glance as they passed, leaving him conscious of his improperly-knotted tie, unsuitable tan sport jacket and slacks, and too thick-soled shoes. Dave bore up under it grimly, conscious that the trip would not last forever and that after seven or eight more trips, the accordion effect would probably present him with some new phenomenon.

A good-natured middle-aged man, carrying a thing like a small riding crop with a silver handle, moved out beside Dave at the doorway, cast a cool glance after the elegant pair, nodded to Dave, and walked down the corridor, carrying the crop turned up inconspicuously against the cloth of his sleeve. From the opposite direction, a beautifully-dressed fop strolled by with a swagger stick. Then two men went past deep in conversation.

"No, no," one was saying earnestly. "I'd have been stuck there for life. A stinking baronet. But I found Carter. He was nobody, then. Nobody. But I saw a possibility. Nothing more, mind you. Just a possibility. And I—"

They disappeared around the corner. From their direction came a thickset man with beet-red cheeks carrying a swagger stick. No, Dave saw, a gold-encrusted baton of some kind—and everyone else in the corridor bowed and stood aside till he passed, whereupon the conversation, respectfully subdued, sprang up again, and the traffic in the hall got moving.

Dave noted that the courtesy was more elaborate than it had been on previous trips. The social phenomenon, whatever it was, must be coming to full bloom. He watched the hustling crowd go past, and became aware of a feeling of loneliness.

Someone banged into Dave, muttered an apology in a strained, suffering voice, and started past into the crowded entrance of the first-class lounge. Dave muttered an automatic acceptance of the apology, started out into the corridor, then hastily changed direction as some grandee came around the corner and they all stood against the wall for him.

Growling under his breath, Dave shoved back out of the way into the lounge, banged somebody, apologized, heard a muttered, "Sure. Sure. That's all right. Never mind," whirled and caught sight of a man in a dark business suit with a thick stubble of beard and horn-rimmed glasses. Dave immediately grabbed him by the arm. The man whirled around, a grim long-suffering look on his face.

From the corridor and all around them came snatches of greetings and conversation:

" . . . Beg pardon, your Grace . . . "

" . . . Be delighted, Sir Philip. I'm much indebted to you . . . "

" . . . Lot of plebian rot, my lord. Hogwash. Income tax, indeed . . . "

" . . . Well, that put me one step up the ladder, but I never hoped to lay hold on the swagger stick till—"

" . . . No, no. What a bore. I wouldn't dream of it . . . "

" . . . Best be up and doing, eh, your Grace? One day a commoner, next a baron, and pretty soon . . . "

" ' . . . Tongue, you insolent dog,' I said. 'Your rank was bequeathed. It's no greater than mine, and it's on the slide. Your children will be commoners . . . ' "

The man Dave had by the arm was staring at him as at some friend temporarily forgotten, but whose features were agonizingly familiar.

Dave said in a low voice, "You're Anatoly Dovrenin. A courier for Sovcom. Right?"

The man nodded. He said suddenly, "I've seen you. Wait—You're David Blackmer? Interstellar Communications Corporation?"

"Correct."

Dovrenin thrust out his hand. Dave grabbed it. They shook hands with the sincerity of two nineteenth-century Midwesterners in a Boston drawing room. The instant they paused the bits and fragments of conversation washed over them again.

" . . . Reconversion dynamometer. Well, I thought, that's good for a step up if I can twist it around a bit, so . . . "

" . . . Incredible callousness. The chap was only a rung above me, you know. It wasn't the snub, it was the way he did it. So offhand. As if I didn't *exist* . . . "

" . . . Of course, my dear fellow. Yes, yes. I assuredly will remember you. Now if you'll excuse me . . . Pardon, gentlemen . . . "

" . . . Lord Essenden, you've met Sir Dene Swope? . . . Splendid . . . Now, if we can find a quiet seat in a corner somewhere . . . "

Dovrenin glanced around and muttered, "It's getting crowded in here."

Dave nodded, "I know exactly what you mean. My room's just down the hall. If you can spare a minute—"

Dovrenin brightened. "I've got a big collection of cheeses they gave me at home for a going-away present. Also, naturally, I have some Vodka. How about—"

"Good idea."

"But, I haven't got any crackers. There was a little slip in the five-year plan, and ah . . . "

Dave nodded knowingly. "I'll go down to the commissary and pick up a couple of boxes. Incidentally, I'm in 226."

"I'll be there. My room is 280, so it will take me a few minutes."

They parted, Dovrenin going up the corridor, and Dave down it toward the gravity drop to the commissary. A few minutes later he was carrying the crackers and on his way back, meditating on the effect of the change in the exchange rate from six dollars a pound to seven twenty-eight a pound.

Thus preoccupied, Dave failed to notice a sudden hush in the corridor as everyone stood back respectfully against the walls. Dave walked past unaware. An elaborately-dressed fop drew his breath in with a hiss, grabbed Dave's arm with one hand, and slapped him across the face with the other.

Dave instinctively grabbed the man by the shirt front and knocked his unconscious form fifteen feet down the corridor.

There was a dead silence.

Dave picked up the crackers.

Coming toward him down the hall was the man with the riding crop that Dave had seen earlier. He smiled at Dave. Dave smiled at him. Dave walked down the hall with the accumulated gaze of many eyes focused on the back of his neck.

As he approached his room, he could see Anatoly Dovrenin coming down the hall from the opposite direction, carrying a box so large that he could see only by looking around one side of it. Behind Dovrenin, a door opened. People jumped to right and left to stand courteously waiting against the wall as a skinny individual carrying a silver-and-gold-encrusted baton emerged from a room behind Dovrenin, to walk behind him in deep conversation with a short fat man who was obviously paralyzed by greatness, and able only to bob his head and say, "Yes, Yes."

Dovrenin, peering around one side of the box, clearly had no idea what was behind him, till a gorgeously-dressed young man indignantly slammed him to the wall, knocking the box to the floor. Dovrenin waited with downcast gaze as the baton-bearing celebrity went past. There was a blur of motion as people began to move, then the magnificently-dressed young man appeared carrying the box, his expression blank, and Dovrenin right behind him with his hand holding something bulky in a side pocket.

Dave opened the door. The big box was carried in and set on the bed. Dovrenin's companion favored Anatoly and Dave with a hard look, and left the room.

Dave shut the door. Dovrenin carried over a chair and jammed it under the door's silver knob.

"I'm not very popular here right now."

Dave nodded. "My own circle of friends is strictly limited."

Dovrenin went to the box, and glanced around. Dave followed his glance:

The room, done in an exotic combination of silver and New Venus mahogany, had a bed, a chest of drawers, a table, three straight chairs, a large mirror, a plush armchair, and a thing like a wide-screen TV set. Another door, partly open, gave a view into a luxuriously-fitted bathroom.

Dovrenin glanced around, saw the two big boxes of crackers, and beamed. "You had no trouble?"

"No. I'd hardly touched my travel allowance. But if that exchange rate keeps going up—"

"It will," said Dovrenin grimly. "We have information that the next jump would put it at about $8.40 a pound. It may be higher yet when we get back."

Dave winced, then shrugged. "No need to worry about that now." He pulled a couple of boxes out from under his bed, Dovrenin in turn began to unload his own huge box. The table was soon laden with a variety of edible delicacies, and an assortment of liquids in different sizes and shapes of bottles. Various packets, cartons, and little boxes appeared, packed with delicate white cigarettes, and big brown cigars. Dave and Anatoly stepped back, grinned and eyed the table. The room promptly filled with the sounds of pouring liquids, tearing cellophane, and can openers at work. For a time, the conversation was strictly limited:

"Pretty good cheese. What do you call this?"

" . . . And of course, there isn't anything in the world like American whisky. However, try some of our . . . "

" . . . Stuff really has a sting, doesn't it? But hm-m-m now suppose we mixed in a little of this . . . "

There was enough food and drink on the table to last most of the trip, but there were only two to consume it, and something in the atmosphere impeded the development of really spontaneous joy. The two men glanced around from time to time, unaware that they had the puzzled looks of couriers just home from a long trip, and still unaccustomed to the changes that happened while they were away.

"Eight-forty a pound," murmured Dave, lowering his glass.

Dovrenin put down a bottle of clear brown liquid. His expression clouded. "You should see what is happening to the ruble. And the fools at home try to pass it off as if it didn't mean anything—"

Dave shook his head. "I guess it's because we see things speeded up. They jar us more."

"Oh, of course," said Dovrenin. "But let me just show you." He got out a piece of paper, and wrote rapidly.

He slid the paper over, and Dave noted that it was headed "Overall Industrial Index." Dave read:

I

U.S.	.98
U.S.S.R.	.86
Gr. Britain	.42

II

U.S.	.99
U.S.S.R.	.89
Gr.Britain	.42

III

U.S.	1.01
U.S.S.R.	.92
Gr. Britain	.47

IV

U.S.	1.00
U.S.S.R.	.95
Gr. Britain	.55

V

U.S.	1.02
U.S.S.R.	.97
Gr. Britain	.69

VI

U.S.	1.01
U.S.S.R.	.99
Gr. Britain	.91

VII

U.S.	1.03
U.S.S.R.	1.01
Gr. Britain	1.26

Dave looked up. "This is accurate?"

"No, it's a summary of our official past estimates. Therefore, it's somewhat biased in our favor. But that can't hide the trend."

"No wonder the exchange rate's going up."

"Yes, and no wonder their ships are beating ours. But *why*?"

Dave shook his head. "All I heard of it at home was an article I read, headed, 'Boom in Free World Economy. Britain Profits from Westward Economic Shift,' whatever that means. The article didn't make sense."

Dovrenin nodded gloomily, and picked up the big glass in which Dave had mixed several drinks together. Dovrenin eyed it suspiciously, took a cautious sip, shrugged, said, "This is certainly innocuous," and drank it down like water.

Dave sat up.

Dovrenin swallowed several times, and looked around vaguely. He cleared his throat. He opened his mouth, and no sound came out. Dave glanced uneasily at the empty glass. Dovrenin tried again, and now words came out clearly, "I will show you what I mean."

Dave eased his chair back, so as to have freedom of action, just in case.

★ ★ ★

Dovrenin came to his feet, and glowered around as if looking over a large assemblage, made up entirely of his inferiors.

"Comrades," he growled, his voice threatening, "unhealthy rumors have come to my ears." He looked around, and said in a different voice, "No, we'll skip that part." He cleared his throat, glowered, and said in a deep, authoritative voice, "The present situation in steel production proves the futility of inexpert analysis. Hasty generalizations drawn from overall figures lead to fantastic conclusions. Steel production is not one monolithic development, but is the resultant of three totally unrelated factors: land-based production, sea-based production, space-based production.

"Water covers seventy-five per cent of the Earth's surface. Do you suppose there is no iron in the water, and no iron under the water? To think so would be an absurdity. But it is the kind of absurdity into which the inexpert falls, to bruise himself severely.

"Clear-headed analysis shows that in *land-based production*, we are breathing fire down the necks of the imperialists, and will soon *forge unshakably into the lead*. Only by desperate attempts at sea-based and space-based production are the capitalists able to stave off for a while their day of ruin. The sea—and space-based production figures are in direct proportion to their desperation at overcoming us in land-based production, and are thus a *source of grim satisfaction* to every one of us capable of a true understanding."

Dovrenin leaned across the table and said moodily to Dave, "You understand that before we came to this part, everyone had been already psychologically beaten into a jelly, so that the reasoning seemed very good."

Dave nodded sympathetically. Dovrenin picked up the empty glass and held it in the air, turning it slowly around and looking at it. "I have had it explained to me that this revolution in productive capacity is purely and simply the result of chance inventions. Little things like innovation in dynamic drift, resonant screening, ionic immobilization, linear-directed pseudo-molecular forces, stress-mold patterns, and so on. Mere inventions. No connection with the usual socio-economic factors." He gripped the glass suddenly, and Dave, expecting to see it smashed against the wall, braced himself to duck the flying fragments. Instead, Dovrenin abruptly sat down, pulled over his paper, and did some figuring on the back of it. Then he wrote on the face of the paper, and slid it across to Dave, who read:

VIII

Gr. Britain	1.83
U.S.	1.04
U.S.S.R.	1.03

"That," said Dovrenin, "is what we can expect to see very shortly."

Dave checked the figures. "Seems perfectly accurate, if the trend holds."

Dovrenin swore. "Dukes and earls all over the place! The verminous nobility are taking over the universe! What an experience for a loyal Party member."

Dave bit back the automatic comment, "Well, at least, that's better than if the Communists should take over." He observed the expression of suffering on Dovrenin's face, finished off his glass, and looked at the figures again. The room was now traveling in slow circles, so that it was with some difficulty that he worked out the next stage of the progression:

IX

Gr. Britain	2.60
U.S.	1.05
U.S.S.R.	1.05

Dovrenin checked the figures, and nodded. "That is exactly it. My friend, I am so glad you came on this ship. Otherwise, I would have been all alone with these rabid imperialists." He poured out two generous glasses of something that had a rocket on the label. After the exchange of several toasts, the room picked up considerable speed.

Dovrenin held to the table with one hand, while Dave braced it from the other side, and the paper traveled back and forth. In time, Dave squinted at something reading:

XIV

Gr. Britain	11.90
U.S.S.R.	1.15
U.S.	1.10 ·

There was another lapse of time while Dave worked out a mixture to reverse the polarity and cut back the excessive rotational inertia the room was building up, and this somehow introduced an eccentric motion that landed them both on the floor, where they shared a fresh piece of paper bearing extended calculations on one side, and on the other an untidy scrawl reading:

Gr. Britain	3,162.4
U.S.A.	.1136
U.S.S.R.	1.149

"Well, well," said Dave, focusing his mind with some difficulty, "blood is thicker than water, and all that, but we can't let this happen."

Dovrenin nodded emphatically, and speaking carefully said, "Together we will smash the filthy cap . . . er . . . imperialists."

Dave shook his head, and struggled to sit up. "Thing to do is get their secret, strain the dukes and earls out of it, and use it ourselves, see?" The beauty of this idea almost blinded him.

Dovrenin considered this, and a light seemed to burst on him, too. He beamed approval, then said, "How?"

"Have to get that first paper," said Dave. He managed to get up, and tried to step over to the table, but owing to the powerful Coriolis force operating in the room this proved to be impossible. He tried again on hands and knees, succeeded, located the paper, but found that the dizzying motion of the room impeded his concentration. He decided that something would have to be done, located a small brown bottle on the table, and after many patient tries managed to get hold of it. He unscrewed the cap and with great care swallowed the faintest taste. His nostrils immediately filled with bitter fumes, and he experienced the sensation of being slammed headlong into a brick wall.

The room had stopped spinning.

Dave set down the bottle, which was labeled "Snap-Out: The One Minute Drunk Cure. By appointment to His Majesty . . . "

"*Whew,*" said Dave. He fervently hoped he hadn't taken too much. When the room began to revolve again gently, he sighed with relief, and carefully poured out a sparing dose for Dovrenin, who was lying on his back counting the revolutions of the ceiling.

Dovrenin choked, gagged, and sat up. After a moment, he sighed with relief. "That's better."

Dave, without too much difficulty from the free-wheeling action of the room, rummaged through his chest of drawers, and got out a glossy brochure. "Listen to this," he said. " 'Passengers desiring information on any subject have at their disposal a most complete reference library, which may be consulted by dialing "L" on any of the ship's viewers'."

Dovrenin looked doubtful. "Would it be that easy?"

"Maybe not, but we ought to get a few leads."

Dovrenin nodded. "Worth a try."

Both men looked not quite convinced, but as the alcohol they had absorbed overpowered the sparing dosage of Snap-Out, they appeared more confident.

Dave bent at the viewer, and dialed "L". A set of instructions jumped onto the screen, followed by a list of general topics. Dovrenin pulled up a chair and sat down nearby. Thirty minutes passed in plowing through a welter of information neither man was interested in. Then the heading "H.R.I.M. Government, Under Act of Revision, A Summary," sprang onto the screen.

Dave scanned the text, then hit the spacer button for the next page. The two men leaned forward, to read:

"Peerage. The House of Lords more drastically affected by the Revision.

"Two basic factors were taken into consideration. First was the unquestioned importance of technological innovation. One basic change of technique can revolutionize an industry. Second was the ingrained national characteristic of respect for titled nobility, a respect for rank and title apart from any immediate political power.

"At the moment of Commission's report, the foreign trade situation was extremely bad, with broadly-based competition holding an accumulating advantage in resources and production capacity. A feeling of desperation had grown up, and this may explain the speed with which the Commission's report was acted upon.

"Two measures were adopted. The principle of *decay of inherited title* provided that the eldest son of a nobleman assumed upon his father's death a rank and privilege lowered by two degrees. The son of a duke became an earl. The son of an earl became a baron. The second principle, that of *acquisition of merit*, provided that noble rank might be acquired only by merit, and *principally by the bringing to use of new technological innovations*. The patent of nobility was awarded, not to the inventor, who was seldom interested, in any case, but to the individual *who brought the useful invention to prominence*. The inventor was rewarded by prize money and a percentage of profits, but received a patent of nobility only if he himself brought the invention to prominence.

"The result of these two measures was to create overnight an interest in inventors and inventions which had not existed for the previous two centuries. The energies of those who wished to rise socially, or who were moved to maintain their ancient rank, were at once mobilized in the search for useful innovations. Ingenious technical persons who had in vain pleaded for at least a hearing suddenly found the drawing rooms of the nation flung open to them.

"The effects were not slow in coming. A scheme for ocean-mining which had been kicked around in a desultory way for twenty years was seized upon at once and given a trial. Serious difficulties developed, but the backer was determined upon a peerage. After a heroic struggle, the process was made economically feasible. The result was a dramatic easing in the raw materials problem. New developments followed swiftly as a favorable climate was created for men of inventive minds.

"There were, of course, and still are, certain shortcomings. Fortunes have been lost on worthless devices. The wild scramble for position disgusts many. The bumptious self-importance of some newly-titled knights and baronets is a continuing offense. The lordly mannerisms of the degenerate scions of once-great families is an irritation which must be experienced to be appreciated.

"The main defense of the system is that it works. The social process it has set in motion is the unquestioned cause of the accelerating rise in Imperial power, dominion, and prosperity. This alliance of genius and worldly society is the hallmark that today distinguishes the Empire from the backward nations of the home world.

"One might wish to confer the blessings of our systems upon these nations foundering in the backwash of history. But repeated missionary efforts have failed, rousing savage passions where enlightenment was intended.

"We must not despair. The inevitable march of history will sweep the doubters along with the procession, if not at the van, yet somewhere in the dusty trail of the column, and at last all will issue out of the abyss and the confusion into the broad royal grandeur of space.

"In the end, all will be one mighty Empire."

Dave snapped off the viewer, and the two men looked at each other.

"All right," said Dovrenin. "Now we see how it works. *How do we adapt it?*"

Dinner time was approaching as, symbolic riding crop in hand, Richard, Prince of the Realm, strode briskly down the hall that ran past Room 226, where Dave and Anatoly still wrestled with their problem. From somewhere up the corridor, the stirring strains of "Rule, Britannia" came faintly to Richard's ears, the word "waves" replaced by "stars," destroying the rhyme but not injuring the meaning. Richard was in a good mood, and slapped his leg lightly with the riding crop every few steps, an outward sign of his satisfaction.

Word had just reached him that young Smythe had cracked the self-repair problem for gravitors in actual use. The silver-handled crop that Richard carried, modest symbol of his position as First Peer of the Empire was his for a time longer. Moreover, this discovery was bound to be so widely useful as to add another few years to his tenure as a prince of quasi-royal blood.

Even if, he thought, eyes narrowed, even if he should lose the first rank—which heaven forbid, but such things did happen—still it was no small matter to be a Prince of the Realm. Damn the accelerated decay on that rank. A fellow could never rest, without getting slammed back to a dukedom.

He rounded a corner, telling himself that it had taken three generations to work up to this position, and he didn't intend to lose it without a struggle. There were those—petty fellows, sweaty upstart barons, backslid

sons of earls, and the like—who complained that a
dynasty like that of his family was unfair to the others.
The beautiful answer to that was, "The system exists for
the benefit of the Realm and of the innovators, not for
the benefit of the nobility." That left the croakers helplessly grinding their teeth. Good for them. Let them shut
up and produce.

His family knew how to produce, how to keep the
inventors happy and working. Hunt them out, keep them
going, doubt them when doubt will stimulate, believe in
them when they doubt themselves. After a time it
became an instinct. He could walk past a tenement, with
the smell of decaying orange peels in his nostrils, and
detect an inventive mind at work in the basement across
the street. There must, he supposed, be some outward
sign that he wasn't consciously aware of, a flash of light
and movement, a fleeting glimpse of apparatus, seen
but not—

"Hullo," he said suddenly. "What's this?"

He'd come to an abrupt stop outside a blank-faced
door numbered 226. There was a peculiar something in
the air, like the almost palpable absence of sound a man
is aware of in an intensely quiet room.

"Something doing," said Richard, his instincts alert.
He glanced up and down the hall, then stepped to the
door, his hand raised as if to knock, and paused, listening.

"So then," came the voice of Anatoly Dovrenin, "each
Party member must sponsor one good invention every
five years, or he loses his Party card. What do you think
of that?"

"It's a good idea," came the voice of Dave Blackmer,
muffled by the door, "but probably it still needs to have
some more work done on it. Now *my* idea is to have

two major leagues of half-a-dozen teams each, see? Each region's got its own team. The New York Bombers, Boston Gnats, Philadelphia Phillies. The 'players' get on the team because they sponsor inventors. Cash prizes, pennants, and gold, silver and bronze cups are given out every six months for the leading team, with special mention and smaller cups for the leading players on each team. What scores points is useful inventions brought to prominence."

Dovrenin's voice came through the door. "This will work? Or did this idea come out of the whisky bottle? Who will be interested? Where will your 'fans' come from?"

"Where do you think? What gets people interested in a little ball batted around the park? It's the *contest* that counts. It's regional pride. Once it gets going, it picks up speed. Listen, they'll have special scouts going around to spot inventors. The newspapers will feature a running coverage—"

Outside the door, Richard frowned, gauging the potential merit of the innovations with practiced instinct. "They've got hold of something," he told himself. "Haven't got it worked into proper form yet, but—"

Habit brought his hand up, to rap once eagerly on the door.

"Just a minute," said a voice, "I'll get the door."

Horrified, Richard realized what he had been about to do.

Some inventors were best left alone, like that fellow who had the plan to turn the polar regions into tropical gardens, and which would, just incidentally, immerse London under the melted ice.

Firmly, the First Peer of the Realm stepped back, said, "Sorry, I misread the number," and strode swiftly down the hall.

The door opened, and Dave and Anatoly stared after him.

"Now," said Dave, "what do you suppose *he* wanted?"

Dovrenin shrugged. "Who knows what goes on in the minds of these grasping imperialists? Let us get back to work."

The door closed.

The ship sped on, carrying twenty-eight assorted dandies, fops, and ne'er-do-wells, thirty crewmen, four hundred and seventy-eight status-conscious noblemen, sixteen inventors and assistants in specially outfitted workshops, one proletarian, and one free-enterpriser.

Not one of these travelers was aware that, between them, they had the long-sought, supposedly-mythical entity to turn dross into wealth. But they went on using it just the same.

HARRY C. CROSBY,
who wrote as CHRISTOPHER ANVIL,
1925–2009

"I've done a lot of reissues of past authors, but this one was always special for me. Anvil was the only one of those authors who was still alive, and my hope was that he'd live long enough to see the project completed. He didn't quite make it, but he came close. . . . He died before he could see the final volume but he knew it was in the works. . . .

"The truth is that first and foremost, Harry Crosby was a satirist—and that manifests itself, one way or another, in practically everything he wrote. His stories concerning conflicts between humans and aliens were just as likely to needle human foibles as they were to poke fun at aliens. He was one of the wittiest authors our field has ever produced.

"Try his work for yourself, if you never have, or refresh your memories, if you have. You can find it all here: *Pandora's Legions* (2002), *Interstellar Patrol* (2003), *Interstellar Patrol II* (2005), *The Trouble with Aliens*, (2006), *The Trouble with Humans* (2007), *War Games* (2008), *Rx for Chaos* (2009), and *The Power of Illusion* (forthcoming)."

—Eric Flint, *Locus*